The Forging of Frost

Donna Croy Wright

Dedicated

to Cedar and Willow,
always turning toward the sun.

"My god is all gods in one.
When I see a beautiful sunset,
I worship the god of Nature;
when I see a hidden action brought to light,
I worship the god of Truth;
when I see a bad man punished and a good man go free,
I worship the god of Justice;
when I see a penitent forgiven,
I worship the god of Mercy."

Edna St Vincent Millay, from her diary, 1908

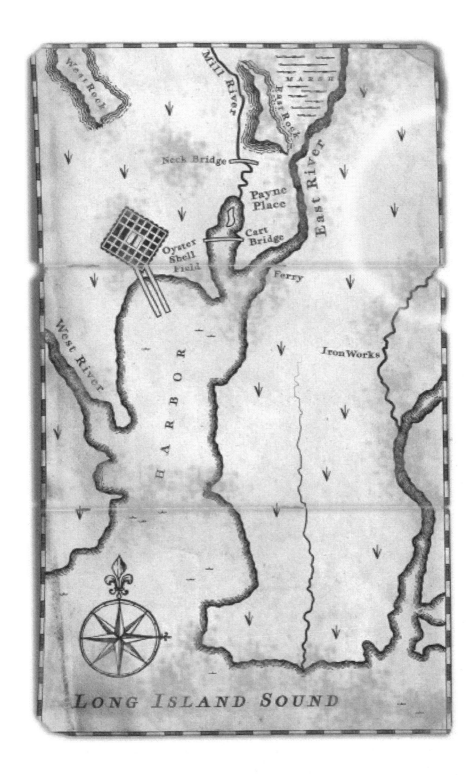

PART I

1654 (and the present)

...everyone that hereafter should be admitted
here as planters should submit and testifie,
namely that church members onely shall be
free ...

Code of New Haven

*P*lace matters, as does the moment, and two old books sitting on a bookseller's table just discovered that their time and place is now. After centuries of waiting and one near miss, their chance has arrived; they can feel it.

A year ago, they came close. They were stuck away on a shelf—at that antique store with the rickety screen door—when she walked in. They throbbed in anticipation, but she passed them by, distracted by a stronger force. A shot bag near the back of the room called out to her. It wrapped its energy around her, and the books could not compete.

Today, though, is different. Today she is alone, wandering the aisles of a convention center packed with genealogists. Of them all, it is her who ripens to the call. They vibrate their desire, and she stops to scan the room. They pull her away from the clutter, the vendors, the distractions of the conference hall. They pull her in.

She runs her fingers along the spines of books laid out, row upon row, in wooden boxes. She is so near. They pulse, begging her to touch them. But the merchant intervenes.

"Can I help you?" he says.

She looks at him, blinking. They make it hard for her to concentrate. "No, not really. I just..." She stumbles on her thoughts, and the books grab hold. "Maybe," she says. "You never know." Her hand falls like magnet to iron and she traces their spines.

The merchant sees her fingers stroking them. "Oh, are you interested in New Haven? Those books were published in 1858. The transcribed records of New Haven Colony. Written in the 1600's. There weren't just thirteen colonies in the beginning. You know that, right?"

They feel her smile. Of course, she knows. They glow, heating her fingers. She tips one up. But a tensile strength holds the two volumes together. They protest the separation.

The merchant voices their thoughts. "I can only sell them as a set. They're an amazing find."

While he talks she lifts the second volume from the box. Their energy ripples from her hand, through her arm, to her heart. They are part of her.

"I want them," she says and hands the merchant a card.

He flips it over in his hand. "Margaret Carter Smith. Been into genealogy long?"

"A while," she says, "and I go by Maggie, just Maggie."

"Well, Maggie," he says, returning the card, "sign here, and enjoy your read."

She fumbles, tucks the card into her bag, and pulls up the shoulder strap, freeing her hand so she can sign. She does not put them down; she holds them to her breast. Then, finally, she opens the bag and slides them home. They nestle in, contented, because now it begins. Maggie Smith can read between the lines. She reads souls. And they have a story to tell.

⤚✦⤙

The ship lurched, its cargo of wine, salt, and human indenture swaying in response. The hold held the wine and salt, even the pottery jugs well enough. But human cargo did not belong. It existed; John Frost existed.

Freedom and bondage had taunted John the voyage long, both as deception and delusion, and always as a sea-born spew. He clutched the hammock's edge, rough hemp eating into his palms, a sea-born fury eating at his gut.

Out from the dank, a smooth-faced boy emerged; he jerked at his hammock. "John, friend John. I come to fetch you," he said and jostled him once more.

"To fetch me?" he murmured, his mind lost to the sway and the smell. He buried his face in his arm, repulsed, attempting escape. But he was its source—an amalgam of sweat, offal, and vomit born of his battle with the sea.

"Stop the swinging," he pleaded. Then a name stirred within. He steadied himself and cried, "Edward! Stop!"

Edward held up his hands. Though twelve like John, he was bigger by half, a looming shadow in the darkened hold. "Sorry," he said, steadying the hammock, "but we are nearly there, and Mister Meiggs asked me to ready you for land."

John's lip twitched into a wary smile. They had arrived.

He swung his legs out, jumped down, and hit the deck. His knees buckled. And he fell into Edward's arms.

"Steady, friend. Lord's breath, the heft of you. Not more than a bushel. You best lean on me." Edward raked John's arm across his back, grabbed his waist, and maneuvered him through the narrow passageways.

As they circumnavigated the towers of crates and barrels, John checked his stomach. The ship—The Cockerel—glided gentle and true, a contrast to the turmoil he had endured over his long months at sea. Some little strength returned to his legs so that, when they reached the ladder leading from the hold, he managed it on his own, though Edward steadied him from behind.

He stopped at the top, eyes shut, anticipating the sunlight's glare. Edward prodded. "Go, John, before I faint from the stink of you."

A swell of determination nudged him forward. He tumbled onto the deck, then balanced on his knees, swaying. A world of colorless shadow greeted him, the hint of morning still trying at the horizon.

"Night," he said, an attempt to make sense of his world. Then it accosted him: the idle creaking of the The Cockerel's masts; the flapping of sails taking wind; the banter of the sailors lobbing jabs at each other; and Edward's gull-like squawking in his ear.

"I am here for you. See? Have cared for you from the beginning. Didn't get off in Boston. Wonder why? Signed a new contract. Indentured two years more, but to be a currier when I finish." John looked dubiously up at Edward, pushing back his hair, sand-brown and matted with grime. "Well, besides," Edward continued, "they threatened to toss me overboard if I refused. And how could I leave you? On your feet now. We go to Mister Meiggs."

John held up his hands, his wrists thin inside Edward's sturdy grasp. With his friend's help, he stood and adjusted to the ship's sway. Then, with a jerk of his chin, Edward directed him to the bow.

Trailing behind Edward, his gait labored and uneven, he crossed the main deck and climbed five steps to the quarterdeck. There, looking out across a quiet sea, stood Mister Meiggs and Captain Sylvester.

When they reached the men, Edward spoke, his voice emboldened by duty. "Begging your pardon, sir. Mister Meiggs? I have him here. John Frost."

Meiggs turned to them, scowling. He lifted his arms, shaking them so his ruffled sleeves fell away from his hands. "This, Captain, is the last of my indentures, an evil sickness turning a strong boy to the semblance of one of your galley rats."

John took measure of the man's voice. It returned him to his father, pulling him arm first along the dock and stopping, simpering to this man, "Old enough to be useful, he is. But through prayer and beating, the devil remains."

It was this man who led him onto The Cockerel, who took him from his mother, buried deep in England's soil—this iron-faced man, reeking of lavender, saying, "Fear not. We shall cast his evil out."

Devil and evil. John had swallowed those words whole, and now they bubbled up like bile. He seethed. But, confronted by this unknown world, he battened down his anger and pretended subservience. Besides, his head swam, and he feared he might topple to the deck if he stood any longer.

Captain Sylvester shook a handkerchief beneath his nose. "The devil, boy, go aft. You will find wash water, buckets of it. Your new master would have you less...troublesome."

Meiggs seemed to take the comment as an affront. "Our choices are small now, Captain, with Cromwell in control of Parliament. Purists like New Haven's staunch Congregationalists feel safer now, so free passage is less of an incentive. And the difficult voyage is no help. I started with ten indentures only, and three died at sea. This boy... Edward is it?" Meiggs glanced at Edward for confirmation. "He chose, through God's providence, to extend his contract and learn a trade. God willing, John will grow strong and serve his master well. Now, Edward, do as Captain Sylvester orders and assist John in a cleansing."

He fluttered his fingers aft. "Do so now."

John backed away under Edward's lead. Then they broke into a run and scrambled down the stairs to the main deck. Still unsteady, John stumbled and caught a splinter in his heel, sending a shock of pain through his foot. "Not the best of beginnings," he thought as he limped behind Edward.

At the starboard railing, Edward presented John with a bucket and brush. But his impending future, and the head pounding it produced, distracted him. Across the water, in the direction The Cockerel sailed, was his new home.

The crew shouted words John little understood as they tacked into the wind. The ship veered right and gentled into a thumb-shaped inlet. At the base of the cove, sat a town, square, gridded, and angled into a low-lying plain. A wood-spiked wall protected it, and two long wharfs jutted out from its gate.

But what took John's eye, and his breath, was what stood behind the town. In the distance, two buttes rose like crowns, east and west, shadows in the pre-dawn light. "Beautiful," he whispered. "And I am done with both Father and the sea."

He scrubbed at his skin, white as the lye soap Edward provided. Then, slick from his cleansing, John stooped, lifted the bucket, and poured the remaining water gushing over his head. He scoured his scalp and brushed his hair smooth while staring out beyond the village stockades.

"So, is that it, Edward? Out there, where the red rocks stand?"

Edward elbowed him and nodded, "It is, John. New Haven. A colony all its own. A pretty place, I think."

The New Haven ground that young Samuel Payne walked would forever be his home. Yet, before this moment, he would remember nothing; and from this moment, his every memory would unfold.

He lived between two rivers that flowed into New Haven harbor. The largest, the East River, rushed from the mountains and then bogged down, creating a brackish marshland before gathering speed and slicing in an arc to the harbor. Its gentle cousin, the Mill River, flowed from its source beyond East Rock, ducked beneath Neck Bridge, and rushed along ill-fenced pastures before skirting the eastern edge of Oystershell Field and entering the sea. He lived between them on the land called The Neck.

Samuel looked pensively from East Rock to his house, a two-story structure with a porch, a door-side garden, and a shelter-shed for animals. Seeing his home bathed in morning's first light settled his uneasy stomach.

His father had asked him to fetch his mother from the river so they could walk down The Neck to attend an upcoming trial. Being only five, the request flattered him, but it also unsettled him. Mama unsettled him.

He maneuvered the uneven ground, first running then slowing to a walk. A heron announced its presence with an unsettling squawk. It soared above him, its wingspan half again longer than he was tall. He startled and twirled, its bluster pointing him toward Mama.

She danced, milk vetch feathered at her feet. Her fists punched the sky, railing against it, lecturing like his father lectured when he was displeased. Or perhaps she sang—the way the parishioners sang Psalms on Lord's Day. He realized, walking nearer, that the words were neither lecture nor psalm. She rambled. And she laughed—at nothing—the sound high-pitched and endless.

Her mass of golden hair whirled, and she faced him.

People said he looked like her, with her white-gold hair and startling blue eyes. But he was not like her; he could not be.

Then her visage, once distant and diffused, focused on him.

"Ah, my little one, my angel." Her hair flew over him as she knelt. "I shall miss you," she said, "I shall. Did you know? I leave this place. I leave it soon."

A high-pitched song fluttered from her, and she swirled. "Not what kills the body, but that which kills the soul." She sang the words over and over until they melded with the wind

Samuel trembled, unable to voice his need. He wanted her to come with him, to calm herself, to hold his hand, to talk of gardens and bird songs. Then his fear broke through, and he ran for home. He ran to his sister's comfort.

He tried to avoid the sedge, but it scratched at his bared legs and caught in his breeches. His legs ached from his uphill race. He tripped on the porch steps, and he fell through the door. His sister, Mercy, stood at the table packing a bundle for the outing. A sob caught at the back of his throat, and she stopped, bent, and gathered him in her arms. Curls fell loose from her cap, framing the shelter of blue-grey eyes.

He reached up, wiping at his forehead and the confusion in his mind.

"I...I found Mama by the river." His stomach gripped, and Mercy, as she always did, saved him.

"Shush. Go tell Papa she is ill and unable to attend the trial." She led him to the door, her hand caressing his shoulder. Her eyes trailed away, toward East Rock and then back to Mill River. "I will fetch her," she said.

The Cockerel brought New Haven closer to view. The glint of sun, just rising, washed the town with shadow, and a rosy flush bloomed on the eastern buttress. In John's mind, it was a beckoning.

His father considered New Haven's name apt, a haven from evil, a new beginning for those seeking freedom from the bondage of sin. Then he had forced John into indenture, saying it would set him free.

"A confusion of contradiction," he thought, gazing at the idyllic scene.

Then, in a jangle of chains and the splash of an anchor, his musings vanished. Edward twisted John's head in his hands. "Look there!" he said. "Look there!"

A flat-bottomed craft with two wind-filled triangular sails skimmed over the distance between them. Edward poked John with his elbow. "They call it a shallop, a tender for transporting goods from ship to wharf—people as well."

"So, an expert at the sea, are you? Something you learned while I puked out my innards below deck?" John turned, ready to give Edward a good-natured jab, but he stopped.

Mister Meiggs, his nose falling cliff-like from an equally angular forehead, stared down on them. "Still bedraggled, but far better smelling," he said. "Follow me, boys. We go ashore."

They disembarked on a rope ladder ranging from ship deck to shallop. Captain Sylvester descended first, then Meiggs, a leather satchel at his hip. John limped behind, followed by Edward and the other indentures.

Meiggs strode to the back of the shallop and gestured John to sit next to him. Captain Sylvester ordered the shallop to shore and settled on the other side of Mister Meiggs. The captain blustered, "The crew will return to fetch the cargo after we make shore. A good haul, pipes of Madera wine, hogsheads of salt, porcelain, items craved by the Magistrates." Then he lowered his voice, conspiratorial. "All while the colony struggles under the weight of debt."

Meiggs readjusted the satchel's strap and bent close, his voice a whisper. But John was near enough to hear and grew intent. "Take care, Captain. The Magistrates think they rule with God's hand. Any criticism and they call it sedition. And, by law, sedition is death."

Captain Sylvester leaned closer. "They meddle too much in a man's affairs. Discontent grows in the colony's plantations—Southold and Stamford."

Meiggs nodded, "I confess, their ever-changing laws breed bitterness. But watch yourself, Captain. New Haven likewise breeds busy ears, always ferreting out evil."

Their talk made little sense to John, but he stored the information, adding it to his growing picture of the world around him. He took stock of Captain Sylvester, a sunburnt man, blunt in features and, based on the exchange, blunt in his dealings. The man slapped his cocked beaver hat to his knee and fingered the pearl pendant anchoring the brim.

"No court of Magistrates will dictate my ship's cargo."

Meiggs scowled. "Unwise talk, Captain. Watch for tattlers and keep your crew close."

⌒✳⌒

The shallop was tied to a wooden landing extending to shore. Its iced-over deck slicked beneath John's feet. He shivered and curled his toes, his mind dizzied and his legs weakened from the voyage. Relief and trepidation battled inside him—relief at leaving the ocean's turmoil behind and trepidation at meeting his master. A seven-year indenture might earn him a skill and eventual freedom, a far away thing in his mind. Both lay at the feet of a master he was yet to meet.

Edward's hair tickled at John's neck. "We might have a shallop someday and tender cargo from ships. Would that please you?"

John tottered forward, his left foot swollen from the splinter wedged in his heel. "Lord, Edward, you're apprenticed as a currier. Tanning hides is a foul-smelling job. No shallop awaits you, just tannins and dyes and stink. Besides, I want land under my feet—and maybe a walk in those red hills."

Mister Meiggs raised his chin and glared a silent reprimand, so they walked the rest of the wharf in silence. The air brimmed with the omnipresent smell of fish, seaweed, and salt. But John's stomach did not rebel; now it grumbled.

Meiggs stopped and stretched, glancing toward New Haven, scanning to his right. His brows furrowed, and John followed his gaze.

On a treeless isthmus east of a river, maybe twenty people, far distant, crossed a bridge to a shell-littered field and entered the town through an eastern gate. They reminded John of the processional of mourners who had come to stand at his mother's grave, the day a cloud crossed his father's face, and he was left alone.

Next Meiggs turned his attention to an assemblage of men milling at the end of the dock. He tugged at his waistcoat and strolled out to meet them. John limped behind. As Meiggs drew close, the congregants parted like the waters for Moses to reveal an imposing man dressed in a dark-blue doublet, waistcoat, and breeches. His lace was plain compared to the lace of Meiggs or the captain.

Mister Meiggs bowed low. "Governor Eaton, your humble servant. I pray you are well."

The governor nodded. "I am. And you?"

"Well enough...but I notice a gathering, and not on the Lord's Day. The occasion?"

"A reason not to tarry. A trial. Goodwife Knapp was judged a witch and punished by hanging. Then came whispers that Goodwife Staples was a witch as well. Her husband claims she was defamed. The trial begins within the hour, and the town is astir." He glanced to the gate behind him with a shake of his head. "But to the business at hand. These are the servants you bring from England?"

The men's discussions droned in John's ears. His heel throbbed, his gut churned, his fingers tapped uncontrollably.

A short, barrel-chested man, pale-skinned and ruddy, sidled up to Eaton. He stretched, his chin aloft, as if to gain height. "Like a peacock," John thought, near to laughing.

He was about to whisper as much to Edward when the peacock man strutted away from his flock, hands clasped behind his back, and stood so that his breath fluttered across John's face.

"Ill-clothed, Mister Meiggs. Not well. Scurvy?" He whipped up a pointed finger. "Still, I abide by our covenant to lead every soul to God's light." He preened, smiling toward Eaton, then glared at Meiggs. "You carry the necessary papers?"

Meiggs loosened the strap securing his satchel, flipped through the contents, and retrieved a single parchment document. "It only wants your signature, and your payment."

John looked from Edward to Meiggs. He forgot his heel and came down hard on it, winced, and shifted his weight to favor it.

"John Frost," Meiggs was saying, "attend. By your father's judgment and the contract he signed, this man takes you for his servant. Indentured to him for seven years."

John stared in confusion at the peacock's buckled shoes while Meiggs finished his introduction. "Mister Gibbard, your servant, John Frost."

❧

Mercy Payne left Samuel with instructions to find Father and ran down the slope to Mill River where Mama danced. Then, through lies and cajoling, she coaxed her to the house. But Mama refused to go inside. She fidgeted in a fitful fury at the door-side garden gate. Mercy tried to draw her in, but she twisted Mercy's every word into fanciful notions, smiling and swaying and singing her repeated song, "Not what kills the body, but that which kills the soul."

Father appeared with Samuel clutched in his arms, and, with eyes cast red, he handed him to Mercy. "Not yet eleven and you shoulder so much. But I must tend to your mother."

Mercy cringed, thinking what her father would do. He would bind Mama to the bed and call it an act of love. He tied Mama down so often now that Mercy's heart cried out. She prayed for a cure. She begged Him, but He did not answer.

She warned Samuel to stay put, though he seemed disinclined to move, and stepped silently into the house to retrieve their basket of food. On the way out she heard her mother's wispy voice. "Sweet husband, dear William. Did you know I sail home? Away from the ears and the eyes? Soon, very soon." Her father responded as he always did. He hushed Mama, told her to settle and to sleep. He walked away.

Now they followed their neighbors across the cart bridge spanning Mill River and traveled the barren Oystershell Field. Mercy clung to Samuel's hand and Father held the other.

She had not wanted to attend this trial, to involve Samuel in it. But Father had insisted. "Our absence," he said, "would draw suspicion."

She lauded Father's courage, his grip, of necessity, on duty. Her mother's strangeness had expanded over the past two years. She neglected their care, spending more and more time along the river. Mercy took some of her duties and, finally, all of them, including tending to Samuel. Papa spent his time keeping the pigs and the corn and the cow and protecting Mama from the watchers. Her mother was their shared secret, their uncommon bond.

Samuel squeezed Mercy's hand, and she looked down to his white-gold hair, falling like silk into eyes as trusting as the sky. A beautiful child, she thought, the visage of his mother, but saved from her temperament.

"These trials are long, Samuel, so be patient. I put in honey and corncakes, with cider to wash them down. We might sneak out early."

Samuel's smile shook, but he lightened and that made her glad. For, of all her prayers, and she embraced prayer like a personal communion, her most fervent was to keep Samuel safe.

John waited a few paces back from his new master and eyed the sentry positioned on a rampart above the open gate to New Haven. His heel throbbed, as did his head, from lack of food or water, both difficult to manage on his grueling three-month journey.

Edward hovered behind his own newly appointed master and mimed an aching belly. He clutched his gut and contorted in conjured agony. John laughed, a silent snicker that lifted both his shoulder and his spirit. He cherished this newfound friend, always breaching the barriers he built, willing himself into John's heart.

His friend's new master, a tall, hunched man, sensed the silent communication between them and challenged their antics with a grim-faced stare. He said something to Edward that John could not hear, then marched toward the gate. Edward followed, smiling back at John from under his arm. He slicked back a mass of brown curls and, with a wink and a grin, was gone.

John squirmed, half-listening, as Meiggs finalized some transactions and made arrangements to meet with others at the ordinary where he and Captain Sylvester were staying. They talked of the prices, the drink, and the food. The mention of flummery pudding set John's mouth to watering, and his memories wandered to his mother and her kind hands setting a dish of the white fluff on the table before him.

Then Mister Eaton announced his departure for the trial. Mister

Gibbard darted toward John, dithering, "Follow me, boy. Keep the pace," then dashed back to Mister Eaton like a fawning sycophant. Eaton's entourage hustled through the gate, each member vying for his attention. They called him Master, Mister, Magistrate, and Governor. "For these men," John thought, "Eaton is The Word."

He hobbled behind his master, balancing on the ball of his left foot and cautiously stepping to his right. They traversed a lane, two carts wide, lined on either side by fenced-in acreage. Clapboard houses with door-side gardens crowned every parcel. Then, at the end of the lane, the town opened onto an unexpected expanse.

A square of near twenty acres occupied the center of the town. Splendid chestnuts and oaks provided a welcoming shade and, at the near corner of the green, a spring bubbled into a cistern, beckoning John's bone-dry throat. He worked saliva into a ball at the back of his teeth and swallowed.

At the clay-lined tank, he waited while a team of oxen finished their drink. Then Gibbard signaled, and he fell forward, gulping from cupped hands until his gut constricted and begged him quit. The cistern's rock wall called out, and he leaned against it, shifting his weight from his heel, a savored release.

Then Governor Eaton made to walk to the center of the green where a square building stood. Gibbard trotted after him like a dog currying favor. John sighed, ready to follow, but his master vacillated, indecisive, as another man strolled toward the spring. He had a stubborn nose framed by gentle eyes. Pale, curling hair popped from a square, black cap. A dower woman hung on his arm.

Gibbard moved to follow Eaton, looked back, reconsidered, and positioned himself to wait for the couple. "Begging your pardon,

Mister Davenport," he said, his head bowed. "I hope you are well."

The man greeted him with polite reluctance. "Mister Gibbard. Will you join us at the trial?"

"I would not miss it, sir, and support you always. Word says Goodwife Davenport testifies?"

Davenport scowled, about to reply, when another man, followed by a girl and a towheaded boy, interrupted. "My humble pardon, Reverend Davenport."

"Mister Payne?"

"Sir, I bring apologies regarding my wife. She suffers again with lameness and regrets she is unable to attend the trial. And one so important to our congregation."

"And our covenant," the reverend added.

Gibbard intervened, again stretching to gain height. "Indeed, should the woman be possessed of the devil—not your wife, Mister Payne, of course, but Goody Staples—God will reap his due. Reverend Davenport knows the woman's condition, I am sure."

Mister Payne stiffened. "Ah yes, but Satan can be wily," he said, and, with an artful redirect, he moved the conversation from the devil to John. "So, Mister Gibbard, you have a new charge?"

John cringed and shifted his weight, wincing from the attention more than the pain in his heel. He straightened, not wishing to look slovenly, and again balked at the pounding in his foot. The girl, who until now had stood behind, stepped forward, eyeing him with concern. "He favors his foot, Papa. It hurts."

Her father's eyes widened, pointedly chastising her. "Daughter, be seemly!"

But the girl was undeterred. She shook loose the hands of the little boy holding her arm and walked straight toward John. "Look, Reverend. Look to his foot."

She stared with blue eyes that trailed to grey. John avoided them and roamed her freckled nose and the reckless curls trapped beneath her cap. Then, to his shock, she hoisted up his foot. He grabbed the edge of the cistern for balance, and she gentled him like a farrier examining a horse's hoof, presenting his heel to the three men standing before him.

"Swollen, sir," she said, and gently prodded his heal, but not gently enough. John gasped.

She pulled again and a sharp agony radiated up his ankle.

He stood now, pulling from her grasp.

"Enough!" The word barked from his throat before he could retrieve it.

Still he stood, looking it back and studying those around him— first, the girl's father, who turned up it to avoid a [illegible] next, his new master, who shifted his [illegible] going to Reverend Davenport for direction, and lastly following Gibbard's lead, but he peered who hinted at an unexpected smile.

"The girl, dear boy, has found you out."

Then Reverend Davenport dealt his pronouncements: "Elzbeth Payne my best wishes, William. We shall miss her. And Gibbard, I know your passion for God's judgment and your [illegible] attend the trial, But it must proceed without you. We are [illegible] covenant with our servants—to educate them in the way [illegible] provide for them in all ways, Therefore, with my [illegible] God's blessing, take the boy home and into your wife's [illegible]

John surveyed the reaction of these new players in his [illegible]

Mister Davenport," he said, his head bowed. "I hope you are well."

The man greeted him with polite reluctance. "Mister Gibbard. Will you join us at the trial?"

"I would not miss it, sir, and support you always. Word says Goodwife Davenport testifies?"

Davenport scowled, about to reply, when another man, followed by a girl and a towheaded boy, interrupted. "My humble pardon, Reverend Davenport."

"Mister Payne?"

"Sir, I bring apologies regarding my wife. She suffers again with lameness and regrets she is unable to attend the trial. And one so important to our congregation."

"And our covenant," the reverend added.

Gibbard intervened, again stretching to gain height. "Indeed, should the woman be possessed of the devil—not your wife, Mister Payne, of course, but Goody Staples—God will reap his due. Reverend Davenport knows the woman's condition, I am sure."

Mister Payne stiffened. "Ah yes, but Satan can be wily," he said, and, with an artful redirect, he moved the conversation from the devil to John. "So, Mister Gibbard, you have a new charge?"

John cringed and shifted his weight, wincing from the attention more than the pain in his heel. He straightened, not wishing to look slovenly, and again balked at the pounding in his foot. The girl, who until now had stood behind, stepped forward, eyeing him with concern. "He favors his foot, Papa. It hurts."

Her father's eyes widened, pointedly chastising her. "Daughter, be seemly!"

But the girl was undeterred. She shook loose the hands of the little boy holding her arm and walked straight toward John. "Look, Reverend. Look to his foot."

She stared with blue eyes that trailed to grey. John avoided them and roamed her freckled nose and the reckless curls trapped beneath her cap. Then, to his shock, she hoisted up his foot. He grabbed the edge of the cistern for balance, and she gentled him like a farrier examining a horse's hoof, presenting his heel to the three men standing before him.

"Swollen, sir," she said, and gently prodded his heal, but not gently enough. John gasped.

She poked again and a sharp agony radiated up his ankle.

He cried out, pulling from her grasp.

"Enough!" The word barked from his throat before he could retrieve it.

Still he tried, sucking it back and studying those around him—first, the girl's father, who twisted as if to avoid a punch; next, his new master, who shifted his dumbfounded gaze to Reverend Davenport for direction; and lastly, following Gibbard's lead, the reverend who hinted at an unexpected smile.

"The girl, dear boy, has found you out."

Then Reverend Davenport dealt his pronouncements. "Send Elzbeth Payne my best wishes, William. We shall miss her. And Mister Gibbard, I know your passion for God's judgment and your desire to attend the trial. But it must proceed without you. We are bound in a covenant with our servants—to educate them in the way of God and provide for them—in all ways. Therefore, with my permission and God's blessing, take this boy home and into your wife's care."

John surveyed the reaction of these new players in his life, weighing the nuance of each. The girl smiled in triumph; her father rolled fear-filled eyes toward heaven; Reverend Davenport looked on with righteous pity.

But it was Mister Gibbard's reaction that sickened him—even more than a heaving ship. The man's lip curled, his nose twitched, and he glared at John with loathing. This trial, these Magistrates, meant something to his master, and John had thwarted his plans.

~❀~

After the scene at the cistern, Mercy's contempt for Mister Gibbard swelled to revulsion. The man regularly wheedled Father regarding her mother, even spying from Neck Bridge on his stout little pony, and today he offered that poor boy not even a thimbleful of kindness. Now he hobbled away, dragged by Mister Gibbard whose squat body pumped from side to side like a rutting pig. She swallowed a giggle.

Pleasuring at that pompous meddler's deflation was, no doubt, a sin. Self-shamed, she whispered a prayer against bedevilment. Then, when the boy stepped into a pile of the cattle dung littering the green, she recanted her prayer. The man was a mean-spirited and undeserving toady. She pitied the boy's fate. Gossip said Mister Gibbard dealt with his servants through the unrelenting lens of scripture—and the rod. Those same pernicious tattlers approved of Gibbard's actions, considering him a virtuous interpreter of God's word. A vision of her mother's bound wrists sent a fire burning in Mercy's chest. As Mister Gibbard and his sandy-haired charge disappeared behind an oak, she scrunched her nose and stuck out her tongue—just the tip, quick as a viper. It was the most she could do for now.

Mercy's father walked with long strides toward the meetinghouse. It loomed before them, large, square, and decrepit. She rushed to catch up, with Samuel in tow, stepping high to avoid the muck generated by animal hooves, mud, and manure. Father walked with Mister Cooper who rose, tall and gangly, above even her tall father. The men launched into a familiar conversation.

"The place decays more each day, Brother Payne. The result of shoddy workmanship. We require craftsmen—tanners and boot makers and carpenters. We may be blessed of God's spirit but we are sorely lacking in the necessary skills."

Her father agreed. "We hail from educated families, Mister Cooper, and the trades elude us. But, without funds, no matter our skill, I fear the meetinghouse stands as it is."

Mercy glanced up at the two-story building ringed with windows high and low. A soldier stood guard in the small tower fastened to the top of the meetinghouse's hipped roof. She worried for the man. Could the building tumble with him in it? Did he know his danger? A triangular roof covered the turret and pointed skyward. She had always thought it heavenly, but now? She looked down, squeezed Samuel's hand, and pulled him closer, then fell in behind her father.

Samuel tugged at her apron. "Will it fall?" he asked.

"I think not, Samuel, or they would not allow us entry." Still, she listened to the creaking of the stairs as they walked up to the meetinghouse door and took note of the curling clapboard siding. A mustiness wafted from the foundation. She bent to Samuel's ear. "It will not, at least, fall today."

Three doors, one at the center of each wall, opened into the meetinghouse. The back wall held no door. In its place, facing the congregants, stood the pulpit and the Magistrates' benches, barred off by a wooden railing.

They walked through the east-facing door, the one opposite the pulpit. Her father stopped her just inside the door, near the stairs leading to a balcony. His hand fell heavy on her shoulder as he leaned to face her. "Be not meddlesome, daughter. For the sake of your good mother, take care in your speech and choose meekness, a choice adornment for a woman. Do you understand?"

A firebrand of anger worked into her throat, but she swallowed it down. For her mother's sake, she curbed her tongue and nodded. Her father left her to walk the central aisle and take his assigned seat. Mercy turned right and led Samuel along the back wall.

The militia occupied the last three rows on both the men and women's side of the central aisle. Come sixteen years of age, every man, freeman or servant, served. The Magistrates imposed fines on any soldier late for duty or lacking the necessary musket or powder. Fines flew with ease from New Haven courts. The court once levied a fine against Mercy's father for a pig that broke loose from his fencing. Her father had grown angry, saying they collected fines for no more than a sneeze and a fart. Then he cautioned her never to repeat his words.

Freemen now flowed in through each of the meetinghouse doors. They took seats assigned to them by their prominence in New Haven society. Mother sat at the back of the meetinghouse on the women's side in a pew mirroring their father's, just in front of the soldiers. Those seated nearer the front garnered greater stature.

As Mercy guided Samuel up the aisle to their mother's pew, Midwife Potter caught her eye. The woman took up no space in her seat but held her wizen body straight and stern. As Mercy walked past, she reached up with a gnarled hand and tugged at her sleeve.

"Goody Potter," Mercy said, a reluctant greeting.

"Again your good mother begs illness?"

Father's words vibrated inside her. She wanted to tell the old woman it was not her concern and huff away. She refrained. "Yes, still ill, but recovering."

"Well, perhaps I will visit her. Elzbeth misses so often. It concerns me."

Mercy wet her lips. She felt every eye press in on her, but when she glanced around, found everyone distracted.

"Be not concerned, Midwife Potter. She mends. Thank you for your thoughts, but Samuel and I best take our seats. We block the aisle." She hustled Samuel away, head down, shamed by her deception, a breath of anger in her chest.

Relieved to reach her mother's pew, she hoisted Samuel up to sit in her lap. Only five-years-old, he was still heavy, and he slipped from her grasp. She caught him under his arms, repositioned him, and collapsed into the pew, her apron wadded beneath his sturdy frame.

"I want to sit next to you," he said, wriggling and tugging at her petticoats.

"No room. Now hush."

Goodwife Cooper nodded to her as she passed to take her place at a front row pew. While one of the more important freeman wives, she never acted haughty, and Mercy liked her for it. The woman stuffed four children into the center pew three rows from the front. Her housemaid must be detained. To gain space, congregants with servants usually sent one to watch their children in the gallery. Lacking that convenience, Mercy and Samuel crowded into the pew with their mother or sat at her feet or in the aisle.

Samuel squirmed. Mercy nudged him close and used her sleeve to wipe a rivulet of sweat forming on his hairline. The women's pews and the upstairs gallery were filled to congestion. They sweltered in a suffocating spring heat amplified by a sizeable attendance. It was, after all, a witch trial.

Widow Sherwood squeezed past Mercy and plopped her bulging body next to her. "Now we shall see what comes of a witch's confession," she said. "Take it as a lesson, dear Mercy. Befriending one who is bedeviled will indeed bedevil you. Mister Ludlow named Goodwife Staples a witch. He says Goody Knapp, overcome by the chain slipping round her neck, stopped everything to confess, not to her evil, but to the evil of Goody Staples. Humph. Do you believe it?" She readjusted her mass, and, deprived of space, Mercy scooted with Samuel to the edge of the pew.

Widow Sherwood rarely stopped talking, nor did she now. "Mister Staples calls it false, says Mister Ludlow spread an unfounded rumor about his wife. He claims the reverend and his wife passed the ill-begotten story on to others." The widow adjusted her collar and leaned near, the fragrance of new-baked bread on her breath. "What I hear is that Goody Staples did consort with Goody Knapp—not as a witch, but as a friend—so take care in your friendships, dear." The woman tucked in her doubled-chin, considering Mercy. "But, child, you come once more without your mother. Has she taken sick again?"

With minds focused on witchcraft, this attention to her mother's absence sent Mercy's stomach churning. Worse, Widow Sherwood proved a happy gossip, waddling from one household to another under the guise of a good neighbor. Thankfully, a soldier behind the widow knocked the butt of his gun to the floor and cleared his throat, admonishing Widow Sherwood to quiet.

At that moment, Governor Eaton stepped to the pulpit. The rumble of the crowd receded to murmurs. The governor's appearance signaled the commencement of the trial, but due to her small stature, Mercy saw nothing but a sea of caps and backs.

"Stop wiggling, Samuel." She tried to keep her voice quiet, an effort under the weight of his bouncing body.

"I cannot see," he said.

"And you think I can?"

"Sister, please...the aisle. I will be still. I promise." He lifted his soft blue eyes and smiled a wide rosy smile, the one he used to gain her favor. Of course, he won. Though only ten, she considered him more her child than her brother. He was her duty. She favored him and loved him, always.

"Hold tight to my petticoat and do not scoot away. And no more squirming. Or talking!" She whisked a strand of white-gold hair from his forehead and kissed him. Triumphant, he slid from her lap and settled in the aisle. With her petticoat serving as a lever, he leaned out for a better view.

Sweat trickled along Mercy's neck. She dabbed at it, set her back straight, and closed her eyes, listening to the proceedings. First came the deep, kindly voice of Governor Eaton.

"Thomas Staples, you charge Mister Ludlow with defamation. You claim he spread falsehoods to Mister Davenport, his wife, and others, that he called your goodwife a witch. You claim he told others that your wife searched Witch Knapp after she was hanged and, seeing her teats, said 'if they have the marks of a witch then I myself am one.' Is that correct?"

Samuel reached up and pulled on Mercy's bodice.

"A witch's teats, sister? What do they look like?"

Mercy flushed. She raised her eyes to the gallery. Was the whole of New Haven staring at them? "I know not, Samuel. Now shush!"

Samuel slumped back to the floor, pulled hard at her petticoats, and wrapped them around his tucked knees. Mercy ignored him, attempting to follow the words of the trial.

Mister Ludlow, the one accused of calling Goody Staples a witch, was not there. He sent an attorney to speak for him. Many a man deserted the plantation before his trial, fearing the Magistrates and their verdict.

The man's attorney asked Reverend Davenport to testify under oath. Offended, the reverend refused, but after some sermonizing, he acquiesced. Dissembling, he prattled that he thought the accusations of witchery false, but Ludlow spread the rumor with such intelligence that he became convinced. So he repeated the gossip to others.

The trial continued on and on, mostly it repeated itself, witness after witness. The next Mercy knew, her head bobbed to her chest then jerked awkwardly upward. She lurched into awareness with a startled gasp and glanced down to Samuel. He sat at her feet, using her petticoats as a prop for his sleeping head.

The bench wobbled with Widow Sherwood's muffled chuckle. "Seems you are blessed to sleep straight as a rod, Mercy Payne. Here is the trial so far." The widow nuzzled close; a yeasty odor seeped from her pores as she spoke. "According to the new witness, Witch Knapp had opportunity to save her life by naming Goody Staples a witch, but she refused. Said she knew nothing of it and would not breed difference betwixt her neighbors nor spread malicious seed."

"She would hang rather than name the woman a witch?"

"So the witness says, if she be trustworthy."

Samuel tugged at Mercy's apron. He rubbed his eyes, glum and disoriented. "I am hungry, sister, and need to..." He grabbed at himself. A flush of heat engulfed Mercy, fearing all must be watching. But, she likewise rejoiced. A gate had opened, an escape route from the trial—and the widow.

"Forgive me, Widow Sherwood. I must—"

"Say no more, dear one. A good daughter you are, to serve your father and mother so. Go care for the boy."

Mercy retrieved their basket of foodstuffs at the entry and hurried Samuel outside. After he relieved himself, they sat to eat on the rickety steps by the meetinghouse door.

Samuel licked the honey that oozed from the corncakes, then sucked his fingers to catch the last drips. "Will she hang?" Samuel asked.

"It is not even about hanging, Samuel, only gossip, and lies." Mercy sipped cider from a small pottery crock, washing the liquid around in her mouth to clean residual bits of cake and honey from her teeth.

"But is Goody Staples a witch?"

"I'm not even sure poor Goody Knapp was a witch, nor if witches are real at all."

"Enough, daughter."

Mercy scrambled, startled, to her feet. "No one was around, Papa."

"And yet I heard you."

"I am sorry, I—"

"Do not dither, child. I understand." His eyes had softened. He smoothed her cap and tweaked her cheek. "We go now, children.

Captain Sylvester is finishing his account of damages for goods not paid, and aside from some issues of estate, they are finished. I begged leave to care for your mother."

Mercy corked the crockery jug, slid it into her basket, and took Samuel's hand. They hurried to catch up to their father, already hustling across the green.

"Papa, what of Goody Staples? Did they decide?" Mercy asked.

"Ludlow did her wrong, and more. They fined him ten pounds with another five to Mister Staples for his trouble. And daughter?"

"Yes, Papa?"

"You are right. Witches are not likely, and man meddles too much with too little wisdom. But, take care. You see how things went. They would conjure a devil from dust. So be wary."

⤺❀⤻

John's new master hurried him, with snatches and yanks, along the shell-strewn streets. He followed with a lop-sided limp, favoring his aching foot. They angled down a side street, then turned away from the harbor and skirted the palisade wall. His master stopped. With a jerk, he wrenched back John's arm and pinned him to a post.

John stared at the man's stiffened collar, stomach muscles clenched against the pain. Gibbard's breath blew out, thick with onions. "You caused me to be late for trial, boy, and I will not have it. I know the devil when I see it, and this is what he earns." He buried his fist twice into John's stomach. John doubled and blinked his watering eyes.

While unexpected, coming from this new lord of his life, the blows were not uncommon—just another version of his father's punishments after Mother died. But they battered a lingering hope for something new in a new world. Gibbard pulled back harder on his arm. "Stand, boy, and say nothing—unless you wish for more. Now move."

Near the end of the street, they came to a fine two-story home with a summer kitchen and a good-sized barn, not so nice as an English country home but fine enough. Gibbard hustled him up the stairs to a porch spanning the length of the house. A thin-boned woman holding a ladle in her hand greeted them at the door.

"Our indenture," Gibbard said. He shoved John forward, and he fell to his knees at the woman's feet.

She looked down at him and held out her hand, her countenance one of buttery warmth. "I am Mistress Gibbard, child. And you are—"

"No time for that, wife. Care for the foot. I shall deal with him later."

John scrambled to his feet and bowed his head, biting his lips, unsure how to proceed.

Gibbard bounded down the porch stairs, continuing his harangue. "The boy be ill-gotten, already putting me late to the trial. He is an eye-servant, wife, one to be watched. And not to be trusted." The man left in a fury to his all-important trial. John deemed his appraisal of the man complete. He hated him.

Mistress Gibbard placed a gentle hand on his back and eased him across the threshold into the house. "Your name?" she asked. The smell of fermented cider lingered on her breath.

"John Frost, mistress."

"Well then, John Frost..." She touched his arm and led him to the hearth fire. "Sit here and I shall see to your foot."

He sat on a long wooden settle facing two slat-backed chairs. The woman placed her ladle on the hearth, crossed the room, and paused, glancing up a short flight of stairs leading to the second story. Four stocking feet fidgeted there. "Not now children, I must see to his needs and then you may greet him." She smiled back at him. "My two daughters. They are anxious to meet you since you are charged with their care. But time enough for them later, after you rest."

So Goodwife Gibbard fussed with his foot. He pretended the splinter was minor, his only concession to the pain a slight upward twitch of his lips, one he hoped would seem a smile. He balanced on the settle, and she practiced her housewifery. She doused the heel with a decoction of witch hazel and lowered his foot into a tub filled with cornflower and goldenrod. The water, hot from the hearth, had bled to a pale urine yellow. He curled his lip, finding little faith in the remedy.

"The color comes out of the petals, John. Are you one who doubts even what stands before your eyes?" She paused, turning inward, then burst out laughing. "Wise in that, boy, for the devil hides often in plain sight. Let the foot soak until the water turns cold. I shall see if there are shoes in the house near your size." She slid from the stool, her body as lean as her husband's was square. Her brown and ocher petticoats swished up the narrow stairs, and she disappeared.

John closed his eyes. He retraced his steps from the cistern in the square and across the green to the meetinghouse. He drew a mind map as he rehearsed the route, reversing it. The way veered south and then east along the walled fortification. From there he could make the harbor. He swallowed down the spit rising in his throat. If ever necessary, the memory of the route and Gibbard's fist in his stomach would be useful in escape—to wharf and ship and safety.

With time, the soaking water cooled. He lifted his foot, balancing it on his right knee, and studied the wound. By applying pressure with both thumbs, a tar-brown point appeared just beneath the surface. He pinched harder and a thick mass crept forward. With foot held steady, he pushed with his left thumb and seized the culprit between the thumb and forefinger of his right hand. He pulled with precision— neither hurrying nor jerking, a patient act—and the splinter slid free, though a biting pain remained.

He marveled at the devilish slip of tarred wooden decking, more than an inch long. This burdensome bit of wood, wedged deep in his heel, had harassed his every step, and now he was done with it—but not all. He whispered a curse and flipped the sliver into the coals behind him. Again he pressed at his wound and winced as a clear burst of liquid emerged, followed by a trickle of blood. He spat on his fingers and dabbed at the leavings, then rinsed the puncture clean with the witch hazel Mistress Gibbard had left by the hearth. Though his heel throbbed like the devil, it would heal. Some things, though, might not repair.

The spite and malice of Gibbard's words festered. This flaw his master ranted over— his father's preaching had condemned it, as well. "Our lots," he had said, "are predestined, and our sins ordained."

John poked at the puncture once more and a thin thread of red-tinged liquid trickled out. A shivering, residual ache remained.

"If I am an eye-servant, to be watched and not trusted," he whispered to the fire whipping at the hearth's grate, "then I too must be watchful. And wary."

The volumes wait on her nightstand, their patience a lesson of time.

*After their return from the conference, Maggie had sat them at the
top of her stack of books, and they waited. She needs to finish one title
before going on to the next. She likes to finish things to the end, a habit
the volumes appreciate, a habit they will need. But last night she had
completed the intervening competition and tucked it on a shelf with a
pleasured sigh at the story's ending. Together, the books decide—the time
for waiting is done.*

*They sense the tickle of her shorts' frayed cuff as she pulls them up,
feel the cotton camisole tumble over her head. She scowls, annoyed by
the creeping of her skin, and wonders how to stop it. They chuckle at the
notion. She needs perspective; life is so much more than creeping skin.*

*The summer day hangs glum and smoky, a product of drought
induced wildfires. The air, too unhealthy to spend time outdoors,
provides them with a perfect opportunity. So they encourage her, ask her
with all politeness to spend time with them.*

*Still she flounders, like one of those wind-up ducks from an import
store, skittering and circling without clear direction. So many things tug
at her: a list of research possibilities, the laundry, the bills—and them,
two volumes sitting at the top of her stack of reading. They refuse to leave
her alone.*

*She walks away from them, into the kitchen. But distance changes
nothing. They travel with her, cord connected to her soul. She slugs down
a handful of vitamins and minerals, her attempt to extend a meaningful
life. They intercede, wheedle her even, attempting to draw her into the
lives they hold between their pages, lives as important to them as hers.
She looks up at a multicolored India ink drawing of Yama, the Lord of
Death, hanging on the wall. His mouth opens wide, regurgitating the
world and its endless wheel of compassion and suffering.*

She wishes—almost "wishes to hell"—but she won't go that far, not with old Yama staring down. Still, she wishes she could cough up all the ideas, every possibility rumbling inside her head, and fling them out, once and for all, in a magnificent mouthful. The volumes understand and sympathize. They too experience urgency. The older you get, the more urgent doing becomes, and they are exceedingly old. Their empathy works on her. She shakes her head. "Those damn books keep calling me," she says and walks back to her library to retrieve them. But not them. Only one.

She decides to start at the beginning and picks up Volume I: 1638-1649. The books ache at separation, but it is necessary. She needs to read the first volume to understand the story hidden in the second. Volume I floats off alone, cradled in Maggie's hand.

Her step springs; she likes purpose. Besides, Duncan will enjoy having her beside him. He's been a little perturbed lately, bemoaning those days away at the conference and all the time she spends in the miniature office tucked into their back bedroom. At least this way she can sit next to him in the front room while she reads.

"Oh, coming out to join me are you?" he says as she walks to her chair.

"Yesss." She draws out the word, smiling at him, grimacing really. She gives him the expression that says he'd best not make a big deal out of it, hoping he gets it. She turns the first page, but before she can start—

"What you reading?" Duncan peers over her shoulder, trying to make out the title. "Records of the Colony and Plantation of New Haven, from 1638 to 1649. Wow! A real page turner." He drops his head to his shoulder and begins snoring—a pretty accurate portrayal.

"Smart ass," she laughs. "I'll have you know that New Haven

is a pretty interesting piece of history. These upscale, educated
fundamentalists—some of the richest in the early colonies—sail out of
Boston, find this shallow little harbor, and start their own colony. No
charter from the King or anything."

"Really? So—want to make a bet on how long before you fall asleep?"

"I'll bet that you'll be the one falling asleep first. And I'll win."

"Well, yeah, but that's betting on a sure thing. I always fall asleep.
You carry on like it's a mission or something."

Maggie crosses her eyes at him, and he lifts his grey brows in
acknowledgment. The first volume relaxes in her hands, enjoying their
good-hearted bantering, a combat with no malice intended. Maggie
shakes her head, feigning disgust, and begins to read.

She notices the attention to detail right away, more like wordiness.
Her first impression isn't great. She thinks the text reads like some kind
of early English "lawyer-ese."

The books worry at her reaction. She doesn't get these people,
especially Theophilus Eaton and John Davenport, the two undisputed
heads of the colony. The volume in the backroom badgers, insists the first
gets to work. Help her understand. Tell her the New Haven colonists are
impassioned. They are businessmen.

The first entry outlines the purchase of New Haven lands and their
agreement with the Quinnipiac, the local tribe. The book paints her
a picture. The leaders are educated, upstanding, independent, and
wealthy. Maggie thinks "uptight elitists" might be a better description.
But the book warms in her hand, opening her, willing her to suspend
judgment so she can fathom their world.

One thing intrigues her, a point of consensus. They believe all
freemen should participate in decision-making. They vote—on

everything to begin with. Their first vote is that the scriptures, the word of God, will be their perfect foundation for governance. The next vote establishes church members as the only men worthy to govern. They believed they were chosen by God to establish His order in their new world.

Maggie lets go, reads it all, even the passion between the lines. These men—and they are all men—navigate with an iron-willed moral compass. They use a decision-making system based on their interpretation of the Bible and require a freeman's oath swearing allegiance to their church, the one church that knows the way to God. She doesn't like it; it is so different from her world. Still, she is intrigued. She is learning something new.

"Complex but interesting," she says aloud, an attempt to engage Duncan. "They actually paid the Indians for the land they took. Maybe they aren't so bad." The book invades her thoughts. She goes too far. It offers doubt.

"Compared to now, though? Really different," she says and looks over at her husband, hoping for a little acknowledgment of her enthusiasm.

Too bad she hadn't pushed a little harder on that bet. She would have won.

PART II

1655(and the present)

If any person be a Witch, he or she shall be put to death.

Code of New Haven

Aside from the constant sting of Mister Gibbard's rod, John's winter survival proved the hardest thing. He slept in the summer kitchen, a shed built for cooking during the sweltering months. The barn would have served better, but law prevented him from a bed in the barn—some notion about kindliness to servants.

A plank table at the center of the kitchen exuded the permanent odor of slaughtered chickens. His bed consisted of straw gathered on the table and covered with a worn tarp. Mistress Gibbard had provided him with a warm coat and wool coverlet. Her heart was kind but did not compensate for his condition.

On the coldest nights, he was allowed a small blaze. The place had a stone hearth with no chimney. A hole to the outdoors, big enough to crawl through, had been made to let the smoke out but it also allowed every manner of inclement weather to blow through the opening and extinguishing the fire. He had covered the hole with an old iron grate, but the smoke, thus trapped, billowed into the little room, creating a choking misery.

Fire or not, the wind whistled through the crevices in the plank walls. The slat roof, built only for summer shade, leaked at the seams, and drifts of wind-driven snow cumulated against the walls and froze there.

Any skiff of water turned to ice, whether puddle, pitcher, or trough.

Drips transformed the kitchen eaves into a spiked palisade of icicles. Beyond the kitchen walls, water, fresh or salted, constricted the movement of all living things, including the slow-leaving geese. John felt as equally trapped as one of those birds, frozen to a cold and hapless landscape.

On this rare day, teased out by the coming spring, John ventured to the barn to lounge on the mounded hay stored there. His belly bulged from the early morning meal Mistress Gibbard served, a hardy fare of dried fish and squash stew. His toe ached, so he curled it down and away from the stiff leather of his left boot. The boots were, in fact, fashioned with neither left nor right, making it easier to switch them as they wore out. His feet had grown two shoe sizes since his arrival the year before. It rankled the master to keep providing new shoes, "good money after bad," as he told it, but these kindnesses heartened his mistress. She took pride in his growth and fattening. Much, he thought, like fattening a calf for the slaughter—or a goose—Gibbard's trapped goose, to abuse as he so desired. The abuses, hidden from the mistress, burned. Still, John tried for patience. Spring neared, the ground melted, and opportunity increased with each lengthening day.

He looked around with pride at the darkened barn where each tool hung, oiled and sharpened, just as he had organized it. Rivulets of water trickled off the barn door, creating a soothing susurrus.

Soon the drum would roll, calling the town to Lord's Day services. The master and mistress had left early, as usual. It gave Gibbard time to cozy up to the reverend and governor and puff himself up with his importance as newly elected Deputy of New Haven. With the drum's signal, he would walk the couple's young daughters, Sarah and Prudence, to the meetinghouse. For now, though, he rolled to his stomach, nestled deep in the hay, and closed his eyes, taking solace in the gifts of the coming spring—well-shod feet, if a bit scrunched, a well-fed body, and the chance of escape.

Then, with a thud, a flattening weight plunged his body deep into the hay. Driven to battle, John flailed, spitting at the leaves and seeds jammed into his mouth. He reached back with one pinned arm, then the other, attempting to grab whatever or whoever was holding him down.

The barn echoed with the boon of laughter. "Caught you, John Frost. Dawdling and dreaming." Edward House released his grip and John struggled to his feet, slipping in the hay. He regained his balance and shoved Edward's shoulders. His friend staggered back, rebounded, and flattened John again, stuffing his woolen cap deep over his eyes and ears.

"Enough! Enough," John cried and flung his arms up, lifting Edward into the air. He flew back, still holding John's cap, and landed hard in the hay.

With legs sprawled, he jerked his head up and sputtered, "Christ, John, you are a site stronger than when I last saw you." He glanced up and down John's body, brushed the hay from his breeches, and stood. "Bigger, too, and heavier. Stand."

John obeyed—then registered his own surprise. He stood a hand taller than Edward and his chest and arms were meatier by far. "The mistress is a cook," he said, "and Gibbard works me like his mule. But you, Edward, how go things with you?"

"Well enough. You seemed busy in the hay, John, and grown. I wonder, has that thing between your legs grown as well?"

John clutched his groin. What was it about this friend who sensed everything, including this new feeling in him? And the sensation was new. His feelings fluctuated from distress to excitement. They woke him at night, hard and bursting. They sieged his thoughts, making him wonder what lay beneath Mistress Gibbard's bodice. One thing, though, was clear, the topic horrified him, and he would shift the subject, directly.

"I am a man now, Edward. Thirteen. No boy, if that be your implication. But how goes your apprenticing?"

"Not so well. The man is no currier...has me cutting trees, mostly. Harvesting the bark for tanning." Then, seeing through John's deflection, Edward returned to his needling. "Have you discovered relief? You know, to ease the yearning? No devil in it, trust me, nor is it unclean, no matter what their story." He gestured toward the green, indicating the meetinghouse hidden from view, then leaned close. "Just grab hold and stroke. A grand release."

John looked down at his hands, mortified—and relieved. Sharing this new awareness with a friend, someone trusted, countered the wolf tearing away inside him. It sometimes howled, begging him act. Other times it whined, calling him devilish and dirty, berating him with his father's words, bemoaning his evil. But with Edward's words, he stood taller, more sure of his manhood. He patted his friend's shoulder. "I thank you for the advice, Edward. Now move on, I beg you. Tell me about your apprenticeship. Your master does not support you?"

Edward grinned. "Well, aside from assessing your growth, I am here with grand news. I am sold again, a good thing. As a helpmate to Goodman Brown. He manages the ferry. My master sold me off to him—to his own benefit, no doubt."

"But you were to be a currier."

"That? The stench of it! Not for me. Anyway, a ferryman lives on the water, and Captain Sylvester calls Brown his friend, a good connection. And if the wind blows, instead of poling, they sail the scow. Useful practice for when I become a shipmate and, someday, a captain."

John admired Edward. If nothing else he possessed enthusiasm. Unfortunately, he waded into dangerous territory. "Captain Sylvester's been tried for sedition, has he not?"

Edward lowered his booming voice. "For sharing his view that the Magistrates govern without fair representation, that we are ruled only by members of their approved church, indentures and non-believers be damned. Besides, the captain was rebuked at the trial with only a warning. And spread this not, John Frost. I stand with him. So should you."

Edward tossed back his dark curls and waited. Sedition rumbled in John's ears. It beckoned, but he turned away from it, wary. Gibbard stalked him, a significant danger. He would keep his ideas close to his breast, away from prying tongues. With the end of his indenture, if not before, he would be gone. So he remained silent, attempting to ignore the disappointment on his friend's face.

The drum saved him, its persistent, even beat, calling everyone to Sabbath services. "I'm charged to fetch Mister Gibbard's daughters and take them to the meetinghouse. Will you come as well?" He hitched up the sleeves of his linen shirt and bent to gather his cap and coat.

"God be!" Edward grabbed John's wrist and jerked up his arm. He pushed back the sleeve, and exposed the nagging edge of a bruise, then twisted the arm around, revealing the underside where red, broken vessels mingled with skin tinged yellow and blue. John flinched and tried to pull away, but his friend held tight.

"What is this?" Edward pressed. "Is this how he uses you?"

John's mouth twitched. His whole body constricted, containing his hatred—not for Edward. Edward did not coddle, but he felt safe with him. Gibbard, though, deserved his rage. The dark barn, the tang of manure, and the sting of his arm overwhelmed him. He bowed before his friend's concern.

The truth flew out with a mocking laugh. "A hickory rod where it will not show. Mistress Gibbard would object." His smile contorted. "Fear not, friend. I will have my day."

Edward released John's wrist and paced, his fists beating the air. "I will not be going to the meetinghouse. They give us permission to tend to the river crossings. I will miss this service, all services if I can, and I am not sorry." He took hold of John's hand, his voice low. "You take care, friend, and consider the price." He wheeled from the barn. John followed, torn between friendship and shame and longing. Edward jogged away, and the pounding of the drum echoed cross the sky.

⌖

They searched for Mama everywhere: along the river, behind the door-side garden, and up to what they called The Waste, the land by East Rock, as yet uninhabited. Mama was nowhere. Father wore his voice weary calling for her and, finally, as the drumbeats quickened, he hurried them down the path to Mill River, leaving Mama behind. Mercy sensed his apprehension, compounded by the thought of another fine, this time for being late to Lord's Day services. They could not afford it. Mercy trailed her father and counted his steps. He took no more than ten between each backward glance.

Their usual route down The Neck—along their grazing lot, across the cart bridge, and through the Oystershell Field—would take too long. They traveled the direct route to New Haven, crossing Neck Bridge and taking the road that ran on a diagonal to the northern palisade gate. Father glanced up and down Mill River as they crossed the bridge. After crossing, he faced forward, never back, his stride long and fitful. The clod-ridden road taunted Mercy as she struggled to keep up, taking over Father's searching, stumbling with each futile look back. Samuel skipped ahead free of worry. For him, it was an ordinary day.

They entered the town and the watchman closed the palisade gate behind them. The empty street echoed with their footfall. Even Mister Cooper's house stood vacant. Smoke from banked fires created a pall of grey. It accosted Mercy's throat and nostrils, and she coughed, holding her hand to her face.

"It stinks, it does," Samuel said. He walked backward, facing her with eyes crossed and his nose pinched between his fingers.

"You act unseemly, Samuel," his father said, "and we are late."

They vacillated between run and walk, attempting a calm façade, and almost ran into little Sarah and Prudence Gibbard at the bottom of the meetinghouse stairs. Their servant boy prodded the girls forward as Samuel stepped up to greet them.

"Good friends! Prudy, Sarah!" he yelled out to the girls' backs and then reached out for Sarah's arm.

Father's patience had thinned to breaking. "Samuel, there is no time," he said, then leapt up two stairs and seized his forearm. Samuel smiled back at the girls, limp bodied, as Father dragged him away. Mercy lifted her petticoats and hopped forward in an attempt to skip a stair and catch up, but her left foot caught on a lifted tread and, with her right leg still in mid-air, she fell backward.

Mister Gibbard's servant boy caught her with an outreached arm. He clasped her to him and then set her upright on the step above. He smelled of stored hay and hearth smoke. She glanced up in confusion, and he reached out to straighten her cap, pulled it down by both wings, and smiled, then licked at his full lips, pondering her. She looked away, but when she glanced back, green eyes greeted her. They unnerved her, as did his voice, soft and low.

"Your humble servant, madam, I...I pray you are not hurt. That was a near thing."

Mercy bit her lip. "No, no. Taken aback only. I thank you." She pushed down on her disheveled gown and looked around, unsure how to continue. Her father was already inside, and Samuel waited for her at the door. "I must go...post-haste." She motioned toward Samuel. "My brother waits."

The boy nodded, stepped back and beckoned to the two girls beside him. "Sarah, Prudy, quick now. The drum has stopped, and we are near late." Then, precluding all decorum, he called out to Mercy as she blundered up the stairs. "If you like, twixt sermons, the children might enjoy some merriment...together on the green? We might watch them."

She glanced back. "You are kind, sir. Yes." Then she gave her full attention to the stair treads. Two quick hops took her to the door, and Samuel. "Post-haste?" she whispered as they walked. "I sounded like old Widow Sherwood."

Father hustled them away as soon as the second service was over.

Mercy matched his swift yet melancholy cadence. Samuel bounced ahead. He slowed on occasion to examine a bug or budding shoot, showing Father each one before he twirled off on his next adventure. His light-hearted banter contrasted poorly with Father's mood.

"Samuel, we must press home and not dawdle." He pushed Samuel away and strode out in front of them, increasing his pace.

Samuel, undeterred, redirected his bothersome attention to Mercy. She offered an occasional comment of "how interesting" and such, while her mind wandered to Gibbard's servant boy.

The word "boy" no longer adequately described him. He was taller than her and larger. She considered his age. She lagged behind him by a year or two, she thought. He was perhaps twelve. But, no, he had grown so broad and strong and caught her easily—thirteen, surely. No scrawny ill-smelling boy any longer.

She should have asked his name. They had met between services, but she avoided his gaze the whole time, looking at the dirt or the children or the stick he twisted into the ground—never speaking. He sat on a rock near the cistern, a seemly distance from her. She thought he glanced at her between his burrowing, as he created a deepening hole with the length of hickory in his hand. Why, when she finally looked at him, did she become so shy and fumbling? Those green eyes glistened in her memory, and the thought of his full lips caused her own to purse in a narrow, hidden smile—one not so hidden as she hoped.

"What are you smiling about, Mercy?" A small green and yellow frog, dripping with plant slime, wriggled in front of her face. "It's a frog, see it! You hate frogs."

She stepped back and glared. "Samuel! Get it out of my face. Now! It is not funny."

"Well, you were laughing."

"I was not laughing, and I was not smiling, not at that. The thing smells of rot and mold. Go away!"

Samuel skipped off on a crisscross path, taking time to turn back and hold the frog out menacingly. She rolled her eyes and walked on, adjusting her shoulders and neck in a womanly way, too old for such nonsense.

When the house came into view, Father sent her off to find Mother.

"If we find her at the house, I will send Samuel to fetch you. Start at the meadow by Mill River where she likes to wander." He kissed her forehead, a rare endearment, then followed Samuel up the rise to home.

Mercy gathered up her gown and petticoats and tied them into a bunched up knot. Streamlets escaping from lingering pockets of snow crisscrossed the landscape and grew more numerous the nearer she came to the river. A lone willet bobbed his long, thin beak into the mud. Startled by her presence, he screeched, flapped into the air, then landed and scuttled off, only to stop yards away to continue his muddy probing. Mercy looked around, thinking the noise might rouse Mama from some revelry, but no glistening silver-blond hair appeared and no one danced about on the river's shore. The riverbank path beckoned, one she and Mama often took. On fairy hunts, Mama called them.

She inhaled, filling her chest, then exhaled through her mouth, emptying her breath. Her mother would do that, holding up her arms to exalt the wonder of God. "It heals you, Mercy," she would say, "the sweet fragrance of earth and water and sky all breathed in as one." It greeted her, fecund and cool, and inviting. Mercy knew in her heart that her mother had taken this path.

She followed it until she came to an impasse, a tangled mass that had fallen from a willow tree only beginning to leaf. The branches blocked the path and spread out into the river, creating a dam of leaf and fodder. Mercy secured the largest culprit in both hands, jerked at it, took purchase, and pulled again. It would not budge, so she got under the thicket of interwoven branches and lifted them with her body. She heaved them off the path and stepped over the leavings, catching her stocking on a wayward twig in the process.

Wet, muddied, and annoyed by her torn stocking, she plopped on a springy branch sticking out of the fallen bramble, then pulled at the twig, careful to avoid tearing a larger hole. It slipped from the knitted threads of her stocking, and she tossed it out to the river beyond. And saw her. She gasped, stilled, confusion battling her vision.

The river held her mother in its grasp.

She washed on waves of eddying waters. Blue eyes, dull and unmoving, stared into the sky. Splayed arms bobbed in an uneven, peaceful rhythm. Feet, hidden by a sinking gown, drifted into the current, a single willow snag tethering her to shore. Ice crystals clung to strands of her floating hair. They danced along her lashes and the space between her lips.

"You look like a winged angel," Mercy whispered, "as if you're dancing." Then truth settled. "You are gone."

Shock mingled with relief. She sucked in her guilt and hurried away. She would not disturb Mama's floating form, could not. Father must see to her untethering. Her feet worked independently of her mind, half-running, half-walking, taking her away. She shivered as tears, confused, thankful, shameful tears, trickled down her face. She braced to her task. Father would mourn yet understand. But Samuel. How would she tell Samuel?

Samuel dragged his feet into New Haven town holding his sister's hand. He wore his good waistcoat, breeches, and felt hat. His father walked before them. An ox pulling a two-wheeled cart bounced ahead. The ferryman had lent his father the cart for the day, and now Edward, Brown's servant boy, guided it down the rutted lane to the Cart Bridge and through Oystershell Field. They entered the east gate, bumped past Governor Eaton's house, and slogged in a solemn processional toward the village green. Samuel's once familiar world appeared unrecognizable.

The shrouded body jiggled in the cart, but the hemp ropes held true. When Edward came to gather Mama, he had shown Samuel how to tie a lorry and a bowline knot. He chattered on about how he planned to sail one day on a merchant ship, to become a shipmate or a rigger, and, some day, a captain. Edward made Samuel smile, even as he secured Mama, wrapped in her linen shroud, to the bed of the cart.

Samuel's last remembered smile had come on the previous Lord's Day, when he had danced about with a pocket of frogs hoping to tease Mercy. That was before she went to the river. When she returned, her feet plodding and reluctant, she had stared at him as if he were porcelain, tears spilling off her cheeks. She had spoken to Father, but not to him. They bid him wait inside the house, but he did not. The secret sorrow his father and Mercy bore oozed from them. It had to do with Mama. So, he followed.

His father blocked his view for a while, but what he saw told him everything. With arms raised to the sky, Father fell to his knees, muddying his meeting clothes. Then he stood, shaking, and spoke briefly to

Mercy. Together, they lifted something from the water.

Mama's lifeless body came dripping out, dragging the river's waste along behind. He had run away then, to hide, to pretend it was not happening. He stayed concealed behind the feed bin for hours, twisting bits of oat hay until it broke, ignoring his father's calls, and Mercy's.

Mercy found him finally and crawled in beside him. The comfort of soap wafted from her, and he cuddled near.

"Samuel," she had said, embracing him, "take care. Mama found peace, and I shall be here for you, always."

As she was with him now, crossing the green, following a cart carrying their mother. She squeezed his hand and whispered, "Look up, Samuel. They come to say good-bye."

He glanced up. The oaks on the village green shimmered in blue, and as the cart rolled beneath the first tree, a fluttering mass of butterflies lifted and eddied in the wind. Flutterbyes, his mother called them, Fairy Flutterbyes. His lips quivered, out of his control. He blinked and offered Mercy a smile. She nestled her arm on his shoulder, and they continued, following the cart to the burying grounds at the far edge of the green.

Every oak greeted them with a flurry of blue. Samuel whirled his head about, scarcely containing his body. He refrained from chasing the Flutterbyes, curbed his desire to twirl around with them. It would not be seemly, not now. Yet in his mind, with his eyes, he flew.

The congregation waited at the gravesite by a mound of dirt the length of a body. Samuel, Mercy, Father, and cart passed one last oak where another flickering mass of wings greeted them. Prudy and Sarah played by the oak while their servant boy watched. The girls danced about trying to catch the butterflies. Their servant did not stop them.

He raised his hand in greeting, calling Edward by name, and then addressed Samuel's sister, rubbing at the cap on his head.

"It be sorrowful, your loss, mistress, but..." The boy fumbled with his hat, trying to remove it. "But, she goes to heaven happy, I think, led by a raft of butterflies."

Father heard the boy and turned around, his face as tethered as when Mercy had brought Samuel from his hiding place. But now his father smiled, acknowledging the boy's words.

Mercy, too, noticed the smile. "Thank you for that," she said to the servant boy who looked down at his shoes.

The cart rolled on. The parishioners' singing grew louder as they grew near. Samuel recognized the song. It came from *The Whole Book of Psalms*, the book Reverend Davenport used on the Lord's Day.

"The Lord to me a shepherd is," they sang, "want therefore shall not I, He in the folds of tender grass, doth cause me down to lie. Yea though in valley of death's shade I walk, none ill I will fear. Because thou art with me, thy rod. And staff my comfort near."

Edward stopped the cart near the hole dug for Mama. The ox bent its head, ripped loose a mouthful of grass, and gnawed. Edward untied his knots, and Mister Cooper and some other men lifted Mama from the cart.

The linen shroud hid her fairy hair and her blue eyes, just like his. A salty brine slipped over his lips into his mouth. He batted ineffectually at the dripping culprits, and Mercy bent to dab his eyes with the corner of her apron. No Flutterbyes, no rod, no staff could comfort him—none except Mercy.

⤸❈⤷

John stood by the oak waiting. Edward circled the ox-driven cart away from the grave and led it toward the tree. Mister Gibbard, his round face blotched with frustration, had collected the girls after seeing them cavorting with the butterflies. He contained his disgust with John, but barely. There were, after all, important people about. Even so, Gibbard's pulsing fist predicted John's destiny—a beating wrath, come evening—if the man could find him. For now, though, John's mind winged on an idea, seized from a remembered need.

Once Edward came within a cart's length of him, John stepped out to greet him. "Stop for a bit, Edward?"

His friend nodded and eased the ox and cart around and joined him to watch the funeral from a distance. They were silent until Edward nudged him with his elbow. "Nice words toward Mistress Payne," he said.

"Fumbling, foolish words."

"When you are a fool, I will speak it, John. You feel for them. No hurt in that. Anyway, they will survive. They have a father at least, which be a sight more than us." Edward pulled back on the lead as the ox tried to move between them and block their view of the proceedings. "Did you ever have a mother, John?"

Edward came from the London streets. Without the closeness of family, he had never known its loss. Was it easier, never belonging—knowing only loneliness from the beginning? Did it matter?

"I had a mother," he answered. "She passed of a putrid fever. I was about Samuel's age."

"Well, you had a father." For Edward, it was a positive thing, a statement of fact. For John the comment unearthed sorrows he longed to keep buried.

"He was no help, Edward. I was an annoyance. I needed more than an absent pat and a whack to tame me. He was ill suited to the task, lost in memories and grieving, I think. So he gave up on me." He kicked at a patch of grass. "I went seeking my own distractions, and a little trouble."

Edward jabbed him with his elbow. "So you did, and they landed you here."

John shrugged an acknowledgment. "They landed me here."

The services ended. He and Edward stood, silent, while the congregation peeled away. John pushed the dirt around with the toe of his shoe, thinking how to voice his idea, a way to help the boy. With Edward, he could be direct. "That mastiff bitch, the one your master has, with the pups? Think he might give one up...for the boy?"

"For Samuel? Not for the girl?" Edward ducked, avoiding sure retaliation. "Anyway, not a bad idea. Brown favors the Payne family, and the pups are just weaned. He keeps them at the ferry house. We can ask. What about that devil-spawned master of yours? Will he let you go?"

"Truly? No. But it matters little, and I think I'll not ask. I might escape a thrashing if I can avoid him. I still seek my distractions." John gave him a wink. "Could take till nightfall, you think?"

Edward cuffed the side of John's head. "You are one tough nut, John Frost. Tender breathing in and rebel breathing out. Jump on the back of the cart. We can take turns riding back to the ferry house."

❧✿❧

Of all John sought after his mother's death, companionship drove him most, sending him into the arms of criminals, driving his father to his decision. But he remembered a better companion from those days. Mangy and distrustful, the mongrel had latched to him and, against all expectation, made him smile. So a dog, to listen without judgment, to romp with and sooth your sorrows, seemed perfect—for Samuel.

He and Edward bumped along Oystershell Field to the Cart Bridge spanning Mill River, following the rutted path to the East River ferry. John dangled his legs over the edge of the cart, looking back on where they had come. A cool breeze carried the scent of the sea, and trees, budding with a riot of reddish purple, dotted the landscape. A calm crept into his spine as he bounced along, grass swaying at his feet.

"Nice out here, you think?" Edward said from over his shoulder. "I stay in the ferry house. Ferryman Brown gives me a free rein."

John jumped down and caught up to Edward. "Is that the East River coming near?"

"It is. They call it the Dragon sometimes, after the huge seals that gather at the mouth. I stay in that shed up ahead. Brown maintains a home in town, but most often stays cross the river." Edward squinted toward the ferry landing, concerned. "Take the lead, John. Brown readies a passenger for crossing. I'll hurry ahead and ask about the pups."

Edward trotted across the pastureland, leaving John to lead the ox—Stewpot, Edward had called him. Not a kindly name. But Edward told him it was true to the animal's end reward, and they had laughed at the joke. A fresh gust blew over John's face. He inhaled. Far from Gibbard, that puffed up buffoon of a man, he was, for now, content. Making Samuel happy, giving the boy something to put his heart into, mattered. He walked a little faster, anxious to see the pups, but he would not be moving too fast. Stewpot, he soon discovered, lumbered at only one speed.

The pup came to him right off. There were eight, but Ferryman Brown wished to keep the breeders. Mastiffs protected the plantation's cattle from wolf attack so were much in demand. Brown bred them for profit but reluctantly offered up one male in sympathy to the Paynes' situation.

When John called out to the litter, a muddy-faced pup, all tan and brown and black in a muddle, waddled up to him, sniffed at his hand, and rolled onto his back. John rubbed the little fellow's soft underbelly, and its back foot twitched in ecstasy. A twinge of envy, a long lost longing for companionship, rose in him. But this was not about him. It was about the boy, and the perfect gift.

He and the pup walked north along the upland portion of The Neck between the Mill and East River, or rather, John walked. He supported the pup's ample rump at the crook of his arm while it nuzzled its silken jowls into John's neck. Halfway to the Payne house, at least as a guess, John began to worrying he might miss the place. Brown had given him directions and assured him it was an easy find, close as it was to the Neck Bridge, but John had never been there. He decided to walk nearer the Mill River. If he missed the house, he could at least backtrack from the bridge.

As he turned down toward the river, the pup woke. It was neither small nor light, a portent of its future size. It was also restless. Paws near to the size of John's palm pushed against his arm and shoulder. He held the pup tight and its squirming worsened. Then the animal began to nibble at his ear, working his lobe like a nipple.

"Whoa, you big lout, none of that," he said and shifted the pup so it faced forward and hung in his crossed arms. "You are heavy as a feed sack though not nearly so still." The dog laid its head back and stared up at him with woeful eyes and wrinkled snout. It commenced to wriggle, to turn and paw, nearly causing John to drop it. "Want down, do you? No traipsing off if I set you down, hear? You might someday chase the wolves, but right now you look dinner worthy."

John dropped the squiggly mass at his feet. It sprung to the side, squatted, and emitted a stream of urine in a lingering release.

"Well, I apologize," John said. "Now, time to go." He paced out a barn's length and peeked back. The mastiff sat on its haunches where he had left him. "Humph, you may be all sad-eyed, but you are a brute, and old enough to walk. Now come."

It cocked its head to the side, and then pranced forward. John walked on, then turned back to see if the bundle followed, and it did.

"You be a smart little bugger," he said, then maintained a cheerful banter, glancing back on occasion. The dog continued to follow, stopping at times to investigate some moving object like a bug or bouncing leaf.

River seepage boiled up from the ground where they walked, a mossy mixture of leaf and leavings. Each step was like treading on a loosely wrung sponge. After a long while of walking, John glanced behind, expecting to find his charge, but none followed. "Pup? You dog, where are you?"

He backtracked on the trail, but no muddle of color roamed there. "Damn," he said, and headed back from where he came, taking time to search the willow bramble that grew at the river's edge.

He soon found his charge. The pup gnawed at a stick held in its paws, working it deep into the mud. In fact, the animal's whole body, legs splayed out behind, was sunken in the mud. Then it recognized John and jumped up. It dropped the stick and waddled toward him, hips wriggling.

John accessed the situation quickly. "Whoa, dog. Good dog. Stop, now—" He was too late. Circling arcs of mud sprayed up around him and splattered onto his breeches and shirt, into his mouth and eyes.

"You, you—" He clamped down with his teeth, his mouth twisting between irritation and amusement. "You little oaf! Now look at us, a fine sight. Hereafter, you ride." He grabbed the pup and headed for the bridge.

⤟❁⤝

Samuel spied the boy as he walked up their hill. It was the Gibbard girls' servant, the one who talked about Mama and the butterflies. He ran up the stairs and yelled into the house. "A visitor Papa, coming from the bridge."

Father straightened his waistcoat as he came out the door, the way he did when the governor or another important person from the town stopped by. And these last few days, they had been inundated with visitors. His father narrowed his eyes at the sight of the servant and walked forward to greet him. His sister appeared in the doorway but went no further. Meanwhile, Samuel hopped in behind his father and followed him down the walk.

The servant boy carried something in his arms. The family had received loaves of bread and pot pies from neighbors since—since his mother. But this was not a loaf or kettle, it moved. It moved a great deal. Samuel stepped out from behind his father to see better. A small animal hung from the boy's arms. Well, not so small, but big and brown and black and tan. The servant stammered, trying to talk while the animal struggled in his grip. Exasperation evident, he knelt, placed the squirming bundle on the ground, and attempted to contain it while he spoke.

"Your humble servant, sir. You...I mean I, sir. I come from Ferryman Brown's place. I brought this pup." The boy stumbled on his words. Scared, Samuel thought, the same as him when speaking to his elders.

Father, so impatient of late, interrupted. "I see it. A mastiff pup. And?"

"I...I thought with the boy losing his mother and all, he might be needing..." Samuel held his breath, absorbing the words and the boy's tremulous inhale as he continued. "I thought the child might want a companion."

"You thought this? Or Mister Brown?"

"Well, Mister Brown offered up one male, so—"

Samuel tried to follow the discussion, but his ears had stuck on "the child" and "companion" and he blurted, "For me? The pup is for me!"

His stomach danced and heat flowed into his face. He padded gently toward the dog, so as not to frighten it, and extended his opened palm to its wrinkled face. The dog stared up at him, its round eyes trimmed by dark brown brows. Then it stretched its nose to his hand and licked it, just once. Samuel loved it, and he knew it loved him. "Mine," he said, to no one but the dog, and looked up to his father.

A curious warmth washed across his eyes. "We have need of protection from wolves here. That may be Mister Brown's thought."

The servant boy stood and shook his head in affirmation. "That it is, sir."

Samuel's sister peeked out from behind. "It would be good for him, Papa."

There was a silence. The dog snuggled against Samuel's body.

"Give Mister Brown our thanks," his father said, then swung toward the house.

The servant boy sighed and knelt down to Samuel. He had a warm inviting smile and soft green eyes. He placed his hand on Samuel's shoulder and spoke to him as though he were older, not a babe. "The pup be a responsibility, Samuel. You must train it to come to you, and stay, and feed it well so it becomes strong. Do you understand?"

Samuel shook his head yes, then ran his hand along the dog's back. "He be a muddy thing."

The servant boy laughed. "True enough. Though you hardly notice. It has the same coloring as mud. Muddy—a good name. A dog should have a name."

"Muddy," Samuel said, and nuzzled his nose against the dog's velvet muzzle. "I like that."

Mercy's voice came from behind. "We thank you, but forgive me. Your name?"

"John. John Frost, madam."

"John," Samuel thought. He was glad for this boy. "Thank you, John," he said.

"Oh, it was not me, it was—"

His sister stopped his talking. "I suspect it was you, John. Your thought and your kindness, and we thank you."

John did not contradict. Besides, Samuel suspected Mercy was right. The ferryman was kind, but not so generous as this—not usually.

Mercy continued, "The neighbors brought us bread and oyster stew. Would you like to eat?"

John fumbled at his words once more. "Look at me, madam. Muddy christened me at the river. I am not fit for visiting." He stood and brushed at his breeches. Caked mud sprinkled down on Samuel and Muddy, and they shook their heads in unison. It made Samuel laugh.

" I can bring the food to the porch steps. Would be happy to do so. Pray stay. And, please, call me Mercy." Her words oozed out, syrupy and sweet. Samuel wrinkled his nose at Muddy, and his dog padded at his face.

John smiled down on Samuel and winked. "I would like that. Besides, nothing awaits me that cannot be delayed."

⌒❈⌒

"Forty damn years of summer should acclimate a person," Maggie complains to no one. She lifts her arms in homage to the cooler blowing a moist breeze over her sweat-ridden body. Forever the conservationists, they use evaporative cooling, not air conditioning. In California's dry climate it is, mostly, good enough. "I guess we have no idea how easy our life is," she says, unsure of the sentiment's source, but suspicious. She glances over to the table where Volume I sits, the portal to her other world. Her current existence recedes further each day, and she slides into her imagined one. Her desire? To nestle in and never return. The book chastises her: too romantic, too false. Her version of the past, picked and chosen, was incomplete.

Duncan stretches out on the couch, a glass of ice water perched next to him on the wooden butter churn they use as a side table. He feels compelled to answer a question unasked. "Well, this year's the worst. Three years of drought. Our average rainfall is 26 inches you know."

Maggie knows. He repeats this information regularly, and his keen knowledge of local weather and precise record keeping makes him encyclopedic in his pronouncements. The book waits; Maggie likes to engage him. "So how many inches this year?" *she asks. Facts are not something she remembers. For her they are gateways to ideas; if she can look something up, she sees no reason to remember it. The volume pulls, wishing her back to where facts falter, to where a gesture, a belief, a tangible offering matters more.*

"Only eleven and five-sixteenths this year," *he says.* "Worst ever. It makes the heat seem hotter."

"Hot is hot. And anything over ninety-five is too damn hot. I hate it."

"Can't change the weather. I'm just glad all the weed-eating is done so we are fire safe. Well, at least safer."

Maggie settles into her chair; the volume distracts her from Duncan's banter.

"Still reading the New Haven thing?" *Her husband proves a challenging competitor for her attention. The book tingles near her hand.*

"Yes," *she says. Then she's up again, restless. She opens the fridge and basks in the cool air. She pours a glass of sun tea, closes the door, then opens the freezer for ice. The cold falls out, turning to mist. She closes her eyes, pretending a frozen peace. The book screams at her. Still, she resists, stealing this gift of time, of now. So the book changes its tactic, cajoles, reels her in, pleading with her to return.*

She plops in her chair, takes a healthy sip of tea, and begins to read. Finally, she's engaged, wrapped in its thrall. Between the pages in which parishioners air what she considers petty issues regarding poorly made shoes and cheap, ill-tanned leather, come the amazing—her word is ridiculous—trials. But, the book makes her wonder. Is her worldview a barrier to her understanding? Could poorly made shoes be a real issue? Still, she can't help it. Her beliefs filter everything.

"God," she laughs, "you won't believe this. Listen." She reads from the trial about a deformed pig and the one-eyed man they accuse of fornicating with it, thus causing the pig's deformity. "The man is blind in one eye and so is the pig. Ergo..."

"You're kidding."

"Nope, the man is adamant. Says he didn't do it. But they make him confess. He hardly has a choice."

"So then what?"

"He hangs."

"They're going to hang him for buggering a pig?"

"If he even did it. But it's another world. Another mindset. People do some stupid stuff because of superstition and prejudice." The book trembles in her hand, telling her what she says is true. It unnerves her. The book slides from her hand. "I need a map...to figure out just what New Haven Colony encompasses."

"To the back room again?" Duncan says.

"To the back room. And no guff, okay?" She is gone before he can answer. The book, and Duncan, feel the vacuum. They both want her near.

They wait close to an hour. Duncan looks over at the volume left alone on the end table, annoyed. He heads through the antique-laden room into her bedroom and office sanctuary. "So, did you figure things out? With New Haven, I mean."

The books sense the smile, the lifted brows. He brings Maggie back with a quick jerk on the line, an experienced tug, like snagging a fish. She reaches for the yellow pushpin holding a map to the wall. In no time she returns, to the main room, to the couch, and to Duncan. She kneels on the floor beside him.

The map shows the New England colonies. Massachusetts Bay, Rhode Island, and Plymouth are all in pink and occupy the most easterly portion of the map. New Netherland, in brown, occupies the westerly portion. "The brown section is what the Dutch claimed as theirs," she says, adjusting the map for Duncan, "but look here. This part cross-hatched with dark pink? That's Connecticut Colony."

"Confusing. They aren't exactly unified pieces of land. More like a patchwork."

Duncan takes the map from Maggie for a closer look. She leans over his shoulder. He kisses her cheek. The volume on the table vibrates with understanding. She carries the same traits as the people in their story. She acts strong and independent, but wants approval, thrives on any acknowledgment of her worth—so like them.

She cuddles into Duncan. "New Haven is even more confusing," she says. "See the dots of pink, north of Long Island Sound, between the two Connecticut claims? That's the main part of New Haven Colony. But all along, dotted here and here." Her finger moves along, pointing out each little outpost. "Milford, Branford, Guilford, even Southold across the sound—all New Haven. Each place with different needs, different ways of seeing things. Different worlds."

Duncan hands back the map. "And they think a one-eyed man throws one-eyed pigs. They need an intervention."

Maggie flops back in her chair, laughing. She sets the map to the side and reaches for Volume I, content. Her husband smiles, glad to have her in the room. Volume I concurs, relieved by her caress, anxious to trans-port her back in time, to where one boy's anguish exacts a terrible cost.

PART III

1656 (and the present)

It is Ordered whosoever shall wittingly and willingly burn or destroy any Farm, or other Building, he shall pay double or treble damages, as the Court shall judge meet; or if not able to make such restitution, he shall be either sold for a servant or severely punished, as the case may require.

Code of New Haven

John used a twig, sharpened and charred in the small fire he built, to write the numbered year on the summer kitchen's wall. By his calculations, he was fourteen years of age, born sometime in February of 1641. According to the Julian calendar, it was now the first of a new year, late March of 1656. His father once told him that popish peoples used a different measure of the years, but since coming to New Haven, his education had ended. He wondered what became of that calendar.

He was determined to track his age, though no one else did. The act served as a touchstone to a world where he might matter—in age, thought, and action. It was a marker in the chill of time.

March ran cold and the ground held to frost, but Mister Gibbard insisted the day be one for plowing. John had hoped to sneak off to visit Samuel and Muddy. The dog was a monster, and when John tapped his chest, giving the animal permission to jump up, it looked him in the eye. Though still a pup, when John raced the dog across the pasture, it won easily. Samuel trained Muddy to be responsive and polite. And as John had hoped, the dog comforted Samuel. The boy held to a happy countenance and was equal to his dog in manners. A curious joy swelled up in John when he was with Samuel and the dog— and with Mercy who joined them when her chores permitted.

But there would be no time for that today. He slipped into his shoes and bundled as best he could for plowing. Skiffs of lingering snow marked the path to the Gibbard house. The clear sky showed gold with the beginning of the day, a good sign, because, while cold, there would be a warming sun.

Gibbard's voice rang out from the house, growing louder with John's approach. "Wife, I tell you, if God be a righteous one, He will rid us of Newman. Sly, untrustworthy, but they keep him governor."

"You were chosen deputy, husband. A good thing," Mistress Gibbard's voice cajoled from within.

John stepped to the porch, adjusted his quilted coat, and pulled off his cap. Mistress Gibbard deserved his best manners. She always took a kindly view, even with her husband's complaining. She also cooked the best food in the village. A whiff of her fish stew, a hearty fair made with cabbage, hovered outside the door and mingled with the aroma of baking bread.

He lingered, hesitant to enter, basking in the smells. From the sound of things, Mister Gibbard was in a stew of his own.

"Fiddle!" he shouted, "I, a man chosen by God, yet barely chosen by those surrounding me. Those votes cost me shillings in beer at the ordinary. They owe me more respect."

"But a start, husband."

"Humph, a start. About starts—where is that eye-servant? Lord help me suffer another day with that ill-chosen boy."

John grimaced and rapped twice on the oak-planked door. Inside, Gibbard grumbled, "Finally. In, boy."

John used his cap to open the latch so his skin would not stick to the icy surface. He coveted decent gloves to protect his hands from the cold but made due with ruined stockings cut open for his fingers.

Besides, he thought, "Gloves or Gibbard? I choose for the devil to take that popinjay to hell."

He stepped in.

Gibbard glanced up from his place by the hearth. "You dawdle. Eat quickly, boy. I expect the work done by mid-day, or you labor through dinner."

Mistress Gibbard handed John a trencher of thick stew with a quarter loaf for soaking and bid him sit. Prudy and Sarah took their places at his feet hoping to engage him. Some small parts of this life made him feel he belonged, but he belonged, also, to Gibbard and his plow and the rod.

⌣✻⌣

John hated plowing. Gibbard led the ox while the hard labor of maneuvering the plow through poor soil fell to him. Beneath a surface of sandy loam, the wooden plow dug into clay better suited to brick and pottery. The plowshare bumped and chattered through the clay underbelly while sand accumulated on the shoe. It threw John back and forth with an ungainly force as he struggled to steady the handles. Days such as these left him bruised and weary. And the bruising came not just from the plow. Like John, Gibbard loathed the activity, so took his loathing out on him.

While the clattering plow battled the frozen loam, Mister Gibbard's harangue reverberated in John's ears.

"Dumb as an ox, you are. Pulling us off course. A useless oaf!"

The words blistered, and John grew ever more petulant, more distant, more venomous. Only luck held his tongue. He plowed on and imagined his red-faced master falling on his bum and biting his tongue hard enough he would not talk for a week.

"Frost, you feeble excuse for a servant, hold it still. You let the cut bounce on the surface. Hold steady." His master whipped at the ox with a righteous bluster. Then he stepped back to check the plowshare's cut.

It happened quickly. The plow hit something—an underground root, a frozen mass of clay? John could not tell. But the plow handles lurched left and swung him to the ground. He lost his grip. The plowshare popped up and to the right, tore into Gibbard's stocking, and cleaved his shin.

"Devil's own!" his master cried.

John clamored to his feet and hurried to Mister Gibbard who limped about in a circle, cursing further.

He bent to examine his master's wound. "Are you hurt, sir? Cut?" He saw no blood, so raised his head to apologize for the accident, and caught sight of Gibbard's rod. It arced down with stinging force against his left shoulder.

"You devil child! That was of a purpose." He brought the rod down again, clipping John's head. John's arms flew up as protection, and the rod whipped to the side catching him in the ribs. He grabbed for it.

"Fight me, boy, and I sell you!" Gibbard's breath rattled with short, uneven gasps. "Years added on! Years." Each word drove the rod down harder than the last, pummeling John's body.

Fury whipped through him as he faced Gibbard, fire whipped through him. The impetus to act burned in him, to thrash the ferret, to destroy him. Instead, he spat. The glob landed on Gibbard's shoe, and John turned to walk from the field.

The rod bit into his right shoulder; it knocked him from his feet. He fell like an ox to all fours, and Gibbard struck him again. John did not count the whip-hard stings that came next, but the blows were many. Most were accompanied by curses, Gibbard calling him a defiler, the devil's consort, his spawn. Tears swelled and blurred the frosty earth beneath him. He did not cry out.

After a time, his master stopped and stepped nearer John's head. He balanced against the rod, his breath heaving. "Finish this alone. And, for God's sake, clean yourself. The mistress would have you to supper this eve time."

John sat back on his heels and waited until Gibbard disappeared, then dropped to his side and pulled his knees to his chest. His body throbbed—his waist and legs the most. By bracing himself, hands to his thighs to contain the spinning, he rose to kneeling, then stood. He took inventory of the damage. There would be bruising and broken skin. He knew this from experience. Yet something more had broken today. The moment cut into him. It robbed him of hope and replaced it with a festering disdain.

Finishing the plowing alone required a draining effort. He wrapped the lead around his waist, flipped it hard on the ox's rump, and held to the plow. It bounced across the ground, taking rare purchase in the frozen clay. The contest he waged, twixt the stubborn ox, recalcitrant plow, and frozen ground honed his anger. The job was poorly done, and he took pleasure in its shoddiness. Even ill done, it took him past dark to finish.

He stabled the ox, rubbed it down, and gave it hay from the haystack outside. Last autumn he had piled the hay high and covered the mound with thatch to keep it dry. They used this stacking method in England and he copied it. Gibbard, all books and no common knowledge, mocked him but let him try. The system worked, and Gibbard, of course, took the credit. John scratched behind the ox's ear and whispered his loathing, calling his master an ass's behind and a strutting cock, words for the animal alone. With Gibbard, he would express himself in other ways.

He washed on the porch, calmed himself, knocked once, and entered the house. Mistress Gibbard bent over the hearth, moving some tasty concoction from the hottest part of the fire to the warming coals. She held her gown back and wrestled with the kettle hook.

"Let me," John said.

She stepped aside, giving him room to take on the job. "Home after dark, John?" Her voice took that gentle, worried tone. "You limp, dear soul, and hold yourself so stiffly. A hard day? God's labors well done?"

"Well, enough," he said. "Stew from the morning?"

"For you? Always. I added more onions and greens, and a turnip to stretch it. The dumplings need to simmer a while longer."

The latch banged in the catch, and Gibbard entered, shedding his tall hat and hanging it on a peg. "Done, boy? Come to take your price in food and warmth at your master's hearth?"

John swallowed, and held to his resolve. He would pay the man his price, not by talk, but by deed. His reply burned in his throat. "Your obedient servant, sir. I did your bidding, the plowing done, and ask only those household pleasures to which you see fit."

"That I see fit?" Gibbard gloated. "Humph, so, now you speak as a servant boy should. The fear of God does do wondrous things, does it not?" With a flutter of his fingers, he added, "Feed him, wife. He may yet learn God's purpose."

John smiled the sweetest he could, wide and friendly. He bowed his head. God's purpose indeed.

The stars hung bright in the moonless sky, a portent of a hard frost. Inside his quarters, John plumped the straw on the table, wrapped himself in a woolen cloak, and huddled under the single cover Mistress Gibbard had spared him. He found no comfort but lay stiffened against the cold. His right side, from back to thigh, ached no matter his position, so he curled up like a babe in his mother's belly, settling gingerly on his left arm to minimize the pain. He deliberated on his strategy, then reiterated and refined it; he could not sleep.

The bite of the rod gnawed at him—he had worked to please the man, though not in the spirit of love, he admitted. Gibbard did not respect him, valued nothing he did, considered him corrupt at heart. An occasional disrespect of the man seemed warranted.

Then his mind turned to the haystack. Clever work, yet Gibbard ignored his effort and took the glory for it. Why should he receive no prize for his industry? Why should Gibbard harvest rewards bought with his bruised back?

He tossed the night away, growing ever more stiff and angry. A desire for vengeance worked in him, and by dawn, he knew what he would do. On this, the Lord's Day, Gibbard and his wife departed for the meetinghouse early; John brought the children just before services began. A perfect day for retribution.

John rose with the sun. He went to relieve himself and pressed at the swelling forming on his bruised thigh. The consequent throbbing informed his task, making it easier, even exciting. He tempered his impatience by bringing hay from his haystack, feeding the animals, and walking them to pasture.

Gibbard refused him a fire on the Lord's Day. He expected John to break his fast with them and spend the morning before services reading from the bible. John would bide his time.

After a simple meal of porridge and clabbered milk, each family member read passages from Mister Gibbard's Bible. Finally, Gibbard fluffed his ruffled collar, squeezed into his waistcoat, and tied his cloak around his neck with pasty white fingers. John helped the mistress with her cloak, handed the master his hat, and opened the door. For the first time, John noticed that he stood a hand taller than his master.

"Be punctual, Frost, and take care that our daughters act seemly." Gibbard popped his hat on his head and, with a quick adjustment of the brim, exited the house. Mistress Payne offered her apologetic smile and followed.

"Your obedient servant," John whispered and closed the door. He turned to Prudence. "Go, Prudy. Take Sarah up the stairs and prepare yourselves."

"Why? We are ready but for our cloaks and caps."

"And your bed is neat? Be obedient now and do as I ask." He hated the lie. The girls knew him, knew he never spoke of obedience. He always joked and played games with them while they waited for the drum's call. Prudence scrunched her nose at him, but she obeyed.

"Come, Sarah. We are to tidy up. I suppose."

"Thank you, Prudy," he said, tousling her hair. "I must tend to an errand. After you finish, don your caps and capes and meet me on the porch."

With the girls upstairs, John went to work. He picked up the ladle, hurried to the hearth, and used the tongs hanging nearby to lift four lively coals out of the banked fire. He dropped them in the ladle. The heat of the coals had worked through the handle and up into his hands by the time he reached the door.

The morning frost hung heavy; he hustled along, sheltering the embers to maintain their glow. The haystack twinkled, the icy dew glazing its thatch cover. John balanced the ladle at his feet, dug deep, pulling back the thatch to make a hole. The hay was dry, smelling crisp, without a trace of mildew. He had thatched the stack well, done a service, much good it did him. Now he slipped the ladle into the hole and twisted the handle to release the burning coals. He covered the hole loosely to allow air to reach inside and listened for the soft sputter of smoldering hay. Convinced his task was completed, he hurried to the porch, eyed the water bucket by the side of the door, and tossed the ladle into it just as Prudy and Sarah walked outside.

On the way to the meetinghouse, he played a game of letters with the girls, each taking a turn to spy things by order of the alphabet. His heart raced and his mind wandered, distracted by conjured images of the stack taking fire, of Gibbard raging against the loss of feed. He rubbed at his prickling palms and dug at his thumbs with his fingernails.

As they neared the meetinghouse, they had reached the letter Q and the game had turned to him. John struggled to focus, pleading that Q was an impossible letter. But the girls prodded, so he tossed his worries aside like a ladle to a bucket. He reached down and tickled Sarah, then walked backward along the lane, smiling wide, a gesture far removed from his queasy stomach. "I say we must be 'quick' girls, for the drummer 'quickens' his beat."

Samuel peeked round the corner of the meetinghouse, hoping to find John, then hurried back to Mercy and waited at the steps. After the gift of Muddy, Samuel started joining John and the Gibbard girls in the gallery on the Lord's Day. The view was better and standing by John made him feel bigger, older. He considered John his friend.

"They are late. He will be punished for it."

"He will be here, Samuel. Patience." Mercy smoothed his hair, and he twisted away from her, checking to see if others took note of his sister's attention. He was seven, after all.

Mercy laughed at him. "I forgot you were a man, not to be coddled by your good sister..." She tweaked his cheek, to which he glowered, then she glanced over his shoulder. "Well, look who comes now, the star in your sky."

John rounded the corner with Prudy and Sarah on either side. Prudy was arguing with John. "It does begin with *S*. For steeple, John."

"It is a turret. Which begins with *T*, Prudy."

"I call it a steeple!" Prudy pronounced and flounced away, chin held high, straight to Samuel. "Good friend! Will you join us?"

Mercy answered for him. "Worry not, girls. You have his company. Like bee to honey. Do you mind, John?"

"Never do—and will you join us?"

"You know my answer. Goody Sherwood would burst from the gossip of it."

John shrugged and clapped Samuel on the back. "Come, boy. The drum quickens, and I cannot risk the rod for being late." Samuel walked the stairs backward, making faces at the girls, while John addressed Mercy with his usual query. "We meet on the green, after?"

Mercy adjusted her cap and looked up, coy and cloying—silly,

Samuel thought, as silly as her talk. "I brought hard boiled eggs. The whisper of spring has brought eggs in profusion." Samuel mimicked her coquettish behavior, then bumped backward into Goody Parson. He excused himself and scuttled through the opened door.

In the gallery, John elbowed through the crowd to create a small space for Samuel and the girls to see over the banister. The reverend stood near the front, arranging his sermon. The last of the congregants hurried down every aisle while militiamen waited at the doors, prepared to close them with the last beat of the drum. One large man backed into a pew and pressed his bottom into the face of Goody Pigg. Samuel and the girls tittered amongst themselves. John did not let them laugh aloud, not in the meetinghouse where they risked Mister Gibbard's notice. So they held their hands over their mouths, shoulders raked, their glances twinkling.

Soon the reverend stepped to the pulpit. He lowered his head and asked for a moment of silent prayer. "As believers, to load your conscience with the guilt of sin." Samuel bowed his head and studied the women's caps to his right and the men's heads to his left. He took to counting the men that were hairless.

The sermon began, and it would be long. This was Samuel's least favorite part of the day, but the view distracted him.

Reverend Davenport raised his arms to God and pitched his voice high, calling for the mortification of the deeds of the body. Then, like an expletive, one musket shot echoed through the room.

The reverend ducked down and covered his head. As a united body, the congregants startled and turned their heads to the source of the sound, the turret above them. Two more and it signaled attack. They waited. Eyes turned to Davenport who rose in hesitant bursts to his feet. Samuel looked up at John for assurance, but his friend twisted side to side. "He worries," Samuel thought.

Then it came, not shots, but a warning. "Fire! Fire! Fire to the west."

Samuel looked up to the invisible voice and then down below him. The congregation rose amongst murmurs and dust, then shuffled from their pews. Governor Eaton pleaded in a booming voice, somehow comforting, "Go calmly now. Set not your heart on evil, but reach to help your neighbor. Take care. As we practiced. As we practiced."

John took Samuel by the shoulders and moved him to the stairs. "Go, Samuel, God, go," he said. Then, as to himself, "The devil take me. What have I done?"

John muscled through the crowd of people pushing into the stairwell. Sarah sobbed while Prudy said, over and over, "Our house is west. John, is it our house? Ours?"

The mass of people in the stairwell shoved at them from the top and crushed in on them from the side. Samuel held to the wall, hanging on the rail to keep from falling. With a sudden, tripping shove, he fell out into the entry. John pushed them through the door and down the porch stairs, gathering them at the corner of the meetinghouse.

John's body trembled; he bit his lip and took a shallow breath. "Stay here. Wait for Mercy. I must...I must go...Samuel, you are in charge." John's eyes, frantic and dark, narrowed; his voice wavered. "Should I not see you again, pray believe me, I did not mean this." Then he was gone.

Samuel stretched to his toes, trying to find him, but John was lost amongst the militia running past, near to twenty of them. He recalled the number, having counted them when he stood in the gallery. Men mounted the plantation horses, and, moved by his responsibility,

Samuel hustled the girls aside for fear they would be trampled. Two carts, hauled by men struggling to run, rounded the turn, heading west. Water splashed from the huge casts they carried. The land was soggy, so the carts lurched and bogged down. Other men joined to push from behind.

Movement swirled around him. He reeled in the chaos, the whinny of the horses, the cries, questions and directions, each one conflicting, all spoken at once. He spun, enveloped in a whirlwind of fear.

As in the aftermath of a tree-splitting gale, the cacophony gave way and softened to silence. The day stilled, dusted by the acrid scent of smoke and ash swirling on a westerly wind. Only the women and children were left, scattered here and there in groups on the green. Samuel clasped his hands behind his neck and twisted, looking to every corner. Finally, he saw her. Mercy lifted her hand to him and clutched her chest. She hurried over and gathered them near.

❧

John ran with the militia through the green, but when the masses moved west, following the smoke gathering on the horizon, he ran straight, to the south and the sea. If he turned left at the end of the street, he would reach the gate to the harbor. With the guard likely torn away to deal with the fire, he could slip through the battlement, sneak aboard a ship, and hide there. They would search—but by the grace of God?

His footfall reverberated in his ears, louder than the distant shouting. He slowed at the end of the street. His mind worked as hard as his breath; he closed his eyes to think. What of grace? If all was ordained, and his soul was doomed, he could turn left and at least save himself from the rod, or worse. But reason abandoned him, and an unknowable force turned him right, toward what his vengeance wrought.

He half walked, half trotted toward the sight of his folly, wary of anyone coming from the side streets. When he reached the end of the street and Mister Gibbard's lot, his pace slowed. He had expected the fire to smolder and cool as it hit the wet thatch, only destroying the feed. But the flames had been whipped by the wind. The barn next to the haystack lay in a burning tumble, a single upright signaling where it had stood. Worse though was the house. An ember must have caught the roof. Flames flickered from the building's few windows, and as he walked closer, heads turned to a crumbling whoosh. The men, who carried buckets and pounded blankets on the porch-consuming blaze, stepped back in a rush. The roof ignited, and the north wall fell. He had destroyed everything, and he crumbled under the shame of it.

Standing off from the crowd of men trying to save what could not be saved, stood Mistress Gibbard. Not four paces from her, three neighbor women congregated, head-to-head, talking. Fearing their own homes might be burning, they had, no doubt, escorted her from the meetinghouse. Now, safe from disaster, they succumbed to gossip. And Mistress Gibbard, isolated from their comments, suffered this tragedy, one of his making, all alone. Ground into humiliation and foolishly wishing to comfort her, John ventured forward. As he did, the stalwarts of the plantation, Governor Eaton and the reverend, appeared out of the smoke-filled haze to offer solace.

He thought to run away, but could not. Something drove him forward, to stand before her, to confess. "It was me, mistress. I am so sorry. It was to be a small thing. I...I was angry. I lit the hay, but pray believe me, the rest..." He gripped her hand with both of his and pulled it to his chest. Two men wrench his arms from behind, and as her hand ripped from his, he blurted, "I did not mean it! I...did...not."

Governor Eaton glared down on him. "You lit this fire? What devil possessed you?"

John could not answer. He collapsed into his handlers and dropped his head, an attempt to to hide his disgrace. Tears streamed down his face. Then he saw familiar feet step into his view and raised his head, defiance overcoming shame. Gibbard slapped him hard across the face and then backhanded him. "I will have you hung, you Satan's spawn. Visited by the rod and hung, do you hear?" He stretched up to Governor Eaton. "He will be tried. I demand it."

A confusion of emotion overcame John. He flailed under his captors' grasp, ready to strangle the man before him—until he saw Mistress Gibbard. She clutched her arms to her waist and shook her head in disbelief; he lost heart and looked away. A hand pinched his chin and twisted it up and forward. Governor Eaton scanned his face, reasoned and calm. "Take him to the prison. We put him to trial." With the release of John's chin, rough hands wrenched him up by his shoulders and hauled him away.

⌒❁⌒

Samuel tossed a stone at the prison wall, trying to hit the small window above him. The building stood at the far corner of the green. It was a squat structure with two rooms, one for prisoners and one for the marshal or watchman assigned to guard them. Samuel had waited until Nate Green, charged with the day's watch, snuck off to meet with

Goody Flemming. He figured he had an hour before the man returned. He threw one more rock. This time the trajectory was right and it flew through the opening.

Two sets of fingers appeared in the window hole, one no bigger than a man's head. John's face followed. Samuel raised his hand in greeting and bent to hug Muddy. "The watchman has left, John." He paused, not sure how to continue, then said, "Muddy misses you."

For emphasis, Muddy let loose with a single low, "Woof."

"Shush, Muddy!" John whispered. "Samuel. You should not chance this. Get away!"

"No, John. Answer me first. Are you well? Mercy asks after you and wants to know. It is past a month since...since they took you."

"And will be a month more, I think, before a trial. The Magistrates say the next is scheduled for May, so...I am well enough. Drier and a sight warmer than with Gibbard. Though I do long for the mistress's pigeon pie."

John strained to hold himself up in the window. His sad try at cheerfulness pained Samuel. And while he wished him no sorrow, he had to ask the question rattling in his mind. "Why did you to it, John? Did you do it? Everyone says you confessed."

"That much is true, Samuel. I confessed my sin. As to why? A wrong is a wrong, is it not? The why matters little, though one good thing has come of this prison. I am free from whippings—for now." He blew out half a snort, as with a joke gone poorly. "Make your master leave, Muddy, before he ends up my cellmate."

Samuel roughed Muddy's fur and nuzzled against his head. The hollow in his chest dropped to his stomach. He would not believe John evil, nor Satan's shipmate, as Mister Gibbard told it on meeting days.

"Samuel," John said, "you must go. Now! I can hold here no longer."

Samuel looked up at the face of his friend, Muddy's friend. The dog stood, his tail whisking back and forth, and nudged Samuel, knocking him off balance.

"See there." John shifted his fingers on the sill. "Muddy knows the danger. Heed him. I am fine enough. Tell Mercy I survive. And, Samuel?"

"Yes?" Hope rose in him at what John might ask.

"Thank you for believing in me."

Samuel beamed. "I'm your friend, John, as are Edward and Mercy. We will be there for you, we will...at the trial."

"Well, my hopes are not high, nor should yours be. But I thank you, friend. Take care. And go!" The face dropped from view and the fingers peeled from the sill. Samuel slapped his hand to his thigh twice and ran toward the cistern on the harbor-side of the green. Muddy leapt forward, soon outpacing his master.

❧❀❧

John slid to the floor and swept his fingers through the greasy mat of his hair. His eyes ached from the sun; spots of light danced across his lids as he adjust to the dank cell. The room was not small, six foot on a side, he guessed, large enough to accommodate others. Not three nights ago, Thomas Parker slept over with him due to a complaint of drunkenness. By morning Thomas had puked in the corner three times. The vomit lent a reek to the room of stale beer and fermented wine, a smell yet to dissipate. Yesterday's watchman, tired of the stench, which had reached his own quarters, consented to a rake of straw, moldy but serviceable. John used it to cover the muck but saved out the better pieces to create a bed.

Whether seeing Samuel and Muddy lifted his spirits or submerged them, he could not tell. Like a hard-plucked harp string, his insides quivered between hope and despair. The same mix of feeling rose in him on the nights Edward slid up to talk in soft asides about sedition around the plantation. During the whole of their conversations he worried over Edward being caught in his deceptions, so paid little attention to his words.

He wanted to believe—in himself, an uprising, God's grace. But he knew not where to put his believe; and therein was his dilemma. Samuel's belief in him tugged at his heart but seemed impractical under the circumstances, and sedition, he thought, led more to hanging than freedom. The notion of swinging on a noose sent him shivering, so he retreated—into considering the merits of God.

The Elect shall be granted faith through the grace of God, or so the sermon went. No effort, no act would soften His heart to those not chosen. John would, or would not, be saved from burning through God's will alone. After his mother died, his father had ground the message into him. The Day of Atonement was close at hand, at the turn of the century, the new millennium. Many thought the same. Still, John felt no irresistible pull to faith. In fact, when he considered the actions of the so-called Elect of God, he churned.

Was Mister Gibbard one of God's chosen, even after beating him? How could God hold that man up and allow a kind man, not chosen, to fall? Rivulets of sweat ran from the back of his neck down his spine. This grace thing troubled him. Were Gibbard's words true? Was he filled with a devil? And what God would offer Gibbard the prize of salvation after having beaten a body raw? John scraped at the quick of his thumbnails, rubbed his hands and scraped again, a habit deep-seated after thirty-six days of imprisonment.

He marked the days, scratched them line-by-line with his fingernail. His nails embarrassed him, cracked and jagged and bleeding as they were. He hid them between his thighs, rubbed them up and down against his breeches. Then he snorted at his pretension.

"Like someone watches or cares," he said to the ceiling.

His mind-born torment ended with a banging at the door. "You there, inside. John Frost. Who you talking to?"

So Nate Green was back, the watchman returned from his tryst with Goody Flemming. John laughed, "I talk to no living thing, Nate. Save the ceiling. It breathes roaches."

"Well, unlike you, they are not locked to one cell. The damnable things skitter cross my cot as well."

"Ah, but you have a bed. So I'll be trading you."

"And trading me at the gallows? I think not. But Goody Flemming says she heard your master and Mister Cooper arguing, taking drink at the ordinary. Gibbard cries for hanging. But Cooper says it's not writ in the law. My Martha tells me Gibbard nearly burst, turned redder than a cock. Cooper—patient as Job, she said—told Gibbard if he thought it be God's court, he must abide by its laws. They liked each other little in the past and even less now, or so says my Martha."

John dare not engage in gossip. He feared a trick to ensnare him further. But he might use the situation to his gain. "Humph, time tells, Nate. But tell me this. Have things changed? I thought Goody Flemming was yet married. Best not be blathering 'my Martha' about the town."

Silence followed.

Had he gone too far?

Then came a scraping, Nate rocking back on a chair, or maybe a stool, on the dirt floor. "I hear your meaning, John. Advice to heed. But would others listen to the likes of you? I think not. Still, a rake or two more of straw might serve you well, and quiet you. Agreed?"

"Agreed, and at your next watch, perhaps a bucket of water?"

"Water? You get light beer every meal."

"A bucket, Nate, to wet down Parker's puking, and one later, to bathe in. I would be clean for the trial."

❧❀❧

Mercy stood at the gallery banister with Edward and Samuel. Samuel insisted they stand together, so Edward snuck her up to the gallery, a place she had never been. She had hidden her head, marking each ascending stair tread, grasping at her fluttering stomach, distraught by her rebellion.

Now, she was glad of it. Freed from Widow Sherwood's blistering pronouncements, she could concentrate on John alone, and here at the banister, no one blocked him from view.

He stood before the bar, facing the Magistrates, appearing still and composed. But, even with his wrists pinioned at his back, he rubbed at his fingers and worried the hemp rope. The chains on his leg irons clattered as he adjusted his feet, and his sandy hair hung long. Her hand moved without thought, wishing to reach out and brush the tangled strands from his eyes as he so often did.

Governor Eaton began the proceedings. "John Frost, a serious complaint, to which you confessed in my presence, of willfully setting fire to the property of Mister Gibbard. As a consequence, a haystack and barn, along with the man's house and its contents, were lost. What say you?"

John's voice wavered and did not carry to the back of the meetinghouse. Samuel tugged at her skirt. "What did he say?" he whispered. She bent down, her finger to her lips. How would she hear with his prattling?

With her hand cupped to Samuel's mouth, concentrating on the governor's lips, she repeated John's words. "He says Gibbard abused him, beat him with a rod."

Samuel pulled her hand away. "So he beat him?" The words spit from him, and, fearful of notice, she admonished him again to quiet and returned her attention to the governor's words.

"And you planned this as vengeance?"

"I...I did, sir. Pray forgive me. I was angry at Mister Gibbard and thought...not clearly." John shuffled his feet, the chains rattled, and dust floated up to dance in the sunlight sliding in from the highest windows. Each of his shaking words ripped into Mercy's chest. She wanted to whisk him away, to save him, but the governor continued.

"And you, Mister Gibbard. What say you to the beatings?"

"I confess, Governor, I was driven to it, him being given to the devil. I applied the rod for his lies, for being an eye-servant unworthy of trust. He shirked his duties. And he acted the hypocrite, pretending kindliness and conforming to my will of an evening, then burning my efforts come morning."

All contrition deserted John. "Not by your efforts, master," he hissed. "That haystack was by my effort and my design."

Mercy cringed at John's blistering defiance. She lifted her hand to her lips as if to silence him, to calm him.

Mister Gibbard showed no calm, and would not be silent. He stomped his foot, and more dust danced toward the rafters. "See, see you! A serpent's tongue, ungrateful and unrepentant. The noose is his due, for the danger he presents to us all. I say hang him!"

Mercy thought the man might burst, he was so red and angry. He stepped a pace right then left, a banty hen trying for flight, while a ripple of support sounded in the pews.

Governor Eaton, a steady man, slowed the growing agitation by standing, head high, looking down his nose at Gibbard's fuming. Without a word from him, the congregants settled.

And Mister Cooper stood.

"I would address the Magistrates," he said, and the meetinghouse fell silent. Mister Cooper was a tall man, strong-boned, with a reputation for fair dealing and hard work. Mercy's father liked him, especially when he spoke his mind, as he often did, to the consternation of town leaders. The governor nodded for him to continue.

"Governor Eaton, Magistrates. I do not condone the boy's behavior. But he is a boy. How old are you, John? Do you know?"

"Fourteen as of February past, sir," he said with conviction. John had told Mercy he could read and write and do sums, good things for a servant. It eliminated the time wasted for schooling, a requirement for even servants in New Haven. But Mercy thought his haughtiness came from his opinion that, at fourteen, he was a man. True in some places, but not in New Haven.

A small grin cheated its way onto Mister Cooper's lips. "Not yet sixteen, unable to serve as watchman, and seven years from maturity.

Beyond that, sirs, New Haven law is clear. In cases of malicious arson, a fine should be levied, and if no restitution is possible, as I doubt it is for John Frost, he should be sold as a servant or punished as severely as the circumstance presents."

Gibbard elbowed his way forward, puffing himself up to fill the room, an effort his stature prohibited. "And a severe enough punishment hanging be!"

Mister Cooper paused and shook his head, his disdain percolating in the silence. "The court, graced by God's wisdom, saw fit to designate in writing every transgression which warranted hanging. It did not include setting anything to fire, wittingly or unwittingly. Would this court go against their own word?"

Samuel tugged at Mercy's skirts. She pulled down on her cap's ties and cocked her head to the side in annoyance.

"Sister, will they hang him? They cannot hang him." Samuel's eyes looked so forlorn, the way Muddy's did when she caught him digging in her garden or chasing the chickens.

She touched his porcelain cheek. "I pray not, Samuel."

"I will pray, too," he said, and then stopped. "But, sister, is it not wrong to pray, except for God's will?"

Heart-weary, Mercy just shrugged. Then Samuel stiffened and scrunched his face, implacable. "I know John Frost, and I pray rightly." He did not pray long.

"We hand the verdict of the court," Governor Eaton said. He paused, cleared his throat, and glanced down at the paper in front of him. "Due to his age, and the childishness of his ways, the prisoner escapes death, but we extend his indenture to one and twenty years more. In addition, on Wednesday next, our market day, we condemn him to whipping with rods to the purpose and next lock him in the pillory until sunset. Henceforth, he shall wear locks on his legs for all to see and a halter on his neck. Should he, at any time, disobey or take leave of New Haven Colony for any reason, he shall pay with his life. Do any here object?"

"I object!" Mister Gibbard yelled. His arm slapped up and down as though swinging the lash. "The boy is an eye-servant. How do we watch him? The neighbors worry what he might do. And a lock on his legs? How do we get our value from him if he cannot be fully used?"

Edward's only response, his first, was a venomous whisper. "The bastards," he said.

Mercy struggled to grasp the verdict. "Why?" she asked. "What about Mister Gibbard's abuse?" Edward only shrugged.

John turned from the governor to Mister Gibbard, trying to understand. His despicable master gulped incessantly, attempting to say something, pumping his arms up and down.

Governor Eaton oozed impatience. He held up his hand, indicating he would hear no more. His words clipped the air, a final declaration. "Should the leg locks be a hindrance, the servant's master shall petition the court."

Gibbard blubbered, "Not enough. The boy is a danger!"

The governor's voice rose. "So then, Mister Gibbard, we shall assign him to Mister Cooper. The boy will work in Cooper's iron works, the one he builds outside the palisade walls, either gathering ore or working the kilns, as Mister Cooper sees fit."

The governor deftly moved on to the next item on the agenda. Using his arms as battering rams, Gibbard shoved his way to Mister Cooper's pew. Cornered, Mister Cooper stared at Gibbard with stoic dignity while the man's belly bumped up against his thighs. His finger waved up into Mister Cooper's stone-still face.

Edward touched her hand. "Look at John, Mercy. You would think they gave him a prize instead of a beating."

John smiled up at them, his chained feet bouncing as the marshal led him away.

〜❋〜

The green at the center of New Haven bustled. Market day drew merchants and farmers from Stamford to Southold. They arrived by boat, traveling The Sound to sell everything from haddock to honey. A few ventured overland from The Waste, outside any protection of the militia, to trade what they could. Carts and small stands lined the square. Tradesmen proffered hides and candles and pottery. The Magistrates walked from merchant to merchant, checking charges and extracting rates in wampum or shilling or pieces of eight. But transactions in trade took precedence and were harder to track. In the midst of it all, out the prison door and down the center of the green, the marshal led John Frost.

The trial had extracted John's guts from his belly, swung them round in a fearful arc, and replaced them with a gentle pat and a hug. From Gibbard's talk of hanging to the unexpected decision to make Mister Cooper his master, it had all dizzied him.

Now he stumbled after the marshal, hobbled and pinioned, the leg irons chaffing his ankles. Yet John thought only of his future—with his new master, Mister Cooper. He imagined that life, free from humiliation and the sting of the rod. Beyond the palisade walls!

But first, he must endure both humiliation and abuse one more time. He was their entertainment.

Women, dressed in their best but simple gowns, pulled their children aside to scold them, presenting John as a cautionary example of Satan's intrigues.

"See there," one said, "forsaken by God. Stay clear of such, mind you. Stay clear."

The crowd clustered round and made the devil's horn, their fists clenched with two fingers extended. They turned their backs and forced their children to do the same. John looked forward, only turning his head aside when two boys, not yet ten and unsupervised, threw balls of mud in his direction. The mud splattered against his breeches and his sleeve, but he ignored them and focused on his future beyond the walls.

The whipping post grew near. First, though, he passed a group of freemen chanting, or praying, if you wished to call it that. "Resist not the spirit of God; harden not his heart." John let their words float past him, dust on the wind. He erected a fortress, a shield against the jeers, the gestures, and the chanting.

Then he saw Mercy. She was there at the edges. She provided solace. He lifted his chest and chin, pretending strength for her. His handler elbowed the crowd, creating a path to the pole, and she disappeared.

Nate Green stood at the whipping post. The rod hung lank from his hand. He offered John a one-shouldered shrug and leaned into him.

"The middle switch is hickory, near to five feet long. Twelve hickory switches round the main rod. Shall hurt like the devil." He raised his brows and chuckled at his joke.

John smiled, his best attempt, the inevitable acknowledged. "Did they decide how many?"

"Forty, the most allowed. But not by me, John. The marshal here does the job, and he takes his role seriously." Nate dropped the rod to the ground and fumbled to untie the ropes at John's wrists. "The knots are tight," he said, smiling up at him.

"Get on with it, Nate. I would be done, truly." The rope slackened, a short reprieve before Nate lashed his hands high on the post with his back to the crowd. They circled round him, wolves ready to feast on his suffering. The marshal stepped forward, snatched the rod from the ground and began.

Nate was right. The marshal was heavy-handed, and the rod stung like a blistering hell. Every hit was true, but did not cut like a lash. The rod whistled with each stroke as air whizzed through the bound switches. The smell of hickory spewed out with each slash. It was a rhythmic wounding, the drummer rapping on his drum with each blow. John counted until some time after twenty. Then he dropped his head against the pole, breathing in on the outstroke and releasing with the hit—until the marshal stopped and walked away. A throbbing interlude.

Nate was there then, to untie him from the pole. "Now the pillory, John, till night falls. Then Mister Cooper collects you. Let me see to your shirt."

John raised his arms and Nate slipped the shirt over his head. The rough linen scraped along his back, sending his shoulders into a spasm. He laid his head back while Nate turned him round. He looked for the pillory but instead caught sight of Sarah and Prudy Gibbard. There father stood at their side. Prudy lifted her hand in a quiet wave, which Gibbard batted down. He then mouthed something to Mistress Gibbard who stood behind the children. In response, she hung her head, gathered the girls, and walked them away.

At that moment, John's strength liquefied and puddled at his feet. Those few white-hot words, of the many spoken at the trial, flared up inside him. They had smoldered while he waited in prison and now rose to a burning. "The childishness of his ways." Shame melted his courage, like iron in a searing heat.

The pillory stood a few rods from the whipping post, a prominent place near the cistern where everyone walked. Nate led him there without allowing him water, and his tongue rubbed ashen against his teeth. The hinge creaked and the pillory came down hard, scraping his neck as it bound him. His arms hung out at an awkward angle, and no matter where he put his feet, however he stood, pain jolted through his hips or neck or shoulders. And the taunting continued. He focused on the ground, watched the ants and mosquito catchers passing, anything but the jeering. He dozed but someone kicked his legs from beneath him, and he jolted to waking.

The pillory cut into his neck. He scuffed at the ground, his throat burning. He coughed, struggling to regain his footing. The culprit was no common heckler but Mister Gibbard. He leaned in and whispered in his ear, his breath that of hard liquor and sweet onion. "You are not free of me, John Frost. Understand? Any mistake and, as God's loyal servant, I will expose you. Then your neck will suffer. And that pathetic coughing? Only a taste of what shall come."

John tried for an iron will. But he melted away—from a sense of future or freedom, from any place beyond palisade walls.

Mercy had pushed through the throng, reaching its edges just as John came toward the whipping post. He recognized her, his face showed it. But his acknowledgment was brief. He stared ahead and walked chin high. She ached for him but sensed a strength there and took solace in it.

Then a line of men encircled him. They wore quilted doublets to protect against Indian arrows in an attack. Only now, these men were the attackers, puncturing the air with their accusations and admonitions.

"Harden not his heart," they said, and Mercy wondered. Did they ask that John's heart not harden toward them? Did they beg his forgiveness? She knew it was the opposite, an admonishment: that he should not harden himself unto God. But how could he not? Their words were torture, twisted words in God's name.

Father dragged Samuel by the hand, taking him away, and he expected her to follow. But she would not. She lingered at the edge of the crowd to watch after John.

Nate Green tied him to the post, and John's sandy hair, near his shoulders after two months locked away, fell over his eyes. He leaned against the post, hands lashed high above him, his back exposed. He did not look around when the switches fell; he saw neither her nor anyone else. Mercy wrapped her arms tight around her waist and watched him count the blows, swallowing each word. Then he stopped counting and stiffened to the onslaught. Sweat trickled down his neck and along his chest, and traces of pink, welted flesh stretched out from his shoulders to his waist. The drumbeat quickened, then stopped, and Nate Green cut him loose.

She walked with the crowd, following as Nate led John to the pillory. Then Gibbard caught her eye. She moved to avoid his gaze and tripped into one of the heckler. He pushed her away, and she recovered, weaving through the press in time to see John forced round to face the crowd. He stumbled, then fell into the pillory's grasp, body dangling.

She cried out. Not loud; only a muffled, "Oh..." It was not John's helpless dangling that squeezed the sound from her, but the deathly sorrow on his face. His soul needed quenching. But how? "The cistern," she thought. "He needs water."

Again she forced her way through the crowd, head down, dodging the rock-hard righteousness around her. At the cistern, Widow Sherwood held court. Her cackling grew louder the nearer Mercy came. "Gibbard says the boy be an eye-servant. Filled with the devil."

Mercy's lungs emptied—in order to endure, not just the righteous, but also the gossips. She slipped between the widow and her followers and unknotted her apron strings. "Boneless blatherers," she whispered, and dipped her apron into the cistern's waters. She wrung the apron out gently, leaving it sopped and dripping, and then she turned in a deliberate rush to leave. Water sprayed in an arc across the widow's chest. A pleasured glimmer crossed Mercy's lips.

The widow curled hers in disgust, then faced her compliant cohorts. "Burn and ye shall be burned, I say."

"Ah," Mercy offered, exuding as much derision as she could muster, "but our Bible does not. Though there is a lovely verse about casting stones." She blustered away, a trickle of water trailing in her wake.

At the pillory Mister Gibbard hovered over John like a weasel, teeth bared in warning. She reached them just as the man swaggered away. An uncommon hatred boiled within her.

Water from the apron ran down her wrists, jarring her to her purpose. She lifted her apron over John's head and squeezed. Rivulets of moisture ran along the back of his head, through his hair, and down his cheeks. He raised his head as far as he was able, then rolled his eyes up to meet hers. He blinked.

"Mercy," he said, then repeated her name once more, softer, evoking its meaning. "Thank you," he said, and closed his eyes, then opened them with a breath, trying to smile. "A disappointment, I am. I'm sorry."

He swallowed, a stiff, grasping swallow. Mercy held his gaze and rung out a twist of fabric, holding it near his mouth. A dribble of water squeezed free. He grasped the twist with his lips and sucked. She used the length of apron handing along her wrist to smooth his brow and pushed a musty strand of hair from his face.

"Daughter!" her father yelled. "Daughter!" He caught up to her, yanked the apron from John's mouth, and pulled her across the green. She never took her eyes from John. She watched after him, until bodies blocked her view.

⌒❖⌒

"The boy needs food, husband. His shivering comes from an empty belly and the beating." The words tumbled over John, returning him to the pillory.

He had watched the sun sink in the sky, tracking the time by it. But it moved at a turtle's pace so he focused on the clouds, layered and tinged with grey, sliding through a vibrant sky. They morphed from turtles to toads and then billowed to expose a ship. It sailed, and he followed until his stomach churned with remembered seasickness.

The memory mingled with the marketplace odor of roasting meat and onions. Sweet onions—reminding him of Gibbard. Bile filled his throat and tingled against the back of his tongue. He heaved. Then his whole body convulsed, one last vicious vomit, yielding little. He had struggled to stay upright, scuffling his feet into the dirt, and then he had felt the touch.

Now, he hunched on a three-legged stool and adjusted a woolen cover nearer to his chin. He contemplated that touch. He had thought it might be Mercy again and looked up. The sun still held its grip on the world, but barely. It balanced at the edge of the meetinghouse turret, the glare blinding him. He squinted to see her, trying to smile, but a man's face appeared, Mister Cooper's face.

"So," John thought, "he comes to claim his prize." He must have spoken the words aloud because Mister Cooper answered him.

"The louse-ridden stench of you is no prize, boy. But we shall see." He had wrapped him in a cloak and brought him here.

The woman's voice broke through once more and gentled him into the present. "Give him this tea to start, husband."

Mister Cooper bent near and put the cup, a porcelain cup, in his hands. It rattled and worried him. "It will b-b-break, sir. I can't..." and he held it out, shaking. Then this big man, dark of hair, with brown, kind eyes, put his arm around him and helped him with the tea. It slipped warm into his throat, smelling of chamomile and mint.

"Thank you," he said. Words uttered twice in a single day, first to Mercy and then here.

Next came a thin soup, and he shook as he brought the bowl to his lips. After he could take no more, he tried to rise but shivered, unable to stop even in the heat of the house, and Mistress Cooper brought him a second woolen blanket. Weary for sleep, he wondered where to lie down, and Mister Cooper laid a mat by the hearth, in the house, and led him to it. So he curled into a ball on his side, and Mistress Cooper rubbed his battered neck and back with a salve and told him the shaking would end, that it was from the effort of the day and the stress to his body. Eventually, long after the house was dark, the shuddering did stop, and he fell into a trusting sleep.

⌒❈⌒

Mister Cooper woke John early, and they struck out north. His master set a speedy stride. John hustled behind, leg irons jangling, occasionally inserting a shuffling gallop to maintain the pace. Mister Cooper made it clear the night before. He was not to stay in the town, not, his master said, because he worried what John might do there, but because he worried for John's safety. A kind sentiment, but mistrust, a well-learned inclination, made John suspicious. Escape still played in his plans.

He hurried forward, holding onto the halter so it rubbed less on his bruised neck. They approached the north gate and the road leading to Neck Bridge. John knew that much, and he brimmed with curiosity about his new life. "Pray sir, where are we going? I mean, exactly?"

"The bog, boy, the marshland. Now hush." Cooper gestured, a sly movement of his chin, acknowledging the militiaman standing on the tower overlooking the palisade. "There is time enough for talk once outside the gate."

Cooper tipped his hat to the guard as they exited, then they walked in silence. John reveled in the beauty of the countryside. He had run with Muddy and Samuel often enough on the other side of Mill River, so was acquainted with the wet, willow-ridden odor of the place, the riot of birds, and the horizon, dominated by the towering red butte. The northern horizon drew him in.

A thought occurred to him and he ran up alongside his master again, but tripped on the leg irons in his haste and reached down, warding off a fall. "The marshland, sir? Edward House—he works for the ferry master. He says there is a great marsh between the East River and the red rock."

Mister Cooper looked down on him. John, at fourteen, stood taller than most men, certainly taller than Mister Gibbard, but this man was taller by far, and muscled. "Stop here," he said, then produced a key from his belt pocket and knelt down to remove John's leg irons.

"You take them off?"

"Should I not?"

John stared at his thumbs and ran his fingernails along the quick. "Well, no...I mean yes. I mean you should, but was that not my sentence?"

"By the discretion of the court. I practice patience, Frost, and I am convincing. Outside the town, you need not wear them. But, for now, you carry them." He handed them to John, then continued up the cart-rutted road.

After crossing Neck Bridge, John ventured another question. "Sir, how far are we now?" Cooper snorted, sighed, and stopped, looking him square in the eyes.

"Your friend was right. A great marshland lies between East Rock and East River, fed by a series of streams falling off the rock and out of the uplands. The water spreads and slows before reaching the river.

These percolating streams seed the marshland with a harvest of iron ore. The bog iron hides in the marsh. If you know where to look, you will find it."

"Find it? How, sir? I—"

"I will teach you. I considered sending you into the forest to make charcoal for the forge. I have a team of men and their families cutting the trees, charring them, and cutting the chars into lengths. But it's dirty work, and the workmen are an unseemly lot, not the best for you, I think. Besides, they work with fire. I thought it best you stay clear of fire. Do we agree?"

John's body retracted, an old fear rekindled, of being judged for his lack. But he looked up to Cooper's growing smirk, his eyes twinkling at his joke. A joke, humor; John recognized it but was unsure how to respond so dropped his head, submissive. "Yes, sir. I understand."

"Whoa, now. I tease you. Too soon, I see. No, John Frost, I give you this job because I think you smart enough to find the best yield of ore and strong enough to rake it from the bog. Now, look at me." John stared up into the man's solemn face. "One thing more. I must trust you out here alone—to work hard, to do your job, and, most important, not to leave. Can I trust you in that, boy?"

John licked his lips, considering. It was a hard promise. "You can, sir."

"I thought it was in you. Mind you, though, if you run off, Gibbard will follow you, out of pride and a self-justified piety. And you will hang."

John heeded the reminder, which held no threat or anger. He could work for this man.

They walked by the path turning off to the Paynes' house, and John scanned for life there. Mercy maybe, or Samuel and Muddy, but no one was in the pasture or down near the river. Smoke curled from the chimney, arced down to skim the door-side garden, and then swooped in grey billows, riding the wind to the sea.

He recalled sucking the liquid from Mercy's apron, the rhythmic intensity of it. He bit his lip and worked it, looking left to the looming red rock, embarrassed by his thoughts.

"The girl is kind, John. She nurtures everything she touches. I have seen it. Do not abuse her kindness, or mistake it."

John had sworn he could be trusted. So, trying to sound certain, he said, "Her, sir? She's but a girl."

Then they edged north toward the Great Marsh and his new home.

❧

Volume II sits in the back seat, Maggie's companion in her escape to the ocean. Of course, her husband came, but it was her idea; an attempt to resist the pull of her other world. She desired the vital reach of now, so chose a trip to the sea where the crash of each wave holds you fast to the moment's churning force. But unaware, she threw the other world onto the back seat of the car; Volume II traveled with her, there and back again.

Duncan turns onto their dirt road. Nothing is changed. The wet of the ocean, the foggy coolness that enveloped them while they searched for smooth palm-sized rocks on the beach, all of it washed away. It drifted from view as they climbed the coastal range and descended into the baked, dust-ridden valley. The drought did not disappear in their absence; the trees lining their Sierra view are still as dead. Escape is an illusion. The book breathes her in, exhales; it could have told her that.

"*Dusty as ever,*" *Maggie sighs.*

"*You expected more?*" *Duncan laughs.*

"*I wanted more. You know—change your place; change your outlook; change your life.*"

"*Yeah, right.*" *Duncan stops at the gate and leaves the car running. He jumps out, unlocks the padlock, and swings the gate free. Maggie questions this locking away of everything, the lack of trust, but that argument is long lost.*

The car dips downhill and rounds the turn leading home. The house, outbuildings, and garden come into view.

"*Everything still here,*" *Duncan says, the same refrain each time they return from a trip.*

"*Yep, still here.*" *Maggie echoes the expected reply, but adds,* "*Dry, dusty, and hot!*"

"*Oh, come on. Don't mess with my good time. I'm happy to be home.*"

She says nothing. The mood moves in her, the usual takeover. She thought the books too distant and dry to generate her usual obsession, too perversely at odds with her world to creep into her psyche. Volume I winces, wishing it were otherwise, wishing her calm. She doesn't see yet; she has no choice. Her mind-creep doesn't just happen. Her time-hops are caused. They infect her and alter her awareness. Or maybe the present infects her awareness of the past. The books aren't sure how it works, but Duncan is right, she shouldn't mess with his mood. Still, aren't they messing with hers?

They wither under her melancholy. It wasn't their desire. The details in the records, even the shocking bits, strike her as soulless, and that worries them. Yet, like a modern Dante, she seeks the humanity within.

Some bits hidden in Volume I excite her. They are glad of that. Mostly she likes the references to her ancestor William Payne: the gift of land in The Neck, his release from militia duty because of a lame wife, a fine levied for shoddy fencing, and a complaint he made saying the marshal was unfair to fine some who came late to Sabbath service and then ignore others. But the stuff of Volume II? It is painful, nearer to the blood running in Maggie's veins. It pulls her deeper in.

She picks Volume I off the seat and pulls some remnants from the car—coats, phones, the succulents they bought. Duncan is already unlocking the door, their suitcase in hand. She carries everything, juggling the plants while wondering what in God's name she was thinking to buy them. This parched environment will squeeze them to dust.

"I'll park the car, hon," her husband says. "Then it's a nap for me."

❧

He flattens out on the couch while she unpacks, a quick chore, not more than fifteen minutes. By the time she throws the last of the dirty clothes in the hamper, his breath has slowed into the soft succor of sleep.

Maggie never naps. So much beckons her, and now she closes the door to the front room and pads through the laundry, past Duncan's collection of tools—from chisels to planes—into her bedroom, holding Volume II. It reaches into her, asking her to persevere.

A dry wind blows. It whistles at the corner of her mind as she opens to where the bookmark holds her place, less than a quarter of the way through its pages. She reads the words without wonder, weary of their brittle dryness and starts to skim and scan. One perspective, one dry wind. Then another vision brews—of now. The rustling song of grey pines beckons her, and something more, on the wind, a fragrance both redolent and sweet.

Duncan slips into the room. "Guess what?" he says. The question alerts her to the sporadic patter on the roof. Her jaw drops, and Duncan nods an affirmation. Outside the window, the droplets scatter randomly on the deck, not yet wetting anything, but still—it rains. She jumps up and hugs Duncan. He squeezes her in turn, and she lets her weight fall forward into his arms.

"Thank God," she says. "Come on!" They hustle through the house and out the front door. They leave the books behind. But their essence follows. They dance with her as she twirls, a child in the rain. Duncan laughs, absorbing her joy. Then he joins the jubilee and lifts his head to the dapple-grey sky.

It is a light rain, a sprinkling. The droplets send puffs of dust into the air as they hit. The straw-sweet fragrance of dampened grass creeps into the air, expanding, fresher by the moment. The droplets' frequency crescendos then slows to a stop, the ground barely wet, still dry under the tree branches. But they stand in it, all of them, to the end. They relish a moment of relief, a harbinger of hope, a comfort.

Afterward, Maggie returns to Volume II, her determination renewed, her spirit refreshed. She enters the meetinghouse, she watches the trial, and she meets the boy—John Frost. He burns down his master's house, but the court ignores the master's abuse. She concedes the boy's guilt. She considers the verdict rational but the punishment cruel. It appalls her, but arson...a harsh revenge. A good thing he didn't end up hanged as some wished. She continues reading, scanning complaints about horses borrowed and not returned, of butter stolen. But the boy doesn't leave her mind, nor does the cleansing rain. The books relax—taste their bittersweet success on her tongue. He is found, and the others will follow, they will flow into her, between the lines.

PART IV

1660 (and the present)

...no Servant Male or Female shall
without license either give, sel, or truck any
commodity whatsoever, during the time of
service, or subjection, under the paine of such
Fine or corporal punishment ...

Code of New Haven

Autumn had seeped into the marshland, and the morning was cool. Samuel found the smoldering remains of a fire burning outside John's half-cabin, but no John. The cabin sat on a gradual incline leading up to the outcropping of East Rock. Samuel visited often, at least twice in a week, not counting the day before Lord's Day. On that day, he and his sister broke fast with John on the East River near their home. Afterward, John continued downstream, his flatboat laden with half-buckets of iron ore, his destination the bloomery, now expanded to a fully functioning iron works.

On Samuel's first visit, nearly four years ago, John had held Muddy at arm's length, laughed at the slobber-filled licks, then begged them both to stay away. He said his master would come soon, and he had a trade to learn. But Samuel and Muddy kept coming. They never stopped. John told him he preferred the silence and safety of his new home, considering people more dangerous than any night roaming wolves or panthers. But Samuel persisted and John relented, deeming Samuel, Muddy, Edward, and Mercy exceptions to his solitude.

John, no doubt, was already at work. He mined the bog with help from three boys picked by Mister Cooper from the colliers' families. They trekked in each day from their home in the hardwood forest where their fathers made charcoal to fuel the kilns.

Samuel patted Muddy's neck then surveyed the marshland below.

He pushed flyaway strands of hair from his eyes and stuffed them under the brim of his cap, annoyed by their intrusion on his view.

Morning winked at the mountain range that guided East River to the sea. Meandering streamlets snaked through the marshlands, making their way to the river below. Many were marked by rust-red flotsam, a sign that iron ore grew beneath the surface.

John had taught Samuel to look for the oily scum collecting along the edge of a run. It marked the best places to mine ore. John called the job harvesting. He filled a flatboat with two tons of ore each week. Then he transported the harvest down East River to the ferry landing where they loaded it on ox-drawn wagons. After an hour's journey overland, the ore was unloaded at the ironworks located by the great millpond. Today, though, was a harvest day, not a transport day. John was here somewhere.

Samuel bent down to Muddy's ear. "Find him, boy."

The mastiff bounded forward and streaked down the rocky slope. At the edge of the bog the dog stopped, sniffed, and let loose with an abbreviated howl. Then he splashed off, following the edge of a stream torn wide by the plowing of a boat.

Samuel tracked the meander with his eyes. Halfway to the river, the course opened onto a miniature pond lined with the rust-red evidence of iron. In the middle of it sat the flatboat, a 16-foot long scow lined with squat wooden boxes, but no John. Sure he was near, Samuel took off at a run, skirting Muddy's messy route and coming round from the south where the way was drier.

He reached the wetland meadow minutes after Muddy, just in time to see John emerge from the muck. Water whipped out in an arc as he threw back his hair. His muscled-back strained under the weight of a massive chunk of iron ore cradled in his arms.

"Call off your dog, Samuel. It's a devil stone. Fifty pounds easy." John worked the jagged bubble of black rock up along the gunwale and dropped it into the vessel's depth. The boat bobbed unevenly under its weight. When the rolling slowed, John heaved his chest over the boat's edge and slid in.

"Devil's own," he said, then leaned back, shading his brow with both hands. "Morning, Samuel. Got away early, did you?" He rose, heaved a long pole into the water, leveraged it, and stepped to the other side of the boat, repeating the action as he glided toward Samuel and Muddy.

The dog circled around his master's feet impatiently. When John drew close, the mastiff lowered his forelegs and leapt into the boat. "Down," John motioned, and the dog flattened between two boxes of ore, nose between his paws.

Next, John held his hand out to Samuel and pulled him aboard. Samuel sat on one of the ore boxes and adjusted his thin frame. The lumpy ore provided an uncomfortable seat. "I left early for school in the village. But—"

"You best go. Your father will find you out, and I will not be your excuse."

"I am eleven years old, John. Near to twelve. And I tire of blabbing out the schoolmaster's words."

"Tired or not, I learned to read and write and so will you. With luck he will not beat the words into you, as was my lot."

"You were twelve when you came here. You told me so."

"And I am no example, so enough from you." He cuffed the cap on Samuel's head, causing it to tumble.

Samuel's jaw hardened. He snatched up his cap, resisting retaliation in favor of a tease. "I came with word about Gibbard. But I can go. Can I leave Muddy?"

John bopped Samuel's shoulder and knelt to scratch Muddy's ear. "Up with it," he said.

Samuel glanced down at the halter John kept near, even after four years, ready to slip on should any official appear, Gibbard especially. Samuel considered John's old master a Beelzebub in disguise, and the edge to his voice said as much. "Gibbard is voted secretary again. He struts about the green, prideful. Says he needs to do a survey of the plantations. To be informed regarding the indentures." Samuel stopped, gaging John's reaction. But John waited, expressionless, so he added, "The schoolmaster told us that last part. He did not say he strutted but it was clear to see."

"And has been strutting for two years now. Not a new thing, Samuel. I see him on his fat white pony often enough. Though he won't come down here. The gallinippers love him." John laughed, and as if for emphasis, Muddy raised his nose to the sky and snapped at a swarm of the maddening mosquitos dipping down to test the soft spots around his face.

John waved the insects away. "Sorry, boy," he said, and ran his hand through the dog's thick brindled fur. "They bother me not at all. Bad blood, some say. Bite me forever and not a welt."

Samuel was not so lucky, but John had taught him to rub the exposed parts of his body with pennyroyal. The plant kept the buzzing annoyances at bay. Samuel, though, smelled a diversion and would not be distracted by idle talk of gallinippers. "That is not my news, John. But this is. Gibbard spies on the indentures because Edward put in a complaint to the Magistrates." Finally, he got his reaction.

"A complaint, a trial? He told me nothing of it."

"Against Meiggs, for breaking the covenant of his indenture. Edward claims he signed the contract under threat of drowning and was not taught a promised trade. He has an advocate. I think someone not kind toward New Haven rules. He goes for trial next month, and Gibbard fumes."

John picked at the quick on his nails, a sure sign he was flustered, maybe even worried. Samuel looked at the boat's hull and hid the smirk teasing at his mouth, an attempt to contain his pleasure at confounding the man he idolized.

John voiced no concern, but he ruminated on the information. Samuel could tell by the way he worried his thumbs and squinted his eyes into the steamy morning sky. "You were right to come, Samuel, and I thank you. But time enough to deal with Edward later. Tomorrow is delivery day, and I need five hundred pounds, at least, to get me to my load line. Five hours work. Easy enough if I get to it."

Samuel leaned over the edge of the boat to check the groove whittled into the boat's side. It marked the displacement level for a full cargo and a week's work. "I can stay and help," he said.

Samuel often helped John. He would use a second rake with its widely placed wooden tines to scrape up the iron ore hidden in the muck. But the work required a quantity of muscle, so he never lasted long. He mostly gathered the ore from John's rake as it came to the surface or helped lift the heavier pieces onto the boat after John dove down to recover them. Samuel knew John would refuse his offer of help. Mercy valued learning, and John never broke from what Mercy valued.

"You get to school. I will leave before dawn tomorrow and buy time to squeeze more information from Edward at the ferry. So tell Mercy, no morning meet this time around. Meet me later this afternoon. Maybe Edward can help me pole up river if work at the ferry is slow. We can talk then."

No pleading would change John's decisions once made. He offered Samuel his hand, pulled him to his feet, and helped him from the boat. Samuel made a face in response to John's slap on his bottom as he jumped off. John laughed. "Learn something more for me, little spy."

"I am not little!" Samuel stood taller, then added, "Send Muddy back before dusk. He guards our cattle against wolves."

Muddy sat up at the sound of his name, alert and questioning. Samuel signaled him stay, and the dog squeezed his muscled body back between the boxes. The thwack of his wagging tail rang out as John poled away.

The morning drizzled, dew-ridden and brisk. John manned the aft pole as the flatboat, laden with his delivery, floated on the current of East River. He redirected the barge on occasion and walked the length of it, checking the stability of the cargo. Young Deliverance scanned afore bow, looking for any unforeseen obstacles or floating debris.

John considered Deliverance. The boy was young, fifteen or sixteen, maybe three years younger than John. John had harvested iron ore since fourteen, and his skill added weight to his years. Deliverance was the son of a collier out of England, only just arrived. His father, skilled at turning the hardwood forest into charcoal to fire the kilns and the new blast furnace, expected the boy to learn all the trade. That training fell to John, and while Deliverance was inexperienced, he was enthusiastic.

"Hazard off the port bow," the boy cried. John anchored the pole to steady the barge as Deliverance shoved away from what lurked in the water.

"Deliverance," he said, as he dropped the pole into the boat and leaned over the side, "this is no hazard." He held up a five-foot willow branch not five inches across. "The boat will slide over it like an otter down a mudslide." He smiled at the boy to ease the criticism. Deliverance was as serious as his name. "Come aft for a bit and let me watch. Just stay to the middle of the river where the current is strong."

The river ran slow and steady, perfect for carrying cargo, and the rising sun vanquished the drizzle and melted the frost dusting the reeds along the shore. John sat at the bow, his mind drifting with the current toward the problem of Edward. He wondered what possessed him. By his calculations, he figured his friend had only a year left until he won freedom, and Edward liked his work at the ferry. Why risk the ire of the Magistrates? Edward's freedom, at least, grew near, unlike his own.

John adjusted the halter at his neck. The old resentment chafed—twenty-one years of servitude. Had he engaged his brain instead of his temper, he would have fulfilled his contracted indenture this year. Oft times he considered the possibility of escape but repeatedly dismissed the idea, determined to use his brain, stay clear of trouble, and wait. He would not jeopardize Mister Cooper's kindness; it softened the passage of time. Besides, if caught escaping, he would hang.

They floated along the meadow below the Payne house, which sat a short distance up a low hill. He searched along the landing that he and Samuel had scraped out for the barge when he visited. No one appeared, nor did he expect anyone. Samuel had given Mercy his message. They would meet in the afternoon when he returned upriver.

He thought of Mercy's hair, gold with hints of brown, curling and escaping from her cap, and her grey-blue eyes framed by freckles running along her nose. Of late, he also noticed the roll of her breasts just blooming above her laces. At the thought, he pursed his lips and lifted his head skyward, suppressing the tingle in his loins. She deserved better than that. So he focused instead on her hands, her long fingers touching his, always in kindness, always with care—for him, for what he thought, for what he said, for who he was.

A log collided with a bang against the flat edge of the bow, and the boat heaved, taking on water. Deliverance jammed his pole to the river bottom and steadied the vessel. With all deference, the boy yelled out, "Was that a hazard?"

John jumped to his feet. He used his pole to push the enormous log along the squared front of the boat. With a last heave, he thrust it to shore.

"Ha! A hazard indeed. I think your enthusiasm may be a better choice than my neglect. Shall we trade places?"

❧❀❧

Later, downriver, they pushed alongside the ferry loading dock. Two ox-driven wagons awaited them, as did Edward. John took his hand and swung onto the dock, careful not to splinter his bared feet. He seldom wore shoes anymore, tired as he was of their poor quality and fit, but the thought of splinters curled his toes.

Deliverance and the wagon men began the chore of hefting the hundred pound boxes onto shore. John slapped Deliverance's back.

"I need to talk with my friend. Can you manage without me?" Deliverance bobbed his head, a serious nod to the responsibility, and John led Edward upriver along the shell-strewn shore.

"Have you something to tell me?" John asked, once out of earshot.

Edward jabbed his arm. "The chinwaggers of New Haven, they reach you even there?"

"Not chinwaggers. My spy, Samuel, told me. But the gossips are busy, and Samuel says Gibbard's in a fit. What demon possesses you?"

Edward shrugged. "Educated men in the outlying plantations encourage me. Meiggs abused me, and I'll not take it. Last year Tom Weed took Meiggs to trial for his tricks against us indentures and won his freedom. I'll do the same."

"But you have less than a year to freedom, Edward."

"Not true, John. My second contract added two years." He exposed his foolishness with a comical grimace.

John skimmed his hands along the reeds while they walked, sensing them spring back as they slipped past his fingers. Edward had taken to helping Captain Sylvester, sailing a small sloop to the nearby settlements, transporting news and seditious pamphlets. Then, upon his return, he delivered the comments and scribblings of the informants. John, so far, stayed free of the intrigue, but he saw its workings. And with King Charlie returned to the throne, and both Governor Eaton and Cromwell dead in the same year, treason whispered in the weeds.

"A trial will draw attention to you. Attention to your conniving."

Edward bumped against him as they walked. "Ah, friend. You worry for me. I thank you, but John Cooper works his quiet ways. He will help me."

"Mister Cooper?" John stopped, winding a handful of reeds around his fist. Implicating Cooper in this plotting brought hammer to iron. His master held high rank in the workings of New Haven. He hardened the game.

Edward fed him more. "I tell you, John. Change comes, as does justice, and not just regarding covenants made twixt master and lowborn. Did you know in Connecticut Colony the vote goes to all? Well almost all—you must still belong to some church. No Catholic or Quaker, of course. Here's the thing. Like New Haven, Connecticut holds no charter with King Charlie, but if Connecticut could gain favor, if we could make New Haven a devil in the King's eyes? Could be the King would put New Haven under Connecticut's control. Anyway, talk to your master. He says it better and with a careful hand, like setting a beaver trap, greasing his words, so as not to be traced." Edward winked and looked back at the ferry landing. "Mister Brown is pulling in with a passenger. I need to go, but if you want help poling up—" He grabbed John's arm. "Christ, man. Is that who I think?"

John glanced over his shoulder. He recognized the horse first, a short stocky mare, her coat a yellowing white. Gibbard stood beside her, equally short and stocky, dressed in his finery, tall hat and all. John looked to Edward, tucked his shirt into his breeches, and shook his legs so the cuffs fell below his knees. No shackles, but he was outside the palisade walls so he was safe on that count. He adjusted the halter at his neck. "He comes to snoop and muster support against you. Trust me, Edward, you should worry...about what he says to Brown for one thing. Gibbard is no servant of God. Of that, I'm sure."

At the ferry landing, John stood sullen, head down. Edward led Gibbard's horse from the ferry and held it while the man nattered away at Ferryman Brown. He was the only passenger, so there was little hubbub, and John caught the last few words of the conversation.

"Like a flood, it will be. The hazards are many. And what shall become of your investment?"

Edward's master wrinkled his weathered nose and shrugged. "The boy works hard for me, and I've worked out a plan to use him to my advantage. Like I said, any loss I suffer gets recouped by Meiggs, so..." He stopped and wrapped his arm around Edward. "A flood maybe, Mister Gibbard, but I shall ride it out."

Gibbard snatched the reins from Edward's hand. His face flushed red as he stared across the animal to John, taking him in, right down to his bared feet. "No irons? Someday, John Frost, with God's help, I will find you out. But for now, I go to have words with Mister Cooper. He owns a goodly number of servants and knows a danger when he sees it." He held his puffy hand out to Ferryman Brown who, of politics and politeness, held it then dropped it away and returned to his boat. With Edward's help, Gibbard mounted and whipped the reins. His pony clomped up the log-lined corduroy road leading to the iron works.

The smell of the man lingered, a sour syrupy odor that forever sent John's head to spinning. He brought his hands to his nose and mouth, squeezing away the sensation. Deliverance sat at the back of the wagon behind the loaded boxes of ore, waiting. John breathed in through his mouth, then blew out. "I'll stay and help unload the next flatboat coming down river, Deliverance. Tell Mister Cooper I will speak with him on my next delivery day."

"And the flatboat, John? Will you pole it up river alone?" Clearly, the boy wanted to visit Mercy, Samuel, and Muddy. Besides, poling alone is a hard task. But his trust did not run so deep today, not with the stench of Gibbard still on him.

"I'll go alone today, Deliverance. But thank you for your offer. Edward might join me. You go home to your family." The word "family" twisted, unleashing a need and an uneasy caldron of anxiety. He sought relief in Mercy.

✿

Mercy lifted her petticoats and broke into a mincing gallop across the open meadow leading to the river. The flatboat skirted the western shore, holding to the river's edge where the current was light. She recognized John immediately. He was free of his halter, a good sign. It meant he felt safe. He finished each stroke with an exclamatory force that sped the boat upstream. It moved faster than one man's effort and, sure enough, as they came closer, she saw two men onboard. She did not stop to determine the other man's identity. It could only be two, Deliverance or Edward.

The late blooming cornflowers brushed against her as she ran. Their fuzzy leaves, just beginning to brown, stuck to her stockings, and the lingering yellow pollen dusted the blue of her petticoat. She jumped over the bent blossoms, stunted by the sandy, shell-ridden soil. An unbidden smile erupted on her face. She looked forward to this time, their time, lingering in the meadow, eating, drinking, and laughing. She talked freely, and John listened. He hung on her words and made Samuel do the same. She hung on John's shy, infrequent smiles.

Samuel was already at the river. He and Muddy bounced along the shore, helloing John and Edward.

"So," she thought, "it is Edward who joins him."

Edward appeared out of the willows. He wore no hat, and his dark curls frizzed out all over his head. He strained as he pulled the stern wide while John guided the boat into the alcove cut into the river's edge. The flatboat shuttered as it hit the sandy beach, a step below the river-worn bank.

John jumped off the squared bow and wound the mooring line to an exposed willow root clutching to remnants of eroding soil. He glanced up, and Mercy slowed her pace, feigning a seemly cadence. She steadied the bundle of food she carried, raised her hand, not too high, so as not to seem anxious, and waved. He grinned, his wide mouth bursting out from a bronzed face. Hair, bleached to the color of his skin, fell forward on his brow. He smoothed it back and lifted his hand, a tentative gesture.

By the time she reached them, Samuel was at Edward's side, immersed in a knotting lesson. Muddy sat at John's feet, looking up with woeful eyes and spraying sand in an arc with his tail. John leaned back from the sandstorm, lifted the dog's muzzle, jostled it, and then stepped up to greet her.

"I have looked forward to this," he said, brushing away the wayward yellow petals clinging to her skirt. "You are well?"

"I am, though Papa disapproves of our meetings. He tried to deter me."

John gave her his sweet worried look, his green eyes narrowed. Two wrinkles formed between his brows. "I am sorry, Mercy," he said, then grew smug, "but not too sorry. He let you come."

"He did, and I left him with a hardy supper of oatcakes and berries, and a hug. His resolve melts away with a hug." She scrunched her shoulders, embarrassed by her admission.

"As does mine," he said, worrying the cuticles on his thumbs.

She reached out and held his hand to calm him, to touch him. They played this game more intently each time they met, connecting to each other as in a storybook, acting out a light and lovely, but trembling, tale. She wanted to pull him out into the meadow and walk along the shore, so they could tease and laugh together, but there were rules to the play that must be obeyed.

"Shall we eat?" she asked, and breathed in the day, to break from her desire. "The breeze, it tastes of autumn, yet still warm." She dropped his hand and beckoned to Samuel and Edward. "Are you hungry?" she yelled out. "You best be. I cut into a just cured ham as a treat."

So the play began. They sat and watched the river and talked. John teased Muddy with a stick, only pretending to toss it out. They laughed as the dog searched aimlessly in the grasses until John whisked the stick from behind his back and handed it to Samuel. Next, Samuel threw the stick as far as possible to give them time to talk undisturbed by the dog's huge wagging tail. She laid out a bundle of food and cider, and Samuel signaled Muddy to go lie down so they could eat. Then talk turned to Edward's trial and grew serious.

Mercy sided with John. "The court worries more and more about our colony's circumstances, Edward. Father says funds grow scarce, which is why they keep raising the taxes and fines. And with Cromwell dead—"

"Good riddance," Samuel put in and puffed himself up with a flip of his hair.

John clipped the boy's shin with his stick. "Take care, boy! Words carry on these winds, and flapping tongues are as common as bird wings. Besides, we are back to a king. How free is that?"

Edward cuffed Samuel's ear. "John is right. About the tongues, anyway." He lowered his voice. "Still, the King's noose is looser than New Haven's Bible."

Mercy would have none of it. "It is not the Bible, Edward. It is the men who read it. And with Mister Eaton dead and Mister Leete in charge, Papa worries he cannot control the factions."

"Really?" Edward's tone, and the look he gave John, worried Mercy. Sedition was a dangerous thing. And Samuel followed Edward about like a mastiff pup. Still, she could not disagree with the damage done to the indentures.

Mercy passed the cider jug, nearly drained, to Samuel and poled away from the discussion, an attempt to diminish Samuel's humiliation at the cuffing received by his two heroes. "Samuel and I will be at your trial, Edward, to support you. I pray Mister Leete shows sympathy for your cause or at least sees the danger of pushing the fringes of our colony too far."

"Too bad Gibbard stirs the pot." Edward stuffed a slice of ham in his mouth, garbling the last of the words.

Mercy bristled. "Gibbard?" John avoided her eyes. She saw it. He looked up and away, crossed his arms, and rocked back, rubbing at his thumbs. She recognized his agitation, paused, knowing not to push, and redirected their discussion.

"Well, we have only one oatcake left. Whoever takes it, cleans up for me. I would not waste this autumn day." She touched John's arm, and he stood and pulled her to him.

She was conscious of her new budding breasts as they came so near him. So she stepped back, straightened her apron at the waist, and adjusted the ties on her bodice. "The meadow is awash in the last of the cornflowers," she whispered.

John followed her into the meadow, and they walked without words. She reached down and ran her hands along the cornflower blooms, watching the pollen billow.

John spoke first. "It is nothing, Mercy."

"Gibbard is something."

"He was at the ferry."

"He follows you then."

"He did not follow me. He stirs the pot over Edward's trial. Seeks to influence Ferryman Brown and Mister Cooper."

"Those are good men, John. And Mister Cooper is your master. He would not betray you."

"Edward says I can trust him."

Mercy stopped and pulled a just dying bloom from the ground, root and all. She plucked the flower head, still whole and lovely, as an offering, dropping the dying part to the ground. "I think Edward right. You can trust him. He has treated you well."

She gentled John's fist around the flower, but he crushed it. Wrung it in his hand, letting it disintegrate. He brushed the crumbs from his palms and paced.

"You think life all flowers and new-cured hams...and...and an autumn breeze. But I don't trust so easily. Everything I know points to the devil. They preach it. Heaven or hell, God or devil, one or the other, nothing can change your lot. The only peace I find comes at the red rock and the marshes. And with you. Gibbard watches me because he thinks me devil's spawn. And, Mercy, if he is right? Well, you and Samuel should stay clear."

"Nonsense," she said. "What foul corner of your mind spews this tripe?" She reached for his hand, but he pulled away, overwhelming her with his glare.

"My father beat it into me, Mercy. The reverend preached his suspicions to me in my cell. Gibbard whispered it in my ear while my back still stung. And today? He again assures me that God will help him put a noose on my neck."

Mercy clasped his head between her hands, frightened by the heat of him. His body stiffened, ready to break away. But he crumbled instead; let his head fall, and his shoulders heave. She ran her fingers along his neck and arms, cradled his hands, and brought them to her mouth. They were rough and smelled of flowers on the edge of decay.

"Men say many things, John. But they are just men, no more or less than you, trying to make sense of words on a page. I say grace is nudged along by deeds. And you are a good man, who does good things." She peeked to his bent head and staunched a welling at his lids with her thumb. "You can choose your own direction." Then she teased. "Though you are a bit tethered." His cheeks lifted into an unwilling smirk. "Look up, John. Please. You reject my flowery world, but I know this, about flowers especially. They always turn to the sun. It is in their nature, and it is in yours."

He looked across the meadow, then back to her. The soft beat of an egret's wings competed with the wind blowing through the reeds. He tugged at the ribbons on her cap and ran his thumbs along her forehead. He kissed her there, the first he had given her.

The heat of him nearly unbridled her, so she worked to rein it in. "Besides," she said, "You would spurn Samuel and me because you fear a devil inside you, but keep Edward near?"

He ran his thumbs out to trace her cheeks and laughed. "Edward?" The devil's playmate, for sure." Then he warned her with his wink.

The night settled, still moonless, below East Rock. John leaned back, his hands supporting his neck, at peace, enjoying the fire outside his half-cabin. But Edward shattered any hope of contemplation.

"You think me blind, John? The girl? You cling to her. An obvious thing. And if it is obvious to me, do you think it not obvious to her father and Gibbard? Get caught with a freeman's daughter and you're dead." Edward threw an alder branch onto the fire and sparks flew. He stood, warming his hands. "Balmy, almost. Hardly need the fire."

"I build a fire every night, to ward off wolves. Cooper gave me that musket over there, but fire makes the devils wary. And, regarding Mercy, Edward, we are friends. I do nothing with her that could bring the Magistrates down on me."

"Not yet, you lunatic. But you will. I can see it, and then what?"

John took up his eating knife, a small bone-handled tool with a sharp blade, one he fashioned with the help of the smithy at the ironworks. The blade shimmered, reflecting the firelight as he turned it round in his hand. He took to whittling the skin he had worried loose from his thumbnail.

"She's a friend, Edward." He contemplated the pattern of shadow and light dancing over Edward's body and then looked up to the stars. They flickered beacon-like in a dark sky. "A friend and a comfort...like the stars." He gestured with his knife up to the horizon then returned to grooming his nails.

"Christ." Edward dropped his neck back and looked at the sky, taking in a full-chested breath. "See those stars. They have the names of Greek Gods. Captain Sylvester is teaching me. And those at the horizon? Squint and you see a bow with an arrow at the center, or so the captain says—it's hard to see. Those they call Perseus, after some boy hero who saves a girl from a sea monster. It's only a story. Not real, you understand? And you are not Mercy's hero."

"So you, Edward? Do you fancy yourself a hero, standing up to the New Haven courts?" Edward glanced sideways at him but said nothing. The wind shifted, blowing a whisk of acrid smoke in John's direction. He lowered his head and coughed. The next words fell from him, disconnected and unbidden.

"I kissed her," he said.

"Kissed her? Good God." Edward dropped his head hard against his chest and kicked at the edge of the alder branch sticking out from the fire. A constellation of embers erupted from the flames. "You best leave, John, before you do something truly foolish. Captain Sylvester can help you. Take you to Boston. You could disappear there. You would not believe the crowd of people."

"And if they catch up to me, I hang." John snatched a handful of drying grass from the ground, wiped the knife blade clean, and slipped it into the sheath tied at his waist. "Besides, I like what I do. I may not be a freeman, but this..." He waved out at the sky and the marshland below. "It's close enough. Mister Cooper says he will teach me the blacksmithing trade. I owe him. And I owe Mercy." He paused, studying the sky, gaging the tension between him and his friend. "Perseus? Was that his name?"

Edward sighed. "Acting like a hero, for a girl—and a master—crying freedom but clinging to a halter."

Though his friend's face was undecipherable in the flickering firelight, John heard the derision in his voice. He wanted to soften Edward's anger, the disappointment he felt, to escape from the discomfort of their differences, so he ran his tongue against his teeth, wrapped his arms around bent legs, and blurted out the first thing that came to him, taking the conversation back to the beginning.

"Know what I do when the fire dims? When I want to sleep? To worry the wolves, I mean."

Edward accepted John's proffered peace and sat on the rock next him, stretching his legs out to the fire, arms crossed. "No idea. But, with the night so dark, I plan to sleep here so—"

Abruptly, John unleashed a formidable shriek. It began low, deep in his chest, and worked into a series of repetitive, trembling growls. They grew ever higher, culminating in a whine that dropped into a low graveled groan.

Edward pulled his feet beneath him and braced his arms against his knees. "What the devil? Scared me to pissing!"

"A panther. I listened to them enough to copy them. Predators, like those wolves, fear the stronger foe. So I fool them. Let them think a panther sits here instead of me."

Edward spat out an uproarious laugh that simmered into head-shaking disbelief. He stood, shoved John with his foot, and rocked him off balance.

"I stashed a jug of beer in my satchel," he said, "and I need a drink."

Geordie Garrison slapped John on the back causing his halter to bounce against his jawline. The brawny old man had, no doubt, left a charred handprint on the back of John's sweat-ridden shirt. Geordie supervised the work on the upper deck of the blast furnace, a two-story stone chimney that fired white-hot, hot enough to extract iron from the ore John brought from the marsh. It required a quick, agile mind to calculate the exact proportion of oyster shells to layer with the charcoal and iron ore, then to heat the mass to a precise temperature, creating the reaction necessary to produce the molten iron that flowed from the bottom of the furnace. Geordie was that mind.

He yelled a good-natured order to the two men loading the blast furnace. White wisps of hair clung to his sweat-beaded forehead. Then, spry and matter-of-factly, he cocked his head to inspect John, gripping his shoulders with scar-ridden hands. "You, boy, are a treasure, finding the biggest, cleanest rock of any harvester. 'Tis like you talk it from the bogs. The makings of a fine furnace man, you are!" He smiled, his toothless grin disappearing into a charcoal smudge face.

By habit, John turned his head away from the loading door as it opened and an assistant dumped a pre-measured quantity of ore down into the furnace. The searing blaze burned at his shoulder and heat flashed up the side of his face. He winced, squinting his right eye. As much as Geordie goaded him, he refused to apprentice at the blast furnace. It was a dirty, backbreaking job. You sweltered even in late September. And in a humid, summer heat wave, men were known to succumb, fainting outright, even dying. To ward Geordie off recruitment, John maintained a distant relationship, never staying long, always polite. Besides, he had business to discuss with Mister Cooper.

He wiped the back of his hand across his forehead. "Thank you, Geordie. But I like the marshland and intend to stay awhile. Keep you in good supply, yes?"

"That you do. But you have a quick mind. Made for more than bogging."

"But here, I wear this thing." John adjusted the halter now chafing the back of his neck. "Gets in the way of shoveling. Is Mister Cooper about?"

"Likely to find him at the new forging shed. Proud as a pigeon over it."

John rolled the vision over in his mind. He never thought of pigeons as particularly proud; they filled the sky in a mass, the easiest of prey, but he supposed alone, strutting about, they seemed proud. Anyway, he thanked the man and walked out onto the charging bridge. It connected the storage shed to the top of the furnace, providing easy access to needed materials.

As he made his way along the path to the new forging operation, men he knew greeted him with a single raised hand, a mumbled hello, or a lift of the chin, never more, intent as they were on their tasks. Each part of the operation depended on another, and production never stopped, day or night, except for three months in the depth of winter when they took time for cleaning and repair.

The image of Geordie's proud pigeon grated on his mind. He adjusted the halter once more. It weighed on him, an embarrassment. His shoulders wanted to stoop under its weight, the pressure of it willing his neck forward, rounding his spine. The weight, more than physical, bore down on his temper as well. He pulled his shoulders back, looked straight ahead, and marshaled an inner resolve. His neck had grown callused where the harness rubbed. So had his attitude. It transformed his face and warned all who saw him to best hold their tongues.

A building, its clapboard siding the rich yellow of new cut wood, stood on a rise just below the ponding basin. Water from the basin ran through two separate sluices to waterwheels, one running the furnace bellows, the other the forge hammer. He heard the rumble of the hammer long before he reached the building's open doublewide doors.

At the far side of the building, a five hundred pound trip hammer, suspended on a swinging arm, lifted and lowered with repetitive, earsplitting precision. It beat down on an oversized anvil set into a maple stump. The beating squeezed the impurities out of the reheated cast iron brought from the blast furnace. Sparks flew, lighting the faces of the finers, the men working the finery and testing the ore for color. Color told them the ore's temperature, and temperature determined its hardness. The smithy would turn this iron, harder and less brittle that cast iron, into horseshoes, shovels, and chisels needed by the colony.

John stepped into the building. A sulfuric blast accosted him, as though entering a brimstone-filled hell. But the occupants here were alive, their actions purposeful. The place unnerved him—the noise abrasive and the smell deleterious. In the middle of it, stood Mister Cooper, yelling, pointing, and grinning. The man turned, hands on his hips, at the hub of his domain, and surveyed the work.

A third of the way around, he recognized John, bellowed out his name and leapt to greet him with his broad, beckoning gait. John liked that about the man. When his servitude first began, he had sulked and planned escape, but Mister Cooper reeled him in. He tugged at the line, gentling him. He teased him with talk and taught him things that mattered. Like how to taste the brackish water, testing for the metallic edge at the back of your tongue, telling you iron ore was plentiful. And he praised John when he succeeded, listened to his ideas, and even asked for them.

Cooper took John's extended hand, pulled him close, and patted his back. Then he lifted the halter from John's shoulder and let it fall again. "Someday," he said, with a quiet edge to his voice, "I will greet you here without bumping into this damnable contraption." Then, louder, he continued. "So, a good quantity hauled in, I hear. Will Geordie be gushing out his praise?" He pulled back and crossed his arms, swaying from one long leg to the other, his way of marking the approach of an extended conversation.

"A measure of ore unloaded. Deliverance stayed at the charging bridge to help with the last two wagons."

"Deliverance delivering. Laughable, that."

"He works hard, sir," John said, not wanting to diminish the boy's value, then he dug at his thumbs, wrapped his fists around them, and began. "Edward House, sir, you know him?"

Cooper squared up to John, his eyes narrowed. "I do."

John inhaled. The sulfuric air raked at his throat. He cleared it, half coughing. "He says, sir—" The words choked, and he brought his hand to his mouth.

His master cocked his head, contemplating; John stared at the man's neck, at his open tie, and then his arms, the sleeves of his shirt rolled to his elbows. He coughed again, buying time to think. If Edward were wrong, if John said too much, he might end up at his own trial, this time for sedition. And with his history, a noose would be the verdict. Still, he had thought throughout the week and had made his choice. He lowered his voice, unsettled and conspiratorial. "He says you support him in his complaint."

"I support his right to fair treatment, John. To freedom earned. The colony has laws, a good thing, mind you." The man's eyes bored in on him, hot as the finery forge. "Laws must be obeyed—by everyone, no matter his station. And, if broken, we should mete out our punishments fairly"

John swallowed, unsure how to continue, or what he wanted to say. He need not have worried. Cooper touched his halter with a one-sided grimace and spoke, cryptic but clear. "This thing, your collar, it was decided by a handful of men with their own tethers, bound by narrow beliefs. They consider themselves the only worthy judges and anoint only those who agree with them. They control the votes that make their rules." He looked around, checking for those within hearing, but the noise of the place prohibited eavesdropping.

John leaned close, and Cooper continued. "These men, some indentures, some just hard-working men whose talents we use but whose beliefs we reject, should they maybe have a say in their lives?" He hedged his words with a shrug. "How much longer is your indenture, John?"

The question was a pointed one, at the core of why John stood before the man. "Less than a year under Gibbard's hand, though I am in your charge seventeen years more." He swallowed down rising bile as he spoke. His sentence reached out before him, interminable, a lifetime in his mind. The halter's weight bore down on him and his head bowed. Cooper took his chin and lifted it.

"A monstrous ruling on a foolish boy. Look, I know Governor Winthrop. He started this iron works and then handed it off to me so he could govern Connecticut Colony. Neither colony, New Haven or his, has the new King's blessing, but it is possible for the King to sanction one and place the other under a rule he favors. Connecticut law tries by jury and all men of property vote for their governor. It is fairer, more inclusive, and tolerant of many churches. Though Catholics and Quakers have no prayer." He laughed at his joke. But to John this was serious, and he needed to break through the innuendo.

"So, if Connecticut ruled, they might throw off old wrongs?"

"They might. But New Haven sees danger and works to position itself. Winthrop tells me our Governor Leete has already approached him, wanting to form a loose union with Connecticut that allows New Haven to continue untouched. Winthrop ignores their advances, for now. So, there you have it. Anything, anything at all, that reduces New Haven in the eyes of the King, anything the Magistrates do to anger him, weakens New Haven and its plantations. Colonies favored by the King stand tall, and those he disdains will bend beneath his will."

Cooper paused, gauging him, John figured, to see if he grasped what was implied. Sweat ran down John's back, and his shirt stuck at his armpits. He pulled at his sleeves, first on one side, then the other.

"So, the more one side knows, the better it can maneuver?"

"Perceptive, son."

John squinted to the ceiling and sucked in, his lips pressed against his teeth. "I am obvious walking about. But I might know people."

"A wonder, it is, what fine-tuned ears hear." Cooper lifted his brows and placed his arm on John's shoulder, fingering the halter. "I could use intelligence—for the good of the colony, of course. Never know what might come of it. But we linger too long. Are you off to see our smithy? He says you take to the work." Cooper jutted his chin out, pointing to the blacksmith's shop. It sat at the base of a corduroy road. Built of logs thrown parallel, it provided a firm surface for wagons carrying wrought iron to the shop.

"Who knows," Cooper continued, "if you ever lose that halter, there might be a place for you."

John closed his eyes to the finery's white-hot glow. Apprenticing as a smithy tempted him, but subterfuge? He was a small cog in what was turning, a confusing and unsure thing. He breathed in the hellish air and opened his eyes to Cooper's face, no longer easy but awash with concern.

Something was amiss. "Well, sir," John said, adjusting to the odd change in Cooper's behavior, "perhaps in time, but for now—" A horse complained, halfway between a whinny and a snort. He swung around, then froze. An old, yellowed mare stood on the corduroy road. On its back sat Gibbard, more pallid and portly than ever.

"Well, it be the boy devil himself," the man snorted. He stared at John's feet, shod, luckily, with serviceable shoes, then spoke. His derisive words skimmed the top of John's head, directed to Mister Cooper. "Our servant boy here should be wearing his leg irons."

John stretched up against the halter's weight, his torso straight and unbending. Cooper crossed his arms and lifted his chin. "My friend, John here, stands outside New Haven town. My arrangement with the Magistrates precluded the wearing of irons except inside the town. Now then, John, go practice with the smithy. And regarding that other matter, the one we spoke of earlier? I would appreciate your service."

John nodded. "Your servant, sir. Happier than ever to help."

❧

The river rolled beneath John's feet creating the impression of a ferry dock, rather than a river, in motion. He swallowed the uneasy sensation and turned to Edward, sitting beside him, to regain his equilibrium.

The gusts of a coming storm ruffled Edward's shirt and hair. He rolled two iron nails along his fingertips then dumped them into John's open palm. "How many did you make?"

The comment lacked enthusiasm. "You could show a little interest, at least. It's no easy thing to make them. It takes skill. I made maybe a hundred. Got pretty good pounding them out after a few tries. Still slow though"

"And he gave you ten? Well, better than none, I guess."

"I was glad of them. Marty Jenkins pounds out a thousand in a day. Give a hundred, get ten. It's the smithy's rule." John ran his thumb over the rough tapered edge of a nail and its neat flattened head. "I spoke with Cooper."

"And?"

"He would be grateful for any intelligence I might discover."

"How grateful?"

"Well, he was not too forthcoming, but led me to think I might lose this." He flipped his halter, ignoring the chafing at his callused neck.

"So, you are in!" Edward swung his legs around, dangled them at the deck's edge, then leaned back, slid onto his side, and balanced on one elbow. "Hear about the King's plan for the regicides? That's what they call the King killers, the ones who signed the paper on King Charlie, the first one." Edward took his free hand and grabbed his neck, making a ridiculous face, his tongue lolled and his eyes crossed.

John smiled. Edward always made him smile. "No, I hear little beyond what you or Samuel or Mercy tell me."

"Revenge is our new King's game. Charles the Second, they call him. He plans to hang them all. Some of them escaped to Boston. Bet

your Gibbard is in a tizzy. He and his cronies thought them heroes...
like Perseus." Edward smirked, amused at his joke, and punched John,
who caught himself from toppling, barely.

"Would you stop? You are forever hitting at me, one way or another."

"I mean nothing of it. Just a joke for Christ's sake." Edward gave him
a jab, and another, testing and teasing.

John pushed him off and stood. He dropped the nails back into the
pouch tied at his belt. "I thought I might give Mercy a few of them. To
give to her father, I mean."

Edward rolled his eyes and fell back, flattened on the deck. "What
a boil-brain you are, John Frost. Nails?" He jumped to his feet and
bopped John on the forehead with his palm, then stepped back to
avoid the arm swinging out in retaliation. "Come with me. You need
help."

The ferry rocked at the deck's edge, docked and awaiting passengers.
Edward hopped aboard and rummaged in a chest at the stern, then
pulled out a small wooden box with a leather-hinged lid. From inside,
he retrieved a wooden bobbin wound with lace. The tatting was of fine
cotton, a thumbnail wide, embellished with roses and a scalloped edge,
rare for New Haven.

"Where did you get that?" John asked, worried his friend was
delving into things less worthy than subterfuge.

"Have more faith in a friend, John. I found it on the ferry. Our
passengers sometimes leave things behind. We keep them a while and
if no one asks, we pocket them. Ferryman Brown corners the most
important leavings, but some are left to me. Give her this. Might win
you more favor than a nail."

John accepted the bobbin, a flutter rising in his loins. The lace would please her, he was sure—once she knew it was acquired honestly. And the prospect of her stretching up to kiss him, smelling of honey and bread? He pulled the leaf of a swamp maple from his pouch, one he had admired, touched with the red of fall, and wrapped it round the treasure. "Thank you, Edward. And, I...I'll be going now."

Edward's sly glance verged on annoying. "And why might that be?"

John feigned nonchalance and tucked the leaf-covered bobbin in his pouch. "I'm to meet Mercy and Samuel upriver, but I will be with you at your trial. Halter, leg irons, and all." He punched Edward's shoulder, setting him off balance. "Beat you to it that time," he said, ducking Edward's swing.

❧❀❧

A near-full moon inched over the hills. It danced in and out of the storm clouds rushing in swirls across the sky and washed the marshland below with a haunt of shadows. Like a moon, Mercy's words rose in John's mind, washing him in light and his own haunt. Of confusion.

Earlier this day, when he met Mercy on East River's shore, he had given her Edward's lace. She slipped it in her pocket with the hint of her smile and a thank you. Her reserve, so far from the joy he expected, bewildered him, so he hung back, shaking his knee in a rhythm that rattled the nails in his pouch.

"What's that?" she asked.

"Another gift, not much." He had shrugged, reached into his pouch, and dumped two nails in her hand. She held them there and rolled them over and over in her palm, gleaming with wonder.

"You made these," she said, "with your own hands?"

She asked him how and hung on his every word as he described both the process and his training. He guided her fingers along the rough-edged point and the smooth turn of the nail's head, pleasuring to the touch of her hand.

"And you give them to me?" she whispered, her voice awed. "They are wonderful."

They had been simple words, but like the moon glow, they showed him the way.

Tomorrow he would walk into New Haven with halter and leg irons, the first time since his trial. Though he worried for Edward and dreaded the morrow, some good shined through. Samuel had jumped at the chance to be John's "official" spy and swore to keep it secret, even from Mercy. The boy's enthusiasm bolstered his own. Maybe, just maybe, freedom was possible for Edward and for him. Mercy saw him—beyond his chains and halter. If she saw him untethered, he should at least try to act it, unfettered by fear.

The beginning drizzle of rain threatened his evening fire. By habit, he called out a warning, low and guttural, to any waiting wolves, turned his back on the sparks and the storm, and entered his half-cabin. He wrapped himself in the warmth of a bearskin provided by Mister Cooper and fell into a restless sleep.

꩜❄꩜

Samuel held his hat and stamped his feet outside the meetinghouse door, then he shook. The wriggle began at his hips, traveled up through his arms, and ended with a flip of his dripping white-gold hair.

"Samuel! We are wet enough without your downpour!" his father growled above the din of rain. It pelted the roof, the run-off creating a curtain of silver on all sides of the overhang.

Parishioners huddled on the porch with limited patience, taking turns to enter. They dripped from capes and hats, they wrung out aprons, they shook petticoats and breeches, and they stomped their muddied shoes. The luckiest shed their oilcloth overcoats, flipping beads of water to the floor.

Samuel looked around sullen and embarrassed. "Sorry, Papa." He bowed his head, contrite, then rolled his eyes up to survey those entering the building. His heart had pounded with excitement when John took him into his confidence, asking his help. Of course, he accepted his given task, to listen surreptitiously for what John called "curious activity or murmurings amongst the Magistrates." Edward's trial provided the perfect occasion to practice his spying skills.

Mercy cupped Samuel's elbow and pushed him to the door. She whispered in his ear, a hard task given the rattle of rain and wind. "You will stand with John, will you not?" The crowd pushed them in the door so that they stood at the foot of the stairwell leading to the gallery. Guilt invaded Samuel's throat, and he swallowed it down. John depended on his spying and had told him to tell no one, especially Mercy.

"I...I cannot, Mercy. I want to stay below, on the edges...to hear better."

"Hear better? You can't hear up there?"

"Not so well. Just leave me be, Mercy. I am twelve." He tried emphasizing his age, to show he was old enough to make his own decisions. And he was. But he had always followed Mercy's lead, tacking with her wind, and now he defied her. He wanted to explain. Instead, he scowled, thumped his hat against his thigh, and walked away. He felt her pull, like the tide, and he rowed hard against her.

After Samuel left, Mercy held to the stairwell and waited for John, fuming. Her brother had walked away, neither offering apology nor saying where he went. She considered finding Father and unleashing his ferocity on her brother. Then she imagined Samuel's pale blue eyes glistening with tears from a likely whipping and set her teeth against it.

She feared for John, knew the conflict in him—between supporting his friend and appearing at the meetinghouse. She forced down her frustration and focused on the door, her thoughts turned to yesterday.

John had overflowed with energy. He held out the bobbin of lace to her, his eyes smiling. It was then she noticed their color. Not only green but also gold-flecked and branched with brown. His mood and the light transformed them as she watched. First, they sparkled with gold, but turned murky like the coming storm when she tucked the lace into her pocket. Then, when she marveled at the nails he had made, they softened to new-grass green.

He had explained each part of the process, a lively discussion of proper heat and the strength of the hit, and her every question opened him more. He had gentled and relaxed—until talk turned to this day and how he must enter the village. Then his eyes browned like summer moss, and she realized coming here, in leg irons and halter, dug into him like dying. "So," she thought, "he falters," and slipped into the deluge to find him.

He stood, back to the door, facing the pillory. Rivulets of rain ran in
sheets from his hat and quilted coat. She leaned into him, her forehead
reaching his halter, and settled her hand on the small of his back. The
coat slogged at her touch, and he jerked away, his muscles tensed, ready
to strike. She stepped back, but held her hand true.

"It's me, John." She added pressure to the hand touching him and
bent round to look in his face. Her voice rose, competing with the
torrential downpour. "Are you coming?"

"Every one of them is whispering," he said, and twisted his head to
face her. His eyes stung, a burdened brown. They challenged her. And
she would not deny them.

"They do, John, and they stare. And you hold more courage in your
worried, whittled thumbs than their wizened hearts can fathom." She
pursed her lips, hiding the smile there, hoping she had pierced his
sullenness, and felt his torso tremble with a half-hearted chuckle. A
rivulet of rain fell from his hat onto her wind-blown cap.

He caressed her face and smoothed her brows with his callused
thumbs. "You will stay with me?"

She would set lightning to gossip if she did, a young maiden standing
with a bound and convicted servant. He knew it and asked her still. It
ran against her way, against her covenant with Father and church. Yet
she did not hesitate; it was but a small courage, and she laughed at it.
"I will stand with you always, John Frost."

She set her hand to John's back and pushed him toward the
meetinghouse. For the second time, she climbed the stairs to the
gallery, each time for the sake of John. He followed behind. The chains
attaching his leg-irons rattled once and then twice, followed by a brief,
but evident pause. Too short from ankle to ankle, the chain required

him to take each stair two hobbled steps at a time. It maddened her to feel his humiliation. So, to draw attention from his clumsy ascent, she matched her steps to his, fawning a girlish pretense of fear.

After reaching the top they worked their way through the crowd to the banister, and Mercy helped John shed his waterlogged jacket and hat. She draped them over the banister's edge and settled to watch the proceedings just as the drum quickened and the doors closed.

⁓❋⁓

Samuel matched his pace to the drumbeat, scooting along the edges, avoiding their assigned pew and the chance of facing Mercy's fury. First, he squeezed up behind the soldiers, thinking they might talk of some assignment or discuss the details of the watch, but the unmarried men only whispered tales about one wench or another, prideful of their dalliances. He listened over-close to the details until Matthew Smiley turned to him and threatened, "If you be so interested in what's under a maid's skirt, discover it yourself. Move on you blockheaded dolt."

Chagrined, he wandered the outskirts of the hall, working his way to the front pews where the well-heeled parishioners sat. He stayed to the men's side, away from his sister's pew, and held his breath, worrying the wall. Shouldering through the crowd, he kept the bulk of the men to his right. Thus he was protected from his father's view. A smirk crossed his lips and his stomach tightened with excitement. Espionage, he found, was an intense, even rousing, activity. He quickened his pace, eyes focused on a bevy of men huddled at the side-door entrance.

He settled in behind the tallest of the men, Mister Crane, a beak-nosed and thin-faced slump of a man, one of the court's Magistrates.

Samuel faced away from the knot of officials and clasped his hands behind his back. He rocked on his heels, feigning nonchalance, as if waiting for someone to come through the door. Congratulating himself on his deception, he set to eavesdropping.

"What have we this day, Mister Leete?" Crane's baritone was an easy one to recognize, as was Mister Leete's rasping reply.

"An issue with a servant and some problem regarding the ownership of a horse. Both involve Ferryman Brown."

Next came a soft and repeated pop. Samuel imagined it a pipe being cleared of its waste. He heard the sound often enough when his father cleaned his own, and the heavy odor of spent tobacco confirmed it.

"The servant's name is Edward House. A rioter, he is, disputing our colony's authority. Should we cower, our stature will diminish amongst other servants craving freedoms. God's grace has given us you, Mister Leete, rather than Governor Newman to judge it."

The voice was overly familiar. It wheezed and sniffled. Samuel twisted his head to see Gibbard's fawning face, a dribble seeping from his pugged nose, then jerked his head away to avoid the man's glance.

Gibbard had other concerns. He moved Mister Crane off to the side, beseeching him, "Brother Crane, I need not remind you, the last thing we need is an uproar from the servants. Too unsettled a time, with this new King Charles."

"It is an unsettled time, but I would listen..." Samuel could hear the hesitance in Crane's graveled undertone, so snuck a sly glance over his shoulder. Crane confirmed Samuel's suspicions by ending the conversation mid-sentence and taking three scuffled steps along the wet floor toward Deputy Governor Leete. "Shall we begin?" he asked and ushered Leete forward with one lanky arm.

"We shall. And Brother Gibbard, record all, and worry not, our judgments are of God."

The drumming stopped, and two militiamen pulled the door shut. Leete led the Magistrates' processional along the bar separating the congregation from the pulpit and toward the Magistrates' benches. Samuel hunched down, ready to make a stealthy retreat, just as the side-door opened, blowing in an overwrought and overly late parishioner.

It was only a glancing blow, accidental, due to the man's efforts to slough the moisture from his cloak, but it caught Samuel unaware. His shoe, slick from rain, caught the puddle accumulated at the doorway, and he slid, at first on one foot only. He flung out his arms and toed down with his second foot. Momentum carried him. His torso, head, and flailing arms followed.

He landed. A wrenching pain deviled his tailbone, followed directly by a twisting jolt at his shoulders. His head fell back with a thunk, and he brought it forward with an involuntary jerk. Eyes blinking, he focused on the banister above.

John Frost stared down, then closed his eyes and dropped his chin to rest on his haltered neck. Mercy stood beside him, her head turned to one side, chin jutting out, incredulous. He winced; a hand seized his collar and lifted him up, rough and lacking in empathy. Thus, his father dragged him—up the aisle, behind the leering faces of the militia, and down the women's aisle to drop him down on his bottom next to Widow Sherwood.

His father glared and then walked away with sullen grace, and Widow Sherwood smiled wide. "Why Samuel, what a pleasure. Let me update you on the proceedings." He shut his eyes, retreating from his stinging pride and the widow's painful prattling, both far more devilsome than the throbbing at his rear.

❧

Mercy leaned against the bannister, drawn with the rest of the congregants to see her brother sliding to a stop on his backside with a double-beat thump. The moment was brief, but Samuel had seen her gasp, she was sure. Then Father caught him up and dragged him from her sight.

"His bottom will suffer more later," she told John in a whisper.

"My fault, I think," he said, head dropped to his chest.

"Nonsense."

John found her hand in the folds of her gown and held it hidden there. "No, not nonsense. He is foolish but brave. And I thank him."

"Whatever for?" Mercy asked, her curiosity heightened, suspecting the two kept something from her.

"Shush, Mercy, not now. The trial begins."

She squeezed his hand, and he repeatedly pressed and released her fingers with an unconscious pulsing. From the corner of her eye, she saw his jaw line palpitating in beat with his fingers. His friend meant more to him than he could admit.

Edward stood at the bar with a man she did not recognize. Lieutenant Governor Leete presided. It seems their new governor, Mister Newman, had contracted a flux. Leete fumbled a moment, letting papers flutter to the floor, then gathered himself and the papers together and read the complaint. Edward accused Mister Meiggs of selling him without right.

Meiggs stood at the bar, tall and imposing, neat in dress and demeanor, an unfortunate contrast to Edward, who stood alongside, wearing a wrinkled waistcoat running a size too small. Adding injury to his appearance, he had used a dark thread on his light brown breeches to mend a right-angle rip at his left buttock. The overall impression emphasized the chasm in the men's stations.

Mister Leete introduced a wizen man to Edward's right, over whom Edward towered, as his representative, a Mister Tate. "Governor," the man said, clearing his throat and stretching his neck high in his ruff, "Magistrates, sirs, my good men of the court."

John bent to her. "He slathers them a buttered bread, does he not?"

"Hush, John. They will hear." Mercy pulled his hand to her thigh, holding him, like a child, from running amuck.

Mister Tate continued. He droned the court's usual convoluted dialog. Edward's circumstances fit the discourse. He had been sold to a Boston man. There were papers to prove it. Then, after threats to his person, Edward agreed to two more years of indenture, this time in New Haven, to include training as a currier. Then they sold him again, to Ferryman Brown.

Mercy jerked at John's hand. "How many years?"

"From seven to nine."

"But I mean, how many has he served."

John's eyes trailed off and his tongue worked, calculating. "Since spring of fifty-four so...six years and five months."

Next, Meiggs presented his argument. He placed his hands on the bar, one over the other, offering an elegant nod to the Magistrates. "Your servant, sirs. My memory of the occasion aboard The Cockerel is that House here was a sickly boy, scurvy by the ship doctor's diagnosis. He agreed to his contract's revision freely. But he proved incapable of his duties. We hoped for better with Ferryman Brown."

John ripped his hand from the folds of Mercy's gown and grasped the railing; his chest rippled as he pushed against the banister. It creaked and rocked. Bystanders on either side of them stepped back, fearful the banister might crumble, a fear compounded by the rain dribbling from leaks in the ceiling. A wrinkled old crone glowered at John, and he lifted his hands, a feigned apology.

Then he rummaged in Mercy's skirt, found her hand, and lifted it to his chest, inclining his head to hers. His voice was stiff, controlled. "He be a lying, pompous..." His head shook. "I am the one who fell ill. Edward, he was the strong one."

Mercy nodded an affirmation, then drew him with her chin to the proceedings. Mister Brown stood at the bar, giving testimony.

"More to my displeasure," the ferryman was saying, "is the time I lose due to the breach of my covenant with Mister Meiggs. I bought seven years and have near to three left. The boy grows more sullen and distracted the closer the day comes to the end of his first contract. Seems to me Mister Meiggs owes me for my losses."

Mister Leete asked some pointed questions about how each contract was obtained, impressing Mercy with his astute attention to the nuance of the case. Meanwhile, Edward stood strong, never succumbing to petty anger, something she found admirable given how the conversation circled round him, as though he were a calf at auction. Finally, the case fell to the court for deliberation. John's grip on her hand showed no sign of abating.

"See him." John nodded to the lectern where Mister Gibbard stood, bent over, quill in hand, scribbling. The man paused. His plump fingers dipped the quill in ink, then let it hover above the page. "Gibbard! Who checks those words he scribbles for their truth? What control do we hold in this?"

Mercy heard the "we" John spoke, and it did not include her. She looked down at John's shackles, then to the meetinghouse floor where the marshal was leading Edward to a backbench to await the verdict. And she understood. Bondage went beyond shackles or halter; it saturated everything in their world.

John dropped her hand and, with a light touch, placed his hands on the railing. He waited in a steaming silence far from her reach. And she waited with him.

The verdict took them by surprise. "The covenant entered into on England's shore was ill-served, and Mister Meiggs acted outside his rights, engaging the boy in a second and third contract, one by duress. Consequently, we judge Edward House free from all further obligation. And we further find Mister Meiggs in debt to Mister Brown for breach of said contract, in a cost to be determined. Also, a fine for the time of the court, 5 shillings."

John yelped and hugged Mercy full on, with all watching, his exuberance overwhelming her. She left her arms to her sides, an effort to diminish the impression they made and looked out to the room below. Mister Gibbard held his quill in mid-air gaping up at them. Mister Meiggs shrugged and walked over to confer with Ferryman Brown. And Edward? Edward's head was flitting from Tate to Leete to Tate again. Then he turned to the gallery, and shouted up, "Hey, John, John Frost. Look at me! I am a free, free man."

Samuel jumped up from the pew, overjoyed at the verdict. He

stumbled on Widow Sherwood's skirt as he turned to see John swing Mercy down beside him, squeeze her in close, and then wave to Edward. Scrunched around in her seat, Widow Sherwood saw them as well, and gasped, grasping at Samuel's arm. He pulled loose and hurried down the aisle.

He rushed to the bottom of the stairwell to await John and Mercy, but the congregation crowded in front of him. As he pushed and squeezed through the bodies nearing the stairs, his father appeared, head bobbing above the crowd. He saw Samuel and held his finger high, admonishing him to wait. The man's scowl made it clear—he had seen the contact between Mercy and John, as well.

Samuel considered escape to the green, then reflected on his earlier foolishness. Unwilling to pile on more punishment, he waited. Puddles of rain had coalesced on the wooden floor. His father dodged them, seized his collar, and pulled him to the base of the stairs. By the time Mercy and John stepped off the last stair tread, Mister Gibbard pushed into view.

His mouth moved furiously. "Mister Payne. Stop. I would speak with you. Stop, sir." His ruddy face splotched white and trickled with moisture. He ran like a bandy hen toward them, skidded on a puddle, and stopped with his finger raised, waggling it in his father's face. Not a wise thing.

"Mister Gibbard, sir! I ask you to lower your finger and proceed with dignity and restraint." Then he stared down at John's hand, cradling Mercy's waist. John jerked it away and stepped near Samuel.

Gibbard missed none of it. "There, you see. They flaunt their familiarity before the entire congregation, a servant boy and the daughter of a free planter, not yet—what age are you, Mercy Payne?"

Mercy stared at Gibbard. Samuel had seen that look before, a viperous glare, auguring an infrequent wrath. "I am fifteen, Mister Gibbard, and old enough to sense intimations affronting my virtue." Samuel snickered. John kicked him, and his chain rattled. Father flung them a look matching Mercy's, a familial thing.

John cleared his throat to speak. "Mister Payne, sir, pray forgive me. My enthusiasm regarding the verdict, it was misplaced."

His father nodded, and Gibbard sputtered. "Unfitting! Not misplaced. I say watch him. Always. He will hang himself one day. And this Edward House, this trial—devil's work. A tide change comes, and we lower our guard. But mind you, I accept my duty as God's watchman, and I will ferret out the devil eating at New Haven." His eyes bugged, his voice tight and venomous. "I will ferret it out in every guise."

⤙❀⤚

The story of the indenture's trial gives Maggie hope. The Magistrates adhere to their rules. They believe in covenants of every sort: with God, with your spouse, with your children, and in business. They are scrupulous with God's word. The volume in Maggie's hand grows cold; the Magistrates' rigor is not warm-hearted. They are business men; nuance eludes them.

An early winter angst creeps into Maggie's spirit. She needs relief—time to absorb the trial and the odd juxtaposition of elation and trepidation she feels. She yearns for a reflective calm, a chance to integrate everything, both fact and feeling, into the story growing in her mind. The books confer and agree; she needs a break.

Duncan rattles the doorknob, returning from the gym. He goes every day, incorporating it into his routine like an old machinist. "That darn knob is getting harder and harder to lock," he says, assuming someone is listening. The books consider this, but maybe he would talk to the lock even if they weren't there.

Maggie answers, assuming he talks to her. "I haven't noticed."

Duncan peeks around the corner. She sits smug in her chair, knowing what he'll say.

"That's because you never lock it." He slips out of his coat and hangs it in the armoire. "Someday you'll be sorry."

Maggie just shrugs. "I need a walk, sweetheart...to clear my head."

Duncan stops. "You okay?" She had called him sweetheart, a term reserved for serious conversation.

"Yeah, I guess."

"Have you eaten? Maybe you need some food."

"Maybe. I'll take a tangerine."

The fruit peels easily in her hands, a sign of sweetness, and a pungent oily fragrance squeezes out from its pores. The sections fall apart. She pockets them and throws the peel in the compost bucket. "I won't be gone long. To the top of the hill and back is all." She pecks Duncan's cheek and heads for the door. The volumes follow.

The jolt of crisp air whisks away her melancholy, and the sweet tang of orange on her tongue enlivens her spirit. The rational conclusion of the trial encourages her, but doubt and suspicion seep into what she reads. The books approve of her caution. They understand the congregants' motives. They sniff endlessly for deviants, convinced that by pointing to another's godless behavior it implies the grace in theirs. Maggie senses it, but breathes in winter's greening, relieved to live far from a long-gone, strangled society. New Haven's level of bigotry and suspicion doesn't exist now. The books ripple and cough up their response: she should know better.

"What a laugh! Like we're the saints, right?" she responds. Then she pops a wedge of tangerine in her mouth and picks up her pace.

She just finished reading about the court's treatment of the "cursed Quakers." The Magistrates make law after law to address people who disagree with them. The last "complaint" was against some poor people who spoke against the New Haven courts, in their own kitchen, no less, a private conversation over a hearth. Someone heard them say that the Magistrates took their money and offered harassment in return; and that "someone" tattled to the court. Sedition holds the penalty of death. Not wanting to go so far, the court labels them heretics and fines them.

The records tell the story. Their leaders have squandered the plantation's money on failed business ventures and the cost of serving their far-flung plantations. They fine their people for everything and overburden their plantations with taxes. She sees the experiment failing before her eyes and wonders why they don't see it. The books attempt to temper her scorn. They are men blinded by a righteous pride, and the need to be right.

But Maggie leaps past the books' counsel, ignoring it. A foreboding overwhelms her. The indenture, the desire to be free, John Frost—the words, the books—they dance before her eyes; she is transported. In that world, as in this, acts have consequences. Would the indenture's trial give him hope as it had her? What might come of it? Would further brazen defiance be met, not with release, but reproach, or worse, reprisal?

Halfway up the road, she realizes she sees nothing but a haze of imagining. Her mind races, but her eyes are blind. She takes a deep breath and looks around. Moss vibrates dark-green on the rocks, competing with the grey, orange, and red of the lichen. The ground squishes beneath her feet, saturated by inches of rain. The land, revived by moisture, radiates life, even in the depth of winter. Her shoulders relax, and she is back, here, now, healing. Somehow she knows—no, she believes—her own centering heals the past as well.

At the top of the hill, she stands. The benches beckon but she resists. She looks out, seeking the landscape, deep and green. But she is captured and looks through it to the past. One man in the colony had the gall to speak his mind. He claimed the devil did not exist. He said that if they followed the light within, it would guide them to God. But "a light within" proved too personal for the Magistrates. It smacked of Quakerism. So they charged him with corruption by devilish thoughts, a "ranter," of all things.

Maggie squints into the distance trying to sort out the mindset, to understand it. How could so much anger and fear be built into differences in belief? The ranter said one thing that sticks with her. It ricochets amongst her thoughts. "God," he had said—the secretary wrote the words as though they were blasphemy, "God gives gifts, but not power. Man takes that himself." The court, though, thought their power came from God.

"Arrogant demigods," she says to the valley, and the books agree. They sneak a thought into her mind. "Perhaps others felt the same."

A raven's caw wrenches her from the cavern of her thoughts. He repeats his call, persistently. Maggie looks around and finds him perched in the dead pine to her right. Never moving, he pauses. Then, throat stretched and head bobbing, he reiterates his low, grating coo.

"I know what you mean," Maggie says, and heads down the hill. Just as she makes the first turn, she hears the mate's response, higher pitched

and multi-syllabled, announcing she is near.

Maggie ponders the Grand Dilemma: grace or freewill, the big religious argument, whether our good flows from chance, choice, or God. How the hell can anyone know, and what's the difference? And why couldn't New Haven have the grace to trust in the goodness of man? The books answer the question for her, as though they are one—because they believe in lost souls and the devil and the power of the righteous. They believe. They are sure. There is only one way.

Maggie walks through the door. Duncan looks up, putting the finishing touches on a sandwich. She goes to him. Kisses his lips. Tastes the mayonnaise and tomato on his tongue.

"I love you," she says.

"And I love you?" His response is a question, not of their love, but her sanity. The volume on her table sighs; Maggie gets it—their love—it makes them sane.

PART V

1661 (and the present)

If any person shall conspire, and attempt
any invasion, insurrection or publick Rebellion
against this Jurisdiction he or she shall be put to
death.

Code of New Haven

Mercy stood at the door-side garden and looked out to where the ice-strewn East River flowed, still obscured by night. The snow shimmered, hinting at a growing dawn. The fingernail sliver of a near dark moon and its companion, a rose-gilded morning star, competed for dominance on the horizon. Winter had plodded by, slow as snowmelt on a frigid day, and March carried no relief.

The last she saw John was in late November when he moved from his East Rock home to help with the winter cleaning at the ironworks downriver. Though the snow held off until January, warm November and December days carried one sullen rainstorm after the next. The burgeoning rivers grew dangerous, and the murky waters and flowing ice barred them from travel.

Mercy wrapped a fur shawl close around her and ran her fingers along its white-tinged hairs. John had caught the rabbits in a trap of his making, a practice piece forged under Smithy Gorman's watchful eye. The pride he showed in his accomplishment warmed her then, as it did now.

He had gifted her other things as well: fishhooks he fashioned, knowing she would pass them on to Samuel; the mended copper kettle, which Father accepted with a grudging acknowledgment of the quality of the patch. John strove to earn his worth, and her love, never seeing his presence as her true gift. She missed him.

The door latch creaked and the hinges on the entry door squealed. "Sister?" Samuel's pale hair stuck up in a tangle. "Shall I bring up water?"

Her annoyed sideward grimace turned to a loving snort. "Are you hurrying off again?"

"John promises to teach me to use his musket. A matchlock, not an easy thing."

"I wish I could go."

"The ironworks is a raucous place, Mercy. John calls it unsafe. And Papa? The devil take you if he knew you even thought it."

Mercy closed her eyes and breathed in the icy air, dusted with the tang of their morning fire. She nurtured these men, and they protected her. But sometimes she wished her role and theirs were reversed. Still, she bent before them; it grew out of the world that met her.

"Go fetch the morning's water, Samuel. I will ready some food for the outing, and you will tell John it's from me. But know this. You are not deceiving me. You are up to more than learning to shoot. Papa can teach you that." She stepped onto the porch and leaned close. Her brother's hand hovered on the bucket handle. "Whatever it is, I will discover it. And Samuel, pray take care—both of you."

⋙❋⋘

Samuel lied to Mercy of necessity, both regarding his visits to the ironworks and to Widow Sherwood. It could not be helped. Their mission demanded it.

The widow's proximity to the reverend's house, along with her expertise as a chinwagger, often brought Samuel to visit.

While last year's humiliation at Edward's trial stung, as had his bottom, he discovered, after being unceremoniously plopped next to Widow Sherwood, that he could glean information in a less direct, more surreptitious manner, and to the same results. Widow Sherwood had talked non-stop throughout the trial, introducing Samuel to a clandestine intelligence before unknown to him. The lonely woman invited him to tea, having found a willing listener, and she became his after-school destination. Between his time with the schoolmaster in the morning, his smiling gossip with Widow Sherwood in the afternoon, and his eyes on the Davenport house while he visited, all New Haven's news danced before him.

He sipped at the chamomile tea the widow served him and inhaled the cinnamon-tinged aroma of baking apples. The woman's wide bottom bumped about at her hearth as she ministered to some sort of apple savory. It was hard to see exactly what delectable morsel she worried over, but she would soon present it with her usual flourish. In the meantime, Samuel monitored the comings and goings at Reverend Davenport's home across the street.

The widow stretched her neck and cocked her head, trencher in hand, to see out the opened door. This late March day proved unseasonably warm and the melting snow sang out in dribbles and crackles around them.

"That house has been a whirl of activity since Governor Newton succumbed this winter." She lowered her voice and placed a trencher of apple fritters on the long table where Samuel sat. "The king killers stayed there, you know." Samuel waited, his stomach growling. Widow Sherwood appreciated manners. She bent to his face, wrinkled her nose, and nodded, his signal to feast. "Mister Newton died of the barrel fever, he did. The man was always in his cups. Drink took him."

Samuel chewed a bite too large and reached for a wash of tea. He did enjoy the widow's cooking, but she ranged widely in her talk, hardly lighting. He swallowed the mass with a gulp, redirecting the conversation where it needed to go. "King killers? Here? At Reverend Davenport's? Have you seen them?"

The widow shook with delight, conspiracy wriggling from belly to buttock. Her bench seat creaked as she settled, elbows wide on the table. Samuel pushed the trencher of fritters toward her, an encouragement. She needed none.

"The regicides, King killers, whatever they call them, are gone. Moved them out. The whole thing put Mister Leete—Governor Leete, I should say—in a frenzy. He visits often out of Gilford. Could hear him bemoaning their presence from here, I could." She bit into a fritter, taking time to chew, then mumbled on. "More worried for his own neck, I think, than anything. Anyway, word is the King's men are in pursuit." She paused, turned her head to the side, eyeing Samuel and cocking a brow.

Samuel took a bite and leaned forward, not saying a word. They had a rhythm, born of a winter of blather. She whispered, "There be a reward. A hundred pounds!"

Samuel's eyes widened, becomingly amazed. And he was amazed, but he also knew sympathy in New Haven was mixed. A person would be pound foolish to attempt capturing the regicides here on New Haven land. "So where are they?" he asked, and the awe in his voice spurred her on.

"Well, I hear the King's men stopped in Guilford searching for them. Leete was there. He stalled them while Mister Meiggs rode here to warn Davenport." She stuffed the rest of the fritter in her mouth. Bits of pastry fell from the corners. She licked some with her tongue, then nipped a crumb with her fingers and tucked it between her lips. "Do not be fooled. Meiggs is no Cromwell man. He informs both sides of the street. To cover his future." Her brows lifted twice; Samuel bit his lips and nodded. It was part of their dance. She reached across the table and fluffed his hair. "You are a smart one, Samuel, a bright young lad. My boy, he was like you. God rest his soul."

Samuel dropped his head, embarrassed. He cared for the woman, and he used her. But he was not so sure she did not know it. How could you be privy to so much knowledge without figuring where it might end up?

He swallowed a last bite. "I must go soon. Shall I bring in wood before I do?"

"Such a good boy you are." She pushed up from the table and set her hands on her hips. "It would indeed please me. Can I ready some fritters for your father? The poor man. He still mourns your dear mother. Perhaps I will visit one day. Oh, but the regicides, where are they, you asked. Now that be a puzzle. However, I hear the Sperry boy might know. You two are friends, are you not?" She squinted down, nose wrinkled, a smile on her smug cherry mouth.

Samuel bowed his head and thanked her, told her how pleased the fritters would make Father. He smiled to himself. He had likely met his match in Widow Sherwood, but his father, it seemed, had met his match in her, as well.

Mercy worked the door-side garden, coaxing out the small budding signs of spring nestled under leaf mulch and other decayed leavings of autumn. Yarrow feathered up all along the bramble fence, announcing itself in shades roaming from grey to spring green. Its brisk, heady odor filled her nostrils. She pulled up wanton blades of grass and other busybody weeds popping up around it and entertained herself with an extended conversation with her charges.

"You look fine and healthy, though I know for sure your bloom comes in late summer. Like tempting me, do you?" She picked up the spade and walked to the circle of river rock near the rickety gate, no more than a lift-and-place section of the fence itself. She scraped at the wayfarer weeds coming up at the edge of the rock and picked around the columbine. She had discovered the blooms in the woods and transplanted them where they received morning sun but, for the rest of the day, languished gratefully in shade.

"Near to blooming, dear things," she said and ran her finger along a delicate lobed leaf.

She talked her way along the garden, engaging bee's balm and sage, a run of lavender, and the milkweed and comfrey that lined the back fence. The comfrey still held to winter, its normally large fuzz-ridden leaves crinkled and shriven. She pulled them back and stared into a moist gloom.

"I see you there," she said to the newly formed leaves, then moved to the milkweed, its pods blown to dust. "And I know you've sprinkled your winged seeds, as well. Coming later, aren't you?"

She pressed her weight into the spade and rose, rocking back and forth, indulging in the warmth, the barest hint of spring. In the distance, the river smoldered muddy grey, the ice of winter stripped away from its edges. Rivulets of steam rose like small fires over the surface. The scene drew Mother to her mind.

Mercy knew loneliness. In some ways, it was her comfort and her friend. With a mother so delicate, she had learned to keep to herself, weeding out the strangers threatening them. But when she lost her to the ice-laced river, a different loneliness consumed her, a too private one. She put her energy into nurturing her father and brother, pulling back their darkness, encouraging them with an illusion of lightness and calm. It was John who pulled her out of pretense into something real. So a winter without his presence burrowed into the core of her sorrow.

She dropped the spade against the fence and whisked away the tear trickling down her cheek. Then she saw him. He pulled a canoe up out of the mist and stood, tentatively looking up, shading his eyes to the afternoon glare. A bloom swelled inside her and unfolded.

She dusted her hands on her apron and lifted the garden gate. In the process, a bit of wood stabbed into her palm. She sucked at where the splinter entered, then picked up the unwieldy gate to close it. "You are no gate from heaven," she said, then kicked the bottom corner, knocking it into place. After examining the half-inch sliver lodged in the heel of her hand, she gave the gate one more kick and hurried to the river.

John was half up the hill when they met.

"I missed you," she said and looked down to conceal the pink blush she felt riding up her chest and into her cheeks. "We should go back to the river. Papa and Muddy are bringing the sheep up from the lower pasture. If they return and he sees us...he still fumes over the scene at Edward's trial."

John clenched his jaw and bit down, the wash of his eyes, near to algae green, told her it hurt him. He garnered the twist of a smile and put his arm around her.

"I am nothing to him," he said as they turned back to the river.

"No, he sees you, I think. He...he wants more for me." She regretted the words as she said them, but they were true. "He will come round, John, he will. Please, can we leave him to his demons...for now?" She leaned into him, goading, bumping his chest. "You are something to me."

The ground oozed winter wet, so they sat across from each other in the canoe. Grounded, half in and half out of the river, it rocked with their weight. Cradled as they were, their talk grew soft. The swaying lulled them and drew them deep. John held his hands out and Mercy offered hers up. He rubbed them, worried them as he did his own, and she flinched from the sliver in her right hand. He flipped her hand over, revealing the short dark stain just beneath the surface of her skin.

"Where did you get that? They can fester you know."

His worry was overblown, and it pleased her. "That awful gate on the garden. Not even a proper gate. You lift it and jiggle it into place. I'll be fine."

"You will not." He pulled his eating knife from his belt, held her hand still, and began to work the skin loose at the entry. Mercy pulled back. "Hold still!" he said.

"Hold still? You are digging at me."

"I am helping you. Allow it for a change!"

Shock stilled her. She stared at him, let him open the wound and lift the fragment of wood loose with his knife. He whisked the blade against his breeches and slid it back into its scabbard.

Mercy sucked at the wound and then cradled her hand to her chest.

"You needn't snap. And I do let people help me."

The canoe rocked slightly as John settled into his seat. "You do not. You help, you serve, and even my gifts you give away."

"Not all of them." She pouted. She never pouted. And John laughed.

"No?" He took her hand from her chest and kissed the wound. "I'm sorry if I hurt you."

They were silent for a long while. The water lapped against the back of the boat; a sweet fragrance eddied on the wind. John's thumb skirted her fingers, a gentle tingling.

"The sun feels good, even with the frost...and the mist," he said. It seemed to Mercy an invitation, and she took it.

"I found my mother on a day like this."

John looked from her hand to her face, searching it. "I'm sorry for that, Mercy."

"I think of it sometimes."

"You know, I lost my own mother, same as you. Well, maybe not the same. She died of a sickness."

"But you feel it? The lonesomeness?"

"Like a veil between you and..." He stretched one hand out from hers, just briefly. "I feel it sometimes. But not with you."

Mercy sighed, relieved, but not wishing to perpetuate the gloom. "Nor I with you. So..." She pulled her hand from his, "shall we enjoy the day?"

She stood abruptly, too abruptly, and the canoe lurched with the changing weight. Her arms flew out and flailed, looking for balance. John seized the sides of the canoe to steady it, then stood, stepping out with one foot to provide anchor. She wobbled again. He clutched her waist and swung her from the boat.

And he laughed. How often had she seen him laugh? His mouth revealed teeth nearly straight, white against his bronzed skin. His eyes brightened, spring green. He hugged her. It happened so naturally. A stream of desire wafting up inside her. Then she saw Samuel.

"What are you doing here?" Her voice cut like a cold wind.

"I came to meet with John." He stood as though he belonged, without question. John had pushed back from her and held her at arm's length. Then he dropped his hand and walked to where Samuel stood.

"Have you news?"

"I do." Samuel looked at her, then John, his face questioning.

Mercy fumed. She felt like fodder. "So you are here to see not me but Samuel. After all this time? And you see him often. Well. Enjoy yourselves." She lifted her petticoats and stomped forward, tripped on a river rock and righted herself. As she flounced past John, he grabbed her arm.

"You are right, I came for Samuel. He's helping me, and it's dangerous. And you have a right to know. But I came for you, too. Or I would have met him at the ironworks as we have all winter."

"All winter?" Dear Lord, she was pouting again. She gathered her emotions and replaced them with a smile, teeth gritted. "So, if I deserve to know, I should hear it all." She swallowed, lifted her chin, and tightened her stomach. "What news do you bring, Samuel?"

⤚❀⤙

A waning gibbous moon backlit the West Rock buttress, casting its shadow over John and Edward's hillside ascent. The delicate fragrance of the star-white flowers rooted to the cliffs above blew out on the breeze. John crawled on his belly, the ground moist from the remnants of a spring rain, wondering what in the world he was doing here. The answer came easy. It was Edward and his seditious intent. What made his friend continue? He was free now, would sail the sea soon, escape to Boston or Barbados on The Cockerel with Captain Sylvester. Still, he crawled, dragging John in his wake, intent on finding the regicides.

The rumors flew on gossip born winds. The King killers were here. Whalley and Goffe for sure, and Dixwell, perhaps. So said Samuel, his eager young spy. John slid through the grass, anxious, his mind jumping into the worst possibilities. Mercy called him cautious. She would doubt it now.

They endangered Samuel by using him so. The boy loved the attention, the sense of manliness that came from helping, and he held a deep conviction that New Haven's constraints had killed his mother and extended John's bondage, but they endangered him none-the-less. Then John considered his own risk should he be caught spying on men condemned by the King and hidden by New Haven—him without the halter they required, plotting against their precious colony. They would hang him. The thought sent his hand to his neck, unnerving him.

"Christ be, Edward, what are we doing here? How far yet?"

Edward's face, angled by moonlit shadows, appeared before him like an apparition. "A while further. Samuel said the Sperry boy leaves food on the boulder there. If we hide behind it, we may hear them."

"And then what?"

"Then we know where they hide, and I send word to my contacts through Sylvester. Shush now."

They scuffed forward. Moisture wicked into John's clothing at his elbows and knees. In his mind, the boulder loomed long in the distance, so he breathed relief when they reached it and leaned their backs against its cool surface.

Trepidation and exhilaration wound together in them, requiring release. They glanced at each other in unison, dropped their heads, and laughed; it burst from them. Though low and short-lived, it eased their nerves. But they were heard.

Up on the hill, a whispered voice carried, just enough for them to hear. "What was that, William? I heard something, a strange sound."

John realized their error. Sound carries up, and their scoots and guffaws had signaled the fugitives hiding in their refuge. Their spying would be discovered, and men with muskets might shoot. He tweaked Edward's thigh and signaled for them to head back east. Edward looked at him, incredulous.

"They are here," he mouthed. His enthusiasm shined out from the shadow obscuring his face.

"So now we know. Let's go. Guns," he mouthed back, his face so close to Edward he felt sure the venom in his eyes punctured his friend's forehead. But Edward just shook his head and pointed up.

Frustration mounted in John; it bubbled into his chest and rumbled from his throat. He shrieked and then growled, the low graveled growl he used when imitating a panther. Edward's eyes widened. John froze. Up above, came a response. "Blessed God. I hear it again. A beast. A big one."

"I heard it, too. Quiet."

Edward brought his hands to his face and leaned into his knees to smother his laughter. John's trepidation disappeared, replaced by a thrill, a newfound rush, playing with danger. He and Edward locked gazes and concurred; John roared. His best replication of a panther on the prowl, low, loud, and long, sailed up the slope.

Silence. John roared again. They heard no prayers, but they felt them. The entreaties trembled from the rock above and stretched to heaven while below laughter shivered in the grass. The moon absorbed it all, including two phantoms, streaking eastward and away.

⤙❈⤚

"You shall not traipse about in wanton dalliance, child. Nor pull Samuel into such foolishness." Father wagged his finger about as they walked home from the Lord's Day service. At rare moments his finger centered on Mercy or Samuel then flitted away. He lashed out like a gander protecting her goslings.

Their father had not shown such emotion since finding Mama at the river. But since the trial, and the embrace, and spotting John's canoe on the East River, he had slipped loose of Mama's grasp, bent on keeping her and Samuel from John's devil ways. Mercy wished he had continued in his winter freeze.

His tirades grew worse on the Lord's Day when Gibbard cornered him and admonished him for shirking his covenant to "protect his children against the devil's lure."

"We are friends, Papa. He gave me Muddy," Samuel said. Mercy lowered her capped head and smiled into her growing breasts. Samuel shielded his friend valiantly.

She had no need to expose herself, but she did. "He is thoughtful, gracious in his gifts, Papa."

"Gifts? 'Tis a break of our laws, a servant giving gifts. Mister Gibbard said as much this morning. He worries the boy plies you with things stolen."

"Not stolen, Papa, and not for me. As practice for his trade, and as a kindness. He repaired our copper kettle."

"Humph..." He shifted his musket from his shoulder and rested it in his hand. After the regicide scare, the court had ordered all men to carry arms. "A nuisance, this thing. For what? To shoot the King's men or the King killers? Which I ask!" He strode out, long-legged, chewing on his anger.

Mercy hoped his mind had turned away from John. It had not. "Kind or cloying, I will not have you befriending a servant. No visits—to him or from him."

Samuel stirred and Mercy whisked him forward before he could respond. "Hush, Samuel. He softens after a day away from Gibbard. The man is a—"

"Toad!" Samuel finished. "A toad, sullying our well."

"But Papa's no fool. He will come round. I know it."

Though she told Samuel their father would soften, she feared the opposite. For an interminable number of years, he had lived in dread, fearing someone would discover Mother's oddity. Now, of habit, he fell into the same protective stance. Gibbard fed his fears, and she suspected the man did so with a purpose.

When they reached Neck Bridge, her father veered off along Mill River for his ritual Sunday stroll. Mercy knew where he went. He wandered to where Mama died. But she said nothing. It was their pretended secret, each from the other.

Samuel and Muddy hurried off to bring the milch cow up from the lower pasture, and Mercy stood, her arms wrapped at her waist looking up at East Rock. Its shadow slid east and dipped into an invisible marshland. Her heart turned north. Her feet pulled her there, but her father's words stopped her, wisely she supposed, as did her own reticence, born of a notion that John preferred Samuel's company to her own. She reckoned it foolish jealousy, but still.

She walked up the hill to prepare supper, stopping at the door-side garden, drawn by the tansy, not yet showing bloom. Then she saw the disturbed ground—a mystery. It was scraped clear at the foot of the gate, and the gate stood sturdy and straight, no longer a shabby annoyance. A quick survey revealed the reason.

Pounded and finely worked strap hinges held the gate by pintles nailed into a new, sturdier fence post. Mercy ran her hand along the post, smooth and splinter free, taking in the heady smell of new-worked wood. Her fingers skipped along the gate slats, equally smooth, to where a new-forged hasp graced the closure.

Understanding rushed through her, and pleasure, like the rush she felt seeing a flower's first bloom. She reached to open the gate, but a slice of peeled willow bark lay tucked in the hasp. She pulled it loose and read the few words written in smudged charcoal with an even hand. "For you alone. J"

Mercy opened the gate, pushed it back and forth. It swung smooth and soundless. For a moment she held the note to her chest, then tucked it in her pocket. She turned round to see Father coming back from his walk and ran down the path to meet him. As she drew near, she called out, "You will never guess, Papa, what a grand gift John has given you."

The green bustled with market day activity and while Father, like most of New Haven, had little coin or wampum, he hoped to barter the sausage just finished off in the smoking shed. Winter was gone, and the June sun streamed down, filling everyone with enthusiasm. Friends greeted each other with a joyful "Good day!", and parents loosened their grasp on the children, allowing them to run free and chase each other at will.

Out of the crowd, came a high-pitched refrain, matched in gusto to the day's cheerfulness. "Samuel, oh, Samuel! Over here young man, here."

Widow Sherwood stood at the edge of the town cistern waving her arm wide. Samuel froze. The widow, seeing she had his attention, hustled over with mincing steps, her whole body bouncing with the effort. She held up a bundle and added voice, once in range, to her gestures. "Samuel, dear. I thought I might find you here. Brought you a treat. Oh, Mister Payne, so good to see you. And how are you, pretty? And Mercy, a treat for you as well. Maple candy!"

She leaned down and tickled his nose at Samuel. He winked at her his hand held out, expectant of his reward.

"Samuel, be seemly." Father stood back, reserved and conscious of the people around them. "We thank you for your kindness Widow Sherwood, but we could not accept a charity."

"Why, Mister Payne, your boy is a wonder, a worthy we all deserve a treat now and again. The apple is a great harvest this year, and the harvesters need, with baked goods. I have a reputation." She word, reputation undulation that rippled along her body and ended with two steps nearer their father.

up at East Rock. Its shadow slid east and dipped into an invisible marshland. Her heart turned north. Her feet pulled her there, but her father's words stopped her, wisely she supposed, as did her own reticence, born of a notion that John preferred Samuel's company to her own. She reckoned it foolish jealousy, but still.

She walked up the hill to prepare supper, stopping at the door-side garden, drawn by the tansy, not yet showing bloom. Then she saw the disturbed ground—a mystery. It was scraped clear at the foot of the gate, and the gate stood sturdy and straight, no longer a shabby annoyance. A quick survey revealed the reason.

Pounded and finely worked strap hinges held the gate by pintles nailed into a new, sturdier fence post. Mercy ran her hand along the post, smooth and splinter free, taking in the heady smell of new-worked wood. Her fingers skipped along the gate slats, equally smooth, to where a new-forged hasp graced the closure.

Understanding rushed through her, and pleasure, like the rush she felt seeing a flower's first bloom. She reached to open the gate, but a slice of peeled willow bark lay tucked in the hasp. She pulled it loose and read the few words written in smudged charcoal with an even hand. "For you alone. J"

Mercy opened the gate, pushed it back and forth. It swung smooth and soundless. For a moment she held the note to her chest, then tucked it in her pocket. She turned round to see Father coming back from his walk and ran down the path to meet him. As she drew near, she called out, "You will never guess, Papa, what a grand gift John has given you."

The green bustled with market day activity and while Father, like most of New Haven, had little coin or wampum, he hoped to barter the sausage just finished off in the smoking shed. Winter was gone, and the June sun streamed down, filling everyone with enthusiasm. Friends greeted each other with a joyful "Good day!", and parents loosened their grasp on the children, allowing them to run free and chase each other at tag.

Out of the crowd, came a high-pitched refrain, matched in gusto to the day's exuberance. "Samuel, oh Samuel! Over here young man, here..."

Widow Sherwood stood at the edge of the town cistern waving her arm wide. Samuel froze. The widow, seeing she had his attention, hustled over with mincing steps, her whole body bouncing with the effort. She held up a bundle and added voice, once in range, to her gestures. "Samuel, dear. I thought I might find you here. Brought you a treat. Oh, Mister Payne. So good to see you. And how are you, pray tell? And Mercy, a treat for you as well. Maple candy!"

She leaned down and wrinkled her nose at Samuel. He winked at her, his hand held out, expectant of his reward.

"Samuel, be seemly." Father stood back, reserved and proper, conscious of the people around them. "We thank you for your kindness, Widow Sherwood, but we could not accept a charity."

"Why, Mister Payne, your boy is a wonder, a worthy son. And we all deserve a sweetening now and again. The maple trees give up a great harvest this year, and the harvesters trade with me, sugar for baked goods. I have a reputation." The word, reputation, elicited an undulation that rippled along her body and ended with her somehow two steps nearer their father.

He stiffened, caught in her blather, and grumbled his reply. "Well, a trade then. A sausage for your candies."

"Not an even exchange, William. May I call you William? I must bake you something to balance the scale. Are you walking the merchant row? I would love a companion." Then she addressed Samuel, in a whisper. "You cannot believe the comings and goings at Reverend Davenport's house. My, my, but I wonder at it. So many about. Could you check on my house for me, with your good sister?" At that, she popped a candy in his mouth, handed one to Mercy, and waddled off on their father's arm.

⤥❀⤦

The reverend's home was, indeed, veiled in turmoil. Three horses stood tied to the picketed fence. A bevy of fine ruffled men, many unknown to Mercy, engaged in heated debate on the porch. As she and Samuel walked nearer, Reverend Davenport hurried up the street toward them.

"Good day, Reverend. sir," Mercy said, the sweet tinge of maple still tickling her tongue. Her brother ran over to open the gate leading to the man's home.

The reverend glanced at Samuel, then addressed him as an after-thought. "You are the son of Goodman Payne are you not?"

"Yes, sir. My name's Samuel, sir."

"Well then, Samuel. I may need an errand, God willing. Pray stay here and await my word." He rushed to the house, took the stairs to the porch all in a leap, and disappeared through the front door, a gaggle of men in pursuit. Only a few remained behind.

"What goes on here?" Mercy stood close by the gate and pushed away the advances of a sorrel gelding nuzzling her hand where the maple candy had been.

"Those are the deputy magistrates, the governor's men. They plan their moves."

"How do you know?"

"I come often." Samuel shrugged. "It's how I keep John and Edward abreast, by watching them and my schoolmaster, a loose-tongued man."

"Well, I suppose John was wise not to involve me earlier. I would have worried to distraction."

"Hush, Mercy, and listen."

The authority in her brother's voice took Mercy back. She was his protector, and this put her in an unusual role, but if Connecticut's success meant John's freedom? She held her tongue and listened.

The men argued; the words jumbled together as each cut the other off. One voice rose, protesting. "A letter to Winthrop will only expose us in opposition to the King."

"The reverend wants it."

"The reverend thinks God wants New Haven. And he supported the regicides."

"Got us into this, he did."

"Shush, he persuades Leete as we speak."

"The King may listen to the idea of a single charter, but one that gives New Haven autonomy—if it come from Governor Winthrop's mouth."

"Assuming he can be persuaded to present the reverend's view. But Winthrop is Connecticut's governor. Where stand his loyalties?"

Then the voices receded to calmer discourse, not so easily heard.

The door flew open and Governor Leete, stretched tall and stately, stepped forward, a folded paper in his right hand. Only a twitch at his jaw line exposed his discomfort. Emerging from the shadow of the door, came Reverend Davenport, who donned his square cap, nose held high in triumph. "God shall prevail on the King, and Governor Winthrop shall deliver His message." He took the letter from Lecte's hand and held it high.

Mercy furrowed her brow, pleading with Samuel for translation.

Samuel's eyes rolled, his face framed with exasperation. "They send a letter to the King, through the Connecticut governor's hands." He moved his face within a nose of her. "Saying New Haven law should continue—unchanged."

She understood. Winthrop wielded power. With his support, New Haven's laws and the judgments of their courts would stand, even as part of Connecticut. And the years of indenture levied upon John would hold. If they wished John free, they must stop this letter.

Reverend Davenport straightened his waistcoat and touched Governor Leete on the arm. "Mister Leete, if I may, a ship leaves from New Haven at mid-day, the last able to reach Winthrop's vessel, anchored out of Southold. He sails soon to England. That boy can run the letter to the harbor."

A giddiness rose in Mercy's chest. In Samuel's hands, the letter might disappear. An opportunity Samuel felt as well. He rubbed his hands together, perked up lively, faced the men, and took a step to the porch. Then, from the same shadow that produced the reverend, stepped Gibbard, pink-faced, his thinning hair not yet covered.

He rolled his hat in his hands and looked out at Samuel, then turned his gaze to Mercy. "Oh," he mouthed, "not the best of choices, sir." He narrowed his lips to a thin wedge. "Best I do it—to safeguard our petition and place it in careful hands."

Mercy glowered at the man, forever a splinter festering in her life. She leaned to her brother's ear. "Samuel, wait until he passes. I will distract him. You must go tell John."

Gibbard had reached the gate, a puffed-up poppycock, too busy with his importance to hear her words. She held his gaze, lifting her chin to greet him, like an equal. It rankled him, and she enjoyed it.

"Mister Gibbard." She oozed maple syrup sweetness and the grimace of a smile. "Samuel, open the gate for the good man. On the way to the wharf, sir?"

"I am, girl. What business it be of yours." He whisked by, a sick, sweet smell trailing in his wake. And she followed it.

❧✿❧

John pressed his weight into the oar, a match to Edward's rhythm. The moon, close to full, lit the night sky, a portent of luck.

After Samuel found him at the marshland, they had gone to the ferry stop where they met up with Edward, who added more information to what Samuel had shared. He had stumbled on Mercy at the dock. She had followed Gibbard and watched him deliver the letter. Because of her spying, they knew the letter sailed with the Constance, and the Constance sailed to Southhold. At Southhold a Dutch ship waited to transport Governor Winthrop to England.

After Samuel sulked off to New Haven, angry to be left out of the excitement, they rushed to the ironworks to consult with Mister Cooper. The man agreed—the letter must be stopped. So, they devised their plan, outrageous and unlikely as it was.

"'Twas a good thing The Cockerel arrived in New Haven when it did, and that Captain Sylvester gave us leave to go ashore. Mercy caught me coming off the shallop. I do love my new life, John. I apprentice under the boatswain. He has me tending the lines, walking the rigging." Edward rowed with quick heady strokes. "Put to, John. I'll unfurl the sail once we clear the harbor."

Their idea of stealing back the letter by climbing aboard the Constance squeezed at John's chest far less than his fear of a bilious sea. He checked his stomach, but the nausea he anticipated had not materialized. Still, they had a distance to go before reaching Long Island Sound where winds blew stronger and thrust waves far higher than in New Haven's protected harbor.

John timed his talk with each stroke. "Need to row...takes...my mind...off the...waves..." He leaned back to gain leverage and harness in his anxiety.

Edward's scornful chuckle was no help. "Never get there in time, if at all, without the wind. The tide comes with the moon, and we row against it." They worked in silence then, the exertion of manning the shallop, designed for a crew of four, took all their effort. Strong as John had become by harvesting the iron ore and pounding out its product on the anvil, his arms and shoulders still screamed with each stroke. When Edward announced a decent wind and unfurled the sail, John celebrated by falling flat into the bottom of the boat, at least until Edward started barking orders at him.

"You think you are Captain House already."

"And you are my swabbie. Look lively!"

Their chatter tempered a rising disquiet, and, once again, the Sea

Gods blessed them, this time with a gentle northwesterly wind. It blew them, with little need to tack, to the tip of the island spit, just east of Southold and not far from Shelter Island. Maneuvering beyond Shelter Island and into the bay took a good portion of the night.

"There," Edward whispered. The Constance loomed before them, illuminated by the moon lingering low over the bay.

As a testament to Edward's navigational skills, the shallop swung wide and glided like a silent cormorant, dark and low on the water, near enough to touch the ship's starboard side. Shadowed by the setting moon, Edward, with John's help, furled the shallop's sail. John gave the job of casting the anchor to his friend, tired of the head shaking that accompanied Edward's whispered instructions. His stomach rolled, so that bile rose into his mouth, but no more. For that he was grateful. He took in the salt air and the musky odor wafting off the ship's hull; then he looked up.

The Constance rose above them, a wood-planked wall. Their shallop swayed like bobbing driftwood near the ship's center, its curved hull receding on either side. John tried to calculate the height of the deck above. They were maybe twenty feet below the main deck, but the poop deck to his left rose half again higher. John stared in disbelief. Before, when he arrived as a boy, his mind was a blur, all focus on himself. Now, though, from where he sat, thinking to scale the sides of the ship? Dear God, it was big.

His nails found his thumbs and tore at their quick. "What now?" he whispered.

Edward looked up, then, with arms crossed, leaned against the mast rising from where John sat. "Not sure." He sounded almost flippant.

"Not sure? How can you not be sure? This be your plan. Your grand idea."

"Well, we have options. You can climb the ship's anchor chain. But that puts you at the bow. The letter is likely in the captain's quarters, there at the stern." He nodded left to where the ship rose higher.

"What if it's on the Dutch ship, already in Winthrop's hands?"

"Not likely. Cargo, even letters, are not transferred at night."

"So we take a chance?"

Edward laughed, "It's all a chance, John."

"Funny. So, if not by climbing the anchor, what's my other option?"

"Climb to the captain's quarters. Ax works well. Hug the tiller and dig in with the ax as a handhold. The ship's planking helps some."

John fingered the ax tucked in his belt. He had fashioned it for small tasks, and this looked to be a large one. "And you can do this?"

"Well, no. But I saw it once. A big fellow, he had fallen from the railing. Made it look easy enough. No problem." Edward laughed, then gave John a good-natured kick. "You can do it."

"Stop knocking at me, Edward. This is no joke."

"Well, it has to be you. You are the shadow man. Should they catch you waiting for me, all New Haven watches you hang." He knelt low, exaggerating the points of their previous conversation. "I am a freeman, you know. Court decreed."

John considered the options. He worked his teeth with his tongue, looked from bow to stern, sucked in, and swallowed the forming saliva. "I choose the anchor chain."

"Means you have to crawl the ship's length."

"A sight quieter than the racket of an ax. Besides, the crew looks to be mostly ashore." He pulled his shirt over his head as he talked, then slipped, feet already bare, into the sea.

The ocean greeted him with a jolt of cold. The June waters held to an icy spring, frostbitten in his bones. Salt stung his eyes and snuck into his mouth, but five quick strokes put him within reach of the ship.

He had not expected the seaweed and sea sludge coating the anchor chain. It slipped inside his palms, and he fell back into the sea. The climb would require a slow-found, tightened grip. He pushed the strings of dripping hair from his face, grabbed the wide arc of a single link, adjusted his grip, and pulled. His muscles strained. He wrapped the chain into his legs, curling it to his feet. He held it to his chest with one arm and reached again. Soon, falling into a strained rhythmic exertion, salt drying at his nostrils with each heaving breath, algae squishing through his fingers, the chain burning at his legs and chest, he reached the deck railing.

He held tight and waited. Eyes closed, he listened, but heard no one, so flung his weight onto the rough, tarred deck and flattened into it. Now the moon played villain, illuminating him like a lighthouse beacon.

"God," he whispered, eyes closed in prayer, then scuttled on his chest across the deck to the shadows. An ocean puddle seeped from his breeches. His chest heaved. He tried to wrestle one of the thoughts whisking through his brain to a stop, any thought, but they raced past. Only his purpose remained. His vision narrowed to the rough-planked deck, and he began to crawl, counting each reach of his hands.

On the count of twenty, he arrived at the quarterdeck and huddled there, hidden behind the steps leading to the next level. Voices spilled from the wall. The dining room, he thought, the inebriated banter of unsuspecting men. He strained to hear but only grasped a passing word or inflection.

He slid along the wall, scuttled up the steep stairs, and raced to the charthouse. The only windowed quarters on the ship, it sat furthest aft over the tiller, high enough to view the vessel's length. He nosed up to look in the open window, a square the diameter of his head set to the side of a low door. The setting moon sliced through a second window, casting its beam on a table strewn with paper. He tried the door, and it swung open with ease. The voices from the dining room grew louder; still, he stood up, skimmed the table with his hand, pushing charts and notes aside. Then, protruding from a basket on a shelf above the table, he saw a handful of folded letters. He shuffled through them. The blue seal of New Haven drew his eye. He flipped it over. On the face, written with a flourishing hand, was the name of Governor Winthrop.

John stuffed the letter into the pouch at his belt, bent low, and scurried from the charthouse, then stopped. The sailors had settled into conversation outside, leaning against the stair railings. John slunk to his haunches in the shadow of the charthouse wall. Sweat trickled along his brow. He held his breath, swallowed it, allowed air to slide in through his open mouth, and waited.

Attempting to compose his roiling stomach, he forced his eyes to wander along the cracks in the deck, looking for calm and the hint of a plan. Nothing came to him except the sight of a small blue stone wedged into a crack in the decking. He inched his hand near and dug at the stone with his finger. It popped free.

The smooth-faced orb glided between his callused thumb and forefinger, and in it, he found his courage. He dropped the stone into his pouch, stuffed the letter deeper down, and turned to the high-backed end of the ship. With a running leap, he hurdled the deck railing, and jumped into the sea.

*The book takes a pleading breath, then breathes out hard, like
a bellows working a flame. A closeted disquiet works at Maggie's
diaphragm. It quickens her heartbeat, and, as with her other out-of-time
experiences, anxiety washes over her like an unexpected intruder. But
this is more; it pushes down on her, and she is drowning, disoriented and
spinning out of time. Her nails rake the arms of her chair, an attempt to
hold to reality.*

*Really, she thinks. Over people in a book? Abandoned, lying next
to her reading glasses, Volume II assures her. She is rational. She is
sane. But the sense of drowning, out of time, overwhelms her. So when
Duncan comes in, rescuing her, she is grateful. She needs the relief of
physical exertion.*

"Have I got a deal for you!" he says.

*Soon she is pressing her weight into the eighth of a series of oak
rounds, this one eighteen inches in diameter. She helps roll it, over
uneven ground, to the road. The effort centers her. "You know how to
show a girl a good time," she quips.*

*Duncan grunts, and they roll the full circumference of the log twice
more before pausing for breath. "Times like this, I'm glad I married a
mule." He jokingly calls her his mule, and she doesn't mind. She likes
being strong, capable of meeting him halfway, more than halfway some
days when his back acts up.*

*"On the other hand," he continues, "the stubborn part can be a pain
in the rear. We need to turn it a little. Ready? Go!"*

*She braces her back foot, using her leg for leverage, and pushes.
"Funny. I just happen to know when I'm right is all, that's not stubborn."*

"You mean as in...always?"

"Hey, I can stop anytime."

"Nope, because I'm making dinner tonight. Fair is fair." They press on, their joint efforts increasing the winter store of firewood considerably.

They lift together and set their oak behemoth atop two equally large rounds already gathered. Maggie stands, pumps her arms, body-builder style. "A seventy-year-old specimen like me deserves a fine meal. And a fine wine, I'm thinking."

Duncan dusts her stomach off with both gloved hands and tugs her hat down, centering it. "A beauty, you are."

"Smart-aleck. Are we done?"

He looks at his watch. "Took an hour between the two of us. Two hours labor. See? An hour a day and we can keep the place up."

Maggie nods in agreement. Hard work, effort—you can look on it as a trap or a road to independence. Either way, it takes you closer to your goal than inertia. Effort out-trumps worry every time, and common effort doubles the effect. She sends the lesson into the ethers; the books approve. The message will come in handy.

She and Duncan walk back to the house, a brief downhill trek. The redbud leaves glisten, heart-shaped, the last gasps of autumn dusting the greening landscape with muddled streaks of maroon and brown. The moldering fragrance of her world, at the edge of decay, summons a smile from her and from the books feeling her near; each of them takes solace in memories spun out of time and woven into their being.

Maggie thinks emotions might not just come from now. Maybe those unexplained emotions—others must have them—maybe they burst out of a recollection imprinted on genes long ago, a genetic past acting on us now. The Volumes feel her thoughts and wonder if she's considered the memories held in things—like books.

But Maggie's mind is flitting now, in an orgasmic volley of ideas. She settles on the question of empathy; perhaps she's too empathetic. She does, after all, cry at the drop of a word, or a Kleenex commercial. The volumes protest. Empathy is her strength. She reluctantly accepts their assessment and, with her angst on hiatus, walks past the old Indian bow, the grinding stone, and the handmade drum decorating their entry toward a rendezvous with Volume II—where hints of sedition surface. Like our own revolution, she thinks as she turns a page, and she romances a fairytale ending.

〜❊〜

The wind rushed along John's cheeks. By instinct, he clutched at his belt, securing the ax head and the pouch holding both letter and stone. He closed his eyes, stiffened, and hit the ocean like a musket shot. It hurt. His first thought was only that. How could water hurt? But it did, slapping the soles of his feet, crushing his knees to his chest. His elbows lurched out, and he spun. The force wrenched his neck back, and he stalled, twisting like a top losing momentum. Foaming bubbles swirled around him, created a disoriented confusion, and he gasped—a mistake.

The ocean rushed into his lungs. He spasmed, his body's effort to reject the salty brine stinging at his nose and chest. He attempted to breathe again. Why did he keep doing that? He kicked, pumped with his elbows, still holding to his weapon and the prize at his belt. He twisted, willing his eyes to open to the sting, trying to find up.

A lighter, shimmering shell beckoned him and he reordered all movement, attempting to surface. Somewhere along the way, a terribly long way up, he floated, dreamlike, drifting with Muddy, sinking toward Mercy. But Mercy shoved him away and when he turned to Samuel, the boy pushed him harder. He ricocheted between them, caught in an undulating eddy. He kicked out, harder than the overwhelming ache in his chest, and gasped, reeling beneath the brackish swell stinging at his throat.

Awareness crashed in on him, a wave, carrying with it the actions of the day; he paddled around in it. The glow of a salmon sky, a morning sky, produced a thought—east. Was the shallop anchored behind him? He arced his right arm down, still holding to his belt with the left, the force of water slipped between his fingers. He broke out of a rolling surf and found air. A hand reached out to him and jerked him up. He flung his other arm out. The edge of a boat. He coughed, retched, coughed again.

"Damned, John, not in the boat. Lord be—did you get it? Did you get the letter?" He shook his head, gasping, and Edward pulled him by his armpits head first into the shallop.

"Ahoy! Below. Who goes there?" The voice fell on them like a distant warning. Edward sat on John's back, stuffing his face sideways into a coiled rope muddled with seaweed.

"You there, again I say, show yourself."

Edward's weight shifted, grinding into John, and he felt the lurch of Edward's arm waving to the ship above. "Sorry, sir, too close are we? Just the two of us, see. My fishy friend here dipped heavy in the rum pot. Turned pot-valiant and decided to row home."

"And you, who are you?"

Edward paused, and John retched beneath him. "Lord above,

friend," Edward said too loudly, making a show of it. "Not you, sir. Forgive me, sir. But the lout is fouling my shallop. I would have him up and rowing us away."

"Damnable drunkard is he? His head will roar tomorrow."

Edward laughed. "Yes, sir. I believe it's true. Now up with you, Charlie. One last heave, and we go." Edward lifted John by the armpits and laid him out with his back to the ship, his head and arms over the gunwale. He whispered, bending low over John's ear, "Pretend you are puking, man. Then keep your head down and take to the oar."

John's gut stiffened. His head pounded and his chest ached. "I need not pretend the first, but the other? God—" He purged the waste in his gut twice over; the rowing he would manage with a newfound, conjured power.

⌇❀⌇

Mercy swung the wooden bucket over her arm and lifted the door latch to go outside. The moon hung low, near to setting, its brightness scrubbed away by a sky edging to light. The coming of day only heightened her concern for John. She had tossed through the night, her anxiety gripping her chest, her breath quick and shallow. Finally, knowing sleep impossible, she rose, taking refuge in what she controlled—stoking the cooking fire, grinding the corn, hauling the water.

She left Samuel and Father to break their fast with light beer, boiled eggs, and cornmeal porridge, then went to do the milking. She pulled the milch cow from the shelter-shed that backed up to the pigsty, luring her with a flake of hay. The cow settled to munching, and Mercy settled to her milking. She inhaled the rare combination of hay and dung, heady and earthen. It grounded her. She grasped the far teats and squeezed in an undulating rhythm, one hand after the next, each stream of warm milk burbling against the side of the bucket. Her mind wandered across her fear-born imaginings—John injured, John caught, John dead—and her part in it.

She had walked with Mister Gibbard to the dock, bombarding him with innocuous commentary on the weather and the day and his errand. Finally, he blistered her with scathing comments about her unseemliness, blathering about her embrace of a servant boy, saying he would not be party to her wanton behavior. She wanted to jump on him and throw him to the ground. Instead, she slunk off, feigning shame, and hid from view.

Mercy watched as he boarded the harbor tender and tracked it, noting which of the anchored ships it sailed toward. Just then Edward and Captain Sylvester's crew came ashore. She grabbed Edward aside and, after dampening his shock at discovering she was an accomplice, told him what she knew.

"The letter is important," he said. After which, he drew her close and peppered her with questions. Then, determining the ship's name to be the Constance, he ran off to find Samuel and John.

She was left to deal with Father. The greatest luck was Widow Sherwood. She kept him occupied with talk, a great deal of it, and maple muffins, thwarting his efforts at escape. Finally, Samuel had returned, pouting over being left out of an espionage. His guess was they planned to steal the letter from the ship. It was then she saw what John risked. Pride had swelled in her chest at her part in it. Then fear squeezed her pridefulness away.

The milk splashed into her bucket, now half-full. Her fingers pulsed in rhythm with her thoughts. This exploit took John out of the confines of New Haven Colony. Under the edict of his trial, the consequence was death. She imagined him dangling from a noose at Oystershell Field or escaped to Boston and lost to her forever.

Exhaustion wore at her spirit; she upbraided herself, knowing John risked all to be called a freeman, to be equal in her father's eyes. Tears ran along her face, asymmetrical rivulets tracing her nose and cheek. She swiped at them with the back of her hand and continued milking, now working the forward teats.

Samuel's footsteps scuffed along the straw-strewn path; he kicked at the ground as he came. "Father has me helping in the field the whole day, then checking the lower pasture with him afterward."

Ever since returning to the market place after warning John, Samuel had brooded insufferably. Her temper broke. "So? We all have our requirements, yours least."

"Well, he keeps me from seeking out John or Edward. I want to know what happened. See if they're safe."

"You mean not in jail or dead?" Mercy leaned out from around the cow's haunches. "And you would have me dredge up sympathy for you?"

"I could have helped them."

"You would have caused Papa to alert the militia to look for you." She stood and kicked back her stool, gathering her petticoats with one hand and the bucket with the other. "Take care of the milch cow, Samuel. I have more than enough chores myself." The bucket fell heavy in her hands, and she jerked it up, biting her lip; milk splashed up and dribbled down the bucket's edge.

"You are angry with me?" Samuel's voice broke, shaming her.

"Not angry, Samuel, worried. Like you. Now go! Loose the cow from the stanchion, take her to pasture, then give Papa your dutiful attention. We cannot afford him to suspect anything. Not now." She adjusted the pail. Samuel held the gate open for her, downcast, his eyes trailing to East Rock.

Mercy filled her lungs, groping for calm, then emptied her breath completely. "I will do something, Samuel, I promise."

And she did do something, not for Samuel, but for herself. As the day wore on, her imaginings grew like leavening. She had never entered the marshland, had always maintained a seemly discretion. But her soul ached, and her mind turned in on itself. She shrunk further into worry.

The sun arced to the west. Samuel and Father ate their dinner and journeyed down the neck with Muddy to check the other pasture. She gathered her courage, poured an offering of the day's fresh milk into a small jug, and headed north, to East Rock, to the marshland, to find John.

❧

The canoe wobbled as John rolled from his side onto his back. The sun baked down on him, and he covered his eyes with his forearm to block its glare. With brow furrowed in an effort to beat back a pounding headache, he reconstructed the events of the day and night before. The decision to retrieve the letter and the actual heist came back in a whirl. But after his jump into the sea, each moment unfolded fog-ridden. He remembered rowing and Edward commenting on the luck of the tide. They must have sailed to the island that sat at the mouth of the river flowing from the ironworks. He recalled Cooper meeting them there, saying he came to gather up the letter—and him. The letter was no more than a soggy smear of ink, little of its content visible.

"A petition left to God," Cooper said, and stuffed it into his waistcoat. "A burnt offering."

He praised them then sent Edward to return the shallop to the harbor and alert Captain Sylvester. John collapsed into the bottom of a canoe and Cooper paddled him upriver. Barely revived, John's next recollection was stumbling into the wagon Cooper used to take him back to the ferry. Then he settled into his own canoe, anxious for his marshlands and a semblance of safety.

"What next?" he had asked.

Mister Cooper smiled down on him with his gentle brown eyes and patted his shirtless shoulder. "We wait, son. We wait."

The rest floated in mist. Obviously, lying here now, he had made it up river to this place in the reeds. This place? He rose to his knees, thought better of it, and sat back on his haunches. Calculating the sun, he determined it must be past mid-day. He steadied the canoe as he rose and looked around.

Like a snow goose, he had returned to the edge of his marsh, grounding the canoe below the red rock and his half-cabin home. Fresh water rippled into the river beyond a nearby raft of cattails. He inhaled the fertile spring air and relished the cooling breeze on his chest.

His shoulders burned, his lungs ached, his gut twisted. His elbows and knees stung. Upon examination, he discovered, buried beneath the skin, multiple tar-coated splinters. He must have earned them crawling across the deck of the Constance. He hurt—more than the worst of Gibbard's beatings. He felt wonderful.

Always, in the past, his pain had come unbidden, punishment for a fault of character he only half understood. But this time every ache, every gnawing hunger, every welt came of his actions, for his purpose, by his choice, and for his good. He had chosen a side, made a decision, and accomplished his goal. And this glorious day only crowned his ecstasy. But he was a mess.

He looked down on his mud-strewn chest and welted knees. He raked his fingers through his hair, but they stuck in salt-crusted tangles. He would meet the day's end with a clean body, washed of the struggle of his adventure. Careful of the ax, knife, and pouch, he loosened his belt and let his breeches drop into the canoe. Then he stepped out, hesitated, and retrieved his knife. The fresh water creek would provide a deserved cleansing and a shave.

❧

Mercy reached John's half-cabin as the sun began its downward turn. His little home was neat, organized in every corner, but he was not there. Her worry worked into shallow breaths. She bit at the inside of her lower lip and scanned the marshland below, her focus settling in heartfelt relief on the small creek at the edge of the bog. Her eyes shut of their own volition, chastened by what she saw, by the shame she thought she should feel. Then they fluttered open, curious, unashamed, embracing her desire.

He stood naked, shaking his ash-brown hair, reaching open-armed to the sky as if in exultation. The sun shown on his body and his skin gleamed with moisture. She thought him beautiful, could have watched him forever, but he slipped into the reeds.

The fact of his safety melded with his image, idyllic in her mind. He was not captured, would not be hung. He was home. She took a single step forward, wondering how to proceed. Then he stepped into view, adjusting his belt to his breeches, barefooted and bare-chested. She lifted her hand to wave.

He bounded up the hill, his smile so wide, his joy so evident, and she hurried out to greet him. They met at a stand of willows edging the marsh, the ground awash in miniature lupine.

"I did it, Mercy. Retrieved the letter." He coughed into his hand. "One step closer to coming under Connecticut's control. Gibbard be damned."

She touched his face, then looked down at his chest and closed her eyes.

He stepped back. "God, I'm near naked. I lost my shirt in our mission. I have one above." He wrapped his arms around his body and lowered his head.

She paused, eyes still shut. The tang of watercress washed over her. "You are not injured?"

"Some slivers, seems I collect them. And I ache. But, Mercy, I feel more alive today than I have ever been. I...I have a gift for you."

She opened her eyes to his. They glittered, green, flecked with gold. "And I one for you," she answered. "A jug of the day's milk." She held the jug up to him, then laughed, thinking it an awkward gesture. "I thought you might be hungry I guess."

"God, yes. I starve. Thank you." Cream ran down the corners of his lips as he emptied the jug in a handful of swallows. He gathered up the droplets with his fingers and thumb and sipped them into his mouth. "You are always there for me, knowing what I need." He stared into her, searching her, then sat the jug down. He fumbled at his pouch, looked up and smiled a slow, wide grin, charming and prideful, then bit his lips as if reining himself in.

He placed a small stone in her palm, his fingers skimming the pattern of lines on her hand, brushing her fingertips.

"I found it yesterday. And I thought of you. The color of your eyes."

She cradled the stone in her hand, pinching it between thumb and forefinger, then tucked it into the pocket tied to her waist. She felt him watching her and looked up to his wide mouth. Her hand ventured up to touch his lips, willed by a power deep inside, drawn by the clearness of his marsh-green gaze, the honesty in his heart. She traced his cheek with her knuckles, her movement tentative and unsure. The grace in that touch moved her further, and her hand roamed the back of his neck, broad and strong, so unlike the thin-formed child he had been.

He cupped her waist, and they met, lip to lip. The taste, the rich scent of cream roamed round her senses, and she shuddered, feeling his whole body falling into hers. His lips, chafed by salty winds, consumed hers—and then slackened. He stopped, still holding her, but pushing her back like a loss.

"I would not take you against your desire, Mercy. I cannot. Yet I do long for you."

And she took hold of him, his whole body, telling him, whispering, that she was drawn by a command. An unspoken command. Word and reason fell apart. He groped for her petticoats, caressing her hips. She responded, falling. The cool grass cradled her, and mosquito hawks swished skyward. He gentled himself into her; a stabbing twinge took her by surprise. She pulled back, her stomach tightening against pain akin to pleasure.

"I would not hurt you," he said. "I would not."

A swell moved through her, thrilling on her skin. Ecstasy, the reverend called it, God-given. It pulled her back and then, with equal force, it pulled her into him. Her eyes squeezed shut and danced with starlight; lids, one moment closed, opened—to sky.

An expansive blue canopy, dusted with feathers of white, lifted her up. A breeze blew through her, rippling, then settling. She looked to him, his eyelids trembling, back arched, and brow furrowed. They road the same breeze and came down together, taking in the deep, musty odor of ground. Spongy and wet, it soaked into her back, and she tucked up to evade it.

He pulled from her and fell to her side, face to the ground, his arm caressing her.

"Dear God, Mercy!" he said, and she laughed, softly, not wishing to shatter the bloom.

"A spirit, surely."

He lifted onto his elbow and look down at her.

"Not an evil?"

Still reeling, a shutter streaming up through her, she shook her head.

"'The skies proclaim the work of his hands.'"

John bent to kiss her but pulled up short, responding to a rustling in the brush. Muddy lunged forward with a woof, shaking dampness and bracken in a mercurial arc. Mercy jumped to her feet, shaking down her petticoats and brushing leaf mulch from her apron. John, working to button his flies with one hand, used the second to push away Muddy's massive tongue.

The next punctuation in their ethereal haze came from Samuel, following after his dog.

"Muddy! Muddy!" he called and burst through the same broken thicket, then pulled up to examine the scene. "I...uh...There you are."

He looked at the ground, noting the imprint there. He tugged off his hat and, with a questioning look toward John, knelt with a pat to his thigh. Muddy circled and sat beside him.

"I worried after you John and...I beg your pardon, sister, I...Papa sent me, tired of your..." She watched him struggle for a word. "...dalliance," he said.

The glory still shimmered in her, turning the world bright and shining, infusing her with its softness. She could not be angry. She reached down to him, jostling his hair.

"My good brother, there be no dalliance here, no evil, I assure you. Naught but peaceable goodness." She looked over at John.

His smile, for her, twisted into weighty resolve toward Samuel. "Walk with me, friend. I think we must talk."

Samuel stood and nodded. "Come, Muddy. And you, sister, you best find your cap."

❧❀❧

They pulled the canoe from the water together. John attempted to distract Samuel from his earlier discovery by entertaining him. He gave a rousing account of how he rescued the letter from the enemy's hand. It worked, to some degree, though the boy still sulked over being left behind.

"I could not chance your father looking for you and catching us before we were off. Though truth be, I could have used a strong shoulder rowing that boat." John tried for playfulness, squeezing the boy's neck and pulling him near. Samuel's eyes narrowed, dancing down John's bared chest. John grimaced. "Lost my shirt and shoes somewhere in all this. I have a shirt, at least, up above. Care to walk with me?"

Samuel said nothing, only scowled and nodded. So they walked to where Mercy stood, silently pleading to know what transpired. Samuel turned his head to the ground as they passed. John gripped his arm. "I would talk to your sister," he said.

Then he went to her and held her hands in his. "Leave us be for a while. I will fetch you." He leaned in and kissed her nose, whispered, "It will be fine," and caught up to Samuel.

"So, I have not thanked you, friend, for bringing us that information. You are a fine spy for sure."

Samuel wrapped his arms at his waist and walked ahead. "What are you doing with my sister?"

His voice was so small John could hardly hear him, but he knew well enough his meaning. He gave up on bolstering the boy and braced himself to deliver the truth. "How old are you, Samuel?"

"Near to thirteen."

"And you know of animals, of rutting, and—"

"I know rutting."

"And you know the feeling you get, say when seeing a girl you like or…Widow Sherwood's teats."

"Ugh, John!"

"Well, if you do, Edward says it best to bang away. It worked for me…till this day at least. Not the best image, I guess." He was doing this poorly. He rubbed at his chin and pulled at the skin there. He needed more time to rethink his approach. When they reached his half-cabin, he begged Samuel sit. "There, on the log settle. Let me get my shirt."

In the darkened cabin he waited for his eyes to adjust, as well as his mind. He cared for the boy and wished not to offend him. But he wanted one thing more. He wanted Mercy—to hold her again—to be with her.

Edward's long-ago talk, the method he used to explain those budding feelings, was not producing the effect he needed. He found the shirt hanging on a peg, slipped it over his head, and tucked it into his still damp breeches. The act centered him, helped him feel less bawdy and sinful in his dealings with Samuel, feelings far from his experience with Mercy. He ducked beneath the overhang and stepped out to sit with Samuel on the settle. He had fashioned it using an adze of his making, and the smooth, flat surface comforted him.

He dug into the quick of his thumb with his fingernail, then slapped his hands to his knees and bent forward. Muddy nuzzled between his legs. John grabbed at the fur on either side of his neck, kneading it.

"I spoke foolishly, Samuel. Though it be true, a good stroking provides a 'grand release.' Those are Edward's words, mind you." He snuck a sideward glance. Samuel gifted him with a sly smile, blue eyes rolling.

With the tension broken, John spoke pointedly. "But that was not what you witnessed with Mercy and me." Muddy butted his head against John's hands and John obliged, digging deep into his fur and kneading his muscled neck.

"So then?" Samuel swept his hat from his head and raked at his hair. "You swived my sister?"

John stiffened, pushed Muddy away. The dog shrunk back, cowering at Samuel's side. "Never speak of her so, Samuel. Not ever." A breeze blew up around them, cooling the dank air, and wind-blown trees broke into the silence between them. "She is sunlight to me, Samuel. Few people have stood with me, cared for me. Edward, Mister Cooper, maybe, and you. But your sister—from the day I met her—she comforted me, touched me, heard me when I spoke. What we did this day was no grand release and never swiving, ever. Understand? It was a covenant, a gift freely given—and received."

"Mercy did this thing willingly?"

John dropped his forearms to his thighs, cradling his head in his hands. A half-snort, half-laugh escaped. "I believe she did; I felt it surely. But that question is one for your sister. She said it was no sin."

"No sin?" A layer of contempt edged Samuel's words. "Why do you not marry then? Reverend Davenport says marriage be the covenant."

"So, you think your father would consent? An indentured man to marry his daughter? One shamed? Shackled?" John stretched out, leaning back against the log settle, and then jerked to standing. Five paces off he returned to Samuel. "I need her, Samuel, and I need you. I need you to stay quiet, to help us, until, maybe someday, I can do what you say. I would have you continue as my spy and our lookout. Please?"

Samuel stared up at him, his young eyes earnest. "Be good to her," he said.

John tousled the boy's blond mop. So, this conjoining encompassed more than just Mercy. It included this boy. "I promise," he said, giving voice to a new covenant.

❧❀☙

July came on with a swelter, on this day tempered by infrequent gusts blowing off the sound. The schoolmaster, dripping with sweat fostered by their overcrowded quarters, released them early, and Samuel took advantage. He hurried off to Widow Sherwood's place to satisfy his cravings—for fine cooking and excellent information. All her doors and shutters hung open to gather any blowing breeze, and she plied him with blackberries, cream, and the latest news carried by a ship come out of Boston.

"Governor Leete is in a fit about it. Seems a "certain intelligence"— I heard him call it that—has informed the King of New Haven's part in harboring the regicides. What did he call them? Oh yes, 'fugitives of the King's justice.' What Governor Leete fears most is to fall from the new King's grace. And the King, well..." She held her soft, round hands to her neck and lolled her tongue.

It was an old joke, one Edward used often, but Samuel rewarded her with a laugh, and she continued, "Moreover, I saw the King killers in Davenport's home of late, frightened from their cave by a panther."

Samuel squirmed, his knees twitching, searching for a way to end his visit and get back home. A panther? And it scared off those lofty men? What a piece of news. He licked the cream and berry stain from his lips and held his hand up as the widow hurried to refill his wooden bowl. "No, thank you, mistress. I must go. Only came to say hello, really."

"But you have not heard all." She held the spoon of berries aloft and swung it, teasing. Samuel saw the trade unfolding—time for tattle—a fair exchange. He lifted his hands in surrender, and she dumped the juice-ridden berries in his bowl.

She doused them with thick cream and continued. "The Magistrates hear nothing from their first letter, so they concoct a second—they do love their letters—one directed to the King this time. No doubt an attempt to placate him. Without admitting to guilt in hiding the regicides, of course. Our good Magistrates could not be guilty..."

Her round face narrowed in on Samuel as she placed the creamer on the table. "Anyway, they plan to deliver the letter to Boston through a non-threatening man, Mister Cooper perchance. What think you?"

Samuel smiled, stuffed a spoonful of berries into his mouth and, forgetting his manners, let the juices dribble off his lips as he spoke. "Mister Cooper? Yes, perfect. Just the man for the job."

Widow Sherwood straightened, shook her breasts, and smoothed her gown out over bulbous hips. "Your father comes to sup this Lord's Day, Samuel. And you and Mercy?"

"No, mistress. We will tend to the cattle—and give you courting time." Samuel winked.

The widow's neck reddened. "Humph," she said, then plopped another dollop of berries in his bowl.

❦

The Lord's Day delivered a new kind of worship for John and, he hoped, for Mercy. With her father trapped, as Samuel called it, into a food-centered courtship with Widow Sherwood, Sunday, from late afternoon to setting sun, became a time of communion for all four of them—John, Mercy, Samuel, and Muddy. But this day John wanted more.

He pushed back the undergrowth of witch hazel and slipped out from the looming chestnuts. Muddy, who regularly met with John after the Payne family left for morning services, had already nosed out Samuel and Mercy coming up from Neck Bridge. The mastiff loped out to greet them. Samuel waved his arm wide, signaling John, and set out running. Mercy nodded her head and offered a shy smile. She would not run. But John saw the signs, the rise in her chest and a faint quicken of her step.

Their meetings exuded a false decorum. They sat on the log settle at John's half-cabin and sipped on his reserve of light beer. They talked, small talk of New Haven's comings and goings, then moved on to weightier speculation on Connecticut's petition to the King for a charter. They walked, listened to bullfrogs chortling, and swatted at the perpetual annoyance of mosquitoes filtering up from the wetlands below. They threw sticks for Muddy and finished their walk with a race back to the settle; Muddy always won and then circled back to encourage the laggards.

After a light sup on whatever Mercy pulled from her rucksack, they separated with an unspoken understanding. Samuel went with Muddy to explore the overlook above Neck Bridge, while he and Mercy disappeared into an isolated nesting place here or there amongst the undergrowth. In it, they would clasp each other with an anxious pent up desire; he would lift her petticoats, fall on her, and find release. She held him then, with his head on her covered breasts, until fear of discovery rousted them and they tidied themselves before going to find Samuel. Today, though, on this waning summer afternoon, John vowed it would be different.

So when Samuel whistled to Muddy, teasing him with a stick close to his muzzle and scrambling back as he nipped playfully at the bait, John faced Mercy, held out both hands, and pulled her close. "I would do this differently," he said, "and know you more."

She looked up at him, all the things he desired present on her face— her gold-brown lashes surrounding blue, her nose still sprinkled with freckles now fading into womanhood, and the precious turn of her mouth, standing ready, seeking opportunity to nurture.

"You know me." She bowed her head, demure, no flirt; it was not in her.

He tweaked her nose and pressed back the curls at her cap. "I do, but we should know each other naked of encumbrance."

"Body to body?"

The words grabbed at his loins; he shied, dropped his gaze, and whispered, "Yes." She lifted his chin so he could see her affirmation. Then he led her to the cabin.

Early in the day, he had mounded fresh grass on his bed and covered it with the woolen blanket Mistress Cooper gave him the night after his flogging. It was but a piece of his preparation.

He ducked through the cabin's opening, while she walked straight in, her frame so small and supple. He had to stop himself from grabbing her to him. And, as though sensing the pulse of his restraint, she crossed her arms over her breasts and stopped inside the open entry. Light washed over the darkened surroundings. Her gaze settled on the flowers bundled on the stool by his bed. "Gayfeathers, and coral vine— the few flowers still lingering. For me?"

His head shook yes, and his tongue squeezed at his throat. He had picked the spiked purple flowers at the bog's edge and tied them together with a sweet-smelling vine. "I didn't know their names. But they smelled of you."

He rubbed his callused fingertips and reached up to pull the string of her cap loose, to slip the knot free. It fell from her head. He folded it so the ties disappeared in the crease and walked over to lay it, just so, next to the flowers on the stool.

There, against the wall, cloaked in shadow, he slipped from his shoes, unbuckled his belt, unbuttoned his breeches. He placed everything neatly, shoes to the side of the bed, belt and breeches to a peg on the wall. He turned around, eyes closed, willing calm. His tongue ran along his lips, savoring mint, another preparation he had made. Then he opened his eyes.

She stood on the opposite side of the blanketed bed. Her fingers flitted over the lacing at her bodice. An apron lay jumbled on the bearskin at her feet. Petticoats fell in a rustled release and swooshed and swirled as she kicked to free her feet of the untidy tangle. Then they faced each other, covered still, he in his hunting shirt and she in her shift. Lace graced the shift's neck, the same he had gifted her.

"You used it," he said.

"In a private way." She fingered it and smiled.

John fumbled with his shirt; it tangled as he pulled it up. He tried to shake his head and arms loose at the same time. Finally, he broke free, hung the shirt on a second peg, and ran his hands along the linen stubble.

"John?" she said, and he looked to her voice.

Her shift was gone. Her eyes shined in the subdued light. She overwhelmed him. He had imagined her, but not the roundness, the fullness, her soft brown fluff, felt and never seen. The breasts that had cradled him covered, lay bare, upturned, the nipples hardened. He could taste her. Then he flinched with a realization—her eyes, too, were traveling. He reached down, cupped himself—and she laughed.

"I think, John Frost, I know its actions," she said. "Naked is naked. Now come to me."

He did what she asked, but as he had promised himself, held back, took her in, smelled her muskiness, ran his hands along her length, free of hindrance. He quickened to the staccato release of her breath, soft against his ear. "Smell the honeysuckle?" she asked and ran her hands, so near. "Smell it?"

"And grass, and you." He pushed her hair away. "You are beautiful, Mercy."

"And you tease."

"No, I cannot, nor can you. Not now."

⌒❀⌒

Fall settled in with a cold, hard frost, and winter soon followed. John could smell it on the wind. Cooper would move the men and their families to the ironworks, and his time with Mercy at their East Rock shelter would end. He regretted leaving, but it was regret peppered with anticipation. All of New Haven awaited the results of Winthrop's audience with the King.

He held Mercy's hand as they walked along the southern ridge overlooking the distant curve of Mill River and Neck Bridge. A trio of dark, bulbous clouds rose in the northeast, framing their rock.

"I can only visit as weather and the work cleaning the furnace permit."

"I know."

"It depends on the harshness of winter."

"I know, John."

He pulled on her arm, bringing her closer. "You know all, it seems."

She made a face, eyes narrowed, dark as the sky. "Do you make fun of me?"

"Yes."

"Well, I do know, and I know more."

"Do you?"

"I do. You will miss me. You will miss...it." She took both his hands and wrapped them round her so that he looked over her head to the valley below. He felt he could gather her up beneath him and soar in consort with the vultures and raptors circling aloft. He pulled her cap away, had come to despise the thing; it contained her so.

Then he saw him and pushed her down, flattening her, covering her, looking out into the valley.

"Gibbard!"

"Where?" She wiggled under him.

"Be still." His hand went to her mouth, gentle, though he knew the man could not hear them from the ridge, or so he hoped. "He's alone on his mare. The devil spies on us." He gathered her under him and maneuvered her behind a vagrant shrub. She sat back, her hair askew.

"He may simply be out on business."

John brushed the leaf and bramble from the petticoats furled out around her, then tucked her hair behind her ears, replacing her cap. She brushed his hands away and tied it beneath her chin. "You need not be quite so...vigorous in your protection."

"Mind me, Mercy. I'm not wrong in this. We stand against evil men, and must be cautious." He snuck out from the bush on hands and knees, then pressed against the ground and inched onto an outcropping. Gibbard nudged his horse along the trail circling East Rock, the one leading out to the marshland, then in a circuitous meander, he swung round to the Payne's house.

"What are you doing?" Mercy stood behind him, hands on her hips.

Frustrated, he pulled her down by her gown, and she flattened beside him. "He goes to our house," she whispered.

"He does, and on a Lord's Day. He spies. I told you."

Mercy rolled to her side and traced her fingers along his cheek and his lips. "You knew." Her eyes twinkled. "Know all it seems." She pressed against him, and he caught her hand, refusing diversion.

"This is no game, Mercy. You must trust me in this. Do you trust me?" Her eyes penetrated, roamed inside him, and as her mouth opened to respond, he laid his fingers on her lips. "Shush. You need not answer. Your soul is trust, as though evil be a myth, regardless of those churchmen. But evil exists, Mercy. I know it. I have seen it, felt it. It exists, even in them, and in me..." He pushed back her cap again, to set her free. "But not, I think, in you."

The winter solstice looms. A bank of clouds from last night's deluge settles over Maggie and Duncan's mountain. The shortened day engulfs them in a chill morning gloom, and they hunker down near the radiating heat of a just banked fire. The book nestles in her hand supporting her as she absorbs the all-important trial—the exclamation point in the books' story.

She now understands her anxiety, so pronounced of late. She wondered at it before—how John Frost could pull the strings, as he did, on her psyche. But the next trial spells it out.

She believes in these echoes through time; she trusts in them. They play out too often not to believe. But she hadn't understood the connection until she read the records this morning. The minutes for

October 15, 1662, spell out what she felt instinctively.

The link between John Frost and her is real.

Maggie stops reading, tucks the book face down on her knee, opened to her leaving place, and looks through the woodstove's isinglass window to the simmering flame. Their fractured world and foolish youth sparked disaster. But after that? What happened after that? The book lays silent, cold in her lap. It has no answer. More pages follow; she will read on, but she knows no answer resides there. She slips a marker between the pages and sets the book aside. The copper bucket beckons, near empty; they need kindling, so she walks out to Duncan's shop.

Maggie scans the open rectangle of his workroom. She takes in every neatly placed tool, nothing in disarray. The kindling is split, stacked in a box by the cutting block, a masterful piece, waist high, a product of Duncan's mind, ever questing to make each chore easier. The two of them sometimes talk of leaving this place when they are older and can't manage the acreage and the daily tasks. Then they laugh and say, "We are older!" Maggie doubts they will ever leave, with each corner of their world christened by Duncan's artfulness, by the wonder of his hands.

She gathers up an armful of kindling, takes it to the house, and arranges it in the bucket sitting by the woodstove. That done, she heads outside, turns her back to the waning gibbous still hanging in the morning sky, and walks into a lingering haze illuminated by the low-lying sun.

What Maggie last read spins her into a spiraling confusion; she wonders where to go next, and the books are oddly mute. So she inhales one breath, full and centering, for the people of the trial and for her. The air tastes cold, refreshing, touched with the tang of green. Her gaze runs over the white, rheumatic fingers of a buckeye, leaves long lost, a three-

dimensional denizen in the winter landscape. Moss-covered rocks grace the land as though placed by a drunken stonemason. Neither plumbed nor square, some teeter but never fall, while others burst up, strong and sturdy, like Stonehenge itself.

She climbs the jumble of rocks, doused with a fairyland of lichen and moss, to a giant granite precipice overlooking a confusion of downward cascading columns. When the children were young, she took them here to hunt for salamanders hidden in the crevices. The place washes her in memories, a fitting reprieve from the trial's litany of prejudice. The thought slips in that maybe now isn't so different from then. Fences grow between differences in every place and time; and cruelty exists, perpetually, both great and small.

But they lived it. How did any of them live it? Did they hope for more? Did they retreat in despair? Or did they rally against it, like cause-crazed rebels? Maggie runs her fingers through her wiry, grey hair; she stands and pulls her pants loose from a soaked rear end; she stretches skyward, relishing this place where memories are dear. She and Duncan will stay because place matters. But so far from her children, her grandchildren, so labor intensive? It's a tired old cliché, a scale balancing freedom and its cost. Anyway, for now, she is here. She needs to finish the books, check other records, reflect, regroup, make plans. So enough with philosophy! She sets her sights on home.

PART VI

1662 (and the present)

It is Ordered, that if any man shall commit
Fornication with any single woman, they shall
be punished, either by enjoyning marriage, or
fine, or corporall punishment, any and all of
these as the Court of Magistrates shall judge
most aggreable to the word of God.

Code of New Haven

Mercy watched the icicles dripping down to nubs on the porch eves. She had watched and waited the winter through, one proving long and snow driven.

John's first visit came at the beginning of the cold time. They walked the frosted river's edge with Muddy and Samuel in tow, unable to chance what they desired most. John had leaned in and kissed her forehead before he left. It heated her for weeks.

Then the snow fell and the temperature plummeted, turning the river to ice and prohibiting all travel. Father brought all the cattle, including the milch cow, two sheep and five pigs to the shelter-shed. The rooster objected, causing a repeated ruckus until the cow clipped him with her hoof. Peace ultimately ensued. The multiple bodies in the cramped space created enough heat to keep the animals from freezing but the stench of them overwhelmed any who entered the shed.

John's next visits occurred as winter loosened its grip. One trip was brief, to bring a snow knocker, a small hammer forged as a gift for Father. Then an early spring thaw drew him, once again, up the ice-strewn river. They walked its banks, now turned to slush, while Muddy raced ahead. She longed to run her hand along the down at the curve of John's back, but instead, they walked hand-in-hand while Samuel talked, incessantly.

"They smelled of manure baked in oat bran with soured urine

sprinkled on top, and it was my job to muck out their leavings. Every day, mind you. And where to put it in the snow?"

"You stack it to mellow, Samuel. Good for the crops in spring." John squeezed her hand, a message. He humored her brother; he cared for him.

"I know, and I did it, but a poor job. I am glad to have them pastured."

John smiled. His green eyes lightened, considering. "You need a barn. With a sturdy roof and room for stalls perhaps."

Samuel perked at the suggestion, but Mercy dampened his dreams. "Which takes a good rock foundation, hewn boards, and what for the roof? Papa makes little from his hams and what little he harvests goes to feed those manure makers filling the shed—and us."

"Well, someday maybe." Samuel looked at John, near straight in the eye, Mercy noticed.

John whisked Samuel's cap from his head and ruffled his hair. "Someday," he said, then scanned their surroundings, looking, no doubt, for Father or Mister Gibbard.

To distract him and return his attention to her, she reached into her bag, pulled out a corn muffin, and waved it under his nose. "We are a long way from barns and closer to food. I say we find a log to sit on and eat. There are oysters, fresh harvested, as well."

The sky darkened as they ate; the wind blew in heavy gusts from the west. A crack of lightning ripped at the sky, soon followed by a warning rumble. John pulled her near, and they ducked as if to avoid what they knew was coming. Muddy whined and cowered at Samuel's feet. The hail hit in a torrent, the icy pellets falling ever larger. Even Muddy flinched, snapping at the falling ice.

"Stay to the lowest trees," John yelled above the reverberating thunder and the hail's din. He pulled her along while Samuel dragged Muddy. As they worked their way to the house, the distance between the flashing of the sky and the roll of thunder increased. The musket ball hail shrank to the size of peas, stinging with less intensity. The ravishing had stopped by the time they reached the door-side garden, now awash in pellets of crystal white. Plants hung beaten by the hailstone lashing, and Father stood on the porch.

"Folly," he said. "Idle time bears the devil's fruit."

Samuel tried to hold Muddy back, but he escaped, seeking safety on the porch. "No, Muddy!" he yelled, too late. The dog already writhed, rippling from muzzle to hindquarter. Droplets arced over the length of the decking, and the length of Father's body.

"Oh, Papa," Mercy cried.

Her father closed his eyes and held his breath. Then brushed at the wet on his face, sleeves, and breeches, exuding a disturbing calm. "You have chores, Samuel. The pastured animals need checking."

Samuel knelt, holding Muddy to prevent further shaking. "Yes, sir."

John stepped in front of Mercy. "I will help him, sir. We met only to eat a bite."

"You, John Frost, can help by serving your master only. Accompany Samuel to the pasture, then be gone. And Mercy, in the house, now. You will not frolic loosely, like your mother."

The words stung like a hailstone. She pictured her mother as neither loose nor frolicking, but as light and love. She stepped from behind John whose mouth had fallen open then shut with a huff. A touch of his arm willed him to patience. Then she spoke. "I am an obedient daughter, Papa. Better than you think." She past by him and climbed the porch steps. With the grating squeak of door hinges, she withdrew, glad for her lie, her obedience not to Father, but John.

The spring reprieve withdrew. Cascade after rolling cascade of inclement weather blew in from the west. The snow-bound earth froze, melted, then froze again. Meanwhile, Mercy waited, and watched, as icicles dripped away the days.

꙳

John awaited word. Mister Cooper tired of his asking, but he asked all the same. The late spring torrents had finally ceased, and the earth eased into summer, bright and glorious. He and Deliverance again carried the ore down river to the iron works, and he again found shelter at East Rock.

Mercy renewed her Lord's Day visits while her father fattened on the courtship bounty provided by Widow Sherwood. Samuel and Muddy returned to their roles of watchmen, vouchsafing he and Mercy's communion. They also reinstated the evening suppers on the days John returned from delivering the iron ore. And sometimes on those days, when his loins cried for her, they would take refuge in the willows. Each encounter deepened his need, unsettling him.

Driven by that need, he had sought out Mister Cooper and found him at the base of the blast furnace where casting molds awaited the flow of molten iron. Restlessness born of waiting prompted him to ask again, "Hear you word from England?"

"Shall I tease you a while or tell you outright?" Cooper smoothed the sweat of his brow with his forearm, a grin growing on his face.

"So there's word?"

"Come lately. Governor Winthrop signed a charter with the King."

John dared a smile. He opened his hands out and raised his shoulders questioning. His master just stared, brows arching. So he teased after all. John had no patience for it. "And? What of New Haven?"

"The King, and the charter, place New Haven under complete control of Connecticut."

John slapped his hand against his thigh. "So, it is done!"

"Well, not done..." Cooper shrugged and headed toward the finery. John hurried after him. As they neared the building, a sulfurous stench accosted his throat. He coughed, his fist to his mouth.

"How so?" he said. "What holds things back?"

"New Haven delays. Already the Magistrates talk of rejecting the charter until they see it, signed by the King, when Winthrop returns. But rumblings have begun in New Haven's outlying towns. Southold and Guilford grumble loudest. They would break with New Haven and side with Connecticut and the King."

The noise and the vibrations coming from the mammoth hammer pounding out impurities in the iron reverberated throughout John's body, compounding his frustration. "So a game, then, of hem and haw?"

"For now. We must bide our time. So return to your work, Frost. And take care with your pleasures. I watch your comings and goings. So does Mister Gibbard and his old white mare."

John fumed. These men played games with their paltry principles while his life, the simple act of living, stood waiting. And on top of it all? Gibbard.

"I hear your meaning," he said, and turned back to the ferry where his flatboat lingered. If he must wait while the mighty played their games, he planned to wait holding Mercy.

Samuel signaled Muddy with a flick of his hand. The mastiff circled and sat to his left. He swiped his arm across his forehead, removing the accumulated sweat of the humid summer day. A rustling in the reeds suggested hidden fowl, likely turkey. And there they were, more than two-dozen dotting the rise above East River.

He and Muddy practiced at hunting, but he was not allowed to shoot anything, not while he was alone, and not while he played lookout for John and Mercy. John permitted him to carry his musket, but not shoot it. He had taught Samuel to hold it in his left hand perfectly balanced to allow for easy maneuvering and told him Muddy must learn to follow the rules of a hunt as well. When they proved their mettle, John promised to teach him to hold the matchstick, a string of long woven hemp that ignited the powder in the prime pan. He had begged John, saying it was time, but John was wary. It was an art, keeping the match lit and far from the powder while you walked. At least without blowing off your face or hand. Too dangerous while John was otherwise occupied. And he was otherwise occupied—with Mercy.

Samuel's constancy guarding the couple earned him these lessons and the use of the gun, so he did not complain. He walked toward the grazing turkeys, bringing the musket to his shoulder and taking aim, fabricating a hunt. The turkeys expressed no interest. They scratched and pecked, oblivious to his presence. He bristled, unfulfilled, and longed for the excitement he felt hunting with John. So he dropped the gun to his side, careful to balance it as John taught him, and signaled Muddy free.

The dog leapt forward and nipped at one fluttering fowl and then another in a zigzagging ramble across the field. The birds scattered.

"Ha," Samuel said. He hefted the gun, took aim and yelled, "Kapow!" Wings beating, the birds momentarily hoisted their awkward bulk, squawked, and bounced away toward the trees. Samuel winced at the unexpected ruckus, not discrete as John required. He glanced back to John's flatboat tethered in the willows, then up to the small clearing where his sister and John lay hidden. Sensitive to every movement in the sultry stillness, Samuel instinctively turned west. A flash of white alerted him. A dusty white mare plodded toward the docked flatboat; the rider whipped at her haunches, urging her to move faster. She broke into a lumbering trot.

Samuel dropped the musket to his side and ran; Muddy circled round to meet up with him. With uncanny understanding, the dog bounded straight for Gibbard and the mare, confronting them just outside the little clearing. He growled, leapt forward with a low, menacing snarl, and nipped at the mare's rear hooves. Emitting a high-pitched neigh, she whirled, ears back, to avoid her attacker. Gibbard groped for the horse's mane. She reared, and Gibbard fell with a wincing crack onto his backside. His hat took flight and skidded to a stop at the feet of John, just exiting the clearing.

Samuel skidded to a stop in front of John who was still tucking his shirt into his unbuttoned breeches. Samuel dropped his head, stared at his friend's bared feet, and then met his eyes. "I am sorry, John, I..." He held the musket up for John to take, an unconscious acknowledgment of failure.

"Not now, Samuel." John secured his breeches, jaw working, then held his hand out to the fallen Gibbard. The man's eyes bugged; a rash of red spread up his neck to his flushed face. He worked his feet and arms like a bug attempting to right itself. Samuel would have laughed, were the circumstance less dire.

Gibbard rolled to his hands and knees with a ragged huff. Ignoring the proffered hand, he rocked, wheezed, then pushed to standing. His pudgy finger flitted before John's face. "I have you now, you indecent philanderer. She is in there. I know it. Sinful! It is sinful! Where is she?"

As he spoke, Mercy slipped from behind John. Her hand clung to her bodice and its undone lacing; her uncapped hair tumbled along her back. "I am here, Mister Gibbard, though what business it is of yours, I do not know."

The man recoiled. Samuel could see him wither, the veins along his eyes pulsing. "You little harlot. Perhaps not my business but your father's." His head bobbed about, looking for his horse, nowhere insight. He pressed his hand to his chest, whipped around, and plodded with determination to the Payne house on the rise above.

Mercy shot between Gibbard and John. Her hair hung over her face, her disheveled appearance frightening Samuel. Muddy circled, frenetic, jolting back and forth, barking repeatedly.

"Damn, Samuel, shut the dog up," John yelled. Then, with a voice softer, still stern, he addressed Mercy. "Move away from the man, Mercy. And you, Gibbard, will not call her harlot."

But Mercy was in a fit; Samuel had seen it before. And in it, she could not be stopped. She jerked at the back of Gibbard's coat as he waddled away and drew up to him, impassioned.

"Mister Gibbard. Please, I beg you. He did nothing. I will swear it. Leave Papa out of this, please!"

Gibbard's lip curled. He grabbed her shift and pushed her away. The shift ripped from his hand, and she fell back in a tumble of petticoats, her breasts half-exposed where the laces fell loose of her bodice. John flew at Gibbard, a guttural roar rising from his throat. He lifted Gibbard, one hand grasping his waistcoat, the other crumbling its collar. The toady little man hung there, a frog on a gigging spear.

Mercy screamed, "John, no! For your sake...My father..."

John stared at her; Gibbard wriggled in his grasp, repeating over and over, "I will tell him, I will. And with a chained servant. A chained servant!" In the midst of the din, John stilled, closed his eyes, and, with a cool detachment, threw Gibbard away. The man landed with a breath-jangling thud.

Samuel looked from Gibbard to John, frozen in the moment. John looked only forward.

"I will tell him myself," he said, his words ensconced in fire. Then he tread, determined, toward the house.

Mercy struggled to rise, but Samuel prevented her. He looked away, fumbling at her breasts, attempting to lace the ribbon through her bodice eyelets. He missed some holes, creating a spider web at her chest.

Gibbard stumbled to his feet and hobbled after John.

"Get off me, Samuel. Hurry." Mercy brushed him aside, her practiced fingers finishing off the work, then took off in an uphill frenzy. She overtook Gibbard who lurched forward with uneven, panting steps, a torrent of sweat beading on his face.

Soon Samuel and Muddy outpaced Mercy. They chased after John as they often had, racing for fun along the riverbank. But this was not for fun, not a lark. The stakes were high, and Samuel feared what would come of it.

He looked back as he ran. Mercy followed close. Gibbard had stopped, his hand to his knee, bracing to gather his breath. Then Muddy barked with a fury, darted forward, and caught up to John's heels. The two turned the corner and disappeared behind the shelter-shed.

Samuel followed—to where tumult had turned to silence. Muddy lay flat at John's feet. Both of their chests heaved.

Father leaned against a hay rake, his shirtsleeves rolled to his elbows, his hat and coat draped on a fence post. "What, pray tell, is this?" He waited with the still, cool intent only his father could maintain.

John's breath expanded. Air rolled up through his chest and shoulders. He lifted his chin and spoke. "Mister Payne, sir, there has been an incident, ill-timed, and I am sorry." Now, he raised his right fist and held it at his chest as if holding in his heart. "But I would marry your daughter." He pounded his fist twice, and Mercy swung round the corner into her father's view.

The horror in Father's face hit Samuel like a chill wind. In the dripping swelter of the day, he awaited an ice storm.

"Daughter? I...what have you done?" Each word sheared away from Father's lips. "What have you done?"

John paled. "Sir, truly. Mercy is no dalliance." His fist still pounded, his left now clutched to his stomach. "She is my friend, my strength." He looked at Mercy who hurried to stand beside him. "My heart."

Mercy reached over to hold the hand John clenched to his stomach. "And I came to him willingly, Papa. Gladly. He is a true, good man."

"And a servant! Branded an indenture for years."

John moved to speak, but now Gibbard gasped onto the scene. Samuel felt his head would screw off, tracking the turmoil swirling around him.

"Fornication, for...ni, fornicating...I saw it." Gibbard bent, bracing his weight on his knees. He inhaled an erratic, fitful breath. "He be the devil...no halter, his leg...irons. The...the Magistrates will hear." He stopped, spent. Sweat dripped from him, a sweet sickness permeated the air, and his face bloomed red. Then it paled, white tinged with blue. He fell to his knees, collapsed on his side, and grasped his collar. Then he was still.

Samuel flung his head around, looking for answers on the faces—his sister's, his father's, his friend's. They looked back with stonewashed stillness, questing for answers, as well, in each other. Then Father bent down. He lowered his face to Gibbard, whose mouth gaped open, eyes blinking. The man inhaled, then exhaled. Two rattling gasps. Samuel stared at the man's breeches. A wet stain expanded from between his stocky legs. Then a rank, fecal odor replaced the sweet, sticky one.

Father's voice broke through the confusion. "He is dead."

The words lingered, oppressive as the blistering air.

⌒❈⌒

Mercy clung to her father. She begged him to lie. "We can say the horse threw him, that he came for help." But Father stared at her, a stranger shaking his head.

"They will question every piece." He looked into the stark, summer sky, then closed his eyes, beseeching, "God, guide me." His answer came from John.

"I will not lie. We cannot, Mercy."

"Why not?" She pushed her hair from her face and pleaded once more. Her voice cracked with the effort. "Papa? Please."

Father spoke to Samuel instead. "Son, go to Marshall Kimberly's house and retrieve him. He may be at the prison. Ask him to bring a cart. Tell him why."

Samuel's eyes narrowed. He had lost his hat in the race home; his hair glistened silver, sweat plastering it to his forehead. He raised his chin, sullen.

"No," he said.

Father lifted his hand, ready to slap, and John seized it, mid-air. "Sir, be easy on him. His loyalty is misplaced. This is my doing, and I take responsibility. I would not have your children hurt."

Mercy wanted to pummel John, beat him for his nauseous prudence. Her face trembled, tears threatened. But Samuel had defied their father, and, for love of him, she flung him a smile, acknowledging his courage. It fed his determination.

"Hit me if you must, Father, but I will not go."

John took a stern breath. "You will honor your father—and you as well, Mercy. My presence makes everything suspect. And I'll not run, leaving you and your father to spin a lie." Then he looked straight into her father's eyes. "I also will not be ashamed. Or sorry. Now, go Samuel. Do as your father asked."

Mercy's neck pulsed and her head ached. She felt lost in a blizzard, so cold. But John's hand warmed her shoulder. He wanted her eyes, but she could not look.

"We are not children, Mercy, nor should we act as such."

"You would rest your faith on...on them?" She swung her arm out to include her father, the Magistrates, all of New Haven.

John laughed and slid his fingers under her chin, lifting it. "No, but I will not run, not from you."

Her father stepped over Mister Gibbard's corpse and wrenched John's hand from her face. "I give you credit. You do show mettle. But understand this. For my daughter's sake, you will not have her. Never as an indenture. It will not be."

John's jaw worked. "I understand. But right now, we have other things to think about."

"In that, you are right. We should carry Mister Gibbard to the porch. It will look more seemly."

They lifted the body, Father at the shoulders and John at the knees, carried it with clumsy steps to the porch, and dropped it with a thump onto the plank decking. Father closed the man's eyes while John arranged his legs and arms, brushing off the duff accumulated on the waistcoat and breeches.

"Where is his hat?" Father scanned the ground, searching.

"At the river." Mercy heard the voice, thin and shallow, then realized it was hers.

John stretched his back and smiled at her, a near smile, his full lips marked in sorrow. He spoke to her father. "With your permission, sir. I would go below, to find my old master's horse and hat." He examined Mercy, head to toe. "Also to gather Mercy's cap and our shoes. And my halter and chains. I need them to enter the town."

For the first time since meeting John, her father seemed to show compassion. "He sees John," she thought, "as a man."

"I am sorry, boy," he said.

The distinction was clear, an acknowledged sympathy, perhaps, but still he addressed John as a servant, not using his name, not seeing a man, not marking him free. Nothing and everything had changed.

"I'll go to the river with you, John." She emphasized his name and did not wait for her father's response but slid past him, her shoulder turned away in a snub. Her elbow clipped him as she passed. The grass slicked beneath her feet as she rushed to the river, hazy in the low-lying sun.

Her name echoed out from behind. She blinked back the anger pooling in her eyes, but did not slow her pace.

"Mercy, wait." John's voice pleaded. It touched her heart, and she slowed for him to join her.

"If he were not my father—"

"Well, he is your father." He touched her forehead with the rough, worry-worn edge of his thumb and ran it down her cheek, then up again, wiping away the wetness lingering there. "How else can this thing play out, Mercy? I lifted him up, threw him." He dropped the implications at her feet.

"So, better fornication than murder?" she asked.

"A sight better." He touched the tear running down her cheek. She breathed him in, the deathly smell of Gibbard on his hands.

"Come help me gather our things," he said. "You can fetch them up while I find that toddling mare."

❧❀❧

John's search was an easy one. The mare had found a stand of watercress on the river's edge and ripped away at its succulence, oblivious to her previous turmoil. Gentling up to her, he grabbed the reins, led the reluctant pony to the boat, and tied her there. Mercy joined him, her head capped, holding Gibbard's hat.

"She will have the green shits soon enough," he said, running his hand along her distended stomach.

"Serves her right. Had she not bucked—"

"Had she not bucked, Gibbard would have stood above us in our glade. Samuel's warning saved that at least." He stared at her, holding her in his mind, her earnestness, her disheveled determination, and he swallowed down his fears. If this colony did not change, if all Cooper and Edward and Sylvester planned fell to nothing, he would lose her. Their only other chance was escape, a hanging offense for him, and then what for her? And how could he ask her to choose? Him over her father and Samuel?

"So," he said, making his voice ring lightly, "our shoes." He tweaked her nose and stepped to the boat.

The leg irons lay near the bow, stashed there for emergencies; the halter leaned against them. The mare balked when he hung them on her wool-lined saddle, so he calmed her, circling his arm around her neck and telling her of her master's demise. John sensed she was happy of it. "As am I," he whispered in her ear, "but keep it to yourself."

"What are you doing talking to a horse?" Mercy laughed, and it eased John's heart.

"Commiserating is all. Well, maybe celebrating." He nuzzled the horse, which snorted a fragrance wet and green. "We have some common experiences, you see."

He sat with Mercy on the boat's edge while they buckled their shoes. Then he tucked a single escaping curl into her cap and snugged it down on her head. With a quick tug on the ties, he kissed her cheek. She placed her hands on his. "No more sorrow, John. I cannot bare it."

All else was precise and efficient. They led the mare to the house and waited, wordless, until Samuel arrived with the marshal and a wagon.

Mister Payne helped Marshal Kimberly move Gibbard's body to the wagon bed. Then John slipped into his halter and iron shackles. It was only when the marshal attempted to tie his wrists to the wagon that his emotions flared, hard-forged.

"I'll not stumble in behind him," he said, "not like a broken man. I will walk at the front, unashamed."

The marshal looked to Payne for consent. Mercy took her father's arm and squeezed it. Her father nodded.

Before walking away, John gave Samuel one last chore. "Go to the marshland tomorrow, Samuel. Deliverance will be there. Return with him and pole the flatboat upstream. Have him care for it. I shan't be home soon." He then addressed the marshal. "Neck Bridge?"

"Neck Bridge," he confirmed, and with a flick of the reins, urged the ox forward. John took the lead.

As they left, he heard Mercy's voice, loud enough for him, but pointed to her father. "I am no child, Papa. I will speak truth at his trial. I will not abandon him."

John held her words to his heart.

⇜❀⇝

Marshal Kimberly peeled off John's halter and released his leg irons. Then he opened the cell room door, only a crack, to push him through. "Your cellmate's name is Taphanse. He speaks no English." The lock snapped shut, and John stared into blackness. From left to right, he scanned each corner of the room, tracing it from memory. From the foot square window on the left, streamed the hint of a dying day. It fell on toes, dark and callused, beating a silent rhythm. As he tracked the bared legs, his sight adjusted. A deerskin was draped at the man's hips. A fur cloak hung loose over his shoulder. The Indian raised his head, revealing a pox-pitted face.

He ran the crook of his elbow across his head, shaved clean on one side, and pulled back the ragged braid hanging long on the opposite. "I speak English. Sometimes," he said. "Who are you?"

The question fell heavy on John. Who was he? The musty odor of the place threw him into the past, to when he was first imprisoned here. He was not that boy, nor was he the one who walked out of New Haven thinking his freedom found. Who was he?

"John Frost," he said, and shrugged, then found the wall and slid down to wrap his arms around his knees.

"Taphanse, of the Quinnipiac."

A long oppressive silence ensued. How could this place be so warm and dank, while, even now, dusk carried its cool swirling breezes round East Rock? He trembled, overwhelmed, took a long breath, and reached up in a feint, wiping away tears as if dabbing at sweat. He would not succumb before this stoic force sitting next to him.

"Why you here?" Dark eyes stared out of the pitted face.

"Fornication."

"Forni...?"

"You know..." Anything John could use to explain the word was humiliating—as if fornication were not. So he gestured to his groin, then stared at his shadowy companion, refusing further mortification, daring him to laugh. But the man did not laugh; he cocked his head, processing, his nose wrinkled and lips turned down.

"You here for..." He gyrated his hips. "This with a woman?"

"Not my wife."

"Someone else's woman?"

"No, my woman." Out of his defiant declaration, came a truth. He took comfort in it.

"You people," Taphanse shook his head and chuckled, soft at first then full bellied. "You people crazy."

John snorted. "You may be right, but why are you here?"

"Murder."

"You murdered someone?" He tried to strip judgment from his tone, but it seeped through.

"I did not do it. I tell them who and take them to the body." The Indian lifted his hands in surrender. "Then I run away."

"Why? Why did you run if you're innocent?"

Taphanse sat straighter and stared into John's eyes, searching. "You know why. They talk good, then do what they want. Do you trust them?"

The man's words girdled him. He had pushed away the issue of trust, but now it shook him, encapsulating him with fear. So he told Taphanse about Gibbard, his hatred of him, how it had brought him here. The man listened—for a while.

"That man is dead, so now you decide to trust? Who?"

John rubbed the linen nubs of his shirt against his chest. He trusted Mercy, Samuel, Edward; but none of them would be his judge. And the deciders? They held ideas equal to Gibbard.

"I don't trust the Magistrates. They're akin to Gibbard, every one." A rat, previously content to linger on the far wall, gathered courage and sidled up, sniffing at John's shoe. He kicked at the rodent twice before it scurried into the background.

Taphanse clapped to scare it further away. "Yes, John Frost. Rats, not to trust. So, you know why I run."

He knew the answer for Taphanse. The man did not trust the Magistrates to judge him fairly. But what of him? Why didn't he run? Not from the fire and not from this thing with Mercy. The day's events bore down on him. His chest ached and his eyelids burned with exhaustion. The conversation died, each of them retreating into separate thoughts, separate emotions, and sleep.

A wheezing woke him, and a shaking at his shoulder. "You, John, you sick?"

He flung his arms up by reflex, then gripped them to his chest in a spasmodic cough. "It be so fetid and moldy in here. God, my chest does hurt."

"Humph." Taphanse's loose braid swung back with the motion of his head, the single movement a signal to John of the man's opinion of him. He was a pitiful case. The Indian reached into the wide leather pouch he had used for a headrest and, after some digging, produce a globe-shaped bag large enough for a man's hand. He held it to John's face. "Bear. Made from these." He grabbed his groin and smiled, revealing a wide gap in his bottom teeth.

John coughed again and pressed his fist to his ribcage. Taphanse placed his hand over it, his dark eyes a comfort in the shadowy cell.

"No matter. I will help you." He opened the pouch to John's face. A collision of competing odors accosted him, an astringent, minty, musky cacophony. John turned his head aside to evade the smells, while Taphanse held the bag close and dug deep into the contents. First his sun-darkened fingers, long and large knuckled, drew out two dark-red orbs encrusted with some crystalline substance that shimmered in the darkness. He held them out to John. "Suck," he said and popped them into John's mouth.

His first reaction was rejection, but a honey-sweet infusion burst on his tongue and slid deep into his throat. "Sweet," he wheezed, "but tart." He puckered, then swallowed, a difficult thing. With a second attempt, his throat opened, less resistant. "It does soothe," he said. "Thank you."

The Indian's eyes twinkled, and John wondered how eyes so dark, in a face so pocked, could twinkle. "Cherry, dried with honey," he explained. "Good for eeeeh..." He held his hand to his throat and mimicked the wheezing in John's lungs. "For cough, too."

John sucked on the cherry orbs and watched as the hand reached back into the sack. Taphanse exuded the same joyful exuberance as Samuel did when he unveiled a newfound turtle or water snake.

Out came a much smaller pouch. From it, Taphanse scooped a wad of grease, wafting out, resinous and astringent.

"What is that?" John held up both hands in retreat.

"Good for chest. Breathe it." He stuffed his fingers up to John's nose. John reeled from the stench, coughing, holding his hand to his mouth to keep from spitting out the drops of cherry.

"Devil's own! What is it?"

"Bear fat." He pointed to his pouch and smiled; his tongue slipped through the gap in his teeth. "Bee flower, pine needles. I grind them." His eyes narrowed, looking from the mass on his fingers to John's chest. His eyebrows rose.

Obediently, John reached down and lifted his shirt. The man rubbed the grease across John's chest in slow, circular motions. The warm pulsating movement sent tremors through his body, his eyes drifted shut, and his shoulders released their burden. He took in a deep breath and exhaled, his first full breath since lying with Mercy.

Taphanse pulled his shirt down and stepped back into the shadows. John floated in a piney haze and considered the will to trust. He curled into a ball, wrapped his arms to his knees, and added one more person to his list.

During the ensuing month, John learned Taphanse's version of the murder in Stamford town. There had been talk of a killing—of a man named Whitmore. Taphanse had told some men what he heard and they asked him to lead them to the place of the murder. Which he did. But fearful, he snuck away. Later they accused him of the murder, saying they found his clothing at the site. Taphanse assured John it was impossible, said he even had witnesses to support him.

Taphanse spoke of his life; of how smallpox had destroyed his village and killed his family, all except him and his father; of how another Quinnipiac tribe adopted them, thinking them charmed because they survived the epidemic.

Then John told his story, from his mother's death to the present, leaving out the traitorous parts. He waxed on about his home on East Rock and how he harvested the iron ore. Out of this, Taphanse shared the story of the rocks and how, long ago, twin giants used the rock ledges as stepping stones.

John reveled in Taphanse's stories. They kept his mind from a sullen truth. In the days since his imprisonment, no one had come. Edward was at sea. That he understood. Even Mister Cooper, of necessity, might maintain a distance to avoid suspicion. But with every noise, he would pull up into the square window, expecting to see Samuel and Muddy, or catch site of Mercy. The sounds were shams, branches dropping, flotsam carried on the wind. He justified their absence, figured their father prevented them from visiting. He hoped it was true. Still, he caved further into a cavern of abandonment.

Finally, on this day, he and Taphanse would both face trial.

The marshal led them to the meetinghouse door and guided them to the front of the hall. Left at the bar, its bannister separating them from the Magistrates, they waited. The shackles on his wrists clinked against the wooden rails. The eyes of the congregants burned at his back. He stared at the wall above the Magistrates' heads, his mind hollow and resigned, believing he was forgotten.

$$\sim\!\!\gg\!\!\text{❋}\!\!\ll\!\!\sim$$

John frightened Mercy. He looked broken and withdrawn and would not turn in her direction. She watched, hoping to give him a sign, to show him she was there for him. Father had controlled her every movement, and she had acquiesced, to soften his anger and to honor John's words. "He is your father," he had said, so she obeyed.

She sent Samuel to the prison once, to tell John she was sick, which was true. Her stomach churned of late. But Father prevented even Samuel and Muddy from going alone to New Haven.

Now she awaited a single sign, a raised hand, a smile, his eyes on hers. She sat straight in a forward pew next to her father and Samuel, expectant, even hopeful. John, though, stared forward with shoulders slouched.

The first trial was for an Indian accused of murder. Pits covered his face. A fur cape hung from his shoulder, and the skin of some animal draped his hips. The congregation murmured amongst themselves, a flutter of chinwagging that reached to the rafters. A man named Minor interpreted the Indian's words so that the proceedings plodded, convoluted and confusing. First came a flurry of guttural syllables unknown to her, followed by an explanation of their meaning, then the process repeated in reverse.

The Indian, Taphanse, according to Mister Minor's interpretation, was not guilty but ran away in fear. Clearly, Governor Leete disagreed and produced witnesses against him.

"He quaked and trembled at going with us to discover Whitmore's body," said one.

"He gave us the slip, he did. We found the body and a scarf and stocking. They belonged to the Indian."

Then they brought in an old woman, Anne Akerly, a dim-witted widow who said he was at the Whitmore's house. "He shook Mistress Whitmore. Said he looked for her friend, he so loved her friend." But, through Minor, the Indian objected, saying he was far away, making wampum with his father.

On and on it went. And Mercy did not care. She watched John, who absorbed every word. He touched the Indian's arm, encouraging him, like he mattered. But to her John gave nothing, not even a glance.

Mister Minor delivered the Indian's final defense. "I have often been among the Indians, sir, when mischief was done, and even those innocent would tremble in fear."

The verdict came, finally. The governor's evidence ran thin, so they ordered the Indian to produce the person he claimed was the real murderer and return within the month. When some parishioners protested, saying Taphanse would run away, Mister Minor translated the man's answer.

"By running away I say I am guilty, and you should hunt me and kill me." So he was granted his freedom until the next month's meeting.

Then John clasped the man's hands, chain to chain, and she heard the Indian speak to him clearly, not in his language, but English. "Good luck, friend. And remember, your people? They crazy."

❧

John lowered his head and contained a smirk, working to hide his secret knowledge from the crowd sitting behind him. Taphanse, that wily soul, ran free—no doubt gone for good. John leaned on the bar for support. His back ached, unaccustomed to standing so long. He expected to be called next, but he was not.

Mister Cooper complained of the theft of a horse. They took as much time with the horse as they had with Taphanse. John wished he could see without looking. See where they sat, every congregant, see how they reacted, how they looked at him. He ran through a litany of blame and anger, toward Mercy and Samuel and Mister Cooper. Mostly, though, he cursed the rotting flesh of Gibbard.

But as he picked away at the bits of skin hanging from the cuticle of his left thumb, the truth snuck in. He felt shamed, stripped of all dignity. He shrunk behind his wall.

A murmur from the crowd at his back stirred him and he chanced a glance. Mister Cooper was smiling. For a moment he thought it was meant for him. But no. His master directed it to the congregation, gloating at having won his complaint, and a horse.

Still other business intervened, this time to set aside a day for thanksgiving. John let his head fall back, close to rolling his eyes at Governor Leete but thought better of it. He widened his stride, and waited.

The governor's gravel-tinged voice barked out the pronouncement. "Good friends, send word proclaiming the twenty-third day of this month of October as one for thanksgiving. Use the day to fast and pray for guidance in the weighty business of joining with Connecticut Colony, a move desired by His Majesty and writ in the charter read in Boston."

The words wandered into John's ears, but clarity came more slowly. The King had granted the charter, this he knew. But now the signed copy was here, the decision immutable? A clamor rose in the room. Heads bent together in a whisper of rumors. The words came at him in disconnected spurts, some comprehensible, some garbled.

"Southhold sent Captain John Young to accept..."

"Reverend Davenport petitions..."

"...await Winthrop's return."

"...the colony falls away. Guilford, Stamford would go to Connecticut..."

John turned from one side to the other in search of Mister Cooper. He sat in his pew, looking ahead, while the man next to him bent forward, talking to him, his finger cutting the air. His master glanced John's way and smiled, then returned to the excitable man next to him and offered a conciliatory nod.

John took heart. This news, lost to him in prison, provided hope. Pieces of the colony were breaking away, and now the Magistrates must consider the charter. But a warning shiver rippled on his spine. Hope could not consume him, having made peace with despair. The bannister became his touchstone, the trial his reality.

Governor Leete clapped his hands three times and waited for the din to diminish, then continued in his rasping voice. "I beseech you, save your thoughts and take the day to offer thanks and bow to the grace of God. Now, we have other business." Leete cleared his throat and coughed. "John Frost, examined September last and committed to prison, appears before us."

Leete looked past John, sighting along his nose. "Mister Payne, you make a complaint against John Frost?"

Feet shuffled, the man stood.

"I do, Governor, a complaint coming, by happenstance, from the untimely death of Mister Gibbard at my home—an accident of health, mind you. No fault of my children or this man."

John considered those words, a sidelong effort to protect the greater scandal.

The governor responded, equally circumspect. "An unfortunate thing. And your complaint—that this man lured your children to the devil's ways, through gifts and enticements. That he did fornicate, unbeknownst to you, with your daughter. Of those charges, what say you?"

"Of that, good sir. I desire my children be held to their truth and beseech them speak for themselves."

∽✦∼

Samuel replayed John's reaction to the Connecticut Charter in his mind. From the shock whirling on John's face, he figured the information was new to him. Samuel felt part of this triumph and had wanted John to celebrate with him. He tried to sneak off to share the news when it came, but Father's nose had grown as clever as Muddy's at sniffing out any attempts to steal away. The man grated on him. Even now, his father's elbow ground into his rib—an annoyance. Samuel wrenched away and glared up at him.

"Stop," he said, then cowered under the menace of his father's glare.

Furrows of disappointment ran from the man's nose to his thin-lipped frown, and he whispered from closed teeth, "You are to make testimony! Stand and address the Magistrates. Now."

Samuel squirmed. He wanted a familiar place, the pew with his sister and Widow Sherwood or the balcony with John. His inward breath shook, and he held it. But he would not be a babe in this; he stood, head high, biting his lip to hold in a growing panic.

"Samuel Payne," Governor Leete pierced him with his pompous, long-nosed scrutiny. "Was it you who found these two out?"

"Found them out, sir?"

"Caught them in their love making. When?"

Samuel wished John would face him, counsel him, but he did not. "Sir...Muddy and I came upon them summer last. But John explained it...that they wished to be trothed, but could not because—"

"So, the accused pressed himself without consent of the father. And you supported him in this?"

Samuel dropped his head, ashamed, not for his part in the betrayal, but for betraying his friend. "I kept watch—to keep them from discovery. He is my friend, sir. And she is my sister. John showed me how men have needs, to release—"

"Showed you? How to pleasure yourself? A blasphemy!"

"No!" Samuel swayed, bewildered, humiliated by the tittering. "I misspoke, sir, please. He explained...helped me understand..." Could his shoulders slope further? "He is my friend..."

The governor shook his head. The gesture mocked his feelings, labeled his loyalties unconscionable; Samuel's lip quivered. He hated the man.

"And gifts, boy. Did he seduce you into duplicity?"

"Gifts, sir?" Samuel's mind reeled. What was this about? "He gave me Muddy...my mastiff. I...only Muddy..."

Samuel's father squeezed his hand and rose. "Governor, sir, the boy, distressed in these proceedings, misremembers. Frost delivered the pup, true, but at the request of Ferryman Brown. Mister Brown offered the gift as consolation for the death of the boy's mother."

The governor turned to the secretary whose quill quivered as he wrote. "Make note of that distinction." Then Leete picked up his own quill, checked on the paper before him, and told Samuel to sit. "Now, to the daughter. Mercy Payne may stand."

❧✿❧

At the mention of her name, Mercy rose and, mimicking her father's elongated stride, walked up the aisle to the bar. She had noted Samuel's frustrated timidity and determined to respond differently. She reached the bar and was standing by John before Governor Leete could settle his quill and look up from his list. "Mistress, you need not stand forward. Return to your father's side for testimony."

John's brown lashes flashed, and moisture lit the gold in his eyes. He offered a wan smile, licked his lips, and bit them down. The scent of lye and fear flew from him, and ripped at her soul. Mercy laid her hand on his folded fists. "I stay, sir."

The governor's words fell from a distance. "Obstinacy will not serve him or you, child."

She stretched taller. Her diminutive frame would not diminish her resolve. "I am no child, sir."

"Well, so you say. Answer then, mistress. Did this man take you as a woman?"

The condescension of the man—she closed her eyes to gain control before she spoke and squeezed John's hands. "He did not."

Governor Leete tucked his chin, confounded. "We have witness—"

"You mistake me, sir. He did not take me. I gave myself. Freely." The murmurs of the congregants billowed from the pews as they always did, a practiced prattle devouring newfound fodder. And she was the fodder.

"You admit to partnership in this deceit?"

"I do."

John stirred. He slipped one hand from under hers. "Mercy, no," he said, beseeching her. "With your absence these days, I came to terms."

A wave of nausea caught at her throat. He had abandoned hope for them. She wrestled to understand, but the governor interrupted her thoughts, his voice coarse and grating.

"Did he give you gifts, things as a servant not his to give? Did he ploy you with them?"

Mercy squinted at the hawk-faced man. "Small things, heartfelt. No thievery, if you imply such. Things made with his own hand, or mended, or found."

"To maneuver you to his desire. Thank you. You may return to your pew."

"No, you mistake me, sir—"

"I mistake you not, I assure you. Now go." The marshal took her by the shoulder to lead her off. But she clung to John, to her desire, until John pried her fingers from his arm.

"Go, Mercy."

He closed his eyes to her and turned away.

"There are procedures to follow."

John denied nothing; he admitted all. His hip hurt. He wanted to lash out, bare his teeth to the tongue-wagging crowd. Instead, he erected a shield wall and hid away behind it, distant and aloof, until, from far away, someone asked him if he would like to say any more. He climbed back over the wall, smiled at the man in front of him, and mustered one small rebellion.

"I would like Mercy, sir. Nothing more."

"Insolence!"

The congregants echoed the governor's refrain, and John withdrew once more, the mumbles receding like a wind-borne squall—until they asked Mister Payne the final question, the answer known to all. Would he consent to the marriage of his daughter to this man, Frost?

"No. Bind my daughter to an indenture, himself bound for years by irons within our town and a halter on his neck? Though failed in her dalliance, my only daughter demands more—a freeman, at least."

"A freeman?" John glanced at his shackles and laughed. "Seems he excludes me, Governor."

The Magistrates conferred, heads bent together, on occasion popping up like feeding sea fowl, until Governor Leete slid away from their floating raft to read the decision.

"By your confession, John Frost, you commit the offense of gifting as a servant and fornicating without consent of the parent. We condemn you to forty lashes laid on by Marshall Kimberly this market day next, and forty shillings as a fine."

John laughed again. Where was he to find forty shillings, except by selling himself to longer service or selling wares stolen from his master? He wished to be done with it, but it seems the governor would continue.

"To, Samuel Payne, as punishment for his collusion, a whipping inside his father's walls. And, for willful compliance in this wickedness, thus confirmed by her confession, to Mercy Payne we levy an allotment of lashes and fine equal to that of John Frost"

This last sentence, John barely absorbed. They condemned Mercy to flogging? Forty lashes? His heart wrenched at the words. He flung round, the chains at his legs tripping him off balance. He grabbed for the banister. His halter knocked against his chin and he pulled up, a garble of words falling from his mouth. "No! For what? Make it me! I will take them. Not her. Please."

His voice flew out across the pews, even as the marshal and his man fastened him at the elbows and held him back. He struggled against their arms, jerked to get to her, called her name. The meetinghouse erupted. He tried to find her, but Widow Sherwood's bulk intervened. The woman scuttled out of her pew and bobbed over to Midwife Potter.

He saw Mercy then and cried out, "It's wrong," slackened in the arms of his handlers, then pitched forward with his full weight to escape them. Their grip held, and they hefted his dead weight to standing.

Marshal Kimberly wrapped his arms around John's chest, clasping his forearms to prevent escape. "Stop, you fool," he said into John's ear. "You help nothing."

By then the widow and midwife had reached Mercy and her father. Samuel nosed into the middle of them, but Mister Payne pushed him away, took stock of the women's words, nodded, and hauled himself up, using the forward pew as support. He raised his voice above the tumult in the room. "Mister Leete, Governor. Sir! Pray let me speak, I...I would address the Magistrates."

The room quieted. John scanned the sea of congregants, confusion pulling him under.

Mercy's father spoke, his words a far off beacon. "Midwife Potter suggests a weakness be on my daughter which would prevent a corporeal punishment." Mister Payne wavered, unsure, and Widow Sherwood leaned in to counsel him. "These women would search her, to confirm it...the weakness...and if it is so, I pray you levy a fine in its stead."

"A weakness?" John asked the marshal. "What weakness?"

The women took Mercy by the elbows and whisked her toward the north-side door. She stood straight, her eyes on him as she passed. He locked with them. "I will be there," she said, "whipping or no." He did not hear her, but saw the words reaching out to him as Widow Sherwood hurried her away, just before Marshal Kimberly attempted to drag him out the same side door.

"Marshall, please," he said, heels dug into the floorboards, "tell them. Me instead. Eighty for me."

Mercy followed Widow Sherwood out the door and along the path leading to the prison. The widow's full-framed hips swayed in rhythm as she walked, her buttocks pausing and plopping with each step. No thought lived beyond the movement. She sniffed, and a burst of nausea overwhelmed her. Her mind writhed, thinking of the trial, and the betrayal. The words, hers and Samuel's, had been perverted to the governor's goal. She tracked the ground. The grey-green of her gown grew wetter and darker as it soaked up the rain-drenched earth.

Midwife Potter prattled on behind her. "It is for your good, child. A quick check may yield reason to free you from the rod."

Mercy sniffed again. She had no notion what Midwife Potter meant. Her head pounded as if in a vise, tightening turn-by-turn. Above, the sky darkened with clouds, and she wrapped her arms across her belly, an unconscious response.

Widow Sherwood opened the prison door. The uninhabited cell loomed dark before her. The watchman's bed, a stool, and a table lined the walls. A latch and lock donned the door to a second room, and she imagined John locked inside with that Indian, an accused murderer.

"He will not be there, child. They hold him off until we finish."

"What do you plan for me?" she asked, staring down at grease-ridden floorboards, worn smooth from table to bed to the cell room door.

"Fear not child. A simple test to see if your body prepares for the entry of a babe." Midwife Potter pulled loose the ties to Mercy's gown and began unpinning it.

Mercy's hands flew up to stop her. "What do you do?"

"Do not feign innocence, girl, you have known far more than this." Midwife Potter narrowed her brows. "We test your breasts and between your legs. If you prepare for a quickening, it saves you a beating. Now undress to your shift."

Mercy reached to undo the tie to her cap, a stall that proved unsuccessful.

The midwife stayed her hand. "The congregants await us, child. No more rebellion or you and that man shall suffer, and more so, your good father. That poor shamed man. Now, your gown."

Mercy slapped the woman's hand loose. She fumbled at the apron tie and let it fall to the floor, unpinned her gown, stepped from it, and unlaced her bodice. It slipped from her arms to the floor. Her woolen petticoat played stubborn with her fingers but soon fell to her feet. Left to her shift, she reached up to find comfort in the lace-trimmed neck, the rent Gibbard had made mended with a near-invisible stitch.

Widow Sherwood reached her plump hands around from behind and slid them under the shift. The hands screamed, icy against her body and Mercy pulled back. "Still yourself," the woman said. "I do this for you, and your father." Then she reached up and squeezed her breasts.

Mercy pressed her arms to her body, trapping the widow's hands. "Pray stop, you are hurting me."

"When last came your courses, dear one?" the widow asked.

Mercy's eyes flitted like a cornered deer. She grasped the widow's groping fingers and pried them loose. Midwife Potter stood before her, small but formidable, blocking escape.

"I...summer, before..." She remembered it, gathering the oak moss on the full of the moon, before Gibbard, before they took John.

"Good. So, you prepare for a child. Now, one thing more. Lay you down on the bed and spread out your legs."

"I will not!"

She pushed down on the widow's hands and turned for the door, but Midwife Potter stepped into her path. She placed a hand on Mercy's cheek and looked up into her eyes. The woman's breath smelled of apple and mint, and her hand soothed, though something deep told Mercy it should not. "Hush child. You are new to this and must trust of God. He has prepared you for a child, but the deed is not complete, or so we think. From this test, we will know. Have you felt a quickening, a stirring in your belly, to tell you He has chosen you for childbearing?"

"I...I do not understand you."

"A quickening. A rumbling in you. More than passing food. You would know."

"I do not think so, no."

"Good, now lie you down. I check for fullness at entry. A final clue."

It was a conjurer's voice, gentling her, a calming breeze after the accusations at the trial. So Mercy sat on the bed, leaned back on her elbows, and spread her legs. Midwife Potter reached up and touched her where only John had touched her before. She turned her face away. Where it had once been a spirit's touch, now it was the devil's. Her degradation, her humiliation was complete.

"She is not yet full, though nearing." The midwife looked at Widow Sherwood standing above her. They communed with one another through silent, pity-filled nods.

Mercy clothed herself, eyes to the latch and lock, but confusion dressed her mind. What next, for her and John, and Samuel?

Midwife Potter maneuvered her out the door, a soft touch to the small of her back. "Come girl. Governor Leete awaits our opinion before his final judgment, though I doubt it fairs well for that young man. A servant is not the husband your father seeks. And your condition requires a further decision, an ongoing communion twixt you and me."

Drumbeats marked the morning and fell against Mercy's heart. They called the inhabitants together for a day of thanksgiving, and John's flogging—fifty lashings, ten extra for her, with her father to pay both fines. She would stand by John at the whipping post and tend his wounds afterward. A soft length of flannel and a bundle of comfrey leaves swelled her apron pockets.

In the night a squall had blown in from the sea, sending autumn leaves whirling to the ground. An ice-hard frost followed. She lifted her cloak from the hook by the door and wrapped it round her before stepping into the morning chill. Her father and Midwife Potter greeted her at the bottom of the porch steps.

Father looked, not to her face, but her belly. "Good daughter, the midwife and I spoke this day past and determined a remedy to your condition."

A pounding rose in Mercy's chest, throwing her back to the examination during the trial. "The drums beat for thanksgiving, Papa. I must go."

"We know the reason you go, and you will not, nor will you join with that man again. He is a servant, condemned to fifteen years more, and I would protect you."

"He is good in his heart, Papa. Ill-treated and unlucky, but—"

"You will obey me, daughter, or I take you to trial. Do you understand me? By God's covenant—child to father. Obey!"

Mercy looked for support and saw Samuel and his mastiff, far distant, beyond the door-side garden. Their silent solidarity was her only protection.

Midwife Potter's spellbinding voice took hold. "Mercy, dear one, go to the garden and harvest the tansy left from the night's frost—a good bundle of it. Mister Payne, did you gather the juniper and deer berries? And the slippery elm bark, shred long and thin?"

Her father handed the woman a small package and whispered, "I pray God keep you, Midwife Potter, and I thank you."

A dark seed germinated in Mercy's mind. "You would end my fullness? Block the child which comes in me?"

"The time is not ripe for it, nor is the man one of my choosing." Her father's words rang cold and distant, and he turned his face away.

Midwife Potter wrapped her thin, big-knuckled hand around Mercy's waist. "Honor thy father, child. It be the law. Now, to the garden, and then we walk to the cart bridge where a fine stand of pennyroyal grows."

Alone inside the door-side garden, Mercy signaled to Samuel who came to stand outside the bramble fence. "You must help me, Samuel. I cannot be with John this day, nor any day further it seems." She bit her lip to gain control. "So tend him, I pray you, or find one who can." She took the felted cloth and comfrey from her pocket, reached across the fence, and placed it in Samuel's hand. "This will help him."

Muddy whined and nuzzled Samuel's leg. "Your dog knows us better than ourselves, Samuel." The distortion of tears played on her vision, and she reached to smooth her brother's silken hair. "Make you haste, now. The drum quickens, and you must not miss your chance."

Nate Green led John along the same path he had walked at his first flogging. Some things, though, were different. Nate would wield the rod this time, thus raising his stature with the marshal, and while John hoped Nate might take a lighter hand, there was no guarantee. Nate had assured him of his sympathy, for, in his words, he "still dips into Goody Flemming's well on occasion."

Different too was his awareness. Before he had none; now memory twisted inside him, playing on his courage. Before, he had expected no one to stand with him. This time he held out hope, an expectation that played him a fool. For, as he walked the gauntlet of gawkers, from prison to pole, he saw no one he trusted.

"Hey, Frost, been diddling with your doxie in the brush, have you?" An uproarious guffaw rolled through the crowd, accompanied by gestures, one after another, of wriggled devil's horns or fingers jammed between a circle of thumb and forefinger. Lewd mocking faces flew up to greet him then backed away, laughing.

The whipping pole appeared, same as before, facing the meetinghouse. He stumbled when he saw it, forgetful, his stride widening beyond his chain's measured length. The crowd responded, pointing and gyrating their hips. A woman jumped into his path and flung her skirt up. A man joined her, miming fornication. John closed his eyes, his anger boiling, then remembered the long ago kindness he had found amongst those faces. So he lifted his head and looked. A white curd hit his eye and slid down, a wet slime along his cheek, sour and astringent, likely clabbered milk past using. He knew the implication. He lifted his arm, only smearing it, then a tug on the rope binding his wrists urged him forward.

While Nate tied him to the pole, John scanned the crowd, looking for a face not mocking, not lewd, not hurling epitaphs. A few faces stood out, worn with pity, but none belonged to the ones he named friend.

"Seems your wench stayed home, John. Just as well. Would you have her suffer that?" Nate nodded to the crowd who bellowed a raucous cheer, then he positioned John's arms high on the pole. "Your whipping rod is longer, with more lines than before. And I must put on a show for Marshal Kimberly."

John tried a half-hearted laugh. "You cast your lot with the wrong colony, Nate. The King granted Connecticut its charter. He hates this place."

"And you talk sedition. A hanging offense. But I watch Meiggs. He plays the game from both sides, ready to bow to the one who holds the coin. He is my mentor." Nate pushed John's head into the pole. "Now, hush, and ready your body for the lash."

This time the rod fell hard, the sting sharper than before. And twenty lashes in, he felt his skin break open and a trickle of wet slide down his back. He looked for her, even then, to the far corners of the crowd circled round to see his pain. But she was not there. At the count of thirty, for the crowd relished the count, he grew numb and retreated into a walled corner of himself. His jaw worked, holding in his fury, and his loss.

Finally, the throng yelled, "Fifty!" His breath faltered. He waited for the crowd to part, for her to come forward to tend him. But he was alone, and her absence festered, painful as the rod.

Samuel's voice cut through the throng's dying jeers. "John, I'm sorry, I come late. Papa..." The boy glanced around, his ill-kept hair flying under his felted hat. "Mercy sent me—with these."

A rag and a weed. His focus blurred. Samuel held them up like absolution. But John would not give it. "Where is she?"

"She needed to be elsewhere. Let me—"

"Go," he whispered, his throat burning with the effort to speak.

A voice flew out from the meetinghouse behind him. "Samuel! Away from him. I demand it, now!"

"No...Papa...Mercy asked me."

A random body knocked John from behind. His resolve shattered. "Leave me!" he cried. But Samuel would not go, just stood there, until Mister Payne wrenched him back by the arm. Then John thought of Muddy and looked for him. Even Muddy was gone. He propped his head against the pole, no pillory this time, but same as before, he waited for the setting sun.

❦

Midwife Potter's house sat facing the delta where Mill River entered the sea. The little clapboard structure was two-storied like most houses in New Haven, but it was small, set on an angle, no more than a bed's length in width. The smell of the wharf, all salt and rotting fish and oysters, permeated the walls. Once inside, the heat of the place set Mercy to sweating. The fire lingered, still bursting to flame here and there, in the hearth.

"Warmed to the bone, you will be," the midwife said. "My thin body, shrinking with age, requires a heat beyond that of youth, I fear. Besides, the fire warms the water for your tea. Now, to work." Mercy stood in the middle of the tiny space, watching the woman. The midwife took a mortar from the hearth shelf and set to crushing the berries Father had given her. A quart crock set on the table where she worked. In it, she dumped the crushed berries. Then she stripped the leaves from the garden yarrow and added them to the crock.

The slippery elm bark lay in thin fibrous clumps on the table. These she gathered up and wound into a small ball as though forming yarn for knitting. Finally, she picked through the pennyroyal, choosing from it carefully, to what purpose Mercy could not guess. Each length was covered with fingernail-sized leaves and the occasional fine root hairs that took purchase along the riverbank. Mercy did not move.

"Your woolen cloak must bake you, child. Take it off and sit. The settle will do."

"I will stand, thank you. And would know what you plan for me."

"We provoke the monthlies. Call God's bounty into play and bring on the menses." The woman surveyed the table, and squinted up at Mercy, only the remnant of the fire providing light. "We beckon God to release you from this burden. And through His grace, you shall be freed." She reached into her apron pocket and pulled out a thumbnail sized morsel. "You must relax, child. Take this sweet treat. Candied violet soaked in honey and calming herbs, then dried in the sun. My own concoction."

She popped it into Mercy's mouth, and, in spite of her trepidations, the sweetness gladdened on her tongue, though her lips puckered from the heady herbal aftertaste.

Midwife Potter smiled. "Good, yes? Now, take this ladle and fill that crock with hot water—there in the kettle on the fire."

Mercy obeyed. It took three short walks from kettle to table to finish her task, by which time a weariness crept up through her shoulders, unsettling her mind. "I think I would sit for a moment, mistress."

Midwife Potter took Mercy's hands and brought them to her mouth. She kissed them. "Of course you must. I have but one more chore. Rest yourself now."

From the settle, Mercy watched as the woman took the ball of elm bark and submerged it in the steeping berry and tansy tea. When she pulled it out, the ball had turned to a gelatinous mass, easy to mold around a root she held. From a little distance, as though wandering through a far away field, Mercy wondered, "That root. Might it be pokeweed?"

"Pokeweed, indeed, child—a good eye. The base for the pessary which I will place inside you to bid the courses forward." The woman began wrapping the strings of pennyroyal around the slippery elm ball, pushing them deep into the mass until the whole thing looked like a flower—green and yellow and round—blooming on a crimson stem.

She walked to Mercy with a cup of liquid from the tea steeping in the crock. "Drink it down, child," she said, and took Mercy's fingers, wrapped them round the vessel's warmth, and led the cup to her mouth. Mercy swallowed; the tea hung bitter on her tongue, the taste as pungent and rancorous as the tansy and juniper smelled. Midwife Potter smiled down upon her and whispered from far away, "Drink again, empty it, then spread your legs and let God's remedy find you."

She remembered nothing after the stabbing pain of the pessary entering her. She might have fainted, or maybe she floated. She supposed she walked home. She remembered a hand at her elbow whispering calming words and the taste of sweet violet on her lips.

By morning, her bed was awash with the scent of blood and fever, and a mumbling echoed inside her—her voice, repeating a single name.

John's dreams sailed him out to sea, and he languish alone in the doldrums. Out of the waves, condemnations echoed, lewd and demeaning. He kicked out at them, an angry flailing, until he collapsed at the bottom of a boat, knees tucked, arms covering his ears, beaten. He struck out again, writhing against a touch, returning.

Mister Cooper draped John's shirt over his back, lifting him from a dream-weary languor, his knees propped against the whipping post. Cooper balanced John against him and cut him down. "Stay quiet now. I cannot risk others observing my sympathy."

"I'll not need your pity."

"Not pity, son."

John pulled away, staggered, his shirt falling to the ground. He caught it, dug deep to find his balance, and maneuvered it over his head. Mastering one step, then the next, he set his path east to the cart bridge, the ferry, the ironworks, the only place he knew to go. Cooper walked at a distance behind him; John could feel him there. "No one came, you know." The words blew out like a bellows, flaming his pain.

"Circumstances prevented it."

"A fine excuse, and a message." They walked in hobbled silence except for the clanking of the chains at his feet. "I would stay at the ironworks, sir. I have nowhere else."

"You will. And you will work as my servant there. You are still bound to me, a good thing."

"A good thing?" John said it not as a jab, nor defiance, but as a plea. His mind wavered low, between hatred and loss, numbed into grieving. He wanted a good thing.

"You are seeping through your shirt, John. You need tending."

"Nate Green performed his task well, but the harness blocked some of the blows. Don't worry, I will survive."

The ferry offered a moment of rest. Ferryman Brown proffered a cloak to block the cold. "A wind coming upriver and strong. The first of winter, early and circling from the northeast." The ferryman spoke with unwarranted brightness; the night was black, the waning moon long set. John offered no thanks for the cloak nor did he reply to the distracting conversation. Brown and Cooper whispered to each other, no doubt about his wretched state. He shifted, adjusting to the aching, and his leg irons jangled at his feet. He shrugged off the cloak, pulled the halter from his neck, loosed the chains from his ankles, and kicked his bondage aside. Then he threw the cloak over his huddled frame and set his back to the wind.

At the iron works, Cooper insisted on tending to his whipping, dabbing the wounds with witch hazel distilled in alcohol. He braced his hands on his knees with his back arched against the sting.

"A good ale might temper the pain. Or something harder?" Cooper asked, his hand on John's forearm, careful to avoid his wounds.

"Harder," John replied. "Much harder."

So by the time Cooper steered him toward a bed in the workmen's quarters, John's thoughts had darkened to a rum-soaked malaise. "Nothing here for me," he mumbled, "The devil take you all." His last memory of the day was Cooper's footsteps as he cobbled away along the wood-planked floor.

⌁❀⌁

"It had to be the sushi." Duncan says, helping Maggie to the couch. Maggie is just glad to be home—ensconced in the safety of her world. She curls into her baby block quilt. The energy she had stitched into it so long ago soothes her. But even nestled inside it, surrounded by the warmth of early spring, she shivers. A restless sleep grabs hold. Tentacles from the past pull her down, an escape from her crumbling gut.

The smell of pennyroyal takes over. They drag the boy away. He recedes into mist, retracting, as she does, into fetal repose. The heat from a fire burns. She pushes away from it, grabs her stomach, and wakes.

It takes a moment to reenter her surroundings—to return. She knows where she was; her body intuits it. The illness untethered her and dragged her through time. But here, now? So unfamiliar. She drifts. How long? Then sits, rocking. She needs the bathroom; so she stands, shaking. Duncan is there.

"Who's John?"

"John?"

"You were talking in your sleep. Mumbling the name over and over."

She looks at Duncan, confused, then it occurs to her. "My research. It's sneaking into my delirium I guess. I'll be all right."

"Like hell. You're scaring me."

"They say it takes time."

"I'll make that electrolyte drink."

"Oh God, how sick do you want me to be?"

She holds her stomach and shuffles to the bathroom—again. Not the most romantic illness, but definitely something she ate. She spent Saturday night at the hospital, her family hanging in the background. The lab work came back positive: E. coli and Shiga toxins. Her intestines battle the invaders and obliterate her will: to eat, think, focus, talk. All she can manage is sleep.

She struggles back to the couch and huddles under the quilt once more. Sleep slinks in, and she relishes it, the only place she is free of pain. How can you sleep and dream and ponder at the same time? But it happens. Her world closes into quiet. No motors rumble; no electronics hum. Only a dog barking somewhere breaks the solitude, accented by a repeated swoosh and whack. The whip, she thinks. They whip him, for making love, for giving gifts. She feels the air breaking as the woody straps fly past. She twists in her bedding until she sinks into a vacuum of darkness.

Talk pulls her up once more. Duncan is on the phone, telling everyone. He worries, imagines life without her. Always expecting the worst, she thinks. The phone calls drag her back to now. Friends check in. The health department drills her. It can't be the sushi. The incubation period was too short. Just ride it out.

"If I ever hear about an E. coli outbreak on the news, I'll have a lot more sympathy," she says.

Duncan hands her another drink, thick and unappealing. She gags, drinking it down. He needs something to do, and she needs something more palatable. "Hon, maybe some rice cereal and rice milk? Could you go to the store for me?"

He grabs the keys before she finishes her last sentence. "You sure you'll be okay without me? I'll come right back."

"I'll be fine," she says. The couch pulls her in. She must return to them,

to help them ride it out. She laughs. Is that the only answer—to ride it out? Then she pulls her knees to her chest, gripped by pain. The books have deserted her. Left to her own resources, she searched other records and her tenacity won out. She found them—found their futures, but only pieces, scribbles from the past.

She knows them, deeper than words or dates or research; they exist in her DNA; they are a soul truth to her. And now it makes sense, why the cord reaches in and binds with a knot so tight. It's Samuel, traced down through time from her great-grandmother; it is Samuel who pulls her back.

༄ ❀ ༄

Samuel stood over his sister, considering what to do next. It had been a full week since Mercy walked home with Midwife Potter and took to her bed. He slept at the hearthside that night, listening to her moaning John's name. Come morning he found her doubled in pain, a pool of blood staining her shift and bed sheets.

Little had changed. Mercy still lay fitful on her bed, not eating or drinking, except for the droplets of watered wine he squeezed from his bladder flask onto her cracked lips. The bleeding had slowed, but the fever continued. The fits were most worrisome. They arched her body and then pulled her down into a collapsed trembling. Over and over he bit down gut-retching thoughts—of Mama, and of Mercy, leaving him alone.

Father sent him for Midwife Potter. The man's fear spilled out of his hands in a repetitive wringing, incongruous to his stone-still body. The old woman came and babbled, "Grace has writ its truth on Mercy

long before this day. You must wait for God to reveal His aspect." His
father had bowed and thanked the woman. Samuel had walked from
the room.

He would not wait for a future seeded in doubt. He had bungled the
message from Mercy to John—should have used better words, should
have understood how much John's wounds stung. Hard as he tried,
John hardly listened and had stared at the felted wool and comfrey as
though it were vinegar. But now, perhaps, John would hear. It was all
Samuel knew to do, and he must do something.

⌢❀⌢

He found John at the ironworks. He sat with Edward near the
casting shed at the base of the furnace, a large tankard between them.
The tailrace ditch separated Samuel from them. Diverted water ran
past the idled wheels, through the ditch, and to the river. Muddy
smelled John before Samuel saw him. Anxious to reunite, the dog took
the width of the ditch with a single bound. Samuel followed, hesitant,
hands roaming from hip to thigh, teeth grinding on the words he
would say, the ones to make John hear.

John leaned back on his elbows, laughing aloud. He was bare except
for breeches and a linen shirt, the sleeves rolled above his elbows, his
halter tossed to the ground. Despite the patches of an autumn flight of
snow, sweat glistened on his forehead.

Muddy, joyful at seeing his friend, waggled up and straddled John.
With tongue, long and dripping, he licked John full on the face. John
laughed again.

His feigned, overloud guffaws burned at Samuel's throat and he clamped his jaw, crushing out every word he had practiced. "Cease, you devil-dog," he said and bopped Muddy on the backside. His dog stepped off John, cowering, and slunk in behind him.

John wiped his face with his sleeve. "A ripe greeting, that one."

Samuel stepped back and kneaded the nape of Muddy's neck in apology, then drew him close. "Stay," he whispered.

Edward's eyes narrowed, but he motioned to the cloak he sat upon. "Sit, Samuel, we welcome you. Do we not, John?"

John said nothing, only raised his eyebrows and shrugged his shoulder. Then he rubbed his back, a telling gesture. "So, Samuel, what of your whipping, the one ordered by the Magistrates? Was your father's rod as heavy as mine?"

"Father? No, not as hard. And I come not to talk of whippings, John." Nor, he thought, was it time to admit that his father gave him none, being so consumed with Mercy. "I'll not sit, Edward, but thank you," he said, trying for dignity.

John leaned back on both elbows, relaxed and easy. Did he not care? It disgusted Samuel. "We must talk, John. 'Tis of Mercy."

John's head lolled back. The haze of him and the lingering odor of rum gave witness to his condition.

"Ah, friend, I know plenty of Mercy. A drink perhaps? I concocted a fine mix of cider, beer, and rum. See here, I set these heated tongs in the tankard and the drink becomes a hot toddy. Quite the luxury you think? Fit for a freeman."

He lifted a cup with a fine bent handle and toasted him. "My handy work, this cup. Little be its worth." He reached forward, dipped a ladle into the tankard, and filled the cup. "I drink my toddy cooled. A servant's work is heat enough."

Edward grimaced. "Take his words lightly, Samuel. I found him tanked, a pity-filled imbibing." He turned his face to John. "Too free I think this noontime."

"Ah, yes, free. Free as I ever shall be. Free of all encumbrance—aside from my servitude, of course." He waved out his hand, taking in the ironworks. "But no grand bondage, given a well-met drink." He toasted Samuel. "Sit. Drink. Be free."

Samuel barely listened; each word turned to steam inside him. "I will not." He reached down and rubbed Muddy's muzzle. The dog leaned into him, and Samuel's foot shot out to keep from stumbling. He lowered his head to conceal the quick motion of his fingers whisking away tears bursting from his lids, then stretched tall. "You must listen, John. It is Mercy."

John rolled his eyes again. He shook his head back and forth. "I know, I know. The poor tempted jilt, drawn into a rebellious dalliance by a devil. Oh, and Edward? That devil be me, a mere servant, void of grace. Marked by Beelzebub himself. And her father, Samuel? Has he found a freeman better suited for a sullied maid?"

Samuel's fists tightened until the pressure burst out through his body. He leapt forward, led by hands now wide-open and circling John's neck. The rattle of tankard and tongs mingled with his angry cries. "She be dying, dying, damn you. The devil take you to hell."

John twisted beneath him, yet held his arms open, not fighting back. Samuel squeezed tighter and tighter. John opened his mouth, bewildered. Then he coughed, again and again, his devil eyes closed, wet seeping from their corners. His fist banged against the ground. He sagged, limp, beneath Samuel, lifeless but not dead. Samuel felt it; it was defeat, and he would not allow it.

"The devil take you," he screamed into his face.

And John opened his eyes and smiled. "Squeeze harder," he said. It was a rasping plea, and Samuel hated him for it. So he squeezed, raving, until someone jerked at his chest. He struggled against his assailant. Edward.

"Samuel, in God's name, stop!" Edward screamed.

Muddy growled a bared-toothed warning, punctuated by intermittent barks forewarning attack. Edward ignored the dog, pinned Samuel's chest, and ripped him away.

He flew into the air and landed in a patch of snow. Muddy moved to guard him, stood astride his chest, hair high and teeth bared, a snarl in his throat. Samuel scooted out and knelt beside him. Edward stood blocking him from John, who sat upright now, rubbing at his neck, the glaze of drink struck clean. He stared through Edward's legs at Samuel and brushed the strings of ash-brown hair from his face. "So...you have word of Mercy?"

Samuel blurted his message, the words forming finally, somewhere between anger and despair. "She has taken a fever, a delirium, John... Midwife Potter, she...I am sore afraid." His head dropped. He closed his eyes, swallowed, and tried to find his breath.

Edward's feet scraped against the ground as he stepped back from the confusion. Muddy followed, stalking Edward, a snarl still breaking through his dripping jowls.

The growling, the slush of water running in the race, and John's rasping cough punctured the air. Samuel pushed up to squatting and signaled Muddy to his side.

Edward looked from Samuel to John and shook his head. "John, I promised you once that if you acted the fool I would tell you. Well, today you act the fool."

John stared with sobered, bloodshot eyes. He rubbed his forehead, then swept his hands back to knead his neck.

"Take me to her," he said.

❧❀❧

John stood dumbstruck at the edge of Mercy's bed. A dull burning pulsed at the center of his forehead. The tankards he had consumed over the last week played havoc with his focus, laying down a fog between him and the apparition in front of him. He kneaded his eyes with his palms, then knelt and took her hand, icy, into his. It was white, bloodless as her face. Strands of hair lay wet and sticky on her cheeks, and, if this was her body, she did not reside there. He touched her forehead expecting the same ice cold as her hand, but heat accosted him. She burned.

John stood abruptly; his world swirled. A touch startled him and he jerked away. Samuel held up one hand, somewhere between protection and surrender.

"What do we do, John?"

"I...let me think." He closed his eyes, willing clarity.

"You do nothing," came a low, slow voice, perfunctory, her father's. "You have done enough. Go."

John opened his eyes to grief. The man stood as white as his daughter, struggling against tears. A chill ran the length of John's back; his decision was visceral. "No...I mean yes. Sir, I go—but to get help. I know a man, a healer, Taphanse—"

"That Indian? His healing is of the devil. We await God's word."

"His medicine helped me. He knows things...about plants—"

"No!" Her father's arm punched at the air, then fell slack at his side.

Mercy's moan broke the silence. Muddy whined, went to her, and settled his chin on her chest. The action stirred the room.

Samuel closed the space between him and his father and reached out to the man's arm. "You would have her die then?"

Mister Payne stared at Mercy's ghost-white form and whispered, "No."

John nodded. "Take care of her then. I will return with Taphanse."

He had the slimmest notion whether the man would come, or where to find him.

⤳❉⤫

The porch step seemed to sway beneath John's feet. He shook his head, an attempt to loosen the vise grip on his mind and muster the details of his imprisonment. The expanse of land leading to West Rock goaded him. What had Taphanse told him in their cell? Where was he at the time of the murder? Not in Stamford or at the cabin where the murder took place, but at his father's home between here and Stamford, on the banks of a wide river. The man's father would know where he hides.

If he headed northwest, some Indian would know Taphanse's father and how to find him or Taphanse himself. But how far was it to that river? A day, maybe? Still, if he ran...could he run? He was weakened by prison and his stupid self-pity, and to go into a wild country, one he did not know? He worked to collect his resources, body and spirit, to the task, an effort broken by the clank of the door's latch and the squeal of its ill-fitting hinges.

"I come with you, John." Samuel's feet paced the porch planking; Muddy trotted over and sat, head cocked, facing John.

"No, you do not." He removed his halter, set it on the step, and check his belt. It held his ax, knife, a cap, and pouch. And in the pouch, nothing more than fish hooks and found treasures. He would need provisions, something to eat. He tugged at his coat, nerves rising. "Someone must stay with her. Someone I trust." He looked into the boy's pale eyes, begging his understanding. "It's dangerous. I cannot risk it."

"I am a man, fourteen years. Not a burden." Samuel plucked himself up. It reminded John of his own fourteenth year, of the fire, his oblivion, and its lesson. He had no time for it.

"Then be no burden now, Samuel. Be a help."

They stood in silent impasse. Then Samuel stepped from the porch, slid a satchel from his shoulder, and held it out to John. "Take this then, dried cod and cider."

John dropped the strap across his chest and clasped the boy by his neck, drawing him in. "Thank you. Care for her, yes?"

Samuel stepped back. "I will. But take Muddy, John. If it is dangerous, he will be a useful companion."

The emotion of the day, dammed up inside John, ripped loose, frayed by the boy's courage. He blinked, shook his head in assent, and broke into a run. Behind him, Samuel gave the command, "Muddy. Follow." And the dog streaked past, his brindled body primed for a hunt.

⌣❀⌣

In the beginning, John set a swift pace; a foolish pace, he discovered. His lungs burned from the start, the cost of his cell time. Like heated iron, each breath seared deep beneath his breastbone, bending his will until, while his feet pushed forward over the uneven terrain, his mind waged war with his body. Ravaged by scorched lungs, his body argued with him to stop, to fall to his knees and surrender. His mind demanded commitment, urged him to stride forward, to overcome. He slowed, found a gait that placated his body's fatigue and his mind's resolve. He let it pulse in him; he let go.

Once he achieved his rhythm, Muddy clung to it, trotting along side. They were long past West Rock, trudging a worn path through a dense forest of red and yellow and brown. The colors blurred into a swirl. He tripped on the uneven ground, his vision deceiving him, muddling the distance from his feet to the leaf mulch unfolding before of him. As a blessing, his mind cleared, focused and calm, all effort centered on his feet, his lungs, and his purpose.

Time emptied into itself. Elevation rose and descended, calling distinct muscles to alert. Vegetation marked its presence through subtle changes in the fragrances he breathed. Finally, at the crest of a hill, on an exposed rock ridge extending out from the shaded foothold of chestnuts and maples, he stopped, hands to his knees, the pain in his chest suddenly vivid. Below, winding through a swampland valley was the fork of two rivers. The mother river ran wide and deep. A second one, smaller, fell into it. The sun sank low beyond them. Near to dusk, he thought, and Taphanse had told him of one river, not two.

Futility and the chance of losing Mercy gnawed at him. His stomach complained, telling him he needed food. He pulled out the chunk of dried fish from his satchel, ripped off a piece, and held it down to

Muddy. The dog bit hold and, with a little maneuvering, swallowed it whole.

"Whoa, boy. Slow down." John jerked off a piece of the cod, stuffed it into his mouth, and chewed, eyes closed. Then he pulled out the leather flask and squeezed a stream of cider into his mouth. With a cupped hand, he offered some to Muddy. The dog lapped it up eagerly and licked John's emptied hand clean. Samuel was right; the dog was a comfort. He jostled Muddy's head. "So, boy, where to now?"

The valley unfurled less than a hundred feet beneath them, no great rise. And in it, he found hope. A footpath, twice the width of the one he followed, headed north along the secondary river. And near it, far distant, clung the hint of an Indian encampment. He adjusted the satchel to his body, settled his shoulders to his task, and trotted off.

They followed a river neither deep nor wide, so unlike the one it emptied into. Instead, it flew, rocky and fast. Except for a single detour to the river's shore, where he lapped up the splashing water, Muddy paced close to John's side. The day fell to shadow, lost in the hardwood forest and the dying sun. A wolf cried out, announcing night, and the day birds' songs turned dark.

Unannounced, the path opened onto a circle of domed wigwams shaped from bent branches and hide. John froze and Muddy stood sentry before him, hackles raised, a deep-seated growl emanating from his chest. All around them, women and children stood at fires built to the close of day. Two dogs flew forward to challenge Muddy but backed away in submission. From the midst of this confusing new world, walked a man reminding John of Taphanse. His dress and manner were the same. He was draped in fur, his hair clipped short on the sides and pulled into a loose tail at the back of his neck. In his hand, he hefted a spear the length of a man. Muddy inched forward.

"No, Muddy. Here," John ordered and clapped his thigh. The dog looked back but refused to move. "Now," John said. He clapped his thigh again. With one defiant growl, the dog returned to John's side and sat, rigid and alert.

With a touch to the ax in his belt for assurance, John raised both hands in surrender, his one purpose expressed in a single word. "Taphanse," he said. "I come to see Taphanse."

The Indian turned his head to the side, suspicious and silent. Immediately, the complication of John's mission assaulted him. Taphanse was in hiding. He had avoided punishment for a crime he did not commit, and John might be in pursuit.

"My name is Frost—John Frost, Taphanse's friend." He mimed everything. Beat at his chest, hugged himself. The Indian's mouth quivered, curled on one side, a version of a laugh.

"Frost? John Frost." He stretched the spear along the path leading through the village. "Come with me," he said in a liquid, fluent English. "I will take you."

❧

By the time they reached the single wigwam set on a ridge north of the village, the day had surrendered to darkness. The Indian who brought him never said his name, never talked, except to order Muddy to stay clear. When he drew open the wigwam's hide-covered opening, John glimpsed a shimmer of light. Then the covering fell, abandoning him to sky-blackened silence.

John waited. His impatience grew unbearable in the brief moment he stood there. His legs trembled from nerves and fear and exhaustion. He shook each one, then worked them up and down, as though still running the trail, pushing toward his desire to help Mercy.

In little time, his guide reappeared. "He waits inside," he said and, spear in hand, jogged back toward the village.

John lifted the hide covering and entered, bidding Muddy take guard outside. Taphanse sat facing the opening. A small warming fire burned in front of him, its smoke curling up through a hole at the center of the rounded ceiling. The ceiling hung low, and John hunched as he entered, more so because, from the arching branches forming the framework of the dwelling, hung a variety of plants, bunched and bound, in varying stages of dryness. John's eyes watered, and he pinched his nose to avoid the pungency of the close space.

"John Frost, my friend, you visit. Sit." Taphanse gestured to the fire before him.

As John lowered his body cross-legged onto the cool dirt floor, his calves screamed, then his thighs. His right eye closed, a grimace to ease his resistant muscles. He took breath and stared past the fire to the shadows dancing on Taphanse's pocked face. The Indian smiled, closemouthed, his dark eyes examining John. His tongue snuck out from the gap in his bottom teeth. "In your trial they said you will hang outside New Haven country. This is not New Haven. So, you have trouble?"

"I come for help, Taphanse. My...someone is sick. With fever and delirium. You helped me when I was sick, so I thought...She is far worse, but..." John waved his arm out to the plants hanging head down above him. "Maybe one of these? You know these things."

He had said what he came to say, had dropped his need at Taphanse's feet. Now he yielded to exhaustion. Slumped, he squeezed his lids with his palms until a breath heaved up and out, making way for despair. But nothing came, only a sliver, a fester of hope.

"This woman, the one from your trial?"

John lifted his brows, shook his head.

"She bleeds?"

How could he know that?

"She burns." The Indian placed his hands on his belly, holding John with empathetic eyes. "They take the child."

"The child?" Confusion fluttered and then settled, trembling at his lips; it turned to understanding. It hollowed him, and his chest caved under the truth of it. His forehead pulsed and he pressed two fingers to his brow to hold back the pain. And the words oozed out, like penance for a sin. "They think me unworthy."

"And I think them crazy." Taphanse said it like truth, then stood to rummage in the darkened recesses, humming a low, four-note tone over and over. He stooped, taking a circular route on the edge of the wigwam, reaching at random to gather clusters of leaves from his larder.

John, bereft of patience, interrupted his song. "You can help her then? You will come?"

The man stopped, a step from him, and looked down. "I help. Not come."

"But—"

"You hang here. I hang there." While clasping a small bulging sack, he pointed his finger at John's face. "You know this, John Frost. And what I give her is important, yes? But who gives her this healing and why?" His fist clutched the bag to his heart. "That matters more." He stretched out his arm, offering John the sack.

John recognized it, identical to the one Taphanse had at the prison, a scrotum sack, holding Mercy's cure. He took it and braced his thigh, willing his legs to lift him up.

Taphanse pushed him down. "You will go with the rising sun. Now you rest and learn how to make her well. The dark is too dangerous. Devils out there. Like the devil they find in you." He laughed at his joke, a rumbling chuckle.

Its humor eluded John, fearing it true. And, if true, how could he be her healer? He held her remedy, but his heart huddled rueful and unsure.

"Muddy, the dog? Can he sleep here with me?"

Taphanse gave his assent, and John crawled to the opening and lifted the skin barrier. "Come, boy," he said. The dog nosed cautiously into the room. John ran his hand along Muddy's back as assurance, for the dog or himself was unclear. Then he lowered his aching body and curled to the fire. Muddy settled near, his musky breath rippling against John's face. Wrapping his arm around the dog's chest, John sunk into the animal's warmth and the exhaustion of the day.

Samuel hauled the milk bucket through the shelter-shed gate.

"I am a poor excuse for a milker," he mumbled, looking at the half-full bucket. The milch cow produced less and less as winter grew near, but Mercy's hands could squeeze the last drop from her teats. His efforts left much behind, and the cow would dry up if he continued his poor performance. Still, his mind focused more on John and Mercy than any dried-up cow. He had waited until the setting moon extinguished any prospect of John's return; his hope hung on this morning.

Father discounted any expectation of John's success, talking of God's will and His hand. But Samuel recognized his father's gloaming. It matched the cynical faith he clung to in the years after Mama and the river.

Widow Sherwood often swept the mood away with tarts and corn biscuits. Even this morning her bounty had quenched their meager appetites. But his father soon dismissed her. Then he ordered Samuel to milk the cow and watch after Mercy, returning to his old habit, wandering the river's edge.

Samuel sat the bucket on the table and went to Mercy's bed near the hearth. Beaded droplets hung on her forehead. He washed them away with a rag kept near, then stretched up, lost to what he would do next. The door hinges squealed, their usual scraping annoyance, and he looked up, expecting his father.

But it was John. He stood sweat-ridden at the entrance, though the morning fell cool and breezy. "John," he said, his chest rising. "Did you find him? Can he help?"

John stared past him. Muddy pushed around John's lax arm, whined a greeting, and sat at Samuel's feet. His tail dusted the floor, anticipating a hail reception. Samuel reached out and patted the dog's head, then signaled him down.

John swallowed, eyes clouded. "What of Mercy?" he said.

"The same," Samuel offered, and John nodded, a twitch edging at his lips. His breath, hard from exertion, slowed, and he reached into the satchel strung across his chest, retrieved a pouch, and held it out.

"Her cure, Samuel." He opened the gathered top of the bag, unleashing a flurry of odors, both sweet and savory. They battled the tang of sweat and exertion haunting John.

Samuel held up his hands, refusing to take the offering. "No, John, not me. What of the Indian, of you?"

John's lips thinned and his eyes pleaded. "I have held onto Taphanse's words, Samuel. Repeated them over and over through the night—the whole way here—and at a pace. I am tired. I need you to listen. Hard." He stared into the bag, and as with a poem pulled from memory, recited, "Three things. The leaves lying loose are for nourishment, and to heal her...her insides. Seep two large pinches in a cup of hot water for her to drink at dawn, noon, and dusk. Do you understand?" Samuel nodded. "And the folded leaf holds a powder to soak in a pint of cider. Two spoons delivered after the tea, just before bed, for pain and so she rests." He paused; Samuel bit at his lower lip. John took it as assent and continued. "The last is important. The two roots. You grind them—do not scrape away the mold. It is necessary. Mix it with enough honey to bind and give her a spoonful four times a day, with food...to kill what ravages her." John reached out and squeezed Samuel's arm. "Three things, can you say them?"

Samuel held out his thumb, then his two fingers, repeating the words as near as he remembered. As he spoke, John's face relaxed; he released Samuel's arm and let his head fall back with a breath. Samuel looked down, his palm open, an unwilling witness to fragility.

John slipped the bag into Samuel's open hand then knelt beside the bed. Muddy came to nestle his head on Mercy's stomach, and John reached over to scratch his ear.

"You have a good dog, Samuel. Thank you for his loan." Then he stood, using his thighs for leverage. "Your father?" he asked.

Samuel dropped his head to one side. "He mourns."

"And blames me?"

Samuel blinked, and John nodded. "Rightly, I think. One thing Samuel, Taphanse says that what you give is not so urgent as who gives it."

Samuel's mind twisted to the comment but thought he understood. "He meant it should be you, John. Did he not? Someone who loves her." John's hands flew up; they shook away the words.

"Not love, Samuel. Please, not now. She needs someone constant, someone who can be here. And I cannot. Not with your father, my station, not...I must go. Winter comes and Cooper would have me at the iron works."

The words rang with finality. To Samuel's ears, a severing. And he fought against it, clinging to the connection he feared he was losing. "But I will keep my ears open, John. I will come when I hear things."

"Your job is here, Samuel, taking care of her. Remember—three things. I trust you to this...and will check when I can." He laid the emptied satchel by the hearth and walked to the door, then paused, not looking back. "And, Samuel? Tell your father. I am sorry."

❧❀☙

Spring glistens. The rains sprinkle dew on the grass, and it reflects the sun's delight. Maggie pulls weeds. They are everywhere. Grass mounds up absurdly around her. Succulent miner's lettuce soaks into her jeans. She should rejoice, relish the youthful fertility, the renewal; instead, she curses it, confounded by the back-bending labor it foretells. How is it possible? How, in one landscape, could glory and despair overlap, melding into one emotion, vibrating like spring itself.

Her sunflowers stand two feet tall. Ever hopeful she weeds around them, coaxing them to grow strong. But she notices already the sign of goldfinches; they ravage the leaves every year, their favorite snack. "I don't know why I keep trying to grow them," she says. "Between the gophers and the birds—" She shakes her head.

The lush glory of spring brings work. First comes the pruning. She begins with the withering roses, nipping them off just above a node of five-leaflet growth. Without trimming, the rose turns its energy to the rose hip. To maintain an ongoing bloom, Maggie prunes, and the bees accompany her with a lively allegro. The bees, working with a vibrating fury, are so numerous that her granddaughter once asked, a touch of concern in her offhanded comment, "Do the bees ever sting you, Grandma?"

She had assured her they did not. "They are busy harvesting, and I'm pruning out what's dead. They know I'm helping them. I cut, the plant blooms, and they have more pollen and nectar to gather. I'm their friend." The child's youthful nod said she understood.

Next Maggie pushes the wheel barrel to where she will uproot some old plants and make way for others more suited to summer's glare. The pansies are spent, so she begins with them. Then she eyes the poppies, vibrant orange masses dotting the yard. Not their time yet, but by summer, up they'll come, carroty roots and all. She'll shake the seeds around the yard in anticipation of the future.

Unbidden, an uneasy fluttering sets in at her diaphragm; her breathing tightens. This feeling isn't the easy one her garden usually offers. The pruning and pulling hurts as it never has. The thought of loss and rebirth grips her; it refuses to let go.

She stretches, lets her shoulders roll. The bumblebees have claimed the

Lydia, her favorite rose. Her ears hone in, distinguishing their hum from the higher, more frenetic frequency of the honeybees. A dove coos, four extended rhythmic notes. She listens to the symphony, time's opus. There is rhythm to life, to any life, she thinks—to her life, to her children's lives, to her grandchildren's, even to lives now past. Life beckons. She walks to the vegetable garden, enclosed, top to bottom, protection against aggressors, and she opens the gate.

Some plants require support. She stakes her early tomatoes, anticipating the weight of the harvest to come, and considers New Haven. When searching a family, you can't just focus on immediate ancestors without considering the impact of an uncle, a sister, a friend, or a neighbor on a life. She expanded her search, looking at other names in the records but has found nothing yet. The nerves skittering inside tell her she is missing something; she is running short on time.

The acridity of tomato plants, the power of now, takes hold. She pushes the redwood stake deep into the soil and carefully wraps the stems with twine. The vibration of a hummingbird rouses her. Returned from his winter hiatus, he swoops in and hovers outside the garden gate. His mate dips down; they have returned to revive their familiar role— messenger—taking up the banner of the books now sitting in quiet repose on her library shelf. It is a passing of the guard.

"I hear you, you little flits," Maggie says. "So. Where do I turn next?" She looks around; they are suddenly invisible, but not gone. Her gaze lifts into the branches of the just leafing maple, but they hide, elusive, a sign. "So I should look deeper? Further afield?" Her bones ache, especially her left knee. She stretches, tightens her thigh. What do they call that muscle? She should remember its name from her college kinesiology class, but Latin gobbledygook was never her forte. "Beyond

even New Haven, you say? Okay then, I'll call some historical societies—maybe in Hartford or Boston." She hates making phone calls, but—

"Who are you talking to?" Duncan's resonant voice booms. He stands at the door, dishtowel in hand, a chivalrous dishwasher in the midst of morning chores.

"I'm talking to myself."

"Hum, to yourself you say? Sometimes I think you commune with ghosts. Come and visit me." He waves the towel out to her and then flings it across his shoulder.

Again, he grounds her. The world still glistens; it will all work out.

"Okay," she says. "How about I make a smoothie? Then I have some phone calls to make."

PART VII

1663-1664 (and the present)

If any child or Children, above sixteen years old, and of competent understanding, shall curse or smite their natural father, or mother, each such Child shall be put to death.

Code of New Haven

The winter proved dark and interminable. Northeasterly storms blew in their misery without relief. Ice floated, knife-edged, down East River, precluding safe travel. Yet in the frozen waste, John healed. Isolated from New Haven, and from Mercy, surrounded by the raucous, easygoing ironworkers, people he more and more easily called friends, he healed—from rejection, from guilt, and from a bowel-deep need. He vowed to move on.

"Nothing like the hammer, the bellows, and a searing heat to harden a man," Smithy Mac would say. He and Marty Jenkins, the other apprentice, called him The Mac, but only out of the man's hearing. He was short statured, but his body burst from his shirt and his arms bulged impressively as he worked. He spoke in platitudes. Certain phrases, he repeated liberally, like the one about "the hammer, bellows, and searing heat," and when he ushered one forth, John and Marty would grin at each other and mouth the rest in unison, "...and through creation, ye clean yer soul."

John doubted his soul was cleansed, but turning pig iron to product staved off the melancholy. It pounded away at a molten impotency and loss. Samuel came twice over the winter, once to tell him that Mercy had revived and walked on her own, and once to bring information coaxed from Widow Sherwood and sweetened by her oatcakes. He devoured what Samuel brought, both oatcakes and news.

Connecticut had appealed to New Haven, asking them to conform to the charter negotiated by Winthrop with the King. The plea fell on stubborn ears. Reverend Davenport harangued Governor Leete, spewing his contrary opinions. He stood like a stone gatekeeper, rejecting any change, and, meanwhile, continued to connive with and hide the regicides.

The widow, Samuel told him, felt sure the Magistrates conjured a plan to put off a vote, thus evading the merger and a conflict with the King. "People hold their opinions to their breasts," Samuel had told him, "unsure which side their neighbors take."

John laughed at the comment. "Here," he said, "away from one church and one opinion, tolerance holds sway."

To this, Samuel rolled his eyes and mumbled as he left, something about John listening to his own words and mustering his own thimble of courage. John heard it for what it was—a scathing appraisal of his reticence regarding Mercy. And it stung. He knew Samuel wanted more from him. But more was not possible, so he tossed the comment away.

John combed through these thoughts, holding tight to the tongs. He maneuvered the end of an iron bar, glowing red-orange, onto the anvil and drove the hammer down to flatten the end of what would be a wrought iron hook. It was one of twenty he made that day. He took pride in his hammer work, each piece pounded into wrought iron beauty.

He moved the flattened end to the anvil's hardie hole and drove a punch into the heated iron, piercing the end to accommodate a nail for hanging. From behind him a voice bellowed out his name. "John Frost. A man could wring you out like a sea sponge!" Its familiarity, after his fitful winter, warmed him deeper than the heated room.

He had missed Edward's hearty laugh. But he knew what came next. So when his friend bounded toward him, John instinctively held out the arm holding his hammer to prevent being kicked, pushed, or slapped in Edward's usual exuberance. Edward halted, arms up, his head cocked in wary appraisal. "Whoa, friend. Relax. Just visiting from the sea. A long time gone for such a greeting."

John lowered his hammer. "No harm intended. Just cautious of being battered. Your way as I recall."

"My character be impugned," Edward mocked. "But are you free? Or can you be? I'm here for the better of three days."

John heated the other end of the evolving hook. "The Mac—I apprentice with him—he might agree to a day. But let me finish here. I can stop for a time." He pounded out the bend and finessed a point for the hook, then lowered the finished piece into a bucket of water, relishing the final sizzle.

"You have a skill there," Edward said, nodding to the hooks laid out evenly on a nearby bench.

John ordered his tools and lifted his char-marked apron from over his head. "I like the work. I pound out my devils here. Though old Gibbard might have disagreed."

"Gibbard." Edward brought his hands together in prayer, eyes to the ceiling. "Your own devil he was...good and gone."

John hustled his friend outside before Marty or the boy at the bellows heard the blasphemy. "The winter has not softened you I see." John elbowed Edward, who stepped back in feigned shock.

"And you worried that I might abuse you!"

They held each other at arms' length and then hugged, the joke bringing them back to the constancy of their friendship. "Come, Edward. I know a sunny spot by the water race. A chance to talk."

The whoosh of the finery's waterwheel pulsed behind where they sat. They played at small talk, shared smoked eel from the coffers of The Cockerel, and gnawed on strips of sugarcane from Barbados.

"I have more here—a gift for Mercy. She is well, I hope. And the boy, Samuel, does he still spy for you?"

Mention of their names silenced John. He focused on the healing ripple of water rolling down the race and took in the sky

"Well?" Edward nudged John, a hard elbow to his ribs.

"Stop!"

"So I hit something tender. What is it?"

"Nothing. She heals. And Samuel brings word on occasion. He says Davenport puts off a response until Governor Winthrop returns from England."

"I heard. A game of fox and hen. Spoke with a Boston man who thinks New Haven doomed. Most of her plantation towns offered allegiance to the King's Connecticut charter. Quietly, of course."

"I tire of it, Edward. But Mister Cooper says wait. That I'll soon have my freedom. Promises to dismiss my sentence once Connecticut rules. Whenever that day comes." John shrugged. Such talk conjured the dank recesses of prison, but worse. Where his old prison cell walled him in, a match to his shackled despair, here, where hope-filled breezes blew, his indenture tormented and teased.

"The Magistrates will bend in time, John. Cooper knows the way of it. But more to the point, why this silence around Mercy? Have you seen her?"

John stuck his hand into the race. The bracing water settled him. It sputtered out, diverted by his fingers, and swelled in an eddy around his wrist. The cold worked deep, numbing his hand, and he lifted it out, shook it, and dried it against his breeches.

"I've seen her."

"How often?"

"Three time over, since bringing Taphanse's cure. Twice she lingered in sickness and delusion. The other time..."

"The other?"

John shrunk from the question, asked with such calm. He turned from Edward's waiting, raised brows. It seemed everyone confronted him with this galling patience. It smacked of solicitude, as though he needed cosseting or cajoling.

"I saw her from a distance, with Muddy. He smelled me and came near, but she called him back."

"And you, with the courage to jump twenty feet into the ocean, lost your nerve?"

John seethed at the thickheaded prodding. "We are separated, Edward. By winter, the trial...her trials. By her father, my station, or lack of one it seems..." His anger coalesced, and he heaved it into his friend's sun-browned face, his pitying eyes. "And by New Haven's damnable saints. The devil take them—all of them." He raised his eyes to the sun and watched as it slid behind a cloud and wrapped them in shadow. "A chasm falls twixt she and me."

"Then stow away on The Cockerel. The weather favored us coming and barring any change, the ship leaves four days from this. She docks in Boston, not for long though. We sail to the Caribbean—salt, you know. Anyway, Boston has no use for New Haven, and you have a skill to trade. For silence. With a name change, you're free."

"Not free, Edward. A fugitive, with a hanging if I'm found."

"But not likely. You know I speak true."

The nearness of spring filled the silence between them with gurgling water and returning wrens. John dipped a single finger into the race, lifted it, then settled it once more, and again, an uneven repetition.

Edward blew out his disgust. "So, if your silence is an answer, then go to her. Face her. Face something."

John glanced at Edward, who shook his head and then offered a smile. "Well, you are a fearful bad seaman. Still, I will talk to Captain Sylvester. If New Haven, or Mercy, or her father, or you prove stubborn—and it will likely be you—Boston awaits."

⇁❋⇀

Samuel found Mercy in the door-side garden. She tore at the tansy plants growing out from the fence. She ripped them up with a fury. Patches of snow still lingered in the shadows, and a chill wind belied the approaching spring, but they did not deter Mercy from her purpose. She grasped the short, feathered spikes by their necks, wrenched them from the ground, and tossed them over the fence into a growing pile. Her pace was not languid. It was frenetic.

"Hysteria," Samuel thought, and memories of his mother shivered on his spine.

The gate to the garden stood open, so he walked inside. Mercy stooped to her task, wearing a shift and single mud-ridden petticoat. Her back heaved with her effort. She raked her hair back with the crook of her elbow, and using both hands, yanked more of the just protruding shoots from the ground, dirt-ridden roots and all. Their pungency, like turpentine, closed in on Samuel. He took three quick strides, stopped behind her, and touched her shoulder.

She whirled, still clutching the plants. Tears painted muddy trails along her cheeks. His eyes roamed the reaches of her, looking for the wild woman of his memories. But she was not there. What he saw was Mercy, whole but hurt. He smiled his sympathy, relieved by the mingled grief and determination on her face.

"I want it gone, brother. All of it." Her face contorted in an effort to hold back her pain. He pulled her to him, as she had always done for him, and let her sorrow break into his breast.

"He came, Mercy. While Papa was gone. He begged me keep watch." She nodded, affirming what he suspected. She knew.

"I was weak, Samuel, and ashamed."

He smoothed her shoulders. They had talked enough for now. "I will help you," he said, and took the crumbled tansy from her hand.

Mercy lived—distracted by spring gardening and the increasing gift of sun. Over time she grew strong, busied by the plentitude of eggs and milk and birthings squeezed from the world by summer's touch. She pretended to shut away the rest, but it was a sham. Samuel spoke to her of the comings and goings of New Haven. Edward had sailed in with spring's early thaw and left again for the Caribbean. Father courted but would take no action because of her. And John lurked, spying from a foolish distance.

The furthest she could move was the garden, wiped clean of tinctures and teas. She ventured as far as the shelter-shed to assist their sow as the sturdy creature pushed out one piglet after another, a host of spotted miracles. And sometimes, when the loneliness seeped in, she walked to East River and scanned its empty shores, seeking relief. But her legs grew heavy and a rock-hard stubbornness settled in her feet with any thought of venturing beyond—to the bridges Samuel crossed, to the reaches of East Rock's memories, or to New Haven and its inhabitants' sorrowed stares. Ultimately, Father lost patience, so on this day, he insisted, and he dragged her across Neck Bridge, to the town, the marketplace, and the gawkers.

The green bustled with news of The Cockerel's arrival. After languishing at sea in a series of late summer doldrums, it had sailed into New Haven harbor carrying its cargo of salt from the Caribbean. When ships anchored, loaded with salt from the island mines, trade grew brisk. The shipping merchants accepted neither wampum nor trade for the costly commodity, only silver.

Mercy's father had come to purchase just enough salt to cure the hams after his next slaughter. It took the last of his silver coin. He strolled the aisles with his purchase of salt nestled in his cart next to the hams he had brought for other trade. Widow Sherwood walked beside him, and Mercy walked behind. Rather, her body walked; her spirit followed, dragging her mind and her energy in its listless wake. She returned to the world unwilling and disheartened, betrayed by the midwife, her father, and John. But she recovered and would proceed, broken and emptied.

Samuel flew ahead, to flirt with the girls come to morning market. Even the Gibbard girls, freed of their father, danced up to him with smitten grins. He unfurled his hat before them, flicked away his white-gold hair, and won them with a wink.

Widow Sherwood bumped Papa with her ample bum and gestured toward Samuel and his admirers. "Your son flatters them. I too have succumbed to his winsomeness. His energy is infectious. Watch them flock to him."

"I will speak with him," Father said, and continued, oblivious to the widow's cloying comment. "No more trials or unwanted complications shall arise in this family."

The widow glanced back at Mercy, pity on her fleshy face. "Now my dear William, he only banters with them. He is an ethical boy, I assure you. And you, Mercy..." She reached back and placed a pudgy hand on Mercy's own. "You are moving forward, with God to guide you. Perhaps a new man?"

"I need no man, nor do I think one would want me." Mercy pulled her hand away, but the woman's attention extended to someone behind her. Mercy swung round to discover her interest and the reason for her comment.

Nate Green, dressed most fine, in green overcoat and brown breeches, doffed his felt cap to her and nodded to her father and the widow. "Beg your pardon, sir, mistress. Has the day found you well?"

He pretended to a lofty station, one of no use to Mercy. She swung her head involuntarily from side to side; her body rejecting him before her mind could. Her words flew off her tongue with an embittered wonder. "Nate Green, of all people. You would whip a man and come for chatter?"

Nate's eyes darted from face to face, concocting an excuse. "Pray understand, I hoped to gain favor with the marshal and performed my duties as required. I doled out punishment as outlined by the court and took no pleasure in it."

Her father stepped forward and held out his hand. Mercy wanted to slap it down, but she had no strength. "My daughter still mends from the year's troubles, Mister Green. Give her time to recover."

Mercy recoiled. "Recover from what? My wantonness?"

Nate Green bowed. "You are not so wanton to me, mistress. I look to the future."

"I am sure you do." Mercy hastened her pace, circling away from him, but the signal she sent bounced off his dull head.

He quickened his steps, now walking backward to include her father and the widow as he spoke. "Have you heard the latest news from England?"

Widow Sherwood perked. "We have not, tell us!"

"Nothing. Ha! But Stamford, Guilford, and Southold are siding with Connecticut, signing loyalties, even sending representatives to Hartford. They say they have a right to choose their governance. Of course, our Magistrates follow the reverend."

Mercy widened her stride, and Nate Green tripped over his feet in an effort to follow, his babble louder still. "They say they won't sign the charter while the plantations rebel. A snub to the King."

Mercy swung past a cart pulled by a woman peddling honey. She glanced back to see if Nate followed, but he had given up and returned to Widow Sherwood's side. "Myself," he was saying, "I watch from a distance, checking the direction of the wind."

Mercy cringed. She had heard enough of politics and predictions; she yearned for certitude—and peace. A haze of sorrow blurred her eyes. She lifted them to a cloud-free sky and blinked to clear her vision.

With Muddy at his heels, Samuel jumped from the ferry and headed to the ironworks—with a plan. He could, with a few chosen words, set a thorn in John's heel and drive him into action. His friend annoyed him more with each passing day. It was October, and autumn's frost would soon turn to winter, and still John refused to see Mercy. A coward, Samuel thought. Oh, John saw her. Snuck around like an orphaned wolf pup hoping to snatch a crumb. But he would not face her.

John judged himself unworthy; he had told Samuel as much whenever he visited the iron works pretending to share information. The news he brought was always the same—a knuckleheaded standoff between New Haven and Connecticut. "And Mercy and John are as stubborn as they. Pig-headed, both of them." Muddy perked his ears, halted, and cocked his head toward his master. He barked once in answer.

Samuel, long ago, acknowledged his dog's understanding of English, and Samuel was equally accomplished in dog-speak. So he continued his rant as he walked through the rain of musk-scented autumn leaves. "They act the same as the colonies, no difference—needing each other but resisting all the same." Muddy whined his response. "But watch. I will up-end John. I have a plan."

Muddy showed no interest. Instead, he dropped his nose to the ground and tracked; a long, high-pitched whimper followed in his wake. Samuel let him run, knowing he smelled John. He trailed the dog below the blast furnace and forge buildings, over the new cart bridge spanning the races, and down to the river flowing from the holding pond. Muddy skirted the smithy's workshop and skidded around behind it. Samuel followed.

John and Edward leaned against the sun-drenched shop wall, arms crossed, looking down at Muddy whose wagging tail sent a cloud of dust billowing in the breeze. Both heads turned to acknowledge Samuel, and Edward waved him over.

When he last saw Edward, he was pummeling John, nearly choking him to death. Edward had pulled them apart, disgusted, so his welcome greeting was a relief. He smiled and scurried nearer.

"Good day, friend," Edward said. "John tells me you still prove a worthy spy. Do you bring news?"

"The response of Connecticut to New Haven's last letter."

John's broad chest swelled, and he blew out a breath of disgust. But Samuel's planned deception required a goodly conversation before its reveal, so he ignored John and continued. "Remember? Their letter said they refuse to treat with Connecticut until all our towns return to New Haven rule."

"Ah," Edward nodded. "And?"

"Connecticut ignored them! And appointed their own constable to Stamford." Samuel waited, thinking the two might see the significance. To his mind it was great. "They showed our Magistrates who really governs. Don't you see? Our cause is nearly won!"

Samuel believed fervently in the cause. He fluttered with excitement, ready to participate at every level. But John and Edward were not impressed. They shrugged as one, shaking their heads.

John kicked at the ground where a shadow crawled, a cloud sliding across the sun. "A clever gambit. And the reverend will prod for another letter repeating their grievances and buying more time"

Edward stepped out to where the sun lingered and pantomimed a swordsman's feint and jab. "A wearisome war of words. But Bray Rossiter over in Guilford readies for a real fight."

John moved to the sun as well. "I thought him a physician and a freeman."

"True enough, but one not happy with a narrow religion. He stockpiles arms and ammunition, and horses. Says he would rally those siding with Connecticut into a revolt against New Haven."

Samuel perked to Edward's words. This might be for him. "I would join him. Hurry what we know must come. In Guilford, you say?"

John reached out and bopped him with the heel of his hand. Samuel stumbled off balance. "What was that for?" he scowled.

"For speaking foolish, Samuel. I will not have you more involved than you are."

"You are not my master!" The words ripped loose from his lips, and he regretted them. They would hurt John, and he needed other words to cut, not those.

John's summer-bronzed face flushed. He licked his lips. "No, I am not your master. Instead, I have one all my own," he snorted. "Still, I would not have you hurt. For your father and Mercy's sake. They care for you, and you should be mindful of them."

Samuel saw his moment unfolding. "I know you watch her. I see you hiding by the river bank."

Edward looked at John, questioning. "You stalk her? Still? I thought you done with that."

John lifted his hands in submission. "Less and less. And not in misery. I have accepted my fate. But sometimes—this plodding through life. I yearn for more."

Edward rolled his head to the shadowed sky. "Christ be, John. You are like a flounder filched from the sea. You put off leaving, but wallow in the muck of living. My offer holds. If you tire of waiting—of plodding, as you call it—The Cockerel will carry you away."

Now, Samuel made his move. "May as well. Nate Green courts Mercy of late. Follows her everywhere. I think she considers it." He watched John's slow turn, the held breath, the narrowed eyes. Samuel smirked, holding the smile from his lips.

"The one who did this!" His thumb flew up over his shoulder, pointing to his back. "She would dally with him?" He paced away, then back. "How?"

"Well, he says he overlooks her...shame, I guess. I think he—"

"Shame? What shame? You fool! He uses her."

Edward placed his hand on John's shoulder. "You say it yourself, John. You need to move on. Stop this—" John flung the hand away.

"You stop. I...I must return to my work. My hammer calls me. Nate Green be damned."

They watched John sulk away, his fists and his stride betraying his feelings. It pained Samuel, but he reveled in the planted seed. He lied, of course, but he watered the tale with truth. Nate Green was trying to court Mercy, though he had no chance of winning her.

Edward stood by, regarding him with a thin-lipped smile. "You play a dangerous game with my friend."

"What do you mean?"

"I mean that if John be jealous enough, you think he might act against his fears."

Samuel blinked. "Nate Green does come round."

"But I know Mercy, too, Samuel. She rejects Nate. Am I right?"

Samuel sighed. "Well, John may call me a fool, but he and Mercy are their own kind of foolish."

Edward laughed. "True, but are you acting in their interests or yours?" He wrestled Samuel's cap and smashing it over his eyes. "Anyway, the ruse might work. But we best let it fester a bit. You and old Muddy need to be going."

So Samuel called to his dog, and they ran home through autumn's russet splendor. Samuel's mind swirled, filled with pride over his plan for John, now set in motion. Meanwhile, another idea formed—to join with that Guilford man, Bray Rossiter, in rebellion.

～❋～

After a series of early November storms, December drifted into New Haven mild-mannered and languorous. The weather lulled the ironworkers to a quiet repose. They worked hard through the shortening days and then fell into their beds with the low-hanging sun. At night, the single men's quarters rang with quiet conversation punctuated by raucous laughter. A few stayed up drinking.

John had joined them often, numbing a loss he could not extricate. Until Mister Cooper drew him aside, chastising him. He questioned whether either John's behavior or his appearance deserved his trust or an apprenticeship. Cooper's words, and the warmth of the man's hand on his back, sobered John.

Afterward, he took to sleeping on a pallet in the blacksmith shop, as he did on this night. The forge fire still smoldered, warming the room and his body while he rested, exhausted by the day's work. As it often did, his mind traveled to the issue of Mercy Payne and Nate Green. He hardened, imagining them together, a fist-tightening but unwarranted jealousy.

Mercy was out of reach, and Nate had whipped him of necessity, trying to find favor in an unpredictable world. Nate's prospects were slim, riding on the politics of unpredictable men. He only tried for an easier life. Except for John's extended servitude, was he so different? He laughed, propped his hands under his head, and stared into darkness.

A rumble of hooves outside the blacksmith's shop invaded the silence—not one horse, but many, beckoning, "Awaken! Come forth!"

John sprung up, covers flying. He grappled with his breeches, jumping from foot to foot, half-tucking in his hunting shirt and buttoning his flies. He stuffed his knife in his belt, grabbed his ax, and ran, barefooted, onto the road. Confusion abounded.

Men on horseback wielded sundry weapons and gestured with them, gathering the workmen who stumbled from the barracks. Meanwhile, the workers, despairing for their lives, brandished what meager weapons they possessed and held them out uneasily. John feared a bloody ending. But one horseman swung his mount in a circle, pumping his musket and yelling, "Calm, calm! We are Guilford men. We come with word."

Geordie Garrison spoke for the men gathered round him. "Then lower your weapons and talk. No reason to frighten us so."

"Weapons down men," the leader said. "My apologies. Bray Rosseter, of Guilford. Your servant, sir. We ourselves are riled up. New Haven denies our King-given freedom to choose Connecticut rule. We come to warn you."

"And what has that to do with us?" Geordie's wispy grey hair swirled in a gust of wind. He pushed it back from his face, his bushy brows furrowing. John balanced on one foot then the other on the frozen ground, waiting for a response.

Rossiter stood high in his stirrups, framed by a gibbous moon sailing through whiffs of fast-moving clouds. He preached convincingly to the men crowded round him. "New Haven's Magistrates see only their way; they deny any other. But Connecticut offers trial by jury, a chance for a freeman's status. And the King ordains it!" He pulled a wad of papers from his waistcoat and held them high in the moonlit sky. "I have oaths of allegiance here. Connecticut will pass an act to honor them. Freedom for allegiance."

John stepped forward. "A piece of paper, and no act behind it. What makes you think our Magistrates will honor it?"

"They likely will not. But the tide shifts. The more who side with Connecticut, the better." He peeled off a single paper and threw it down to John. "Take it. And if the rest of you sign, so much the better. Now, to New Haven."

Geordie laughed, a single incredulous, "Ha!" then continued, shaking his head, "You would ride into the devil's cauldron?"

"We would. A boy traveled clear to Guilford promising to help us. He awaits us at the ferry."

John swallowed, stunned. He knew only one boy involved in subterfuge. He seized Rosseter's rein, pulling down and sidestepping the horse's hooves. "The boy? Is it Samuel? Samuel Payne?"

"The same. You know him?"

"I do. And he's but a boy. You put him in danger."

"He made his call," Rossiter answered, and wheeled his horse away with a single kick to its haunches. "Come on, men. We treat with New Haven itself."

John's mind reeled. Samuel—no older than he when he burned Gibbard's house. Good would not come of it. He whirled around, nearly falling over Mac and Marty, come to protect the blacksmith's shop. Mac laid his massive hands on John's arms, steadying him. "Go," he said. "Watch after the boy. But get ye some shoes on first."

John ran. He ran into the shop, tucked the petition under his pallet, and slipped into stockings and shoes. Then he ran after the horsemen, following them from the ironworks toward the river. He trailed far behind the horses, maybe ten, spreading out in an erratic, fever-induced gallop.

The mass coalesced at the ferry, horses circling and bumping at one another. A random shot rang out. He smelled the burn of the pistol's fire, he was so near. And then he heard Samuel.

"Muddy!" The cry pierced through the crisp, unforgiving air.

Then another voice. "Get that devil away from me."

A horse screamed and reared. It came down and reared again. Then a second cry, "Muddy!" John saw Samuel then. The boy raced forward, his hat falling off in his panic. He fell, laid out flat over a moonlit lump of brindle brown.

The horse reared once more, and another scream, disembodied, broke through the melee, John's own. "Away, damn you, away!" He reached them in five paces, leapt over the bodies, and stood astride them, his hands outstretched. As though he summoned them, three shots rang out from far off, inside the palisade walls. He thanked God and New Haven as never before. Then, timed to his breath, came distant shouts and the welcome beat of a drum.

He tried to lend reason and calm to his voice, but it came out hoarse and grasping. "They sound the warning. The militia gathers. Go! Now! I will tend the damage." A chasm stretched between his words and his fear for the jumbled bodies at his feet.

He needed to check them, to see if they fared well—or not—but he waited, protecting their bodies. There was no movement except the uneasy stir of horses' hooves and the mumble of a man saying over and over, "The dog ran in front of my horse, an accident I tell you..."

John tried again. "Move! Now! I must see to my friends."

Rossiter surveyed the scene, eyes darting from John to his men, and brought order. "Enough, for now, boys. We have yet to reach Guilford. Best save the devil's cauldron for another day."

The stench of lathered horses receded, carrying with it the frenzy and folly of the ruined night. John spent no time watching them leave. He dropped to Samuel's side, his hands gentle on the boy's back. "Samuel? Can you hear me? Talk if you can."

"John. Muddy bleeds, bad. I...have I killed him?" He turned his face so John saw the tears tracing through his mud-scuffed cheeks, lips pursed to hold back his fear.

"First you, Samuel. Can you come off him so I can check?"

"The horse only nicked my shoulder. A bruise, I think." He rolled onto his back, pushed up with his left hand, and knelt by Muddy's limp frame. "The gunshot, John. He was protecting me." Samuel implored him to act.

John ran a careful hand along Muddy's back legs and haunches, reaching beneath, checking for blood. He probed for protruding bones and stopped at the dog's chest to feel for breath and heartbeat, then offered a hope-filled smile. "He breaths and his heart beats strong."

"But he bleeds, John. Somewhere." Samuel presented the blood on his right hand as proof.

"I will find it," he said, an assurance hard to muster, and continued his inspection. He inched his fingers along the dog's right shoulder. Muddy whined, imploring and nearly inaudible.

"Hush, fellow, hush," John whispered. A hand-long slice, hidden by matted hair and blood, ran along the width of Muddy's shoulder. "A glancing blow, I think," he said, more to himself than Samuel, "otherwise his shoulder would be crumbled. We need to get him home for tending."

But how? His canoe lay in winter storage at the ironworks. Besides, a nighttime paddle would be too dangerous. The banked ferry stood ready for their use, a dangerous crossing, and then what? At over two hundredweight, Muddy was too heavy to carry for long, and the jostling might injure him more. Then he remembered the pull sledge used to transfer cargo, the one Ferryman Brown kept near. "Stay by your dog, Samuel. Comfort him. I'll get the sledge from the boathouse."

"I think it locked, John."

"With a lock I gifted to Brown. I can open it and explain to him later."

꤮꧁❀꧂꤮

Samuel walked beside the sledge, steadying it, while John gripped the hand pulls and strained to slide it along. He and Samuel held to a silent dirge. The frozen ground crackled under the wooden runners. The moon winked through the race of clouds and scattered a glitter of stars across the icy ground. John leaned into the straps, pulling harder, speeding his pace. An accumulating shelf of clouds erased the moon now falling into the west.

The weight of darkness and silence and effort pressed down on John until, finally, he spoke, attempting a light-hearted assurance. "It will be well, Samuel. Just steady the sledge."

"I did this, John. I—"

Out of the shadows stepped the figure of a man. John reached for his knife.

"Papa?" Samuel's voice, small and unsure repeated, "Papa."

"Samuel? God be praised. When the guns sounded, when they raised the warning... I looked for you." He held his son by the shoulders and Samuel wince. "You are hurt! How?" Then he turned to John. "You? It was you? You drew him into danger? He is a boy...only a boy."

John lowered his head. The man was right. He had lured Samuel in, to espionage, sedition, to the mind of a rebel. "I am sorry, sir. But—"

"It was not John, Papa. It was me. Only me. And Muddy be the victim." Samuel's single sob broke the darkness, answered by a rising wind. "John saved us."

"Sir," John said. The wind served warning; they must act quickly. "If you could help me? We best get Muddy home—and Samuel— before the weather breaks. They both need care."

A brief silence ensued. "Please, Papa?" Samuel pleaded.

The shadowy figure wiped tears from his son's eyes, then held the boy's head in his hands. "We talk later," he said, then slipped in next to John, grasping one handle of the sledge. "Together?"

"Together," John nodded, and the runners skidded over the ground, an easier burden in a night now lost to the moon.

They followed the worn ruts ribboning out in front of them, and John explained, not the spying and Samuel's part in it, but Samuel's desire to help Rossiter, to side with Connecticut and the indentures out of friendship with him. He used the word "misplaced," but it rang false. The boy acted from conviction, but his age and his methods had collided, creating disaster. John understood.

They soon reached the Payne's house where fast-moving smoke threaded in curls from the chimney. John took a last chance to provide cushion for the boy. "Be gentle with him, sir. Muddy be his punishment."

"Perhaps, but he frightened us and put himself in danger."

"Some lessons come out of the consequences themselves, sir."

"And you would know this?"

"I would know. Twice over."

John lifted Muddy as gently as his weight would allow and carried him to the house. Samuel ran ahead and opened the door. Hearing the familiar high-pitched squeal of the hinges, Muddy lifted his head and whined. "Hush, boy. You are home," John whispered and stepped over the threshold into Mercy's soft blue eyes. He froze, and Samuel pushed past him, shedding his coat as he came.

"Samuel," she said, "what happened? Are you safe?"

"Not me, Mercy, not now. But Muddy—make a bed by the hearth. Hurry, please. He hurts. We—"

Samuel's father intervened. "Sit, son. You are injured and in a muddle. Leave us to help your dog." With a firm-handed caress, he led Samuel to a wooden settle near the fire. "Here, where you can watch."

The weight of Muddy bent John nearly to his knees. "I would put Muddy down if I could. The dog be a burden."

Mercy gathered an old coverlet and plumped it into a bed at the hearth. John lowered the dog so his wound lay free and groaned in relief. Muddy looked at him with wet, distant eyes, and John reached behind the dog's ear and scratched. "You will heal, boy."

Mercy's skirts drift along his back. His whole body vibrated with her nearness. Then she knelt beside him, her arm touching his. She fingered the edges of Muddy's gash, pushing back the fur. "The wound needs cleaning," she said. "Water warms on the hearth. I'll fetch the witch hazel and a rag." She rose, not touching, but near.

"And a needle and thread. It will need sewing." His voice had fallen to a whisper, so as to not to frighten Samuel—and because she had stolen his speech. He took out his knife and began shaving Muddy's crusted fur from the cut.

They worked together wordlessly, attune to each other's role. When Muddy lay sleeping, no longer tensing from what he endured, John looked to Samuel. The boy sat on the settle, his elbows to his knees, hands propping his head, fingers raking through pale hair. He reeked of desolation. "It will pass, Samuel...your pain. It tells you what you value." Then, to Mercy, he whispered, "Go to him. He is troubled and needs your care."

Her fingers skimmed his knuckles. "Thank you," she said.

"Do you need me to stay?" His eyes wandered from her hand to the lacing on her bodice, too afraid to look higher.

The scrape of a chair announced Mister Payne's presence. He cleared his throat and stood. "I think we are settled now, and safe. The night grows late. We thank you. I thank you, boy. But it is time you go."

So John stepped back across the threshold, to where wind-blown snow dusted his face and a path led into a pitch-black night.

⊷❋⊷

Edward arrived at the ironworks as soon as the spring thaw allowed. John basked in their friendship. They stood in the sun outside the smithy's shop and talked—of Edward's travels, of the stalemate between Connecticut and New Haven, of the incident with Samuel.

"Pound foolish, but not wrong. New Haven's blinded," Edward snorted, "holding to the past while the future whacks it in the head."

"I have the petition Bray Rossiter gave me, an oath of loyalty to Connecticut—"

"In exchange for your freedom? I hear of those petitions in every port. No good until Connecticut confirms it in their courts."

A whistled tune drew their attention. A man John knew well traversed the last of the new bridges crossing the wheel races. He pointed to the songster with the tongs he held, his genial mood obliterated. "There," he said, "is that damned Nate Green."

He threw the tongs to the ground, then rethought his actions, picked them up, and walked into the shop. After hanging them on their hook, he began organizing every tool, every piece of equipment in the shop. Edward came and stood by the workbench. His silent stare ate into John, so he spewed his frustration. "I'm tired, Edward. I watch after her; I wait for her attention. I wait for New Haven to comply. I wait for Cooper to free me. And while I wait that whipping boy lurks...no better than me."

"So stop waiting. Act! Find out where she stands. Or not. Sail with me instead."

John picked up a punching tool, sat it down, and took to rearranging them by size. The whistling rose, fell, then stopped, followed by a knock at the open, doublewide doors. John refused to turn.

"John Frost? I come with a job. The marshal sent me. Some locks need repairing."

John answered without facing the man. "Go see Marty Jenkins." There was no response, so he snuck a glimpse. Nate was looking at Edward, questioning. "I said Marty Jenkins," he repeated, and then looked to his arm, where his hammer hovered, high in his hand, ready to swing.

Edward's voice broke through. "Whoa, John. The hammer. You forget yourself." Then he added, retreating, "The day after next, John. By dusk. At the wharf. We sail for Boston the next morning."

Nate watched Edward leave, then faced John with a devious looking smirk. "You are leaving? I thought that was a hanging offence." He adjusted the sack of locks and shrugged. "No business of mine, mind you. Your secret stays with me."

"He said nothing of me leaving." John lowered the hammer and twisted the head in his palm. "But you can be leaving. Marty's at the furnace. I have my own work to do."

John returned to the heated comfort of his forge, his back to Green. That ball of slime wanted him gone from New Haven, to have Mercy to himself; it oozed from him. But what of Mercy? He needed to know. Like Edward said, he needed to act.

꧁✵꧂

Mercy knew isolation. The years spent protecting her mother and serving the needs of Samuel and Papa had taught her to sequester herself in every way. She confided in no one, neither freeman's daughter nor servant girl. Their tongues licked at difference like bear to honey. Besides, she had no time for them. And though she loved her brother and her father, her covenant with them precluded intimacy. In John, she had found solace and tenderness and passion. The void taunted her.

She traveled on this late April day pretending she knew not where. But she walked to the place they called theirs—where the cattails teased and reeds wandered, where a rush of blackwings chortled. The touch of his hand on the day they nursed Muddy lingered on her fingertips through winter gales and meltings, twisting her solitude, once a thing she relished, into a bone-deep loneliness. It set a rueful gait.

Halfway to where John had once grounded the flatboat for his visits, she discovered a flurry of yellow violets. Widow Sherwood called them dogtooth. She picked a bundle, shoved back her cap, and tucked them in her hair. These wayward acts peppered her days—a cap discarded, a small profanity—rebellions against her defilement.

Near the river's edge, the ground, thick with thaw, sucked at her shoes. She lifted her petticoats and advanced prudently, mindful of her footing. Caution took her south of the little boat landing. She skirted the sludge and headed to higher ground, home to a bramble of willows. Something showing yellow-brown nested deep in the thicket. It struck her as familiar, so she pulled back the greening growth to investigate. John's birch bark canoe nestled there, a hidden interloper.

An instantaneous, familiar annoyance outmaneuvered her gloom. "John Frost!" His name echoed on the river. She shook the branches with annoyance before letting them go. "You are a coward. You shield yourself, and not just from my view." She waited. No one appeared or replied. She closed her eyes and willed patience. "I would curse you. I would, but...you are blind! I am here. What of you?"

"Here," he said. "Just here."

She opened her eyes to the wall of willow. John stepped out. She gathered the encumbrance of her petticoats to her knees and, unsteady at the edge of the muck, widened her stride, stable and defiant.

"Your cap is down," he said.

"And?"

He smiled. "The flowers...you look well."

Her mouth worked, attempting to hold back...what? Anger? Relief? Desire? Whatever it was, she was no child, nor was he. They must talk.

"I am well enough. With your help, I hear."

"You frightened me, Mercy...I care for you."

"So you say. But where were you?" The words came out like a verdict. They sliced deep, wounding him. And she was not sorry, except that he used her words to lay another stone on his wall.

"And you! Where were you?" he said. "You think I fiddled while you burned?"

"If a tankard be a fiddle, I hear so."

His fist lifted like a hammer ready to pound. Then contained, he answered. "I had reason enough. And now? A dalliance with the man who broke my skin at the whipping post. You have abandoned me. You—"

"What of trust, John Frost? It is not me who abandons you. You are the one. You abandoned me!"

"But Samuel said—"

"So! You trust Samuel's tale about Nate Green, but ignored his pleading before it? Oh yes, he told me. After Muddy, he told me enough. And you believe a dalliance!"

She stumbled in the muck of her feelings, unsure. "I am lost, John. A chasm...it looms between us."

"And you think I don't feel it...see it crumbling with your father's words? I am nothing here, Mercy. Here, my station precludes us."

"But I am here."

"And we are separate!" He grabbed a fist of her apron. "Mercy, we can leave! Edward is sure. He can smuggle us. And in Boston...he says

I can change my name. My trade will carry us."

"Edward says, Samuel says, Father's words!" Mercy tore her apron from his hand. She stormed back from the muck, to higher ground, to collect her frustration. His hand touched her waist, and she knocked it away, facing him.

"What words do you have, John? What do you say? And can you even hear what I say? Do you not see? It is not where you are that matters; it is who you are. And I think you do not know."

She had refused him without saying the words. He knew it; she saw it in the shock crawling on his face. His eyes stormed a murky green. But she pressed, shook her head, disgusted.

"I wonder more and more of men. They yearn, it seems, for a mother. But women—this woman—yearns for a man."

His wound bled out before her in the pitch of his gut and the perplexed crease of his brow. No words. He swung away, reaching the willows' edge inside a heart's beat. When he turned to her, the fetid weight of spring settled on her skin like a portent.

His voice stabbed, low and slow. "Edward waits on the morrow. At the wharf with a shallop. Meet me at dusk's closing, or not. I am done with waiting." He slapped at the willows. The splash of the canoe followed, and Mercy threw her anger into an uphill stride.

Back near the patch of dogtooth, she stopped and followed the course of his canoe. Driven by a hard spring current, he paddled downstream and away.

The receding tide lapped at the edge of the wharf where John sat cross-legged, his eyes tracing the water, oily with waste. He had arrived late, had waited at the cart bridge—for Mercy and for a dimmer light to avoid the whispers and pointed jabs. The route to the wharf went through New Haven streets, and even after ten years, his leg irons and halter were required, perpetual markers of his sin.

Not that anyone would notice in these times. New Haven's inhabitants swirled in an eddy of uncertainty, as uprooted as the seaweed now curling at his feet.

"She will not come," John said and looked up at Edward who stood waiting in the shallop. It sat low in the water, laden with a final haul of cargo and a crew anxious for leaving.

"Then we go?"

"A minute longer." The sky washed with the closing day, a scurry of pink, saddled by grey. She would not come, would be true to her covenant with Samuel and her father. His heart froze, a winter frost where all around him it melted to spring. The sky darkened. A hidden moon, just rising, ghosted the cloud-strewn sky with an inner glow.

"How long your minute, John? We must be going. We transfer the cargo in the dark as it is."

John stared into the sky. "Look there, Edward, in the parting clouds. Perseus. Remember that night?"

Edward twisted his head as the clouds opened to the constellation. "I remember Perseus well enough. I taught you it up on East Rock, but not so well it seems. Those stars make no hero, John. Perseus hides until autumn calls. By then the stars you see there will fall away. Those stars fashion Virgo, the sky's gift to spring."

Virgo threw down her starry offering; she reflected John's mind like a mirror. He smiled up at the messenger deviling him, then reached down and removed his chains. With an inward breath peppered with sea salt and smoke from the evening fires, he stood, then dropped the chains into the silt-skimmed ocean rocking between shallop and wharf. The links entered the sea with a leaden gulp, hardly ceremonious. Next he slipped from his halter and tossed it far into the bay.

Edward tracked the halter's whizzing flight and waited for the splash as it entered the sea. "So," he said, "you've decided."

"I have."

John was no hero, but he could, at the least, be a man.

⤝❁⤜

The car rolls up to the metal mailboxes stacked by row and column. They stand sentinel, serving the quiet mass of people hidden in the valley and the hills around them. Maggie jumps out holding the mailbox key. It is their last task on the Friday list. Duncan wanted to skip it, pick the mail up in the morning or maybe on Sunday, but she sensed something calling, so insisted. A manila envelope with a few bills folded into its curve leans on the wall of the box. "And there you are," she says, "my message from afar."

She slides in, closes the car door, and examines the envelope, unconsciously pulling on her seatbelt.

"What's that?" Duncan pulls the steering wheel tight, swinging the car around to head up their dirt road.

"Not sure." She twists her head to the side with a smirk, lifting her brows. "A mystery. But something to do with New Haven. I can feel it."

"And the return address?"

"The Otis House on Cambridge Street. In Boston, hum..." Maggie

searches the furrows of her mind and attempts to make a connection, but finds none. "I have no idea." She's already ripping at the taped closure. "I called a few people but no one from there. Still, maybe?"

They are bumping up the road, making it hard to open the envelope and get to its contents, but she manages, completing the task just as Duncan pulls up to their door. The cover letter is handwritten. "A friend of mine at the New England Genealogy Society told me—"

"Come on, Maggie. It can wait. We've got to get all this food inside."

She resists, her first reaction to most roadblocks, but he is right. The groceries, the stuff in the ice chest, all need to be put away, their Friday routine honored. She tucks the mail under her arm, lifts her purse strap over her head, and hefts three grocery bags into her hands while Duncan opens the front door. Her heart races in anticipation. A gift from the postal god awaits.

Learned patience guides her. She has discovered so much, but the Barbour records outlining New Haven's familial relationships don't totally jibe with other records. A thread from the past reaches out begging closure. With everything settled and Duncan napping on the sofa, she gathers up the envelope and the papers it held. She sits, licks the salt from her lips, and breathes, eyes closed, centering. She has often held a manila envelope in her hand, hoping for the gift she seeks. She opens her eyes and reads.

It's from a Marjorie Anderson. She works at a place called Historic New England. Seems her friend at the genealogy society mentioned Maggie's phone call and their conversation. She says it jogged her memory. She recalled archiving some materials donated by the estate of an old shipping family. The daughter showed no interest in the pile of things her father kept stored in a trunk passed down through time.

Most items found inside were ephemera of minimal interest. A few manuscripts, however, were dated from the early 18th century. One of them, Ms. Anderson thought, might interest her. She enclosed a copy.

Maggie's heart races, pulsing at her throat. She slips Ms. Anderson's letter to the back of the photocopy, a color replica of paper yellowed and aged. She marvels at the script, the past flows out with a curving grace, the stroke widens and narrows with the angle of the quill, a smudge stains the corner. It is signed Samuel Payne.

～❀～

John held his head up to the moon-bright sky, no longer hobbled by the trappings of bondage. Virgo led him home. He grew more eager, more enlivened with each homeward step. Everything called him: his workbench, his neatly laid out tools, old Mac and Marty Jenkins, Mister Cooper and Geordie. Until the moment of his choosing, he had not understood how much freedom came from choosing. A euphoria of understanding bolstered and emboldened him. But when he reached the ferry landing, night still loomed, so he waited for dawn.

Morning's light found Mister Cooper at the charging bridge in a heated conversation with Geordie Garrison. Geordie's grey fringe rippled in the wind, and John smiled at the familiarity of it.

"Mister Cooper. Sir!" he yelled, his arm waving. "I would speak with you."

Geordie greeted him with his usual enthusiasm. "John Frost. You are here." He flung down his hand and slapped his knee, dust flying out from his breeches. "Come up."

Cooper held to a solemn reserve that dampened John's enthusiasm, but only briefly. He would not be contained. His feet broke into a run, unasked. And he smiled, wider the closer he came. He held his hand out in an equal's greeting, but Mister Cooper stood aloof.

Geordie clapped John on the back. "You look good, boy. A sight lighter, I'd say." Geordie grabbed both shoulders, and John laughed, relishing the splotches of soot he left on his coat. "Missing your neck piece, I see." Geordie stared into him, one eye winked shut in his grizzled face. "The Mac reported you absent. We thought you gone."

With a rise of courage, John nodded. "I was, but...I do like you fine, Geordie. Maybe I came back missing you."

Geordie laughed. "Sure, and I'm a hard man to leave after all. But I think you came to speak with your master, so I leave you to it." He dusted John's shoulders, turning the soot prints to smudges, and walked back up the bridge to the blast furnace.

A version of quiet settled on John and his master. The forge hammer echoed, muffled and woven into the hiss of the blast furnace. Mister Cooper held to his dour countenance, waiting.

"Sir, I thought the night away and come to ask you—"

"First, do I gather you plan to stay?"

"I do."

"No matter what you ask?"

John swallowed. "And no matter what you answer."

"Well, then. Begin."

"Sir, the town is in upheaval. Tumbling like...like Jericho. You say it will not be long. I even have the paper Lassiter handed me. I signed it. And, under Connecticut rule, I might be a freeman."

Cooper stretched taller. He crossed his arms. He waited. So John continued. "You, sir, have dangled hope before me. Sly promises for the help I gave, notions of a changing government. I have served my first allotted indenture, and three years beyond. And I would not abandon you, would serve my apprenticeship gladly—but I would be free."

"You would?" The man settled one eye on him, expectant.

"I ask you. Now, sir, will you make me free?"

A smiled crept onto Mister Cooper's face. "I wondered what day you would ask."

⤜✦⤛

The hens laid eggs with abandon. Mercy tried to contain them with laying racks in the shelter-shed, but they would not be deterred. They deposited brown and speckled orbs everywhere, including the front porch. She hoped she had found them all. The hunt distracted her from the hollow in her heart, born of her ordeal and compounded by John's leave taking.

She suspected he sailed to Boston, likely already nauseous from the rolling waves. It was vindictive to wish him seasick, but she did. Her kinder heart understood John's choice. Not born to patience, John had waited long, and her refusal wounded him. But had he considered her reasons? Or her promise to Samuel? No, he just paddled away.

Still, she mourned.

She placed the woven basket, brimming with eggs, on the table dominating the room. Her father sat there, entering tallies in his book. Widow Sherwood had connected him to a cooper who made wet barrels for the maple syrup harvest. The man needed good hickory hoops and Father now supplied them, a boon to their prosperity and Father's pride.

"Beaten eggs and ham for our supper, Papa?" she asked.

He looked up from his books, stern-faced, his voice edged with concern. "My stomach says thank you, child. But I worry at your melancholy. Be you well?"

"Enough, Papa. We must all move on. I thought popovers, too. The eggs are plentiful. Samuel should be back from the lower pasture soon."

Her father reached out and took her hand. "You are a dutiful daughter, child."

"A woman, Papa. Please give me that." He patted her hand and nodded. The act repulsed and consoled her within a heart's beat. Her teeth came down hard on her lower lip. She whisked her hand away, gathered a mixing bowl from the nearby shelf, and walked to the back corner of the room where they stored the dry goods.

She was spooning out the flour for popovers when a voice rang out from the porch. "Mister Payne. Pray, sir, we would visit." She recognized the voice, as did her father.

"Good friend Cooper?" Her father's chair scraped against the floorboards as he hurried to greet him.

A curious visit, she thought. The squeal of the door hinges set the shiver of memories along her spine. Would they always grate on her so? She stood with bowl in hand and brow furrowed, annoyed by the intrusion on her closeted world. Then, as the door widened in her father's grasp, she saw him.

"John Frost," her father said, and her heart wrenched loose, then retreated to a protected place inside her. She blinked, smoothing her face of emotion. She would not expose her bewilderment. He was not supposed to be here.

"If we could enter, sir. I would talk with you." John's frame filled the door. He dressed well, with stockings and shoes, his sand-brown hair slicked back into a leather tie. He held papers in his hands but fidgeted at his thumbnails, nonetheless. His eyes flitted to hers.

Father waved him in, and Mister Cooper followed behind, leaving the door open to spring breezes. Her father returned to his place at the table. "Mister Cooper, pray sit. May I offer you a light beer or cider?"

But it was John who answered. "He stands with me to verify what I am about to say, sir. And I would address you myself. Standing."

"Would you? And what can you say to me not already determined?"

John glanced back at Mercy. A breeze flitted through the room, spreading the spell of a greening spring. She watched as it freshen his courage. "This day, sir, I have negotiated my freedom from Mister Cooper in exchange for my apprenticeship at the ironworks."

Her father looked up, dubious. "How? You are bound to twenty-one years. The New Haven court—"

"Void, under the laws of Connecticut Colony—with Mister Cooper's consent. See here? I have my signed oath of loyalty to King and Connecticut. And my freeman papers from Mister Cooper." He stepped forward and placed the documents on the table, then ran his hands across them to flatten any creasing. "Mister Cooper will vouch for me, and the inevitable. New Haven's power over us—over you, sir—is history."

Her father looked beyond John to Mister Cooper, who stood taciturn, chin raised tall to match the rest of him. He smiled, first at Father, then John. His smile, Mercy thought, was one of a father pleased with his son.

"So, I see." Her father turned his gaze to John. "You are free."

"And I would marry your daughter…would she have me." He faced her full on. "A question for her alone."

Mercy squeezed the bowl tight for fear of dropping it but did not falter.

"I would have you, John Frost."

Her father interrupted. "That decision is mine, I think."

A fire burned in Mercy at his words. John stood before her vulnerable, exposed, and her father chided his courage. "Papa, you said I could not marry a bound man. And now a freed man stands before you. You will not deny him, or me. And I say yes."

John walked to her and slipped the bowl from her hand. "I could not leave you, Mercy. But I would have your father's blessing, that we might live in harmony." He stepped back and set the bowl on the table. "If you would write out the banns of marriage for us, Mister Payne, we would post them this day on the meetinghouse wall."

Silence held sway until Mister Cooper spoke his first words. "He is a worthy man, William."

Her father nodded. "True. His actions, over time, have shown as much. Though I have tried, I can no longer refute it. And, as my good daughter makes clear, I set my terms. So, Mister Frost, a small courage on my part—a few words on a page."

❧

They walked through the north gate into New Haven. No past shackles burdened them, though an excitement, bordering on prideful, pulsated between their joined hands.

"John Frost, you come untethered." The watchman at the gate, Thomas Harding, knew his sentence, but he spoke without judgment.

"I am freed, Thomas, on this very day. We come to post our banns."

"Well, congratulations. I doubt you will meet with complaint. Rumor spreads that the King rejected our Magistrates' final petition. The town huddles in a fit over how things will fall. You are much too small a fish."

John laughed. "A throw away as always."

Mercy pulled him close, a brazen act. "He is a fine catch to some, Mister Harding."

They continued down the street to the meetinghouse. No one blocked them; no one noticed. John pulled four tacks of his own making from his pocket, and he and Mercy together tacked the banns, writ in Mister Payne's hand, to the meetinghouse wall. Then, without speaking, they walked as a single soul to the cistern at the edge of the green.

"I have a gift for you, Mercy. One I can lawfully give."

"A foolish law," she said and ran her hand along his neck, stopping to knead the lobe of his ear between her fingers. "Show me."

He pulled out a small leaf-wrapped bundle no bigger than his palm and held it out to her. "Seeds," he said, "from Taphanse. He says they are like cornflowers, but bigger. Blossoms as large as a bowl. They turn to the sun." He dropped his head, shy to her suddenly, and shrugged. She took the package, her fingers tracing his arm, and snuck into his gaze, resting her head on his chest.

"They will be my favorite gift, always."

Mercy snuck the package back into John's pouch. Together they placed their hands on the cool, uneven surface of the rock-faced wall and swung up to sit on its edge. Four plops announced the frogs' retreat.

John lifted his chin to the sky, relishing the sun's warmth. "I first met you here."

Mercy laughed. "A pitiful sight. All I saw was hurt."

"You saw more, Mercy. You saw me. You set the key in the lock on that day."

"But you turned it free."

"True enough. So, we should celebrate." He jumped from the wall and lifted her, spinning, then drew her close. "Shall we go?" His voice rang low and evocative.

"To East Rock?"

"To the rock." He dropped her to the ground, and they ran together, laughing at a common joy, a singular understanding.

At the gate, Thomas Harding, yelled out, "Is it done?"

"It is." John looked at Mercy, and they called back together. "Almost!"

⟶❀⟵

John's half-cabin lay in ruins. "The havoc of two winters of neglect," he said. "But I will not need it now."

"You will live with us then?" Mercy lowered her body to where he lay in a bed of sun-warmed grass. He met her fullness freely, unencumbered, with no sense of one belonging to the other, for belonging, John thought, implied ownership, and you could not own the sun.

"I will live with you, wherever you might be, by choice and need, a new kind of covenant." He traced her jawline with his tongue and nuzzled in her hair. Freed of her cap, it smelled of morning dew and the marshland below.

"A lofty sentiment, that." She lifted onto her elbow to study him.

"So what of this covenant?"

His breath dusted her throat, close and intent. "The issue of grace and will. It came to me, waiting for you at the wharf. Like us, they cannot be separated. Our efforts, our will, the choices we make, they are human things—to increase our personal good. And our lives require a sturdy will." He gathered her to him; his fingers skimmed the small of her back and traveled along her spine. "Only time knows where our choices take us, right or wrong."

"And grace?"

"Well," he said, kissing her arm, tasting the salt on her skin. "Grace is us, turning to the sun."

"Really?" She willed him into her, and his body responded, heated by the warming day. "And freedom, John Frost, what of freedom?"

"A grave responsibility, Mercy. And a relief."

Epilogue

M*aggie reads Samuel Payne's letter, drops it on her desk, and walks to her garden. Tears drip down her face. Why? Where does it come from, this sorrow welling up from the uneven arc of ink on a page? Her hand aches, as though she wields the quill. What strange connection takes her there? Because she is there— reading loss, but also triumph, in the words.*

She tells Duncan about the letter after they crawl into bed, after the books they keep on their nightstands are read, after they turn out the lights. He knows her silent tears by heart, even if he doesn't get it and thinks them laughable. He reaches over and traces them on her cheek. "You're kidding right?"

"No, and don't laugh…I can't explain it. It's just not what I wanted,"

"Well, they aren't some characters from a fairytale, hon."

"I know. It's silly, but still—they're a part of me." She snuggles her back close to his chest, runs her foot along his leg, and falls asleep to his breath on her neck. In the middle of the night, still cocooned in his arms, she awakens. She ponders the cosseted safety of a mate who lays with you, accepting your obsessions, your uniqueness, if not always willingly. And yet you know he will stand with you—through the worst. A gift, she thinks. And the Boston letter loops into her mind. Sleep eludes her. She slides from his arms, not wanting to wake him, retrieves the letter

from the desk where it waits, and pads out to the living room by feel, not needing light. She knows these surroundings, forty years worth of knowing.

The fragrance of an early spring wafts from the letter like a memory untied. And her heart aches from loss—not her loss—but a loss breaking through the rhythm of time. She reads the letter by heart, her fingers moving, tracing each word as if it is her own. With closed eyes, she breathes in a moment and, hovering out of now, offers the healing solace of time.

10 April 1700
To Captain Edward House
Of the Merchant Ship, Perseus
Out of Boston

Dearest Friend,

I write to inform you of the Death of our Good Friend, John Frost. As you know, over the past seven years, after Mercy's Passing, he spent his Days in a searing Fury pounding out his Anguish at his Anvil. It did little to heal the Man. He said always, he had lost his Sun. He spoke often of three things in his Life. He marked of Value our early, seditious Adventures and of Great Merit, as well, was the Day he walked into our Meetinghouse to serve as Juror in New Haven Town's first ever Juried Trial, but foremost of his Treasures was the day he joined with Mercy, bound in Covenant to the Gifts she gave him each Day after.

As I know it will be with You, I Grieve for my Loss, but I do not miss them, for in this Place, I see them at every Turn.

In Remembrance,
Samuel Payne

"Flutterbyes, Papa, Flutterbyes!"

The door had swung open silently on its sturdy-made hinges, making his daughter's stealth an easy one. Samuel flinched, smearing an edge of the just completed letter. "Elzbeth! You gave me a fright." His smile grew, seeing her, the image of his sister, her tiny nose dotted with an arc of freckles.

"Come, Papa, come see them!"

"A moment child. Let me sand and seal the letter to Captain Edward first."

"Is he coming to see us?"

"Perhaps, but not soon." Samuel sprinkled the ink with two pinches of sand, then held the letter up, moving the sand around on the page. He blew off the residue and began folding it into thirds. "I write to him regarding your Uncle John's death."

"He missed Aunt Mercy, Papa."

Samuel frizzled her gossamer hair. If only his sister had seen her, hair like their mother's, but with Mercy's sturdy will. "He did indeed miss her, sweet thing. And where, pray tell, is your cap?" he asked, though he knew the answer.

"I like it best free," she said, flouncing as though it were obvious. He let wax drip from the beeswax candle. Four neat drops on the letter's fold. He pressed the wax down with his forefinger, then rubbed his thumb to dissipate the burning at the tip.

"Now," he said, tucking the letter in the inside pocket of his jacket, "let us find your Flutterbyes."

They walked out onto the porch, and he stretched—like a sunflower, he thought. Those flowers, just now sprouting at the base of the door-side garden fence, were Mercy's pride. Their yellow orbs burst out in profusion every summer, each face opening to the morning sun. In that moment a timeless understanding filled him—the flowers would bloom once more.

"See, see!" Elzbeth squealed, pointing to the winged waifs dancing in a cloud of blue all along the fence. With arms extended, she sprang from the porch and skipped to the edge of the garden. Her hand banged at the smooth and sturdy pickets, and a fluttering of blue rose up out of her exuberance. A memory welled up into Samuel's eyes.

"They come late," he said, "announcing your grandmother. She visits us."

"So do Aunt Mercy and Uncle John." Elzbeth twirled as she spoke, and the butterflies lifted skyward in escape.

"Come, child." Samuel bent low and caught her as she danced near. He breathed in her youth. "Go tell your mother I go to the wharf to deliver the letter."

"But I want to come."

"As I knew you would, but this task is mine alone. And besides, you must help your mother and tend to the mastiff pups."

"Dead old Muddy's great-grandbabies?" She smiled with wide eyes of the palest blue.

Samuel tweaked her nose. His heart filled with her. "Yes, dead Muddy's great-grandbabies. Now off with you." He patted her full-skirted bottom as she scuttled away to where Misty and her pups took refuge in the barn he and John had built behind the old shelter-shed.

He walked the path to Mill River, stopping at the bridge to admire East Rock. It rose unchanged above the stretch of morning shadow. A memory from one of John's old stories, from the early times, glistened in his mind, and he whispered to the shadow of his friend, "A pretty place, I think, after all."

Historical Notes

In June of 1637, Reverend John Davenport and Theophilus Eaton sailed into Boston Harbor with a small group of mostly wealthy idealists. They hoped to find a place far from King Charles I and the violence perpetrated against puritan dissent, a place where they could freely pursue a faith "purer" than England's Anglican Church. Boston's worldliness proved to be a less than desirable location.

They soon established New Haven Colony, without charter from the King, half way up Long Island Sound. Connecticut Colony had been established similarly, but New Haven's founders were more extreme in their beliefs. They limited governing participation, including the vote, to church members, excluding all indentured servants, temporary residents, and alternative sects. Nor, because the bible included no reference to trial by jury, did they provide juried trials, leaving the decisions regarding colonial disputes to Magistrates elected by those with church membership. By October 1643, New Haven had incorporated other plantations (towns) dotting the Sound into their Colony.

In the story, Maggie shows Duncan a map to help explain the location of all these plantations. It can be found at www.nationalgeographic. org/photo/connecticut-1645/

From the beginning the colony was fraught with difficulties. They lacked the necessary skills to live in a frontier environment so relied heavily on indentured servants contracted for a specified number of years in exchange for passage, food, and housing. In later years they also brought in temporary skilled labor. Another issue of contention was their far-flung plantations, often with different needs and opinions. Heavy taxes levied on the plantations for the expenses incurred in disputes with the Dutch and protection against Native American incursions compounded discontent.

When, in 1649, Oliver Cromwell overthrew the monarchy and ordered the trial and hanging of Charles I, New Haven fully supported his rebellion and its Puritan governance. But in the spring of 1660 Charles II took back control and, in the Act of Indemnity, pardoned all involved—with one exception. Any of those who participated in the execution of Charles I would go to trial. Most were eventually hung, but some escaped.

Reverend Davenport, in denial over this turn of events, invited the regicides (King killers) to New Haven for protection. Edward Whalley and William Goffe fled to New Haven and hid in West Rock's caves until Davenport spirited them elsewhere.

As one can imagine, this did not sit well with the King. When John Winthrop Jr., then governor of Connecticut Colony, sailed to England to negotiate a charter for Connecticut and New Haven Colony, he returned with a single charter that put New Haven under Connecticut's governance. Winthrop insisted he never received a letter addressed to him from the Magistrates explaining their desire to remain independent.

While New Haven's Magistrates objected to the charter, many of their subjects did not. Considering Connecticut's comparatively liberal governance a plus, many subverted New Haven and made overtures to Connecticut. Finally, New Haven's Magistrates yielded, though

Reverend Davenport never accepted their decision, and reluctantly joined Connecticut Colony. An excellent, more expansive history can be found at www.connecticuthistory.org under the title A Separate Place: The New Haven Colony, 1638-1665.

From the beginning New Haven Colony chronicled their proceedings in detail, through the recorded minutes of both New Haven town and colony. In 1857-8, Charles Hoadly transcribed the records in two volumes. These are the books that drew Maggie into the world of John Frost and Mercy Payne.

I actually found those records while researching William Payne, my direct ancestor. In the records, which I read from cover to cover, the above history unfolds in an intimate manner, as do the day-to-day disputes and trials of the colony. Out of those records and the trials outlined therein came the skeletal underpinnings of my novel.

Few names were changed. An author would be mad to mess with names like Mercy, Frost, and Payne. I did changed John Payne's name to Samuel. Two Johns would not do. The trials were condensed (they are as long and convoluted as Maggie insists), and Edward's indenture trial was built of a conglomeration of two trials in those records.

All that said, the novel is pure fiction. The motivations, rationales, personalities, interactions, demeanor, even the looks of the characters, come from the empathetic reaches of my mind. Bray Rossiter existed and did ride the countryside warning against New Haven's efforts to subvert the new charter, but his rally at the iron works likely did not occur. No long lost letter from Boston exists. My story reflects no truth beyond the wonder found in imagining a people communing in a world lost to time.

Notes of Gratitude

First, my everlasting gratitude goes to Pam Smedley and my friends at Pam's Writing Gym. Your suggestions, insights, and encouragement are invaluable and sustain me when my confidence dips. Thanks, also, to Pam, Sheila, Maryl, Laura, and Dawn who took time out of busy lives to read my drafts, some quite rough. I considered seriously your every thought. To Linda Zupcic, my mapmaker, and Pam Mullins, who designed the cover, an enormous thank you, both for your talent and your friendship. My appreciation goes out, as well, to Jason Bischoff-Wurstle and The New Haven Museum in New Haven, Connecticut. With their consent, George Henry Durrie's gorgeous painting, *East Rock, 1857*, graces the book's back cover. As always, my husband, Tyler, mustered the patience to endure my obsession, even traveling with me to the top of East Rock in New Haven so I could see the present tense version of my imaginary world. And finally, to family, present and future, thank you, because you are my reason to write.

dcw

Donna Croy Wright holds a Masters in Art from Fresno State University. She lives in California's Sierra-Nevada foothills and spends her time researching, writing, working in her garden, and taking walks with her husband and her cat. Her blog is extensive, including research on her family, general histories of place, her musings on writing, and a link to *The Scattering of Stones* short story prequel. Find out more at www.croywright.com

THE MAGGIE CHRONICLES
Book One
The Scattering of Stones

Made in the USA
San Bernardino, CA
10 March 2019